ESCAPE

By Tony Dulio

Dedication

I would like to dedicate this book to my wife, Barbara, our son, David and his family.

Acknowledgement

I would like to thank Mathew Kelly, the founder of Dynamic Catholic and New York Times bestselling author, for inspiring me to write.

Published by TonyDBooks
www.tonydbooks.com

Prologue

In the Oval Office, August 2026

My question to President Rivera was, "Mr. President, what will be your response?"

My question was about the nuclear bomb that was detonated in Chicago by a young terrorist, Fareed Haddad. Haddad had recovered from radiation poisoning he received from the explosion. The CIA and FBI wanted to know where he and his fellow terrorists were trained.

Haddad wasn't sure about the information he was about to give the CIA interrogators. He was willing to talk. He simply didn't know the name of the location. He hadn't been told where he was while he was being trained, and hadn't asked. But he knew of a place on the border where ISIS recruited young men. He took a chance and gave Frank Yanelli's CIA interrogators that information.

As it turned out, the location he gave the CIA was where he and Adib Malouf learned to shoot shoulder-fired rockets, and where fellow terrorists Ghazi Hijaz, Emir Binhaji, and Abdul Bari were trained to build and detonate bombs.

When I asked President Rivera the question, others were also present in the Oval Office: Bob Reynolds, the director of National Intelligence; Frank Yanelli, the director of the CIA; Joe Madden, the director of the FBI, Sydney Alvarez, the secretary of the Department of Homeland Security; and General Mike Evans, chairman of the Joint Chiefs of Staff.

The president answered my question by saying, "Captain, you'll have to wait until I make my decision. I can tell you this—it will be in the strongest terms. The Islamist terrorists will know the United States means business. The whole world will know the United States means business. First things first. Are we certain the information Haddad gave us is correct?"

DNI Bob Reynolds spoke. "Mr. President, we all know of the site Haddad gave us. It's where ISIS recruits new young people to its cause. The probability of that place being the place where Haddad and the others were trained is very high. He probably doesn't know where he was trained. It's a good bet he's right though. It is in Pakistan, just over the border from Afghanistan. As you know, sir, Pakistan is an ally of ours. Whatever we decide, Mr. President, we must consider that fact. They have nukes, too."

"Well, we've known about the place in Pakistan for years, and I am well aware of their nuclear capability. They've gotten away with sheltering our enemies for too long. Before I decide, I'll wait for a recommendation from General Evans and the Joint Chiefs of Staff. General Evans, please meet with the Joint Chiefs early tomorrow morning. I want your recommendation at that time. The people in this room will meet after that, at ten a.m."

"Will do, sir," replied General Hayes.

"I would like Captain Gonzales and the rest of Covert Bravo, as well as Governor Martinez and her husband, Consuela and her son, and Lucia, to stay in Washington for a while. Of course, they will be guests of the United States government. I want to talk with each of them on a more personal basis. I'll have Pattie Hayes make the arrangements. This meeting is over. Thank you all."

* * *

The next morning the president, Bob Reynolds, Sydney Alvarez, Frank Yanelli, Joe Madden, General Evans, the Joint Chiefs, Gonzales, and Covert Bravo were in the Situation Room. President Rivera began, "We, as a country, need a strong response to this nuclear attack. We must show the world we will not tolerate this kind of attack on our soil. General Evans, what do you think would be an appropriate response?"

"Well, sir, the Joint Chiefs and I discussed this earlier this morning. We gave this great consideration. We talked about using MOAB, the mother of all bombs. A previous administration used one. Although the bomb caused considerable damage, the bad guys were able to get back up and running within a short period of time...several months at most. Therefore, we think a tactical nuclear bomb would be just the right amount of force. It will be targeted at the ISIS camp on the border of Afghanistan and Pakistan. That entire area will be out of action for at least twenty years. That will put ISIS, Pakistan, and the rest of the world, friend or foe, on notice. They will think twice before testing our will again."

"Bob, what do you think of a tactical nuclear strike in Pakistan?" queried the president.

Director of National Intelligence Bob Reynolds answered, "Well, sir, as much as I hate the use of nuclear weapons, I think what General Evans and the Joint Chiefs have recommended is appropriate."

"Anyone have anything to say?" asked the president. "How about you, Captain Gonzales? What are your thoughts?"

"Well, sir, I think it is the appropriate use of force. It will let ISIS terrorists and the rest of the world know we mean business."

The president continued, "Thank you for your input. I'll make my decision by this afternoon. Never in my life did I think I'd have to make such a decision. I know there will be a terrible loss of innocent lives. I can only imagine what President Truman went through when he decided to drop nuclear bombs on Hiroshima and Nagasaki. He wrote later that the decision stayed with him for the rest of his life. Now, I'm faced with the same decision. May God have mercy on me and give me guidance and insight into making this decision."

Early the next evening, President Rivera addressed the nation on national television.

"My fellow Americans, as your president, and after conferring with our top advisers, including Director of National Intelligence Bob Reynolds, Director of the CIA Frank Yanelli, Director of the FBI Joe Madden, General Mike Evans and the Joint Chiefs, I have decided on the response to the terrible and tragic nuclear bomb attack on Chicago by ISIS operatives. I ordered our military to launch a tactical nuclear bomb on the border of Pakistan and Afghanistan early this morning. The camp is in Pakistan."

"As you can imagine, this was not an easy decision to make. I bring this news to you with a heavy heart. However, the United States will defend its sovereignty, and that of its allies, at all costs."

"As for our Russian friends, we now know the nuclear material came from your country. It was sold by one of your ex-generals, who is now a powerful Russian Mafia leader and oligarch. The United States is putting your government on notice. If this ever happens again,

Russia will pay dearly.

"Good afternoon, and God bless us all."

The free world accepted President Rivera's decision. Condolences poured in from all over the world. Israel was the most vociferous. Its leaders applauded President Rivera. The Russians were the first to offer their sympathies to President Rivera and condemned the use of a nuclear weapon on the United States. They said they would find the general, arrest him, and bring him to Russian justice. The Chinese condemned President Rivera and the United States outwardly. But the back channels of diplomacy said otherwise.

Pakistan was most upset because the attack came on their soil. They threatened reprisals, but it was just a threat. They, too, knew they were guilty. They supported ISIS. They would think twice before they let ISIS set up camp in their territory ever again. No one wanted a rogue stateless group of terrorists running over the world.

Chapter 1

The bus driver first heard the *whoomp, whoomp, whoomp* of the chopper, then he saw it. It landed right in front of his bus. At first, he thought the pilot was in trouble and had to make an emergency landing. When he saw two men get out of the aircraft with guns, he still didn't get it. As soon as they began to fire bullets at him, he knew there was trouble. That's the last thought he had before he died. One of the men making the assault shot him in the head.

Two men in cars arrived in front of and behind the bus. They stopped and got out brandishing guns, with masks covering their faces. They stopped traffic in both directions by firing their weapons in the air. No one in the stopped traffic wanted anything to do with whatever was going on. They all stayed in their vehicles. The other guards were killed before they could return fire. Dize Cruz led the attack.

Dize Cruz was Flores's second-in-command of the Los Zetas drug cartel. He was on the bus immediately and shouted, "Benito, we're here!" He took the keys to the handcuffs and leg irons off the dead officer's belt. Benito Flores and Baha el Din were set free. El Din had no idea what just took place, but he quickly put two and two together. Terrorist Emir Binhaji, who was taken down at the Mall of America before he detonated a bomb there, and Ghazi Hijaz, who was caught in Disney World after he detonated a bomb there, were on the bus, too. Emir Binhaji and Ghazi Hijaz were part of an ISIS plot that contributed to the detonation of a nuclear bomb in Chicago.

Chapter 2

Dize Cruz took charge of getting Flores and el Din out of prison. He had men go to Fremont, Colorado, where the administrative maximum (ADX) security prison is located. The men were able to cross the border legally. The new immigration laws put in place by a past administration were working. They were able to get jobs with a landscape company and blended into the Fremont community. When the prison guards got off work, Cruz's men followed them to see where they went. They were looking for a weak link in the system; someone who needed money and needed it badly.

After their shift, a few of the guards went to a local bar for a beer. Cruz's men followed and tried to listen in on the conversation the guards were having. The eavesdropping paid off. They overheard the men talking about one of their friends who was in financial trouble. The friend made some bad investments and was in deep trouble with his bank. He tried to win his losses back by gambling. He was in deep trouble with the bookies and was about to lose his home. His wife was getting ready to leave him and take his kids with her. He was so distraught that his work at the prison was suffering. There was a good chance he was going to lose his job, too. Jack Eagleton had made major mistakes.

Cruz's men finally learned who Jack Eagleton was. He came to the bar one night after work with his buddies and said very little. It was obvious by his demeanor that Eagleton was in a bind.

One night, Eagleton came to the bar alone and had, as they say, a few too many. This was the opening for which Cruz's men were looking. Moises Rios was Cruz's leader for this operation. Rios went into the bar and took a seat two bar stools down from Eagleton and struck up a conversation with him. Just small talk about the landscape work he was doing.

Eagleton told Rios, "I work at the prison in Florence."

"Really," said Rios.

"Yeah, that's right. We house the worst criminals in the country."

"Do you like the work?" asked Rios.

"Sure, I like what I'm doing. There isn't much else to do around here. It's a good job and the pay is steady."

"That sounds good to me. Do you think I might get a job there? It beats cutting grass, and I bet the pay is much better," Rios said, trying to set Eagleton up. Rios bought a round of beer for them.

"I think two or three guards are retiring in a month or so. You might want to look into putting in an application," said Eagleton. "And thanks for the beer."

"It's my pleasure, my friend. I'll go there tomorrow, after work, and apply for one of the positions."

"You do that, and let me know how you make out. I'll be here after my shift. We can talk some more then."

"Thank you, Jack, thank you. I'll see you tomorrow."

The next day, Rios went to the prison and applied for a guard position. He had forged documentation that verified he was a citizen of the United States. While filling out the application, he looked around and took in as much of the prison as he could. However, there wasn't much for him to see, which caused him to think, *I guess they do mean maximum security!*

After work at his landscaping job, Rios went to the bar and met Eagleton. They had a few beers, and Eagleton began to open up to Rios. Rios thought he'd gained the trust of this man. It was so easy. Eagleton told Rios, "I'm in very bad financial trouble, Moises. I'm about to lose everything—my house, wife, and family."

Rios just listened and said, "Gee, that's too bad, Jack. Is there anything I can do to help?"

Eagleton replied, "Sure, do you have an extra hundred grand?"

"That's a lot of money, but maybe I can help."

"What are you talking about? Are you telling me you have that kind of money laying around?"

"No, I don't; but I may know some people who do. Let me get back to you."

Eagleton was stunned but managed to say, "OK, what do I have to do?"

"I can't say right now, but I know people who may be able to help you. I'll talk to them and see what they can do for you and you for them. I'll talk to them tomorrow and get back to you the day after tomorrow."

Eagleton just nodded his head and said, "That's fine with me."

Chapter 3

Rios knew he had Eagleton's interest. Jack Eagleton would do whatever it took to get the money; money he needed to save his life. Rios wasn't too concerned about it.

Rios got word to Cruz and told him about Eagleton. "I'm not sure he has the information we need, but I'm sure he'll do anything we ask of him."

"Great. You need to ask him if he has what we need concerning Flores and el Din. When and where are they being brought to the prison? If he doesn't know, he may be able to find out. Feel him out some more. Ask him next time and see what he knows. Do you think he would go to the police?"

"I will put the deal to him tomorrow night. I don't think he will go to the police. He needs the money. His wife is threatening to leave and take his kids with her. He's about to lose his house, and maybe his job."

"When you talk to him, offer him two hundred grand. That should get his attention," said Cruz.

"Okay; if that doesn't get his attention, nothing will."

* * *

Eagleton and Rios met the next night. They had a few beers before Eagleton asked, "Moises, have you talked with those people? You know, the ones who may be able to help me? Do you know what is expected of me?"

"Yes, I do, Jack."

"Well, tell me."

"These people need some information."

"And what would that be?"

"They need to know the time and route Benito Flores and Baha el Din will be brought to the prison."

Eagleton sat there dumbfounded and didn't say a word. "You've been setting me up, Moises, haven't you? I can't believe it! What if I don't know the answer to your question?"

"Well, maybe you could find out. Jack, they will pay *two hundred grand* for this information. No strings attached. You supply the information and you get two hundred grand...simple as that."

Eagleton almost choked when he heard how much money was involved. He thought to himself, *Two hundred grand!* and said, "Why do you need the information?"

"You don't need to know why. You tell them the answer and they pay. It's as simple as that. No one knows any better."

"I'll know, Moises, I'll know. I don't think I can live with that on my conscience."

"That's your decision, Jack. Do you want to lose everything you've worked your whole life for? I don't think so."

"Can I take a few days to think about this?"

"Jack, they want to know tomorrow night. That's all the time you have. That's the best I can do."

"Okay," was all Jack Eagleton could say.

Chapter 4

Jack Eagleton didn't sleep much that night. As he twisted and turned in the bed, his wife asked, "Jack, what's wrong with you?"

He answered, "Nothing, go back to sleep."

He kept going over what he and Rios had talked about. He thought of the two hundred grand and how it would affect him and his family. He had no idea who Rios was or for whom he was working. Eagleton knew he'd been set up. Rios must have known all along he was in financial trouble and that's why they picked him. He thought about reporting this to his boss at the prison. And he thought about the money. He tossed and turned the rest of the night and didn't sleep much. Neither did his wife.

Eagleton went to work the next morning knowing he didn't have the information Rios wanted. He worked in the warden's office, and knew the warden would know. The warden said, "Jack, I'm stepping out for a minute. Please answer the phone if it rings."

"Yes, sir."

Eagleton knew this might be the break he was looking for. He nosed around the warden's desk. There it was. The time and route for the bus carrying Flores and el Din. He memorized the information. After work, he wrote the information down on a piece of paper. He still hadn't decided on whether he would give the information to Rios or not. He knew the money would make things right again with everyone, especially his wife. No one saw a thing. Jack couldn't believe it. He pulled it off.

The next night, he met Rios at the bar. They had a beer together and Rios asked, "Okay, Jack, what have you got for me?"

"I do have the information you asked for, Moises. I work in the warden's office. The information was right on top of his desk. I memorized it. I wrote it down on this piece of paper." Jack Eagleton was still not sure he was going to do this. He showed Rios the piece of paper but not the information. As he showed the paper, he thought of the two hundred grand. He thought to himself, *What am I getting into?*

Rios looked at the paper and said, "If you have the information, I have the money in my car." When Jack heard the money was outside in Rios's car, he choked on the swig of beer he was trying to swallow. "Take it easy, Jack. The money is yours. All you have to do is give me that paper."

As he passed the paper to Rios, little beads of sweat broke out on Jack's forehead. Rios looked at what was written on the paper and said, "If this is not correct, if you are playing us, you and your family are dead."

Jack couldn't believe what he'd just heard. "This is the information you asked for. Now give me my money."

"You'll get your money when we get what we want."

"When will that be, Moises? You just told me the money was in your car."

"I lied. But if the information proves to be correct, you will get your money. I'll contact you and you will be paid." Rios left Eagleton sitting on the barstool. Jack felt like he'd been hit with a ten-pound sledgehammer.

Eagleton went to work the next day. He walked around in a fog. He didn't know what to do. Should he confess to the warden and tell him the whole story? He wasn't sure if he had committed a crime. Was it a crime to give that information out? Would he be arrested? What would he tell his wife? Would he tell her, I did it for us? He decided not to say a word to anyone. He didn't know who Moises Rios was, but thought, Rios must be working for some really bad guys. He couldn't make the connection to a drug cartel or jailbreak. He knew he probably would not get paid and felt he was lucky to be alive. He thought, *This isn't the way it is supposed to work.*

Rios took the information and reported it to Cruz. "Dize, the information Eagleton gave me says that Flores and el Din will be delivered to the prison in a week. The estimated time of arrival is at five o'clock in the afternoon. I know this route. I'll have time to scout out the road for an ambush site. It'll be difficult, but doable."

"How reliable do you think this information is?" asked Cruz.

"I'm positive the information is good. Eagleton is in a real bind for money. I told you his story. He was mad as hell because he didn't get paid. What's he going to do now? He can't say anything to anyone. I think the information is solid."

"Okay, Rios. I'll be there in a few days. I'm in Nuevo Laredo now. I can be there in a day or two. You find a good place to set up an ambush. When I get there, we can look it over together."

"Okay, I'll be waiting for you."

Chapter 5

The bus was headed for maximum security prison ADX Florence in Fremont County, Colorado, where Flores, el Din, Ghazi Hijaz, and Emir Binhaji were to spend the rest of their lives. When Flores heard and then saw the chopper, he knew immediately what was taking place...a rescue. He had been expecting it. He just didn't know when or where it would come.

After the carnage took place, Flores asked, "What took you so long?"

Cruz answered, "We came as fast as we could, Benito. I'll explain later. We must get out of here, pronto. What do you want to do with the rest of these guys?"

"Kill them all, except el Din." Emir Binhaji and Ghazi Hijaz sat with their mouths agape. They couldn't believe it. They were going to die here and now. Cruz gave each a double shot in the head. They were gone forever.

Flores ordered, "Let's go, let's go! Help el Din. He has not recovered fully from the kneecap he lost. Vince Gonzales shot it during his interrogation. He can't walk very well." Flores's men helped el Din to the chopper. Once they were in Flores barked, "Get this thing in the air!" The chopper took off.

Chapter 6

The chopper headed southwest toward Arizona and landed in a deserted place in the Navajo-Hopi Indian Reservation. There were a dozen ATVs waiting for them. Cruz told Flores, "We have to use these ATVs to get to the SUVs I've got waiting. They'll get us out of here. It's not far."

Flores responded, "Okay, let's get out of here!"

As it turned out, not far was about ten miles to a deserted road outside of Tuba City, Arizona. As expected, the terrain was rough, but they made it. There were two customized SUVs waiting there. They both had their third-row seat taken out. The seats were hollowed out to give Flores and el Din a place to hide and were replaced when Flores and el Din were in them. It wasn't perfect, but then, it didn't have to be.

Cruz said to Flores, "We made a place for you and el Din to hide in the third-row seats in both of the vehicles. You and el Din can hide there until we get across the border. I thought the Americans would be looking in the air for a chopper."

"Good work. I'll get into one and el Din will get into the other. How did you know I would need two vehicles?" asked Flores.

"I didn't. I did it just to be safe," replied Cruz.

El Din had a look of suspicion on his face that couldn't be overlooked by Flores. Flores said, "Look, if I wanted to kill you, I would have done it back there. If you keep your end of the deal, you have nothing to fear. We were successful for you. You and your friends will keep

your end of the deal or you will die. I want that heroin...
now get in the car."

"You'll get the heroin as promised. We will keep
our deal. If not for your help, we wouldn't have been
able to do what we did. The Americans know they are
vulnerable and that we can get to them anytime we want,"
responded el Din.

"Listen," said Flores. "All I want is the heroin you
promised."

They got on Route 160 just south of Tuba and
traveled southwest and then took Route 89 south to
Interstate 17. They traveled through Phoenix very carefully,
obeying all the traffic laws. They didn't want to bring any
attention to themselves. They hooked up with Interstate 10
and then Interstate 19 to Nogales.

Flores had border guards on his payroll on both the
Mexican side of the border and the United States side. It
seemed everyone has a price. It was one of the best ways
to get his product into the US. When the guards worked
the same shift, they let all the product Flores shipped cross
the border unchallenged. Since the new immigration laws
were put in place in the United States, the border was more
secure. Because Flores had border guards on both sides
of the border on his payroll, however, tractor-trailers full
of Flores's product moved safely through the crossing and
into the United States.

When Flores and Cruz got to the border, the guards
on both sides were waiting. They crossed without incident.
Cruz drove to a safe house. It was a rough trip for el Din.
He was not in very good physical condition to begin with,
and his knee was cramped in the back of the SUV. Flores
did much better. They were not in a maximum-security
prison. They were free. They had escaped.

Chapter 7

The people who witnessed the rescue of Flores and el Din and the killing of the bus driver and the guards were in shock. As they came to understand a little of what happened—and after Flores's helicopter had left the scene—they began to call the police. One man got out of his car, walked to the bus, and looked in it. He had never seen anything like it.

When the police arrived, each person was questioned. There was not much to tell, except what happened. Some knew the bus was used to transport prisoners to the ADX prison. Others had no idea what the bus was doing there. None of them knew who was on the bus or who did the shooting.

The police knew immediately where the bus was going and who was on board. Two of the most dangerous men in the world had just escaped. The men who orchestrated the escape knew when and where the bus was going to be. But how did they know? That was the question.

The local authorities called the FBI and FBI Director Joe Madden was informed. He called President Rivera. "Mr. President, Flores and el Din have escaped. According to witnesses, they killed Emir Binhaji, Ghazi Hijaz, the bus driver, and four guards before leaving on a chopper."

"What did you say, Joe...Flores and el Din escaped? They got away on a chopper? How could that happen? More importantly, what are you doing about it?"

"Mr. President, my men are investigating and

interviewing all prison employees. They're the only people who may have known when Flores and el Din were going to be delivered. We are looking for any clue. Someone who is tied to the Los Zetas or ISIS. All employees of the prison have passed security tests. Something would've shown up if anyone had those kinds of connections. We think the one responsible needs money. Someone in a financial bind. We have uncovered three guards who may be in that position. I'm going to Fremont, Colorado, tonight. I want to interrogate these guards."

"Well, this is certainly a setback, Joe. Let me know as soon as you know anything."

"We'll cover all the bases thoroughly. I'll keep you informed, sir."

Joe Madden arrived in Fremont at eleven o'clock that evening. He was greeted by the warden of the prison, Jeffrey Miller. Miller had been the warden at the ADX maximum security prison for five years. He was considered one of the best in the business. He and Joe Madden had known each other for at least ten years and had a good relationship.

"It's good to see you, Joe. I can't imagine one of my people being in on this."

"This is not good, Jeff. The president is very upset about this. Frankly, so am I," responded Madden.

"Despite my feelings about the people who work for me, my people think there are three prison guards who look suspicious. I think there is one man who stands out. To think that one of people is tied to this is really upsetting. It's really hard to believe."

"Great; who is he, and why does he stand out?" asked Madden.

"His name is Eagleton...Jack Eagleton. We found out that he is about to lose his house. His wife is about to leave him and take his kids. Some of the other guards Eagleton works with know his situation. They think he's up against the wall financially. We haven't talked to him yet, but we are about to bring him in for questioning tomorrow morning," answered Miller.

"That's a good start. I've come here to be a part of the interrogation. My folks from the local FBI office and I will question this man. Let's hope it leads somewhere. Do you have any information from the witnesses?" said Madden.

"From what witnesses have reported, a chopper landed in front of the transport bus. The guards, the driver, and prisoners Ghazi Hijaz and Emir Binhaji were killed on the spot. Flores and el Din left on the chopper. They had a pretty good head start and could be anywhere."

"What time are you going to bring Eagleton in for questioning?" asked Madden.

"Nine in the morning."

"I'll see you at nine tomorrow, Jeff. I've got to call President Rivera and fill him in on the progress you've made."

Madden made the call. "Mr. President, Warden Jeff Miller has made good progress with the investigation. He's interviewed many of the prison guards and employees. During the interviews, three people have been discovered to be in financial trouble. One of them stands out from the rest. He's about to lose his home, and his wife is about to leave him and take the kids."

"What're you doing about it, Joe?"

"The man's name is Jack Eagleton. I'm going to interrogate him tomorrow. I'll keep you posted. One more thing, sir."

"What's that, Joe?"

"Flores made some strong threats to Gonzales,

Covert Bravo, Consuela Hernández, Joe and Governor Lisa Martinez, and Secretary Sydney Alvarez. They threatened Consuela's uncle Domingo and his wife, too. Precautions should be taken to protect those people. Gonzales and his men can take care of themselves, but they too should be notified.

"As soon as I get any information on Eagleton, I'll inform you. We are looking for the chopper now. From what the witnesses say, it must be an old Huey from the Vietnam era. It carried seven men and the pilot. We'll be looking in all directions. It will turn up somewhere. They will head south to Mexico for sure. So, we'll concentrate our efforts in that direction. But we can't overlook the threats Flores made to our people. Flores won't tolerate any disloyalty by anyone. He never has. He will try to get even."

President Rivera took in all this information and tried to process it. "Keep me up to date, Joe. I'll get things going on my end."

"That's fine, sir. Make sure the secretary, Consuela, and the Martinez family are protected. We should try to get Consuela's uncle Domingo and his wife out of Mexico. If you don't object, I can send some of my people to get them," replied Madden.

"If you have the time, Joe, go ahead and send your folks to Mexico. Get Domingo and his wife out of there. I'll set that up with the president of Mexico. When he considers the circumstances, I doubt he will have any objections."

"I can handle it, sir. Since I'm already in Florence, I can set things up in the next hour or so. After I issue the order, my people will leave immediately. If Eagleton is who we think he is, I want to talk to him personally," said Madden.

"Great. And good luck, Joe."

Chapter 8

The president called Secretary Sydney Alvarez, DNI Bob Reynolds, CIA Director Frank Yanelli, and Captain Vince Gonzales and Covert Bravo to his office the next morning. FBI Director Joe Madden was in Colorado. When Gonzales and Covert Bravo got to the White House, Pattie Hayes, the president's secretary, met them. On the way to the Oval Office, Pattie took a long look at Manny Sanchez. Gonzales noticed, as did Covert Bravo... especially Sanchez.

The president, Secretary Alvarez, Reynolds, and Yanelli were waiting. By that time, the news agencies from all over the world had the story and were running with it. Even though the media had little information about the escape, they knew there was an escape and who escaped.

They sat down, and the president filled them in on what Joe Madden had relayed to him. All were angered and amazed at what had taken place.

"How could this happen!" blurted Gonzales.

"They had to have someone who has access to the necessary information. Someone on the inside. The time the bus left for the prison and the route it would take. The time of arrival. Madden is going to interrogate someone tomorrow morning. His name is Jack Eagleton. He seems to be the most suspicious person right now. We'll get his story soon. We must make certain you're safe, Secretary Alvarez...and that Consuela, her son, Lucia, and her uncle Domingo and his wife are safe. Madden is sending his agents get them out of Mexico now. He doesn't think we should wait. I agree. Flores is on the run right now. When he gets where he's going—and we think he'll get there because of the head start he has—he'll send someone to assassinate Domingo and his wife," said the president.

The president ordered Frank Yanelli, "Make sure our best CIA agents are on the detail to secure the secretary, Consuela, and the Martinez family. I've called the president of Mexico and told him we're coming for Domingo and his wife. With all that's happened, I doubt he will argue the point."

"Mr. President, I'll get right on it." Yanelli left to make those arrangements.

"What's your take on this, Bob?" asked the president.

"I think all is being done that can be done right now, sir," was Bob Reynolds' thinking. "I think Flores and el Din will head straight to Mexico. Flores has men all over our country. Some we know about...others we don't. We should watch the ones we know. But don't forget, Flores is running for his life right now and hasn't had time to set anything in motion. That's my opinion, sir."

The president looked at Gonzales and asked the same question. Gonzales offered, "I agree with Director Reynolds, Mr. President. Flores is on the run. I think he will head for the border as fast as he can and will get to Mexico because he has such a head start. I think he will try to make a hit on the secretary, Consuela, and the Martinez family. He never forgets a betrayal. My men and I have seen his revenge and it isn't pretty. I think the border guards should be notified immediately. We know Flores has some of our border guards, as well as guards on the Mexico side of the border, on his payroll. So, if he tries to cross into Mexico by a land vehicle, it may have been set up already by Dize Cruz, his second-in-command."

Secretary Alvarez sat through the meeting and never said a word.

Chapter 9

When Flores had been questioned by Frank Yanelli, Joe Madden, and Gonzales, he'd said, "Everyone involved with my capture and the rescue of Consuela Hernández—Sydney Alvarez, Lisa Martinez and her husband, but especially you, Vince Gonzales, and your men—will all die a very painful death. I promise you that. All of you will suffer a very slow death."

"If any one of those people is hurt in the least way, you'll answer to me and it won't be pretty," retorted Gonzales.

Flores looked at Gonzales and just grunted.

* * *

After the bombings, the United States bounced back just like it always does from a tragedy. Memorials were held for all the people who had lost their lives. The effort to decontaminate Chicago was underway and was directed by the Federal Emergency Management Agency (FEMA) and assisted by the secretary of the Department of Homeland Security, Sydney Alvarez.

As the process got along, it was discovered Chicago wasn't nearly as contaminated as first thought. It might take no more than a year to finish the cleanup before the area would be accessible to people, as opposed to the first estimate of ten to fifteen years. Rebuilding could start then.

President Rivera kept the country up to date on how things were progressing with the cleanup in Chicago with weekly news conferences. Disney World and Las Vegas were back in business and receiving customers. People were starting to feel safe again. The country was getting back to normal...whatever normal was.

Chapter 10

The day Consuela, her son, her son's nanny, Lucia, Governor Lisa Martinez and her husband Joe, Gonzales, and Covert Bravo got back to DC, the president asked them to stay in Washington for a few days at the Hyatt. He wanted to talk to them personally.

* * *

Joe and Governor Lisa Martinez spent the time together privately. They went to their room and just held each other. "I wasn't sure I'd see you or the children again, Joe." As soon as she said this, she buried her head into his shoulder and began to quietly sob.

"I know, honey, I know. But it's over now. Let's just try to relax. The children are fine. I called my folks. My parents don't know what happened; neither do the boys. They are very anxious to see us." They ordered dinner from room service.

"It's so nice to be together again, Joe. I don't know if I would have let you make that dangerous high-altitude high opening parachute jump. I know you made those jumps before, but you were much younger."

"Are you calling me old?" Joe remarked kiddingly. They both got a chuckle out of his remark.

"If something would have happened to you and me, too, what would the children have done? I must admit, there was a moment when I thought I'd never see you or our children again. Still, Syd and I were confident Gonzales and Covert Bravo would come for us, or we might escape on our own. We were about to when you showed up. I can't believe I ran into your arms. What a coincidence! Or maybe divine intervention."

"Those are all ifs and maybes, honey. I would not have done it if I thought the rescue would fail. Gonzales and Covert Bravo, our best combat vets, were with me. As it turned out, they needed Major Williams and me to pull it off. I'm truly sorry this had to happen to you and Syd. It's over now, and we can get back to our normal life." With that said, they ate their dinner and went to bed. They made love most tenderly. They told each other how much they loved each other and fell asleep in each other's arms. Lisa clung to Joe tightly all night.

* * *

Consuela went to her room by herself with her son and Lucia, just like Gonzales and each of the men in Covert Bravo. She felt like going for a walk, and decided to go down to the hotel lobby. She looked through the shops and sat down and had a cup of coffee. She looked up and was startled to see who was coming her way...Bob Chavez. He stopped by her table. "What are you doing down here, Bob?"

"I called your room. Lucia said you'd gone out for a walk. I got a little worried about you. So, I came looking."

"Thank you for your concern."

"It's more than concern, Consuela. I think you know that." She gave Chavez a coy, quizzical look.

Chavez responded to Consuela's look, "Are you saying you didn't feel something when I was driving you in Mexico or when I grabbed you on the beach the other night? I know I did. I haven't had feelings like this for anyone in my life."

"Yes, I do have the same feelings for you, too. I'm thinking, where am I going from here? I'm not in the country legally. I have nowhere to go. I have no money."

"I don't think President Rivera will let you down. Your contribution to the country's security has been invaluable. You alerted the president of the danger that was out there. I wouldn't worry about not having a place to go or not having any money. The president, I'm sure, will take care of those things. Now, let's take a walk and get some dinner."

"Bob, I'd love to go with you. But I'm wearing the same clothes I had on when you rescued me. They're clean. I sent them to the hotel's laundry. I hope I didn't overstep myself." She wore a pair of black slacks and a white blouse.

"You look great, Consuela, just great," replied Chavez. "Don't worry about how you look; you look terrific. Don't think you overstepped by getting your clothes cleaned."

Consuela blushed at the compliment. She said, "In that case, I accept your invitation. Where do you want to go?"

"Let's just take a walk. As we walk, we'll find someplace to eat," answered Chavez.

They had dinner at a bistro in Georgetown. After dinner, they kept walking.

"I have never felt this way about anyone before in my life, Consuela. The only thing in my life has been the army and the Rangers. I've never even had a steady girlfriend. Oh, there have been women, but nothing serious. I think I have fallen in love with you. I'm certain of it. I feel responsible for you. I want to take care of you. I can't believe I'm saying this to you. I almost feel like a fool."

"You're not a fool, Bob. I have the same thoughts.

I had them almost from the first time I saw you. I knew you were strong and tough, but there was a tenderness about you too. I was completely at ease with you from the first time Benito let you drive me. There was something about you, Gonzales, Sanchez, Ramirez, and Gomez. You were different from the others in Los Zetas. I knew you were there for some other reason than working in the drug business." She hesitated and looked away. "You know about me and Benito. If I were you, I don't think I could get by that."

Chavez gently turned her face to him and replied, "Listen to me; I don't care about that and I told you so back in Mexico. If I were in your position, I would have done the same thing. Those people killed your parents, and I understand." They walked back to the Hyatt. There was not another word spoken between them. Chavez took Consuela back to her room, kissed her on the cheek, and said goodnight.

* * *

Secretary Sydney Alvarez was trying to come to grips with the feelings she had for Vince Gonzales. She had been attracted to men in the past. This was different, she thought. But why? She lay in bed and couldn't answer her question. She wondered why she wanted to get to know Gonzales better. When she ran into his arms on the beach in Mexico, she felt electric and above all, safe. Who was this man, Vince Gonzales? Why did these thoughts come to her?

Down on the next floor, Vince Gonzales tossed and turned in his bed. He thought of the rescue, but in the back of his mind, there was something else bothering him... Secretary of Home Security Sydney Alvarez. He thought of how he felt—or the buzz, as he called it—that went through him when she landed in his arms on the beach in Mexico. Why should he be thinking of her that way? He had done his job and conducted a very daring rescue successfully. He thought, *What's wrong with me?* He got out of bed and turned on the TV in his room when the phone rang. He thought it was one of the guys wanting to go out for a beer. Gonzales picked up the phone. "Hello."

"Hello, Captain Gonzales; this Secretary Alvarez."

"Yes, Secretary Alvarez, what can I do for you?"

"Meet me in the lobby please."

"Yes, Madam Secretary. I'll be right down. If you mean now, that is."

"Yes, I do mean now, Captain!"

Vince put on his dress uniform as fast as he could and went to the elevator and pushed the button for the lobby. He couldn't think of any reason Secretary Alvarez would want to see him. His thoughts went back to the beach. When he got down to the lobby, she was waiting for him.

"Secretary Alvarez, I'm sorry to keep you waiting. How can I be of service?"

"You can start by calling me Sydney; or as my friends call me, Syd."

Gonzales felt like he'd been hit with a rifle butt in his stomach. The startled look on his face was obvious. He couldn't believe what he'd just heard. *Why would the secretary want me to call her by her first name? What is going on here?*

"Relax, Captain. Do you mind if I call you Vince?"

"No, I don't, Secretary Alvarez. You can call me anything you like; but I prefer Gonzales. I am at your command."

"Gonzales it is. Now, take me out to dinner,

Gonzales. I know a place where we can go and have some privacy."

"You want me to take you out to dinner? You want to go to a private place?"

"That's a good start, Gonzales; let's go."

She grabbed a cab. They got in. She gave the driver the address of the place. They rode for a while. Gonzales couldn't contain himself.

"Where is your security? You don't travel without security."

Sydney looked him right in the eyes and said, "Gonzales, you're the only security I need."

When Gonzales heard this from the secretary, he took a big gulp. The cab stopped outside a townhouse in Georgetown. Syd and Gonzales got out.

"Are you sure this is a restaurant, Madam Secretary?" queried Gonzales.

"Of course, I'm sure," answered Sydney.

As they walked to the door, Sydney took out a key and unlocked the door. They went in. When she wanted to be alone, this was the place she went to, just to think and to get out of the Washington spotlight.

"Sit down and make yourself comfortable." She went to her wine cooler and opened a bottle of Rodney Strong Russian River Pinot Noir.

"Do you like wine, Gonzales?"

"I haven't had that much, but I'm open to it."

"Good, I think you'll like this wine. It's a Russian wine."

Gonzales said, "I didn't know Russia was in the winemaking business."

"Russia does produce wine. But this wine is from the Russian River in California. This Pinot Noir is unique. The weather conditions there make the grapes extraordinary. The quality of the wine is complemented by the sediment deposit from the yearly valley flooding. The wine is excellent."

Gonzales just looked at her and drank what she gave him.

"Well, what do you think?" she asked.

"This does taste good. A lot better than the beer I usually drink."

Sydney Alvarez was just as surprised by her forward approach as Gonzales was. She was amazed that she'd brought him to her place.

"Do you like steak and lobster?"

"Do I like it? It's one of my favorites. Of course, there's nothing like Mexican food. I mean good, authentic Mexican food," answered Gonzales.

"Great! I'll remember your desire for authentic Mexican food for another time!" exclaimed Sydney. Gonzales thought, *What's this about another time?* He kept the thought to himself.

She went to the refrigerator and took out two eight-ounce filet mignon and two eight-once lobster tails. She prepared the food perfectly and served Gonzales. She took note of the fact that he ate like he hadn't eaten in weeks and was pleased with her effort. After dinner, they drank another glass of wine.

"Secretary Alvarez, if I may ask, what's this all about? What do you want of me?"

"I want to thank you for rescuing me and Lisa."

"No thanks necessary, it's my job."

"Well, when I ran into your arms on the beach, I felt something I never felt before. I felt your courage and tenderness. My body felt electric like it never had before. I think I saw the same thing in your eyes, too. Am I wrong about that, Gonzales?" declared a blushing Sydney.

Gonzales almost dropped his glass of wine and just looked at her. The country was in danger. He'd sworn to defend it. And here he was doing what, and with whom? He couldn't process this fast enough, but was able to say, "You're right, I did feel a buzz. I can't believe you felt the same thing."

"Well, I did. I'm just as surprised as you. I don't do this sort of thing. You're the only man I've had in this place. I think there is a mutual attraction between us. I don't think we should let it go."

"I've thought about the beach, too. I didn't know what to do about it either. I didn't think I should call you, but I'm glad you called me. You know I'm an Army Ranger, and may get sent anywhere at any time. I've never had a real relationship with a woman. Are you sure you can with me, under those circumstances?"

"I think we should take this a little slower. Get to know each other better. You may find me bothersome."

"I don't know what could be more bothersome than being deployed in an instant. I could be gone for months at a time. I love the Rangers. Would you have me deny my chosen life?"

"I would never ask you to stop being you. The thing that attracts me to you, Gonzales...is you."

"Another thing to consider is your position and station in life. I doubt if I'd fit in with your friends."

"Well, you let me decide that. You fit in anywhere at any time. Like I said, we know we have some attraction for each other. Let's just see where this takes us."

"I agree, Syd. It may not take us anywhere."

When Gonzales used her name, Sydney Alvarez smiled broadly and thought, *That's what you think, soldier.* They caught a cab back to the Hyatt. He took her to her room. They looked longingly into each other's eyes. They kissed softly and said goodnight.

Chapter 11

The next morning, Vince got up at 4:30 and had a workout in the hotel's facility, then showered and got dressed. He went out the door of the Hyatt. He made the short walk to St. Patrick Catholic Church. Vince was a practicing Catholic, like most Latinos, and went to Mass whenever he could. Not just on Sunday. It was a practice his parents taught him. Sometimes, when he was deployed, he went weeks without Mass and the Eucharist. He got his faith from his parents, especially his mother, who went to Mass daily to receive the Sacrament. When he was deployed, he depended on his faith to sustain him during the hard times. His men in Covert Bravo were the same.

Gonzales went into the church and up the aisle. He entered a pew and moved halfway down it. He knelt in prayer, closed his eyes, and thanked God for giving him the ability he needed to do his job.

He sensed someone next to him. The church had just a few people at this 5:30 morning Mass. Who was entering his space? He looked over and saw it was Sydney Alvarez. She knelt beside him and closed her eyes in prayer. Vince experienced something he'd never felt before. Goosebumps. They eventually looked at each other and participated in the Mass and received the Eucharist together.

After Mass, she asked, "How about breakfast, Gonzales?"

"Sure, why not."

She met with her security detail and told them she

would be going out to breakfast with Gonzales. She took Vince to a little, out-of-the-way breakfast spot where she knew they could have privacy. The security detail had breakfast a few booths away, but not close enough for them to hear the conversation Syd and Gonzales were going to have.

They ordered and waited for it to come. They talked as they ate. Gonzales, as would be expected, had an enormous appetite. He had four eggs, two orders of bacon, and the restaurant specialty: griddle cakes, coffee, and toast. Syd had an egg white omelet with spinach, mushrooms, and goat cheese, whole wheat toast and coffee.

"You've got some appetite, fella."

"Yes, I do. I don't get to eat like this very often. I mean, I usually eat in an army chow hall. Not that chow hall food is all bad. This chow, I mean breakfast, is fantastic."

"I'm glad you're enjoying it. But I want to know more about you, Gonzales."

"What do you want to know?"

"For starters, how did you come to be an Army Ranger?"

Gonzales said, "It's a long story. I think you'd be bored."

"Let me be the judge of that."

"Okay then. I was not a very good student in high school. School just didn't interest me. My grade point average was 2.03, but I did graduate on time. I didn't see a future for me. Gangs tried to get me to join them. But I took my parents' advice and stayed away from gangs and told them to stay away from me. My parents didn't have money for me to go to college. My parents worked themselves to death...literally. There wasn't any scholarship for me, either. Even if there was money to go to college, I doubt I would have been successful."

Sydney stopped him and asked, "Why would you say you wouldn't have been successful?"

"What I mean is, I don't think I was ready for college. So, I took a job flipping burgers. It was okay, but I felt the urge for something else...not necessarily better, just different. Don't get me wrong, there's nothing wrong with flipping burgers.

"One day after work, I walked by an Army recruiter's office at a shopping mall. I went in and the recruiter asked, 'What can I do for you, son?' I told him about my situation. He asked, 'What are you interested in?' I told him, 'I'm not sure.' He told me the opportunities the army offered. I went home and told my parents. Although they were worried about my going to Afghanistan, they gave me their blessing. I went through Basic Training, Ranger Training, and survived two tours in Afghanistan. The army sent me to Officer Candidate School and Arizona State University."

"What was your major?" queried Sydney.

"Political Science. My grade point average was 3.5. Not bad for a C student in high school. Now here I am talking with the secretary of the Department of Homeland Security, who for some reason asked me to breakfast." He smiled at her. "Now, I want to know how a Latina got to be the secretary of the Department of Homeland Security."

"That's a long story, too. I've got some time. So, here it is. Lisa Martinez, the governor of Arizona, and I, grew up much the way you did. Our parents worked hard. They told us the only way to get ahead was to stay in school, get good grades, and go to college. We did that, and wound up at Stanford on an academic and athletic scholarship. Lisa played volleyball. I played basketball. We are both tall girls and have some athletic talent.

"When we graduated, we went our separate ways,

so to speak. I went to Harvard Law School. After law school, I clerked for a Supreme Court judge. After a few years of working in private practice, President Rivera asked me to be on his staff. Then he asked me to be the secretary of the Department of Homeland Security. After some deliberation by Congress, I was confirmed. That's a thumbnail of my life. Lisa went back to Arizona, got into politics, and now is the governor. She married Joe Martinez, who is a very successful restaurateur. They have three beautiful boys."

Gonzales was mesmerized as Sydney told her story. He listened to every word. When she finished, he asked, "How come a beautiful woman like you never got married?"

"Good question. There was a time. I went with a man. We did get serious. But it just didn't feel right. So, we—I—broke it off. There were more important things in my life." She shrugged, then looked up at the clock on the wall. "It's getting late and I have to get to work."

Gonzales said, "Breakfast is on me. Let's get you on your way."

"Thanks, Gonzales. Keep in touch."

"For sure. Let's do this again."

Syd said, "Oh, we will, we will. I think we'll be attending a meeting together at the White House. Covert Bravo will be there, too."

"I figured you'd be there."

"You figure well, Gonzales." Which brought a big smile across his face.

At that, she was joined by her security detail and left to continue with her daily duties and extending any help she could to FEMA in its effort to clean up Chicago. She had to meet with the president this morning and give him a briefing on the progress being made in Chicago.

Chapter 12

President Rivera called the meeting with Secretary Alvarez, Captain Gonzales and Covert Bravo, along with directors Bob Reynolds (DNI), Frank Yanelli (CIA), and Joe Madden (FBI) in attendance. The president asked Secretary Alvarez for an update on the Chicago cleanup.

"Mr. President, I'm happy to say the cleanup is going better than expected. We will be denied access for no longer than a year. Initially, we thought it would be ten years, and then five years. We are estimating less than a year and a half. Hopefully sooner than that."

The president said, "That's great news, Sydney, great news. Has there been a final number on casualties?"

"Sir, we are still working on that. We should have a good number soon. When I get those numbers and have a name to go with each number, you'll be the first to know."

The president said, "I need to know soon. I want to get in touch with all the relatives of the dead, and of course, I want to talk to the survivors. I have spoken with some of the survivors. We are taking good care of them. Some have since died from their injuries. I've spoken with their relatives. I know the Mercantile Exchange is burnt to a crisp and all perished there. The Mart did have its data backed up in Charlotte, North Carolina. So, people invested there need not worry. Their records and money are secure.

"I've called this meeting for another reason. Bob, Frank, Joe, Secretary Alvarez, and I have a question for Captain Gonzales and Covert Bravo. We would like you fellas to think about coming to work for us. We need a team we can depend on in sensitive situations."

Gonzales and his men just looked at each other. They fully expected to be deployed again as Rangers.

"Does that mean we won't be Rangers anymore, sir?" Gonzales asked.

"No, you will still be Rangers. But we want to use you for special operations. The information you have provided concerning the Benito Flores cartel is proving to be invaluable. Marijuana has been legalized in our country. The demand for illegal marijuana has significantly gone down. There's little profit in it. However, the demand for hard drugs in this country has gone up just as significantly, especially heroin, cocaine, and Ecstasy."

"Mr. President, we know the border may be more secure now. We know there are border guards on both sides of the border who are on Flores's payroll. When these guards work at the same time on both sides of the border, big tractor-trailer loads of drugs come through.

"We can't forget the Pacific and Atlantic oceans or the Gulf of Mexico either. Flores has begun to launch drones from those bodies of water and the desert on the Mexican side of the border. The drones can carry more weight, which means more of his product gets through. As the drones get bigger and can carry bigger payloads, the profit margin is bigger.

"The semisubmersibles are getting bigger and safer. They will be able to carry huge loads. They will travel long distances. Flores makes more money. He is back in Mexico now, or someplace where he can conduct his business. He has been promised all the heroin in Afghanistan by ISIS... Baha el Din, specifically.

"If not for Flores, the terrorists would not have been successful. The nuke in Chicago would not have detonated. Flores had his men ambush the bus that was taking him to prison. Despite what happened in Chicago, Flores and the Los Zetas still enjoy the protection of the Mexican government—not all the government, but a lot of it. He has many high-ranking government officials in his pocket. Although I think some of them may want to get away from him, they may be too scared to do so.

"Another issue is ISIS. They've been taken down with your tactical nuclear strike. I think ISIS will slink back into the woodwork, so to speak, but will slowly reemerge."

"Captain Gonzales, you've just made our point. That's our thinking, too. That's exactly why we want you to work with us. We need to stop the hard drugs from entering the country and we need to fight ISIS. I want you and your men to think about this. We need you now more than ever. Look what they did to us! I think they will keep coming at us."

Gonzales looked at his men and said, "Let us sleep on it, sir. We thought we'd be deployed shortly. We should give this a lot of thought. Maybe we should take some R & R. Someplace where we can wind down from our mission in Mexico."

"Where would you go?" asked the president.

"I'm not sure, sir," answered Gonzales.

"We need you and Covert Bravo now, Captain!" exclaimed President Rivera.

"We hear you, Mr. President."

* * *

Gonzales and Covert Bravo went back to the Hyatt. They met in Gonzales's suite. He asked, "Well, guys, what should we do about the president's proposition?"

Bob Chavez said, "I think it's a good idea. We'll be

together on any operation he sends us on. We know each other and we know we can depend on each other. What about the proposition you gave to the president? You know, about going somewhere for R & R? Where would we go?" Manny Sanchez added, "I agree with Chavez. This is a good opportunity for all of us. Our military is out of Iraq and mostly out of Afghanistan. We may have a better chance to do some good for the country staying here with the president. I, too, want to know where we'd go for R & R."

"I was thinking of going to a casino. There's one at the Mohawk Indian Reservation in Hogansburg, New York," answered Gonzales.

"A casino? You mean a place to gamble on an Indian reservation?" exclaimed Chavez.

"That's exactly what I mean. I've never been to one. I doubt any of you've been to one either," replied Gonzales. "I've played some blackjack when I've been deployed. It was fun. I didn't lose any money. I didn't make any money either. I just thought going to a casino would be a good change of pace for us. Anyone have any other ideas?"

Jose Ramirez jumped in with, "I went to a casino in Vegas. I was on leave and went to see my parents. They lived on the outskirts of Vegas. So, I went to the Flamingo. I don't keep up with popular music. A guy was singing there named Bublé. He was the featured singer there. I did some gambling, but not much. I lost a little money. I didn't expect to win. Those casinos aren't there to lose. The casino is there for people to lose their money and have fun doing it. I think you've got a good idea, Gonzales. I think we should go somewhere and unwind. I know I could use a few days away.

"Getting back to the president's proposal, I like the

idea. I've got one question. Where will we train? We can't let ourselves get soft. You know that."

Gonzales said, "That's the right attitude, Ramirez. And I'm sure, or at least I think, the president will set those things up for us. We may have a private place. I doubt many people will know about what we'll be doing. I think just the people in the Oval Office will know."

Raphael Gomez said, "I'm not so sure about this. We're Army Rangers. We should train and deploy with one of our units. As for the R & R, I'm all for it."

"Well, let's give it more thought and talk some more tomorrow. We don't all have to stay on with the president. If one of us wants to deploy with a Ranger unit, more power to you. If any one of us decides not to take President Rivera's proposal, he shouldn't think he's letting anyone down," Gonzales ended the conversation. They all left for their own rooms.

Chapter 13

Gonzales and Covert Bravo were on their own for the rest of the day and that evening. Bob Chavez called Consuela and asked, "Consuela, this is Chavez. How do you feel about going out to dinner with me tonight?"

"Bob, I was hoping you'd call. Oh, yes, I would enjoy that very much."

"That's just great. I'll pick you up in your room at about five o'clock. We can roam around Georgetown and find another place to eat."

"I'll be waiting," said Consuela. Chavez hung up and thought to himself, *Perfect.*

Consuela was waiting when Chavez knocked on her door. When she stepped out of the room, she looked lovely. She had on a new outfit. Chavez lost his breath. She noticed his reaction. After he regained his composure, they took the elevator to the lobby. They didn't see any of the others. They walked for a while before Chavez asked, "Consuela, has anyone given you any information on what you'll be doing or where you'll go?"

"I'm glad you asked. I had a meeting with President Rivera this afternoon."

"And?" Chavez anxiously asked.

"Well, we had a nice conversation. He asked me if I wanted to stay in this country. Of course, I said yes. He asked if I had any plans. I told him I wanted to finish college."

"And what was his answer?" Chavez asked.

"He told me both were possible. He said he had documents for me to stay in the United States. And if I want to go to college, it is possible. The president told me that he made arrangements for me to live in a townhouse in Georgetown."

"Wonderful! Now tell me what the president said about college."

"He said I could enroll at American University for the fall semester. And he got me a job at the State Department as an interpreter. I asked if my credits from the Universidad Tecnológica de México could be transferred. He said he'd have Pattie Hayes help me do everything...get into my townhouse, help get my application to American University ready, and see about getting my credits transferred from Mexico.

"On my way out of the Oval Office, Pattie Hayes told me to get my things together at the Hyatt. She said she'd help me move to the townhouse. When I told her all I had were the clothes I had on and a few things someone put in my room before I got here, she said we'd go shopping this afternoon. What do you think about that?"

"Tell me about your shopping trip. Honestly, Consuela, you look beautiful wearing any kind of clothes," said Chavez.

Consuela blushed again and said, "We went shopping in the best boutiques in the DC area. She took me to Style Etoile, where I got the outfit I'm wearing now. She helped me pick out everything. All my new clothes are in my room here at the Hyatt. She and I will move them into my townhouse tomorrow. Isn't that amazing?" asked Consuela.

"I told you President Rivera would take care of you, didn't I?" Chavez said with a delight he could not hide, and added, "That's just great. I'm so happy for you. But did President Rivera say anything about providing security for you? Anything about bodyguards?"

"Yes, he did, Bob. He said I'd have two guards assigned to watch me day and night, starting tomorrow. He said the same applied to Alejandro and Lucia. I'm so relieved. But I still feel safest when I'm with you. Pattie said something to me I think is funny," said Consuela.

"Well, I'm glad to hear you'll have protection," said Chavez. "Flores may be running for his life right now. When he gets to Mexico, if that's where he's going, he'll feel safe. He may think about getting even. What did Pattie say to you that's so funny?"

"Pattie asked me if Manny Sanchez had a girlfriend."

"She asked you about Sanchez? If he had a girlfriend? If that doesn't beat all. Every time we're in the White House, and after she directs us to the Oval Office, she gives Sanchez the look. We all get a chuckle out of it... all of us except Sanchez. He's beside himself. He hasn't said anything to us...but we know he's thinking about it."

"Well, does he have a girlfriend?" asked Consuela.

"Heck no. I'm sure he doesn't. If he did, we'd know about her. When you live like we've lived, you get to know everyone. Sanchez does not have a girlfriend!" answered Chavez.

"Do you think I should tell Pattie?"

"Why not? Sure, tell her," answered Chavez.

"When I see her tomorrow, I'll tell her."

"It can't hurt, Consuela."

"Bob, do you think Benito will come for me and Alejandro?" queried Consuela.

"He made the threat. It must be taken seriously. He may try in time. Not only you and Alejandro, but Secretary Alvarez, Governor Lisa and Joe Martinez, and Lucia. I think he wants his son back. I don't think there's anything to worry about right now though. So, let's find a place to have dinner and enjoy ourselves."

"That sounds good to me, Bob. But I must say, what you said scared me more than a little. Are you and the rest of the team going to be here in the area?"

"The president has asked us to stay and work with him here in Washington. He wants us to work on special projects. The president said we'll still be Army Rangers. We may take a few days off to make our decision...you know, some R & R."

"What do you mean...you're going to take a few days off?" asked Consuela.

"Gonzales said we should take some time to consider what President Rivera has offered. Go someplace where we can clear our heads for a few days. The president has asked us to stay here with him. We'd work on special projects. The president wants an answer as soon as possible."

"That makes me feel better. Where are you going on this R & R? That scares me a little."

"You'll be safe. The CIA agents who are looking after you and Alejandro are the best. I'd trust them with my life."

"Bob, I feel better and safer when I'm with you."

"Thank you. You'll be safe when I'm gone. It'll only be two or three days."

They walked down Connecticut Avenue NW for a while and came upon the little Italian spot. "Hey, Consuela, how do you feel about Italian food?" asked Chavez.

"I don't know, Bob. I haven't had much of it...but I'd like to try some."

"Great, I think you'll enjoy it. I didn't have any until I got into the army. It's good food, but different than our food."

The place, Vace Italian Delicatessen, was famous

for pizza and pasta. They were seated in a booth in the rear of the place. It was quiet and cozy. The waiter brought menus and water to them.

"Do you like wine?" asked Chavez.

"Sure, I'd like a glass, but you choose."

Chavez answered, "I don't know much about wine. I'll ask the waiter to suggest."

The waiter suggested Casa Emma Chianti Classico. Chavez said, "That sounds fine."

They looked over the dinner menu and Chavez asked, "How does a pizza sound?"

"That sounds good to me. I've had some in Mexico. I went to a Little Caesars and had some when I was living on my own. I liked it."

"Have you ever had a mushroom, pepperoni, and cheese?" asked Chavez.

"I don't think so. Let's give it a try," answered Consuela.

The waiter brought the Chianti. Chavez ordered the pizza. While the pizza was being prepared, they enjoyed a glass of wine. The pizza came out and was brought to their table.

Consuela took a bite and said, "Bob, this is much better than what I had in Mexico."

"Well, I'm glad you're enjoying it. It is good. I know this place is a famous Italian delicatessen. I heard people talking about it at the hotel."

They ate and drank until they were full. Chavez asked for the check. When they got back to the hotel, it was 9:00 p.m. Chavez took Consuela to her room. She asked, "Would you like to come in, Bob?"

"You know I want to come in with you." With that, she put her arm through his and they went into her room.

Chapter 14

Ramirez, Sanchez, and Gomez had already left for dinner. Gonzales was alone with his thoughts. He jacked up his courage and thought, *This is tough. I've never felt fear like this.* But he picked up the phone and dialed the room of Sydney Alvarez.

"Hello, this is Secretary Alvarez," was the answer Gonzales got. He swallowed hard.

"Hey, Syd, this is, uh, this is Vince Gonzales."

Sydney chuckled to herself because she heard the tension in Vince's voice. "Hello, Gonzales. What can I do for you?"

Gonzales stammered and finally said, "How, uh, how about dinner? That is, unless you've already eaten."

"I'd love dinner. Where shall we go?"

"You pick."

"I know just the place, Captain. I'll meet you in the lobby in thirty minutes."

"I'll be there," responded Gonzales.

It was just enough time for him to jump in the shower and put on his dress uniform. Thirty minutes later, they were in a cab heading to one of Sydney's favorite dinner spots, with her security close behind.

Syd directed the cabbie to the Proof Restaurant. They got out and went in. Secretary Alvarez had made reservations so the restaurant staff was waiting for them. Gonzales and Sydney were escorted to a quiet booth. The place had a great ambiance. Gonzales spoke. "This is a pretty classy spot, Syd. I'm glad I wore my dress uniform."

"You look great in anything, Gonzales."

Gonzales stammered, "Thank you, but you look terrific too."

"I was hoping you'd like this outfit."

"I do...I do. I feel like a sixteen-year-old kid on his first date."

"You're doing just fine, Gonzales. Relax." The waiter brought them a dinner menu and left.

"You're going to have to make the choice, Syd."

Syd looked through the menu offerings and asked, "What do you have yen for?"

"I'm thinking about seafood."

"Great, I'm favoring seafood as well."

The waiter asked for a drink order. Vince looked at her and shrugged his shoulders as if to say, I have no idea. She said, "I'll select a wine."

"That's fine with me." She chose a Pinot Noir labeled Ballard Lane. It came from a boutique winery in California. The waiter brought the wine to their table. Sydney tasted it and gave the okay. They sipped the wine while they looked over the menu.

"What menu items are you looking at, Vince?"

"Well, to tell you the truth, I've never heard of these items, but I'm gonna give it a try. I don't want any help."

Sydney said, "So, you've changed your mind about wanting my help."

Gonzales said sheepishly, "Yeah, I guess I did."

"Go for it."

"Well, I think I'll start with the butternut squash soup and the potato gnocchi. For the main course, I'll have striped bass and asparagus."

"Very good selections, Gonzales." She ordered Ahi tuna tartar, the squash soup, and followed with scallops with broccoli for the entree. They ate and talked about their time in Mexico.

"What was it like for you and your team when you were with the cartel?" she asked.

"Well, as you can imagine, it was very different from the other duty we've had. In Afghanistan, we were fighting an enemy all the time. In Mexico, we were working for Flores and trying to disrupt his operation. We hated to see him use kids as mules to carry his dope across the border. Not only kids, but women with babies were used to get the dope through. I think the most useful information was how Flores is using drones and semisubmersibles to get his product across the border. He's buying bigger drones. They can carry more weight. Flores is making bigger semisubmersibles. They're safer and will carry more of his product. We did our best to get information back to the president. Now tell me about you and the governor. How did they treat you while you were captive?"

"They were very good to us. And we never lost hope of your rescue. I knew you'd come for us."

"You knew about us all along?"

"I did. I had to let Lisa know that you and Covert Bravo may rescue us. She had to be ready. But we thought about escaping on our own, and as you know, we ran right into you and Covert Bravo during our escape. I'd say that was either quite a coincidence, divine intervention, or just plain luck."

"Well, I like divine intervention...but it's over now. You and the governor are safe and back to work. Your work with FEMA on the cleanup in Chicago is outstanding."

"Thank you, but we have a long way to go before we're through. Have you given any thought to the threats Flores made? How he said he would get every one of us and make us pay?"

"I've thought about that, but I don't see how he can

do us any harm from where he is right now or where he's headed. He escaped and is running for his life. I'm sure he's in Mexico by now. He may think about it. We have a little time before he makes his move. That is, if he makes a move. He still wants to run the cartel. Most of all, he wants heroin from Afghanistan. That's why he didn't kill el Din. He wants to keep him alive to ensure he gets what he's been promised. He kept his part of the deal. Now he expects el Din to keep his. If Flores does make a move on us, he'll wait until we feel secure and safe. Maybe six months to a year," said Gonzales thoughtfully. "Another thing. He wants his son, Alejandro, back. I'm more sure of that than anything. If he makes a move, and that's a big if, he'll make it on the boy...just my opinion. I'm sure he'd like Consuela to pay, too. He'd put her in one of his brothels for as long as she lived. I'm not as worried about you and the Governor Martinez and her family."

"You're not worried about me!" exclaimed Sydney.

Gonzales put up both his hands and said, "Now wait a minute, Madam Secretary, I didn't say I wasn't worried about you. I said I wasn't *as* worried about you. Here's the reason. You didn't hurt Flores in a personal way. That's what I meant to say."

"Well, that sounds better. I hope you're right about the time. It will give us a chance to get used to the extra protection President Rivera is providing. I think about how powerful Flores is and I get a little concerned. Not for me only, but for Lisa and her family and, of course, Consuela and her family. Now, I want to know where you are taking Covert Bravo for R & R."

"I was thinking about keeping it a secret."

"Hold on, Gonzales. You're not keeping anything secret from me...at least anything concerning what you and Covert Bravo are doing," interrupted Sydney.

"Well, Madam Secretary, I thought it would be nice if me and the guys could sneak away for a few days without having to worry about being under any supervision. If you know what I mean," countered Gonzales.

"Of course, I understand where you're coming from. I just don't know why you can't or won't tell me. I won't tell anyone," replied Sydney.

"I'm not even going to tell the president."

"Not even the president!" exclaimed Sydney.

"We aren't going to tell anyone where we take our R & R. Not even the president. We've talked about places we've never been...close to DC. That's all I'll say right now," responded Gonzales.

"How about me? What about my protection? I don't want to rely solely on the CIA. The only time I feel safe is when you're with me," said Sydney.

"Listen, the CIA is the best in the world. You have nothing to fear...nothing."

"That's what I thought the first time...look what happened."

"Syd, look at this logically, please. I'll ask President Rivera to increase your CIA detail. I'll ask him to double it. He won't refuse me."

"You're not telling anyone, not even the president, where you're going? And you're going to ask him to double my CIA detail?"

"Not even the president. I promise the president will double your CIA detail. I'll even ask him to double Consuela's and her family's. Does that make you feel better?"

"Well...it does a little. How long are you going to be gone?"

"Three days, tops," answered Gonzales. "We'll go someplace where we can unwind. We can talk about the president's proposal. This is no small thing for us. I think you know that. It's a big decision for us. The president is asking us to change our lives completely. Isn't he?"

"Yes, I know that," answered Sydney.

"How are Governor Lisa and Joe Martinez taking this? How are they dealing with the CIA around twenty-four hours a day? Have you spoken to them about this?" asked Gonzales.

"Yes, I'm concerned about Lisa and Joe. I called Lisa yesterday. They don't like it...especially Joe. She told me Joe's carrying a Glock. She can't move as freely as she thinks she should, nor can Joe. Joe is concerned about Lisa's safety. She said he doesn't let her out of his sight. She's afraid he'll let his business suffer. He's built a great restaurant chain. He's worked very hard. It's been a good business for him and his family."

"Joe's a really good guy. I doubt he fears anything. Look how he performed during the rescue. We couldn't have done it without him. They'll learn to deal with this. The same goes for Consuela and her family. We finally got her uncle Domingo and his wife out of Mexico. They are with Consuela. However, I think your imagination is running a little wild. That's not your way. You're a smart and brave woman...a formidable woman. You rose from nothing and became the secretary of the Department of Homeland Security of the United States. Why, you could run for president someday. I don't think you're afraid of anything," said Gonzales.

Gonzales saw how her eyes welled up when he said this. She didn't know how to respond to such a frank assessment of herself. There was a small band there playing all the old standard tunes. The band began to play "All of Me." It was in a nice dance tempo. She grabbed his arm and said, "Let's have a dance." He held her close and surprisingly, they moved perfectly with the music. After the dance, she said, "That was nice...now let's get out of here."

"What about your security?" asked Gonzales.

"When we got to the restaurant, I gave them the night off."

"You gave them the night off? Are you nuts?"

"Maybe a little. But not about what you're talking about," said Sydney. "I think you and Covert Bravo need some R & R. You need to discuss this amongst yourselves. You said three days. Didn't you?"

"That's what I said, Syd."

When they left, she gave him a coy smile and hailed a cab. She directed the cabbie to her place in Georgetown. Vince began to squirm a little when the cab drove up to her place. He thought she was going to send him on his way. Instead, she said, "Come in with me." They got out, and she put her arm around his waist and walked him into her Georgetown townhouse.

Chapter 15

Covert Bravo met the next day and talked again about the president's offer. Gomez was the only one to express some concern in their first meeting. He spoke first before anyone else and said, "If all of you are taking the president up on his offer, I'm aboard too."

Gonzales looked at the others and said, "All in favor of the president's offer, raise your hand." He looked at all the raised hands. "That settles it. We stay with the president. Although we've decided to take the president's offer, I don't think he should know we've accepted it. As far as our R & R destination, I think this is our time off. We should be allowed to spend the time the way we choose. Does anyone have any thoughts about keeping this to ourselves? I'm going to ask the president to double the CIA detail for Secretary Alvarez and Consuela and her family while we're gone. I don't think we need more than three days to clear our heads," said Gonzales.

When Gonzales said he'd ask the president for double security for Consuela and her family, he looked directly at Chavez. Chavez nodded his head in agreement and with a smile on his face said, "Thanks."

"I thought you'd like that, Chavez. I'm glad to help. I'll call the president and ask him to set up a meeting."

The president called for the meeting the next morning. Gonzales and Covert Bravo were fifteen minutes early, as usual. They were met by Pattie Hayes. She directed them to the Oval Office.

"May I get you anything?" queried Pattie.

Sanchez said, "If it's not any trouble, I'd like some coffee."

"Anyone else?" asked Pattie.

Gonzales answered, "Why not. I could use a cup. How about you guys?" The rest indicated in the affirmative. "I'll be right back," said Pattie. She came back. Showing respect for his rank, she served Gonzales his cup first. Then she went to Sanchez, and then the rest were served. As Pattie Hayes left, she gave Sanchez the look. Sanchez almost dropped his cup of coffee.

President Rivera came in and took them to the Situation Room where Bob Reynolds, Frank Yanelli, Joe Madden, and Sydney Alvarez were waiting. The president spoke first. "Well, men, have you reached a decision?"

Gonzales said, "Mr. President, "We'd like a little more time to think about it."

"Captain, how much longer will you need?"

"We need a few more days to think about this. This is not an easy decision for us to make, Mr. President. We've always been deployed with a Ranger unit. This is a little different for us. Most of our troops are out of Afghanistan now. We also think we may be able to make a valuable contribution to our country by accepting your proposal. We would be at your and our country's service. We'd like to take some R & R. Go somewhere where we can talk about it. A place where we can clear our heads of Mexico."

The president looked at Bob, Frank, Joe, and Sydney. He smiled broadly and said, "How long will you take and where will you go?"

"Maybe three or four days, sir. I think we need to take a few days to just relax. You know, R & R; rest and relaxation. We'd like to keep where we're going private, sir," answered Gonzales. As Gonzales said this, he glanced at Sydney. She turned her head away.

"If that's the way you want to handle your R & R location, it's fine with me," said President Rivera. He turned to Sydney, Reynolds, Yanelli, and Madden, and asked, "Do any of you have a problem with this?" No one said a word. The president said, "You take three or four days off. We are hoping you and Covert Bravo will accept our offer. We think you and your men could do good things for our country. When you get back, and if you sign on with us, Frank has a place in Virginia where you will be housed and where you will continue your training. I'll leave the details to Frank. He'll fill you in on what you can expect. That's it then, Captain Gonzales...keep in touch. When are you leaving?"

"This afternoon, sir. If that's okay with you and your team."

"I have no problem with you leaving this afternoon. Does anyone have a problem with that?" No one gave any indication to the negative. "You have my and Director Reynolds's number. Let me know as soon as you get back. Is there anything I can do for you, Gonzales?"

"Mr. President, there is."

"And what would that be?"

"We need a vehicle to travel. And I'd like you to double the security for the secretary and Consuela and her family."

"That's easy. Is there anything special you'd like to drive?"

"An SUV would be great, sir. How about security?"

"I'll have a Cadillac Escalade gassed up and ready to go. I'll have it parked in your parking spot. Director Yanelli will take care of security. If there's nothing else, this meeting is adjourned."

On the way back to their hotel, Gonzales said, "Chavez, make sure the Caddy is ready to go. The president said it would be in the parking garage in our reserved parking spot. Get it out front so we can pack our luggage and get going."

"Roger that," replied Chavez. "Is it okay for me to call Consuela? I want to let her know I'll be gone for three days. Are we counting today as day one?"

"Yeah, sure, give her a call. Tell her this is day one. We'll be back the day after tomorrow. We should be able to work out any misgivings about the president's offer. Although, I think we're all in agreement."

"Thanks, Gonzales," responded Chavez.

Chavez called Consuela. "Hi, Consuela. It's me, Chavez."

"Hi, what can I do for you, Roberto?"

When Chavez heard Consuela use his first name, Roberto, he almost melted. He took a deep breath and said, "Listen, I'm leaving town for three days, taking the R & R I spoke to you about."

"Okay, Roberto, go on your R & R. I'll be waiting for you. Is today the first day?"

"Yes, it is. We'll be back the day after tomorrow. Try not to worry. The president is going to double the protection for you and your family," answered Chavez.

"I know. The protection is here already. I do feel safe...but not as safe as when I'm with you. You go and have a good time on your R & R. I'll see you day after tomorrow," replied Consuela.

Chapter 16

Once Flores and el Din got to the safe house in Mexico, they were exhausted. They turned in for the night. The next morning, Flores and Cruz had breakfast together. Flores felt invincible after escaping from the United States.

Flores said, "I'll not tolerate disloyalty or betrayal. I want you to get in touch with our man in Washington, DC, Leonardo Ortega. He's proven his loyalty time and time again. I want him to put a tail on Consuela and that Alvarez woman...not every day. Maybe once or twice a week on different days...just to get a feel for their daily activities. Find any weak spots in their security. Tell Ortega to use the new MS-13 men. Men without tattoos that say they're MS-13. I put eight young men through college...paid their tuition. They studied Political Science. If I remember right, they should be finished with their studies and should be looking for jobs with a lobbying firm. It's my hope they'll be able, in time, to have some positive effect on my business. Maybe hear something that will help me to avoid a problem. At the least, I'll have men in the United States government working for me. Anyway, tell Ortega to use those men. They look clean-cut and are clean-cut. They don't have records with any police agency.

"The Alvarez woman will have the CIA or FBI watching her. They won't let her out of their sight." Flores slammed his fist on the table, making the dishes rattle and move. He screamed, "I want my son back! Alejandro will be with Consuela!" After gaining control of himself, he continued. "We have to assume Consuela will be guarded, too, probably by some type of security. I know, if I were

President Rivera, that's what I would do. We beat them once. We can beat them again with good intelligence. That's what Ortega will get for me."

Cruz answered, "Okay, Benito. I agree with everything you say. Ortega should use his new men, men without tattoos. The ones you sent to college. MS-13 stopped insisting their men use tattoos to identify themselves. Tattoos are a dead giveaway."

"You set this up for me. I'll wait six months or longer before I make my move. I want them to feel safe. Consuela and that Alvarez woman will be the bait. I'm sure Gonzales and his men—what does he call them?—Covert Bravo, are sure to come looking for them. They will come for Sydney Alvarez, the secretary of the Department of Homeland Security, Consuela, and Alejandro. If need be, Chavez will come looking for Consuela and my son by himself. He's in love with her and he probably wants to make Alejandro his son. This will never happen...never!" said Flores emphatically, slamming his fist on the table again. This time the slam was so violent that dishes flew off the table. "You tell Ortega to watch for my son. When he goes out with his mother. Maybe he's in school. I want him back!" Flores slammed his fist on the table again.

Chapter 17

Chavez drove the Cadillac Escalade SUV to the Mohawk Casino in Hogansburg, New York. Once Gonzales and Covert Bravo checked in, they went to their rooms.

"Let's get freshened up a bit...take a shower and maybe take a nap. It's five o'clock. Let's meet for dinner at, let's say, seven o'clock in the lobby," said Gonzales.

Gonzales went to his room and made a call from the cell phone given to him by the president. It had special apps on it that wouldn't show his location. He turned on the app and made the call.

"Gonzales, is that you? I wasn't expecting a call!" exclaimed Sydney. "For heaven's sakes, where are you?"

"It's really good to hear your voice, Syd," said Gonzales. When Sydney heard this, she began to tear up. She hoped Gonzales wouldn't notice. "Now, Syd, you know I can't tell you where I am. Aren't you glad I called?"

"Of course, I'm glad you called. I just wasn't expecting a call from you. I wasn't expecting to hear from you for three days from now. I mean two days. You're counting this day as the first day. Aren't you?"

"Yes, this is the first day. So, I'll see you the day after tomorrow. I just wanted to let you know we got here safe and sound. I miss you already, Madam Secretary. I can't believe I said that."

"But you did say it. I can't tell you how much I like hearing it. I'm so glad you called," was all Sydney could say.

"Well, like I said, I just wanted to talk with you and hear your voice. I'll see you the day after tomorrow. Take care."

"You take care, Gonzales. See you in two days."

* * *

Chavez thought about calling Consuela. He thought better of it. He figured it would only upset her more.

* * *

Gonzales and Covert Bravo met in the lobby at seven o'clock that evening. "Let's see what's on the menu," said Gonzales. They were met by a seating hostess who was a Native American, a true Mohawk. She took them to a table for five and said, "Your server will be right with you."

The server was a Latina. She brought water and menus for each of them. She said, "You may order from the menu, or you might like to try our all you can eat dinner buffet."

Sanchez said, "I think I'll look at the buffet. I'm hungry. Anyone else interested?"

Chavez said, "Yeah, it deserves a look anyway. How about you guys?"

"Buffets remind me of standing in a chow line. But I'm hungry, too," said Ramirez.

They went up to the buffet and looked. Gonzales said, "It looks like everything is on this, guys. This doesn't look like any chow hall food...and it's all you can eat. What do you think?"

Gomez said, "I'm in."

They went back to their table. The server came over and asked, "Have you gentlemen decided?"

"We are going to have the buffet," answered Gonzales.

"Good choice," said the server.

Gonzales was first in line. They filled their plates and sat down. No one said a word. Gonzales was the first one done. He went for another round. Covert Bravo did the same. The server came over with coffee and said, "Now, have you gentlemen saved room for dessert? There's a dessert table with chocolate and white cake, cherry and apple pie à la mode, strawberry shortcake, build your own ice cream sundae, assorted cookies, and our specialty, bananas foster."

"Where's this dessert table?" asked Chavez. "We didn't see it when we went through the chow line. Oops, I mean buffet line."

The server gave a little laugh and said, "Are you men on military leave?"

Gonzales said, "No, we aren't in the military anymore. We just got out. We still use military terms...like chow, chow hall, and chow line. We were in the military for a long time."

Before the Latina server could ask another question, Gonzales said, "Let's see the dessert table."

"Okay," said the server. "The dessert table is on the other side of the room and in a far corner. It's hard to see from here...especially since we're so busy right now. Otherwise, you couldn't miss it."

When the server left and was out of hearing distance, Gonzales said, "I don't think we should deny we were in the service. But we can't let anyone know we're still in. Okay? That's our story."

Chavez said, "You're right, Gonzales. Where'd you get that story?"

"I dunno. It just came out. Well, let's get after some dessert."

After Gonzales and Covert Bravo had their fill of dessert, they wandered into the casino. "I think I'll try some blackjack," said Gonzales.

"Go for it, Gonzales," said Ramirez.

Gonzales played for about an hour. Much to his surprise, he was up five hundred dollars.

Chavez said, "I'm going over to the roulette table and try my luck."

"Good luck," said Gonzales. "I hope you do as well as I have."

"Me too."

Even though Gonzales's money clip was a little heavier by five hundred dollars, he decided to follow Chavez to the roulette table. Chavez played for an hour or so. He, too, was lucky. He managed to win two hundred fifty dollars. Sanchez, Gomez, and Ramirez stood and watched.

Gonzales said, "Let's call it a night. Let's go back to my room and talk a little about the president's offer. I know we're all in agreement to take the offer. I want to discuss what the president might ask us to do."

Back in Gonzales's room, Sanchez said, "Does it matter what the president asks us to do? We've agreed to take his offer. He might want us working on the drugs coming into the country. Maybe in a different capacity than in Mexico."

Gomez said, "Truth is, we just don't know. We'll have to go with whatever he gives us. But your speculation, Sanchez, may be exactly right."

Gonzales said, "Well, that about sums it up. Unless Chavez and Ramirez have something to add. I agree with Sanchez and Gomez about the president wanting us to work on drugs coming into the country. If I'm not mistaken, I think a lot of drugs come through this Mohawk Reservation. I either read about it or heard it somewhere. Maybe we can start right now. You never know what we might hear. We're just tourists...you know, looking for a good time."

"You know, I've heard the same thing about this Indian reservation. Maybe we heard about it in Mexico. We know a lot of the drugs come into the country through the Indian reservations on the southern border," replied Gomez.

"Does anyone have anything to add?" asked Gonzales.

Chavez and Ramirez each indicated they had nothing more to add. "That settles it. We go and do as ordered. Just like we've always done. Let's turn in for the night and meet for breakfast in the dining room."

* * *

Gonzales and Covert Bravo met in the lobby of the dining room and were seated by the hostess. She brought the menus and said, "Your server will be with you shortly."

The server, a young man, brought water and coffee with him. "This is all regular coffee. I can bring a pot of decaf if anyone wants it."

Chavez said, "Regular is fine with us. Leave the pot and bring another when you get a chance."

"I'll do that, sir. You may have the all you can eat breakfast buffet or order off the menu."

Gonzales looked at Covert Bravo and said, "I think we'll go with the buffet."

"Very well, sir. You guys look hungry. I'll be right back with another pot of coffee."

Gonzales led Covert Bravo to the buffet. They loaded up their plates. When they finished, they went back again. Just as they were finishing the second helping, a man came up to their table and introduced himself.

"How are doing? I'm Chief James Roberts of the Warrior Tribe. I'm on the hospitality committee for the casino. I hope all of you are enjoying your visit."

"Thank you for the welcome, Chief Roberts. I'm Gonzales, and these guys are Chavez, Sanchez, Ramirez, and Gomez. It certainly is nice to meet you."

"I'm equally happy to meet you, too. We don't see many Mexicans gambling here. I understand you're just out of the military?"

"To answer your question, we just got out of the United States Army. If I may ask, how do you know that?" asked Gonzales.

"I make it my business to know my customers."

This irked Chavez. "What do you mean, you don't see many Mexicans gambling here. That's a racist attitude! We have every right to be here or any other place in the country! Why do you have to know about us? We've fought for our country. What have you done? Are you snooping around talking to your employees about us? We come back and can't find a good job. We've never been to a casino. We had a few days off. So, we thought we'd try yours...and we get this crap!" exclaimed Chavez.

"Now hold on a minute. I'm not a racist. I'm an American Indian. I know about racism. I meant no offense. I can see you took offense. So, you say you've fought for our country...and you've never been to a casino. I thank you for choosing our casino, and by the way, thank you for your service. Here's what I'm going to do. Your stay here is on the house. We try very hard to make your stay enjoyable. If you and our buddies would like a job—a good job—let me know. Just to set the record straight, I was a United States Marine. I served my country, too," said Roberts.

Gonzales thought fast about what Chavez just said.

He thought he knew what Chavez was doing. "Now hold on, Chavez, just hold on. I don't think we should air our dirty laundry with Chief Roberts. He's a patriot, too. So, let's relax a little. I apologize, Chief Roberts. My friend Chavez has had a hard time with it. He suffers from PTSD. He was a very good soldier. Sometimes he gets a little strung out," said Gonzales.

"There's no need to apologize. I can relate to your friend's feelings. I know a few Mohawk Indians who suffer PTSD. I meant what I said. Your stay is on the house...and here's one hundred dollars for each of you to play with. If you are looking for good jobs, maybe I can help. Does that sound like a racist? By the way...how long are you going to be here?" replied Roberts.

"We are scheduled to leave tomorrow. Thank you for your generosity, Chief Roberts," said Gonzales.

"My friends call me Jimmy. You can, too. I'll try to see you before you check out," answered Roberts as he walked away.

Gonzales said, "Chavez, where did you come up with that story? Don't answer now. We should take a walk after lunch."

"Why take a walk?" asked Ramirez.

Gonzales, speaking as softly as possible, answered, "I don't feel comfortable inside this place. I feel like we're being watched."

On the walk, Gonzales said, "Chavez, that was good thinking with Roberts. I tried to go along with you. Where did the story of not finding jobs come from?" asked Gonzales.

"I thought we'd maybe get a head start for President Rivera. That's if there's something to get a head start on," replied Chavez. "I tried to set Roberts up. I think he bought it."

"Anyone else have any thoughts on what Chavez tried to do?" asked Gonzales.

"I'm not too sure about his sincerity," said Sanchez. "He called us Mexicans."

"Yeah, he did...but he might be looking for people like us to work for him. We are Mexicans. Aren't we?" remarked Gomez.

Sanchez said, "Yeah, we are Mexicans. I wonder if he sees many Mexicans gambling here. I bet that's what threw him."

"Well, let's see what he has to say tomorrow morning when we leave," said Chavez. "He may not even show tomorrow."

"I think we accidentally stumbled onto something. If he does say something about working for him, we'll find out just what it is. As for his referring to us as Mexicans and not seeing many Mexicans gambling here, well, like Sanchez said, we are Mexicans. Do you see any other Mexicans here? I don't. I'm wondering what kind of jobs he was referring to. Maybe he'll make an offer tomorrow before we leave. The chief is on the welcoming committee. He wants us to feel welcome. He may have put it the wrong way. We should enjoy our time here, especially since it's on Chief Roberts. We each have one hundred dollars to start with...courtesy of the chief. Let's see if we can leave here with more of the casino's money. He'll be there tomorrow morning...I guarantee. Let's meet here for dinner," said Gonzales.

"That sounds right to me," said Ramirez.

"Me too," chimed in Gomez.

Gonzales asked Chavez and Sanchez, "How about you two?"

"I'm good," said Sanchez.

"Yeah, I'm good, too, I think," answered Chavez.

Gonzales and Covert Bravo used the money Chief Roberts gave them. Gonzales lost the one hundred dollars Chief Roberts gave him and the five hundred he'd won at the blackjack table the night before. Ramirez and Gomez were lucky at the craps table. They walked away with more of the casino's money. Ramirez took the one hundred dollars and added another one hundred fifty dollars. Gomez was not quite as lucky as Ramirez. He walked away with another seventy-five dollars in addition to the one hundred Chief Roberts had given him. Sanchez and Chavez walked away with the original one hundred but nothing else. So, in effect, they were one hundred dollars to the good.

What Gonzales and Covert Bravo didn't know was Roberts was watching them when they gambled. He was in a booth. The booth had cameras in it to watch for people who may be cheating...either customers or employees. Roberts saw it all.

Gonzales and Covert Bravo met for dinner. "How did it go this afternoon?" asked Gonzales. They gave him the rundown on how each had done.

"Well, it sounds like none of us got hurt in the casino. You all sound like you had a good time. I know I did," remarked Gonzales. "Now, let's put a hurt on that buffet. I'm done gambling for now. After dinner, I'm going to get some rest and turn in for the night."

"You know, Gonzales, that sounds like a good idea. I'm going to do the same thing," replied Sanchez.

Chavez echoed Sanchez and said, "I'm going to my room, too."

Ramirez said, "I've been lucky. I'm going to give it another shot."

Gomez said, "I'm with Ramirez. I think I'm on a lucky streak. So, I'm going to try to keep it going."

"Okay, then, we're on our own till breakfast

tomorrow morning. We meet in the casino's restaurant. And good luck, you guys. I hope you break the casino's bank," said Gonzales.

* * *

The next morning, Gonzales and Covert Bravo met for breakfast. They were seated by the same hostess. "Good morning, gentlemen. You know about our breakfast buffet. You put a dent in it yesterday. I'm assuming you'll be having that this morning."

"You've got a good memory, young lady. We've been thinking about this breakfast since we got up this morning," said Gonzales with a little chuckle. "And listen, we hope you make a lot of money today and that all of your dreams come true. That goes for everyone working here."

The hostess was taken aback. When she recovered, she said, "That's the nicest thing anyone's ever said to me. Thank you, sir. I'll tell the other workers what you said. Your server will be over with coffee or any other beverage you want."

Before they left for the buffet, the same young man from yesterday brought two pots of regular coffee. He filled each cup with fresh, hot coffee.

When they returned to the table the second time, Chief Roberts came over to their table and said, "Good morning, fellas. How did your gambling go last night?"

Gonzales answered, "Gomez and Ramirez were the only ones who gambled last night. Ask them."

"We did okay. We lost a little of what we won. We're happy," said Ramirez.

"That's what we want to hear," said Chief Roberts. "You fellas are leaving this morning, right?"

"That's right, Chief. Right after we finish breakfast," said Gonzales.

"Well, I hope you've had a good time. You sound like you have," said Roberts. "I hope you come back soon."

"You never know, Chief. Who knows? You may see us again. We've had a great time. Okay, guys, let's finish our breakfast and get going."

"Thanks for coming to the Akwesasne Mohawk Casino. Have a good trip. If you do come back, I might have work for you," said Chief Roberts.

"What kind of work are you talking about?" asked Gonzales.

"All you've got to know is, if you come back, I might have something for you to do. I'll say this; it'll pay more than what you're making now," answered Roberts.

"Okay, Chief. If we come back, we may take you up on the job offer. I've got a feeling it may be on the shady side of the law," said Gonzales.

"I'm not saying it is on the wrong side of the law. But if it were, would that be a problem?"

Gonzales thought for a moment as he looked at Covert Bravo. "Probably not."

"Well, maybe I'll see you again. I hope I do," replied Roberts as he walked away.

"Wow, that was something," said Chavez.

"It certainly was," replied Gonzales. "Now let's put a dent in this buffet."

After breakfast, Gonzales said, "Chavez, get the Escalade. We'll get our baggage ready to load."

"Okay."

Chavez brought the Escalade to the front of the lobby. Gonzales and the rest of Covert Bravo were waiting. They loaded their baggage and took off for Washington, DC. They were anxious to report to President Rivera.

Chapter 18

Chavez drove. When he was approaching DC, he asked Gonzales, "Where are we going to stay? Where am I driving to?"

"Drive back to the Hyatt. I think the president will have rooms for us there. Drop us off at the front door. I'll go in and ask the front desk about our rooms. You guys wait out here," answered Gonzales.

He went in the Hyatt, walked up to the front desk and addressed the attendant. "Hi, I'm Vince Gonzales. I'm wondering if me and my friends have rooms reserved for us."

The attendant replied, "Captain Gonzales, it's so nice to see you again."

"Do I know you, miss?" A light went on in his head. "Oh, yes, you're the lady who directed me to the tour of the monuments. Am I right?".

"You're exactly right, Captain. I'll look and see if there are rooms reserved for you and your friends." She clicked a few computer keys, then smiled. "You must have friends in high places, Captain. You have the five best rooms in the hotel reserved for you and your friends. By the way, how did that tour work out for you?"

"As it turned out, the tour was exceptional; I'd even say it was outstanding. I made a friend on that tour, although I've been so busy I haven't had a chance to contact her since I had dinner with her...right here. I'm going to call her. She gave me her phone number; I should have it somewhere."

"Captain Gonzales, I hope you haven't blown an

opportunity for romance," she smiled.

Gonzales felt himself blush but said, "This is not that kind of friendship. Jenny is an older lady. We met on that tour. Her brother was an Army Ranger who was killed in the Vietnam War. She couldn't finish the tour, so I excused us and we had lunch. I called an Uber to bring us back here. She was staying here too...what a coincidence."

"That's a very nice story, Captain. I hope you can find her phone number. I'm sorry for her loss."

"Thanks, I'll find it. I'd never lose something like that. And thanks for finding our rooms."

"Like I said, you must have friends in high places. These rooms were ordered from the White House. Good luck, Captain Gonzales."

Gonzales went out and told Covert Bravo, "I told you the president would have rooms for us. The desk clerk told me they were the best in the hotel. Chavez, park the Escalade. We'll get our baggage up to the rooms and meet you inside."

After checking in and bringing the luggage up, the team met in the lobby of the Hyatt. Gonzales said, "After the six-hour drive from the casino, we should probably grab a bite and get some rest before dinner." They decided on room service, and went to their respective rooms.

As Gonzales entered his room, he thought he should call the president and Sydney to let them know they were back. He decided to call Sydney first.

"Hey, Syd. I'm back."

"When did you get back?"

"Just now."

"Great! I'll see you at the meeting tomorrow, if not before," said Sydney.

"What meeting?" asked Gonzales.

"What meeting? The one the president called. You

must know. The meeting about what he wants of you and Covert Bravo!" she exclaimed.

"It's the first I've heard of it," replied Gonzales.

"Are you saying you haven't called the president?"

"No, I have not called the president. I called you first," he admitted.

"Well, if that doesn't beat all. You called me before you called the president."

"That's right."

"I feel honored. I can't believe you called me first, Gonzales."

"Well, Syd, believe it. I was going to call the president next and let him know we're back. Are you busy tonight?"

"No, I'm not. Why would I be busy with you gone?" she joked.

"I thought Jody might be there," said Gonzales.

"Jody? Who's Jody?"

Gonzales started to laugh. "Jody is the guy who is there when soldiers are away. He's a mythical figure. While they're away, some soldiers worry about Jody being there in their place. You know, when they're away on duty."

"That's not funny, Gonzales."

"I'm sorry, Syd. I'm just kidding you a little. I'll ask again. Are you busy tonight? If you aren't, I'd like to come over and see you."

"Gonzales, you can come over any time. And remember, Jody will never be here."

"I'm on my way. That is, after I call the president."

"I'm looking forward to it."

* * *

Gonzales called the president.

"Gonzales, when did you get back?" asked President Rivera.

"Mr. President, we just got back, sir. I called just as soon as I got squared away," answered Gonzales, knowing he'd just lied to the president. But not really. He did call after he got squared away—with Sydney.

"I appreciate your timeliness. I figured you'd be back today. This is the third day. I've called a meeting for tomorrow morning at ten. The usual people will be there. The secretary, Reynolds, Yanelli, and Madden."

"I'll be there, Mr. President. Do you want Covert Bravo there, too?"

"Yes, they should be there with you," answered President Rivera.

"Very well, sir. We'll be there."

* * *

On the way to Sydney's place, Gonzales suddenly remembered his conversation with the front desk clerk when he checked into the Hyatt. He thought about where he'd put Virginia O'Dea's phone number. Suddenly, it came back to him. He'd put it in his wallet for safekeeping. While on a tour of the Washington, DC, war memorials, she recognized Gonzales's Army Ranger patch. Her brother was an Army Ranger who was killed in the Vietnam War. As they parted, she had given Gonzales her phone number and asked him to call her every once in a while. She said she was genuinely interested in him. He decided to give Jenny a call.

* * *

"Hello, Jenny. This is Vince Gonzales. Do you remember me?"

"Of course, I remember you, Vince. I'm so glad you called me. Where are you?"

"I can't tell you how happy I am you remembered me. I'm in Washington, DC. If you don't mind, I'd like to take you out to dinner. I want you to meet someone."

"I'd love to see you, Vince. When were you thinking of coming?"

"If it's not inconvenient, how about tonight? I still have your address in Baltimore; I'll pick you up. How does five sound to you? That is, if you don't have any other plans."

"Why, Vince, I'd love to see you any time. I'll be waiting for you. You said you wanted me to meet someone. Who might that be?"

"Great, I'll be there. As far as who that someone is, you'll have to wait and see." She could hear his grin in his voice.

Gonzales disconnected the call and said to himself, *Okay, this is going to be great—I hope.* He called Sydney.

* * *

"Hi, Syd. I've finished my call with the president. He told me about the meeting tomorrow. I'm looking forward to it."

"Great. Let's go out for dinner tonight," replied Sydney. "I've got a new place we've never been to."

"Listen, Syd, there's someone I'd like you to meet. Is it all right with you if we swing by and pick this person up before we have dinner?"

"Do you have a secret admirer I don't know about? Do you have a Jody I don't know about?" asked Sydney in her teasing way.

"No, no. It's someone I met when I went on a tour

of DC. It was just before we went to Mexico." He paused and joked, "Are you busting my chops with this Jody thing?"

"It's fine with me, Gonzales, and yes, as you say, I'm busting your chops," laughed Sydney.

"Okay. I get it. Now tell me about this place I've not been to."

"It's a place I go to once in a while, you'll see," answered Sydney. "Well, let's get going. We don't want to waste the whole night."

"What do you mean by that, Madam Secretary?"

"If you've got to think about that, you're not the guy I know."

"Are you referring to the dessert? If you are, I know exactly what you mean. I don't need to think about it. In fact, I'm just turning the corner on your street."

Sydney was waiting at the curb as Gonzales drove up. She jumped into his Buick SUV the president had for his use. "I'm anxious to meet this lady," she greeted, fishing for clues.

"Well, she's a special lady, Syd, just like you; only in a different sense."

When Sydney heard this from Gonzales, she leaned over and kissed him on the cheek. They pulled out. The CIA security team followed.

Gonzales drove to Jenny's Baltimore address.

"So, tell me more, Gonzales. How did you meet this lady?" asked Sydney.

"I will tell you all the details, but not before I tell you about where we're staying. Just before I called you, we stopped at the hotel to see if the president had kept our rooms reserved," answered Gonzales.

"And, did he?"

"Yes, he did. In fact, he bumped us up to the best

rooms in the hotel. The clerk at the front desk said, 'You must have friends in high places.' She remembered me from the first time I was there. The clerk is the reason I thought of my friend in Baltimore."

"That's quite a coincidence. Aren't you going to tell me her name?"

"Yes, it was quite a coincidence. No, I'm not going to tell you her name. You'll have to wait till I introduce you to her.

She doesn't know who you are either, Syd. She was just as anxious to know your name. I gave her the same answer I gave you. She'd have to wait." said Gonzales.

Gonzales pulled into Jenny's driveway. He and Sydney got out of the SUV and walked to the front door and rang the bell.

The door swung open. Jenny stood there with a bright smile on her face. "Hello, Vince. It' so nice to see again. Won't you two please come in?"

"Thank you, Jenny. It is very nice to see you too. I'd like you to meet Sydney Alvarez."

"It's very nice to meet you, Madam Secretary. It is indeed an honor," responded Jenny.

"Gonzales holds you in very high regard, Jenny. I'm just as honored to meet you." The two ladies shook hands.

"Jenny, we have reservations at one of Syd's special places. She won't tell me the name of the place, but we'd better get going."

"Well, this is getting better all the time. Let's go!"

Sydney gave Gonzales directions to Bourbon Steak on Pennsylvania Avenue. The valet park the car.

When they entered the restaurant, they were greeted by the maître d'. "Good evening, Madam Secretary. We have the quiet table you asked for. Follow me, please."

"Thank you, Richard."

"You are welcome, Madam Secretary. As you requested, your server tonight will be Andrew."

Andy came with menus. "Madam Secretary, would you and your guests like to place a drink order?"

"Yes, I think we would. Tonight is a very special occasion. Let us think about it."

"Very well, Madam Secretary." Andrew moved unobtrusively away from the table.

Sydney asked Gonzales and Jenny, "What are we feeling like tonight?"

Gonzales looked at Jenny. She looked right back at him. She had a look on her face that said, *I haven't a clue.*

"What if we let Syd make the selection?" suggested Gonzales.

"I'm fine with anything the secretary chooses," responded Jenny.

"That settles it," said Sydney. "I had a bottle of Caymus Napa Valley Cabernet Sauvignon the last time I was here. It had a dark color, with a lush flavor and aromas. Would that be all right?"

They both nodded their heads in agreement.

"Very well."

Sydney caught Andrew's eye. He came over immediately. "We will have a bottle of Caymus Napa Valley Cabernet Sauvignon, please."

"An excellent choice, Madam Secretary.

Before Andrew left to get the wine, he asked, "Have you looked over the menu, Madam Secretary?"

"No, we have not. When you get back, we will have made a selection. Thank you, Andrew."

Sydney turned to Jenny and Gonzales. "If I may offer a suggestion, this *is* a steakhouse. The steaks are fabulous. I'm going to have a shrimp cocktail to start.

I want a filet mignon for an entrée, a side of asparagus spears, and mashed buttery potatoes."

"Wowzer," said Gonzales. "What do you think of that, Jenny?"

"That sounds wonderful, Vince. I think the secretary has made my selection, too."

"I think she made mine as well."

Andrew returned with the wine. Sydney was ready. She ordered for them.

"Now, Gonzales, how did you meet Jenny? I'm dying to hear the whole story."

Gonzales related the story. Sydney listened intently.

"That's quite a story, Jenny. I'm so sorry for your loss. Your brother must have been a brave young man."

"Yes. He was. He was so proud. My parents never got over it. I learned to live with it. Madam Secretary, I'm not used to eating in such a fine place. The dinner has been extraordinarily good. I want to pay for my meal."

"Nonsense, Jenny. Gonzales will pay for both of us. He has two dates tonight," Sydney replied with a warm smile.

Jenny blushed. "Well, I have not been on a date since my late husband took me out. You know, before we were married."

"Jenny, I'll take you out on a date any time," remarked Gonzales.

Jenny blushed again. "Why thank you, Vince. You are, indeed, a gentleman. Madam Secretary, I want to thank you again for such a wonderful night out. You are a wonderful woman."

Now it was Sydney's turn to blush. "Thank you, Jenny. Now I'd like to ask you for a favor."

"Of course, Madam Secretary. What is it?"

"Would you call me Syd, please?"

"Oh my. I don't think I can do that, Madam Secretary."

"Will you just try, Jenny? Please."

"Well, how's this, Syd?"

"It's perfect, Jenny. Thank you."

Gonzales sat back and took in the conversation Sydney and Jenny were having, and thought, *How lucky can I get? I've got two beautiful women in my life.*

"I've got a busy day tomorrow. I've got to get some sleep," Sydney announced after a bit.

"Okay. I'll have the valet get our car up front and pay the check," said Gonzales. "If either of you need to use the powder room, now's the time." The ladies looked at each other and grabbed their purses.

Once they were all safely buckled into the SUV, Gonzales drove them to Jenny's home. Gonzales and Sydney walked Jenny to her door.

"Thank you again for a wonderful night," said Jenny. "I can't thank Vince enough for not forgetting me. And you, Syd, for your graciousness. I hope we can do this again sometime."

"Don't worry, Jenny, we will; and sooner rather than later," said Sydney.

"Count on it, Jenny. You are one great lady," remarked Gonzales.

Jenny came to Gonzales and gave him a motherly hug. Gonzales hugged her back. Jenny turned to Sydney and gave her the same kind of hug. She whispered in Sydney's ear, "Take good care of Vince, please."

Sydney whispered back, "I will."

Chapter 19

Sydney Alvarez was busy with other national issues concerning homeland security and assisting the Federal Emergency Management Agency (FEMA) as the cleanup of Chicago continued. She didn't want to get in the way of their operation, but stayed close to those in charge of FEMA and offered any assistance she could. She was very concerned about another attack, and directed all her effort and assets to that end. She pushed for more security not only on the southern border, but on the northern border as well. The United States border with Canada stretched fifty-five hundred miles, including the shared Alaskan and Canadian border, and had not been given the same emphasis of security as the southern border. She was determined to strengthen security there. She wanted more done at US seaports. Although the Coast Guard was deeply involved with protecting United States ports, she wanted them to get more funding to further their efforts.

* * *

Gonzales and Covert Bravo were met by Pattie Hayes. She delivered them to the Oval Office. This time, she didn't ask if she could bring anyone coffee. President Rivera came in followed by Sydney, Bob Reynolds, Frank Yanelli, and Joe Madden. Before asking them to move to the Situation Room, the president asked, "Gonzales, did you and your men enjoy your R & R?"

Gonzales answered, "As a matter of fact, sir, we had a great time."

"If you don't mind my asking, where exactly did you and your men go?"

Gonzales figured he'd get this question and was ready to answer, "We may have something to share with you and your committee, sir. I'll wait till we get to the Situation Room."

"Very well. Let's move to the Situation Room."

The president began, "I see things are going pretty well in Chicago, Madam Secretary."

"They are, sir. We still have a lot to do. FEMA is doing all they can right now. The cleanup is going as scheduled. As we all know, the bomb did considerable damage, and the loss of life is going to be very high. The property damage will be great. They let us know they can get to us."

"Yes, they did!" exclaimed the president.

"As you know, Mr. President, the country bounced back after 9/11. It will bounce back from this, too. Most of the deaths and building damage were caused by the initial explosion. The radiation extended to a one-mile radius of the Mercantile Exchange. We can thank our lucky stars the Windy City's wind was mostly calm that day. If the wind had blown like it usually does, the radiation would have spread further. Radiation levels increased to unsafe levels, but not by a lot. The human body can easily handle that amount of increased exposure. FEMA got to Chicago almost immediately. All of the population who were subjected to radiation have been decontaminated and shouldn't suffer any side effects."

"Yes, the country is bouncing back," said the president. "However, the country is mourning for those families who lost loved ones and friends. We must never forget this act of barbaric terrorism. We will not forget. The world knows how we feel about the attack. Our response was appropriate. We need to strengthen our defenses—which brings me to another topic I want to discuss with this group. Our southern border is more secure than ever. We've built a wall in places that needed one. We are using new technologies. We've significantly increased the Border Patrol by ten thousand. It has been successful in stopping illegal immigration, human traffickers, and a lot of drug traffic from coming into the country." The president stopped for emphasis. "Yet, look at what happened. Given what happened in Chicago, I think we should reexamine our southern and northern border security strategy... especially the northern border. That border is wide open."

Secretary Alvarez interrupted the president. "Sir, the last time our government did anything to secure our northern border was in 2012, when secretary of the Department of Homeland Security Janet Napolitano unveiled the National Northern Border Strategy. That was fourteen years ago. As we know, our border with Canada is the longest shared border in the world. It is fifty-five hundred miles long, including our Alaskan border with Canada. It presents unique challenges, including geographic, weather, and enormous legal travel and trade. The border crosses varied terrains that can be very rugged, with diverse climates. It crosses huge populated urban areas and massive unpopulated rural spaces. Approximately three hundred thousand people and one and a half billion dollars in legal trade cross the border daily, which represents the largest bilateral flow of goods and people in the world. We have communities and businesses that reach over both sides of the border. The markets and security of the United States and Canada are forever linked. When we discuss northern border security measures, we must consider these dynamics. Whatever security enhancements we consider, we must not disturb the legal flow of people and goods coming from Canada to the United States or from the United States to Canada. The flow of illegal immigrants coming across our southern border has mostly stopped. Our immigration laws have been changed. People no longer have to come across the southern border illegally to work. However, drugs are still a big problem and are getting into the country at alarming rates. Captain Gonzales has given very good intelligence on how semisubmersibles and drones are being used to bring drugs into the country. However, our northern border is still a big concern of mine. There are a lot of drugs and human traffic coming across from Canada. Although we have no evidence yet that drones are being used in Canada to bring drugs across our border, we can't discount that possibility. My biggest concern is another nuclear bomb coming across from Canada. After Captain Gonzales shot Baha el Din in the knee, Din talked plenty. We learned from el Din that Flores and Baha el Din got one of the nukes into the country using a tunnel that led to a gas station in Laredo, Texas. The other was delivered by a semisubmersible to a fishing boat in the Gulf of Mexico."

Joe Madden sat and listened. The president looked over at him as if to ask, what do you have to say about this? Madden thought he'd better put his thoughts on the table. He knew, as did the president and Sydney Alvarez, that the northern border was still wide open, despite the National Northern Border Strategy.

"Mr. President, I do have some thoughts on the northern border. Even though past administrations have done things to plug that border up, we still, as you said, have a lot of illegal drugs, human trafficking, and illegal immigrants coming across the border. The illegals are mostly Asian, Korean, and Chinese, who fly to Canada and with the help of smugglers, come across the border.

Of course, these people must pay as much as five to fifteen thousand dollars to get into our country. That's in addition to the other related expenses to get to Canada.

"As we know, sir, the Mohawk Indian Reservation straddles the St. Lawrence River. This was a result of the Jay Treaty of 1795, which settled, among other things, a boundary issue with Britain. The treaty left the Mohawk Reservation on both sides of the St. Lawrence River. Half of the reservation is on our side of the St. Lawrence and the other half is on the Canadian side. As a result of that treaty, the Mohawk tribe, as you know, Mr. President, was able to cross the St. Lawrence unimpeded, and still do today. The Mohawks are proud people. They are governed by three tribal councils...the St. Regis Tribal Council manages the American portion of the reservation, the Mohawk Council of Akwesasne manages the Canadian side of the reservation, which splits between Ontario and Quebec, and the Warrior Society. The number of members in the Warrior Society is unknown. They promote a militant brand of nationalism and are interested in reclaiming Mohawk land. They don't favor our government intervening in Mohawk Reservations business. The United States government and the Canadian government enforce external boundaries. The Mohawks have a police force of their own. They police the reservation and work with our law enforcement people with drug and human trafficking problems—"

As soon as Gonzales heard Mohawk Indian Reservation, he thought he'd better tell the president about where he and Covert Bravo spent their R & R.

"If I may, Mr. President," Gonzales interrupted.

After being interrupted so abruptly, Madden had an incredulous look on his face. As if to say all right, he nodded to the president.

The president said, "Of course, Captain, please

do."

"Thank you, Mr. President and Director Madden. As you know, we took R & R the last few days to help clear our minds and to consider President Rivera's request. We went to the Mohawk Casino in Hogansburg, New York. Before we left, we'd decided to stay on with the president. We thought it might involve drugs coming into our country."

When President Rivera and his committee heard this, everyone on the committee sat up a little straighter, including the president and especially Sydney Alvarez. Gonzales continued.

"We believe we may have stumbled onto something by accident." After he said this, everyone's ears perked up.

The president said, "Let's have it, Captain."

"Yes, sir."

Gonzales related all that took place and what was said. The committee listened intently as Gonzales told his story. They all had an astonished look on their faces.

"So, you thought you'd get a head start by engaging this Chief Roberts? Roberts is a Warrior Chief," said the president.

"Yes, sir, we did," answered Gonzales.

"Well, that's quite a story, Captain. You say you could go back and may wind up with a job in the illegal drug business?" responded President Rivera.

"That's right, sir. Roberts offered us jobs that pay well. The only way to find out is to go back up there and find out," replied Gonzales. "We haven't talked about going back. Well, I wouldn't say we haven't talked about it. We think we stumbled onto something we didn't plan on. When your briefing got into the Mohawks, I thought I should speak up."

"Well, you're right about speaking up, Captain.

You said you had made your decision to stay with me and my committee. That's what we were hoping you'd do. Do any members of this committee have anything to say?" asked the president.

CIA Director Yanelli spoke for the first time. "Mr. President, if I may."

"Of course, please do," replied the president.

"We believe a few Warrior Society people have allied with Asian Transnational Criminal Organization, or TCO, and MS-13 to facilitate the illegal drugs coming into the country, as well as human trafficking. The TCOs are Vietnamese thugs and gang members. They are responsible for producing and supplying the drug Ecstasy, or MDMA, and facilitating high-potency Canadian marijuana to the markets in our country.

"When governments talk about the Mohawks, they tend to lump the bad with the good. The fact is, most Mohawks are good people. The good apples are not happy about being lumped in with a few bad apples.

"Mr. President, there is a very small Latino population living on the reservation. We think the population is growing. But just a little. Just enough to do the illegal work. As you know, sir, Mara Salvatrucha, or MS-13, as it is known on the streets, is in our country and is getting stronger every day. As far as we know, MS-13 has eighty thousand members worldwide...give or take. We estimate thirty thousand are in our country and Canada. We know Benito Flores has MS-13 on his payroll in our country. They receive his illegal drugs and human traffic and sell them to the markets in our country. We shouldn't disregard MS-13 and its capabilities. We must bolster our security along our northern border. We know that drugs and human traffic are being brought across our northern border by gangs...specifically Transnational Criminal Organizations in cooperation with MS-13. MS-13 is bigger than ever right now. MS-13 recruits juveniles. Kids as young as twelve years old. MS-13 is considered the biggest, most ruthless gang in North America, Mexico, and Central America. The violence they cause is mostly against their own. Someone who is just thought to be disloyal, and may not be, will suffer horrible consequences...sometimes death by machete. This sends a powerful message to other gang members...toe the line or suffer the consequences. The DC police found a young man who had been stabbed over one hundred times. They think the weapon was a machete. His heart was cut out of his chest."

President Rivera said, "MS-13 is as ruthless a group of people there is anywhere in the world. We need to better police them and get them off the streets...put them in jail or deport them. Gonzales has stumbled onto something we should give careful consideration. Chief Jimmy Roberts may be able to shed some light on illegal drugs coming into the country. As Secretary Alvarez pointed out, the last time our Department of Homeland Security increased Customs and Border Protection Border Patrol agents was in 2012. That was fourteen years ago. At that time, the Department of Homeland Security increased the number of Border Patrol agents to three thousand seven hundred. We need more Border Patrol, drones, military radar, and sensors on the ground. Although ground sensors can be set off by a falling branch or an animal, many times there isn't a Border Patrol to answer the alarm. In time, technology will catch up with that gaff. I'll make our case with Congress. Hopefully, both parties will come together to fund this project."

"That's all you can do, Mr. President," said Madden. "We have hard evidence that supports our position. We just caught Aaminah Abadi in Eureka, Montana, at the

Roosville point of entry. She's a Canadian citizen who emigrated from Syria. She said she fled Syria for fear of her life. On that basis, she was granted asylum in Canada. She was given food and shelter by the Canadian government and eventually gained Canadian citizenship. When she was caught, she had a trunk full of explosives. She won't say for what purpose the explosives were going to be used. She made the same mistake Ahmed Ressam made. She tried to cross the border at a remote location in Montana. She thought the border guards would not be as efficient there, as opposed to a busier point of entry. If she had gone west a few miles, she would have crossed with ease. She could've met someone there and gone off and done her dirty deed. Aaminah, which means 'Lady of Peace and Harmony,' is now incarcerated for forty years at ADX Florence, in Colorado. She is the only woman incarcerated there. Ahmed Ressam, who is also serving out a thirty-eight-year sentence at ADX Florence, made the same mistake in Port Angeles, Washington. If he had moved a few miles east, he would have made the crossing easily. My point, Mr. President, is that we are at risk. Those are two examples. How many people get through our border undetected? We simply don't know. Both Aaminah Abadi and Ahmed Ressam had the correct identification...passports, driver's licenses, and credit cards. Massena, New York, is where past administrations have bolstered the border with more Border Patrol. There have been more on-scene arrests because of increased Border Patrol at Massena. Massena is still an area that is right in the middle of the illicit drug and human trafficking. As we know, the St. Lawrence River, which separates Canada from our country, is full of islands. It is where two countries, two Canadian provinces, the state of New York, and an Indian reservation meet in a maze of confusion. These islands are used by smugglers during the winter when the river is frozen, and in summer, when the river is thawed. As smugglers cross the river, they use the islands to hide from the local Mohawk police and Border Patrol. There simply aren't enough border guards or local police to cover the area.

"Mohawk law enforcement are doing their best to help. They don't have enough officers, either. The Mohawk Reservation is a sovereign nation, which makes it difficult for our law enforcement to enter. When one of our Border Patrol agents goes onto the Mohawk Reservation, they'd better go with a tribal police escort. If not, they'll be subjected to intimidation techniques. Like having their vehicle blocked in, people screaming and yelling at them, or just a bunch of people surrounding them.

"We have three thousand seven hundred Border Patrol agents to cover our four-thousand-mile border with Canada. That still isn't enough people. When a point of entry is bolstered, the smugglers have learned to go downriver five or six miles, where security is not as good. They make the crossing there. Transnational Criminal Organizations, which include Asian gangs, mostly Vietnamese, motorcycle gangs, and MS-13, have become partners. We believe the Warrior Society Mohawks are helping to get a lot of illegal drugs across the border to markets in our country. They're cooperating with the aforementioned groups to increase profits for all concerned. With the help of the Mohawk Warrior Society, drugs, mostly high-potency Canadian marijuana and Ecstasy, are crossing our border in greater quantities. We have information from Canadian officials that Flores's Los Zetas have been and are now cooperating with the ethnic gangs. The gangs don't fight amongst themselves as they once did. The Bureau of Indian Affairs Office of Law Enforcement is doing all it can to help with border security. They don't have enough people to be that effective. We simply don't have enough people," finished Madden.

"We've been aware of these things for some time, Joe. I've got an idea. Captain Gonzales, you and Covert Bravo have agreed to work for us in any capacity. Why not send you and Covert Bravo into the Mohawk Reservation? It's a good bet this Chief Jimmy Roberts is part of the illegal drug business. He offered you jobs. You and Covert Bravo may be able to find out who on the reservation is involved," said President Rivera.

Sydney jumped into the conversation. "That's a great thought, Mr. President. Maybe Gonzales and Covert Bravo can collect more specific intelligence on what is going on in the Mohawk Reservation. Just like they did in Mexico. If they go, maybe they can get intelligence on how and when the illegal drugs and human trafficking are coming into our country."

"What do you and Covert Bravo think of going back to the Mohawk Reservation...talking to Roberts about a job?" asked President Rivera.

"Well, I think Covert Bravo and I should discuss this. I'm confident we'll do the right thing for the country," said Gonzales.

"That's reasonable, Captain. You have the rest of the day and tonight to think it over. Be back in my office at eight a.m.," ordered President Rivera.

"I've got one more question, sir," said Gonzales.

"What is it?"

"Are we going to be to staying at the Hyatt indefinitely? We aren't complaining, sir, but it's kind of high off the hog. There must be another place around here that we can use as a base."

The president said with a little chuckle, "We have set up just the place for you and your men...as you say, a base. I think you'll find it more than acceptable. Director Yanelli will take you there right now."

Chapter 20

Frank Yanelli drove Gonzales and Covert Bravo to a farm in Virginia. There were five bungalows, one for each of them. Each was furnished with a full kitchen that extended into the great room. There were two bedrooms and two full baths. The main house was a big farmhouse that had been refurbished into a beautiful home. The big, fully equipped kitchen also extended into the great room. There were five bedrooms and five full baths. The study had all the latest technology equipment in it. It could directly communicate with President Rivera, Bob Reynolds, Frank Yanelli, and Joe Madden. The converted barn and the bungalows had the latest security systems in them. The old barn had been made bigger to accommodate the state-of-the-art training zone. It was equipped with a workout gym with all the equipment...free weights, universal machine, treadmills, stair climbers, elliptical walking machines, an Olympic-sized swimming pool, and an indoor running track. There were running trails throughout the farm. It had all the weaponry the men of Covert Bravo would need to keep their skills sharp. The weapons included all the weapons with which Army Rangers were trained. The men were more than pleased with the setup. Each man had his privacy. Something they never had when they were deployed. When deployed, they lived with one another and on top of one another. They each had a Buick SUV to drive and were free to use it anytime they wished. After Frank Yanelli gave them a tour of the place he said, "I hope this meets with your approval."

Gonzales looked at Covert Bravo and Yanelli

and answered facetiously, "It's a little rough...but we'll manage." Then he burst out laughing. Covert Bravo followed.

Not to be outdone, Yanelli said with just as much sarcasm, "Make yourselves at home." He turned to leave, looked back, and then burst out in laughter. He walked away laughing with Gonzales and Covert Bravo.

After Yanelli left and everyone got control of themselves, Chavez said, "I never expected this kind of setup, Gonzales."

Sanchez agreed, "I don't think any of us did."

Gonzales jumped in, "We know for certain we're going back to the casino. It's our second operation. Going back to the casino could be hazardous."

Gomez chimed in with, "Yes, it could be...but we're more than qualified to handle any situation. We agreed to stay on with the president. He could send us anywhere in the world."

"When we go back to the casino, we should be prepared for anything Roberts throws at us. He doesn't know we're Rangers. When he finds out we were Rangers, he'll be confident in our ability to do most anything. I'm fairly certain he'll ask us to be mules," said Gonzales. "In the meantime, let's get comfortable with our new place. It's a little rough...but we can manage."

Gonzales and Covert Bravo got comfortable with the place almost immediately. They would train at this facility every day and would love every minute of it. This is what they loved to do...be Army Rangers.

Chapter 21

Gonzales met Sydney for dinner that night at her Georgetown townhouse. Despite Gonzales's objection, Sydney dismissed her security. The detail stayed outside for the night. They stayed because the president ordered them to stay. It was reported by the CIA that she'd dismissed them once before. However, Sydney never felt safer than when she was with Gonzales.

During dinner, Gonzales asked, "What did you think of the meeting this afternoon?"

"I thought it was productive. Are you going to go back to the Mohawk Reservation?"

"We've agreed to do what the president has asked. We know we're going to go up to the casino to ask for jobs. Or at least let Roberts know we'd like to work for him." Gonzales said with a chuckle, "This was a great dinner. You cook Mexican food like my mother."

"Thank you, Captain Gonzales. That's a high compliment. Now, let's clean up the dishes."

"It was meant to be the highest compliment. As far as KP goes, hey, I'm an officer. I don't do KP," said Gonzales with a chuckle.

"You're in my army now, Captain. You will pull KP. I'll put some music on my cable music station. What are you in the mood for?"

"I'm at your command, Madam Secretary. I'll listen to anything you play."

Gonzales got that grin on his face and Sydney knew what that meant. Although Frank Sinatra had been gone for decades, his music lived on. Gonzales and Sydney loved Sinatra's music. She dialed the Sinatra cable station. They listened while they did the dishes. When the task was complete, they sat together and finished a bottle of wine. When the wine was finished, they held each other. Since getting out of Mexico and back to DC, they'd spent as many nights as they could like this.

The next morning, Gonzales woke up at four thirty. Sydney was already up and in the shower. He let her finish before he went in to take his. When he got out, the smell of bacon and eggs wafted into the bedroom. Gonzales came out dressed in his dress uniform. He was ready to meet the president and said, "You're the best, Syd."

She gave him a wry smile and said, "Best at what?"

Gonzales looked at her and said, "Do you want to start over?"

"I'd love to, if we had the time. So, let's eat up. You and I have a meeting to get to. We can take up where we left off some other time. How does tonight sound?"

"Like I said, you're the best."

They ate breakfast. Sydney's security detail was there to escort her to the same meeting Gonzales was going to.

* * *

Gonzales got back to the farm at 6:00 a.m. Covert Bravo was ready. "I don't know when the president wants us to leave for the casino. Maybe we should ask for a day or two to get ready."

"We talked about this for a few hours, Gonzales. It's not what we trained for, but neither was getting embedded in the Los Zetas cartel. I think we can do this," said Chavez.

"So, we're good?"

"Yeah, we're good," answered Chavez.

Gonzales and Covert Bravo arrived at the White House at eight o'clock. They were met by Pattie Hayes, who directed them to the Oval Office. She offered the usual coffee, tea, juice, and pastry.

Gonzales looked at Covert Bravo. They nodded their heads yes. Gonzales said, "Coffee, black, please. And thank you."

Pattie Hayes smiled and said, "Well, this is new." She gave Sanchez the look. He almost fell out of his chair. It didn't go unnoticed by Gonzales and the others. She returned with black coffee and said, "The president will be with you shortly. Enjoy your coffee." As Pattie left, she gave Sanchez the look again. The team took a seat, drank their coffee, and waited for the president. They all chuckled a little at Sanchez, who sat with his mouth agape.

President Rivera came in followed by Sydney Alvarez, Bob Reynolds, Frank Yanelli, and Joe Madden. The president directed them to the Situation Room. Once settled, he began.

"Gonzales, have you and Covert Bravo decided?"

"We're all good with this mission, Mr. President," answered Gonzales. "We're here to do whatever is needed to protect our country, sir. You want us to gain intelligence on the Mohawk Reservation's involvement in illegal trafficking of drugs and human. How MS-13 and Asian gangs are involved. Maybe we'll get a chance to find out who in the Latino community is involved with Roberts. We think getting jobs from Roberts will go a long way to that end, sir."

"That's great," said the president. "There are some things you should know about the drugs coming through the Mohawk Reservation. The demand for illegal marijuana isn't what it once was because most states have made it legal. However, British Columbia produces a strain that has a higher potency. It's called BC Bud. There is a big demand for that strain in our country. We have information that says fifty to seventy percent of British Columbia marijuana is being smuggled through the Mohawk Reservation. That statistic is probably incorrect. It's probably more than that. We just don't know for certain."

Gonzales asked, "What makes marijuana from British Columbia so powerful?"

The president asked Joe Madden to explain. Madden didn't hesitate. "Captain Gonzales, the climate in British Columbia is the major factor. Although British Columbia is in a latitude that is considered cold, some areas of the province enjoy a relatively mild and humid climate. These areas are called the 'Banana Belt.' There are numerous geographical and wind factors that are responsible for the mild climate.

"This product comes into our country at different places across Canada, but the Mohawk Reservation is where we've seen a big increase. The market is immense. It stretches from New England through the southern states to Miami, Florida.

"We also want intelligence on Ecstasy. There has been a very high increase in Ecstasy coming directly into the country through Canada."

Gonzales interrupted and asked, "Ecstasy? That's a highly powerful drug, isn't it? I remember reading about it some time ago. It wasn't called Ecstasy then. I think...I think it was called MDMA. The chemical name is complicated. I won't go there. MDMA had been administered to patients who suffered psychological problems. Some of our guys came back from Vietnam and Afghanistan with PTSD. They were given MDMA on a trial basis. The drug was supposed to help them better communicate their feelings. I think those trials failed. The drug was discontinued largely because of lack of success and the FDA didn't approve it."

President Rivera said, "Gonzales, that's pretty good. MDMA stands for methylenedioxy-methamphetamine. You're right about the chemical name. It's a mouthful. It's the main ingredient in Ecstasy. Ecstasy is made by mixing MDMA with other toxic chemicals, like mercury, formaldehyde, and ammonium chloride. Ecstasy is cut with many other drugs, like cocaine, heroin, caffeine, and amphetamines. In many cases, the buyer doesn't know what they're buying, which puts the buyer in lethal jeopardy. After consuming Ecstasy in a pill—or any other form—one will have heightened emotional warmth, energy, and sensory perceptions. When Ecstasy is taken, dopamine, serotonin, and norepinephrine are introduced to the body. They are three neurotransmitters that regulate mood and emotion. These symptoms occur when certain parts of the brain, which are associated with those feelings, are stimulated by the drug.

"The drug causes many adverse symptoms. For example, one may experience jaw clenching, teeth grinding, profuse sweating, and it could be accompanied by panic attacks and disorientation. Ecstasy pushes the body to its limits and beyond. When one takes Ecstasy, the body loses control of temperature regulation. In some cases, the body temperature can spike to levels that can cause kidney, heart, or liver failure. These are all conditions that can potentially cause death. The Chinese send raw MDMA and the machinery, the pill-making machines. The machine is called DZ-2E.

"Transnational gangs in Canada get the machines and set up assembly line production in Canada. Ecstasy's precursor chemicals are brought into Canada from Asia to gang-operated labs for processing.

"Let's not forget human trafficking. People are entering the country illegally. We don't know who they are or what they're up to. That's not good. Look what happened in Chicago...and those men were here legally. We've got our hands full. My first duty as president is to protect our citizens...period."

"Who would have thought," was Gonzales's reply. "Once we're working for Roberts, hopefully, we'll be able to collect intelligence on the drug trafficking."

President Rivera responded, "We hoped you'd respond that way."

"Do you have a timeline, sir?"

"Not really, but the sooner, the better."

Chapter 22

Leonardo "Little Lenny" Ortega was the boss of MS-13 in the Washington, DC area. He was Benito Flores's go-to guy there. He took a call from Dize Cruz. "What can I do for you, amigo?" asked Ortega.

"Benito Flores needs you to do him a favor."

"For sure, he can count on me. What does he want me to do?"

"You know Flores escaped from the Americans."

"Yes, I know. It's been in the news everywhere."

"You know he kidnapped the secretary of the Department of Homeland Security, Sydney Alvarez, and the governor of Arizona, Lisa Martinez. They were rescued by some Americans from Flores's home on the Gulf of Mexico. A guy named Vince Gonzales and his men did it. Gonzales has a name for them...I think he calls his men Covert Bravo. Flores's girlfriend, the mother of his son, and the son's nanny, were rescued at the same time."

"Hold up a minute. You telling me Flores's girlfriend and his son were *rescued*? Why would they need to be rescued?"

"The girlfriend turned on Flores. She took his son and the nanny, Lucia, with her. Flores wants you to put a tail on the secretary, Flores's girlfriend, Consuela, and his son, Alejandro. He wants you to use the men he sent to college. When they joined MS-13, they were just young boys. They didn't have any MS-13 tattoos. You told me about them. You said they were good kids but wanted in MS-13. That they didn't seem the kind of kids who could beat up or kill people to pass the initiation to get in MS-13. They seemed intelligent and were still in high school. I told Benito about them. He said to not put them through any initiation and to make sure they didn't get any tattoos. He wanted to see how they did in school. When they turned out to be top students, he knew he had better plans for them. He sent them to college to study Political Science. They should be done with college. Do you know where they are?"

Ortega listened as Cruz spoke and answered, "Of course, I know where they are. They are at home. I'll ask them to come to see me. They've been looking for jobs at a lobbying firm. That's what Mr. Flores wanted. Isn't it?"

"Yes, that's what Benito wanted. He'd like you to have them learn how to tail a person. They shouldn't have any trouble with that. Should they?"

"I'm sure they can learn to tail someone."

"Okay. Benito doesn't want you to use the same men two times in a row. He only wants you to tail them two or three times a week, on different days. This way, you can see their schedule every day of the week...including weekends. Flores wants to know about his son. Get as much information as you can on him. When he goes out with his mother or his nanny. He may be in school somewhere. What kind of security he has. The secretary and Consuela will have security details watching them day and night who are very, very good. So, make sure you follow what Flores says. Can you do it?"

"Si, amigo, yes, I can do it. How long will I do this?"

"Until you are told to stop, okay? There is one more thing. The secretary and Consuela have men friends. So, watch out for them."

"Whatever the boss wants," said Ortega.

"Flores has a big shipment of marijuana coming from Canada in a week or two. It's coming through the

Mohawk Reservation to Massena, New York. Are you set up with our guy, Remus Escobedo, in New York?" asked Cruz.

"Yeah, I talked with Escobedo. The product is coming through the Mohawk Reservation in two weeks. The St. Lawrence River is frozen over now. So, they'll use snowmobiles or hovercraft to transport the drugs. The Mohawks and Latinos will provide scouts to spot Border Patrol agents. We'll get Flores's product through with no problem. We're good. Escobedo will distribute some in New York City. I'll do the same in DC. And the rest will go down the pipeline to Miami, Florida."

"This is Flores's first attempt to get his product through the Canadian border. He bought the land a few years ago. He grows marijuana in British Columbia," said Cruz.

Ortega asked, "What about cocaine?"

Cruz said, "Yeah, there'll be cocaine and heroin too. It'll go back to Canada. You and Escobedo be ready to take the marijuana. Okay? Now, Flores wants good intelligence on Consuela, her son, Alejandro, and the Alvarez woman. Do it just like he said."

"For sure. He'll have it. I promise."

Chapter 23

Back in the Lacandon rain forest, Flores said to Cruz, "We'll see how the land I bought in British Columbia to grow the high-powered marijuana turns out. It'll be transported by trucks to the Mohawk Reservation. The trucks will travel through rough territory. It's the hardest way but the safest way. That'll be our first big shipment from Canada to the United States. The northern border has been, like the Americans say, 'a sieve.' It's wide open. It's the perfect place to bring my product to market. We have a good relationship with the Mohawks. I'm anxious to see how they perform for me. If they are successful, we will do business with them. If we are successful this time, I'll buy more land and grow more of my product in British Columbia, Canada. Our contact is James Roberts, a Mohawk Indian. He is a Warrior Chief on the US side of the border. He is involved with the casino on the Mohawk Reservation and is involved in tribal politics. He's been— and should continue to be—a big help to me."

* * *

Mohawks call themselves Kaniengehaka, people of the place of flint. They are one of the original five members of the Iroquois League and were known as the "Keepers of the Eastern Door." The Mohawk guarded the Iroquois Confederation for hundreds of years from attacks from other tribes. The Mohawk first encountered the Dutch and French during the seventeenth century and established trade with them. The contact with Europeans resulted in a smallpox epidemic. Because they had no immunity, the Mohawks lost two-thirds of their population. However, they recovered and regrouped into three villages. During the American Revolution, the Mohawks allied with the British, with whom they'd had a long-time trading relationship. In return, the British promised to prohibit colonists from encroaching on their territory in the Mohawk Valley. When the British lost the American Revolution, they gave up their claim to land in the colonies. The victorious Americans pushed all British allies, including the Mohawk tribe, out of New York. The British Crown gave the Mohawk land in Canada and they went there. Some went to Fort Niagara. Others went to Montreal.

The Mohawk signed the Treaty of Canandaigua on November 11, 1774, with the United States, which allowed them to own land in the US. Present-day Mohawks are organizing and are asking for more sovereignty over their lands in Canada. They want more authority over their people.

In 1993, a group of Akwesasne Mohawks bought three hundred twenty-two acres of land from Palatine, New York, in Montgomery County, New York. The Mohawks returned to their native ancestral land. The Mohawk named the land Kanatsiohareke and view the reservation in the United States as a sovereign nation that shares jurisdiction with the State of New York and the United States. The St. Regis Tribe is in the casino business. Governor Mario Cuomo and the tribe entered the Tribal-State Compact between the St. Regis Tribe and the State of New York. This took place in 1993.

Chapter 24

Leonardo "Little Lenny" Ortega was recruited into MS-13 when he was thirteen years old, orphaned, and homeless. MS-13 offered protection. He jumped at the chance. He passed the gang's initiation by physically beating an older man. The older man didn't die. Ortega was permitted entry into MS-13. He did as he was told and gained more respect from the other gang members. When the leader of MS-13 needed to have someone roughed up or killed, Little Lenny was called to do the job. Little Lenny was twenty-three years old when he took charge of MS-13 and became a ruthless MS-13 gang leader. He didn't want to disappoint Benito Flores. He was the main distributor of Flores's products in Washington, DC, Virginia, and Maryland.

He talked to one of his best men, Carlito Dario. "Carlito, I've been asked to put a tail on two women."

"What? You want two women tailed? Who are these women?" asked Dario with a chuckle.

"Don't laugh. This is very important. If you don't want part of this let me know now!" retorted Ortega.

"Okay, amigo, I do what you ask," said Carlito Dario. "Who're the women?"

"That's better, Carlito. I want you to put a tail on the secretary of the Department Homeland Security and Consuela Hernández."

"Who are they?" queried Dario.

"Who are they? Who are they? The secretary is Sydney Alvarez. She oversees threats to the United States, or something like that. She's a top person in the United States government. Consuela is the mother of Benito

Flores's son. Flores wants us to see what they do every day. You know, where they go. How long they stay in one place or another. He wants to know about his son, too. Don't tail them every day, just a few times a week. Use the men who just finished college. They don't have MS-13 tattoos, do they?"

"No, they don't have tattoos," answered Dario.

"You've gotta teach them how to tail someone without being caught," said Little Lenny. "They should dress in suits, you know, look like businessmen. Look clean-cut. That's what the Americans say, clean-cut." Having said that, Ortega laughed again. "My idea of clean-cut is ear to ear by my machete on someone's throat, or to clean-cut someone's head off. What do you think of that, Dario?" Little Lenny said, laughing a little louder this time. After hearing Ortega define what his idea of clean-cut, Dario shuddered. He knew Ortega's reputation. He knew Ortega meant what he said.

"We can do that, Lenny. I know these guys can pull this off."

* * *

Elio Cabrera, Fabio Iglesias, Chaco Lugo, Edwardo Vicario, Cato Guerrero, and Donato Desoto were the men Flores was thinking of when he asked for men without an MS-13 tattoo or any other identifying marks on their bodies. They were college-educated and spoke perfect English. They joined MS-13 when they were fifteen or sixteen years old and didn't have to pass the usual initiation. They were good-looking Latino young men and intelligent.

When they came to Dario to join MS-13, he recognized something in them. They didn't have the typical MS-13 look. He told Ortega about them, who told Cruz, who then told Benito Flores. When Flores heard about them, he called them for a visit to his home in the mountains in Mexico. After seeing and talking with them, Flores thought they may be used for some higher calling. So, Flores paid for their college education to study . Political Science. While they were in college, Dario used them exclusively to sell drugs in the affluent areas of DC.

Dario got his men together. "I've got an important job for you. First, I've got to teach you how to tail someone without being caught." He explained that Benito Flores, "El Gato," wanted Sydney Alvarez and Consuela Hernández followed. "He wants to know where his son, Alejandro, is. If he's in school. Where he goes with his mother or with his nanny, Lucia. These women will always have security with them. The boy will have the same security, too. The people who will pull security detail for the women and Alejandro are very, very good at what they do. If you get spotted, it won't be good for you. If they spot you, they may just let you follow them and do nothing. Or they may try to grab you, take you somewhere and start asking questions. That won't be good for you.

"There's one other thing you should be aware of; the women have men friends. The men are US Army Rangers. They were involved with the rescue of the women from Mexico. They are also very, very good, and they're tough, too. The secretary's friend is Vince Gonzales. Consuela's friend is Bob Chavez. We have pictures of the women, but not of Gonzales or Chavez. You will be trained to follow people without being detected."

One week later, Dario felt his college men could follow anyone without being caught.

Dario said, "I want Cabrera and Iglesias to follow the Alvarez woman. We've not been able to find the addresses of the secretary and Consuela. These are pictures of the women. Flores sent them. They aren't the best. They'll have to do. We know the building where the secretary works. The Department of Homeland Security headquarters is at a Nebraska Ave. complex, 3801 Nebraska Ave. Northwest, so, you start there. I'd wait till late afternoon. If she's there working today, she probably won't come out till late afternoon maybe five o'clock. You should start surveillance around four thirty. She must eat dinner. When you see her come out, follow her? See where she goes. She may go to her home or some other place. That's why you follow her. To see what she does.

"Consuela wanted to finish college. For some reason, Flores thinks she'll enroll at American University. Maybe he thinks she wants to become an American. Who knows? So, Lugo and Vicario, start there. We don't know for sure if she's going to school there. You may have to pick a place on campus and sit there for a while. But don't do anything suspicious. Like sitting in the same spot all day. You've got to change your spot. When you spot her, follow her.

"The secretary's and Consuela's CIA detail is with them night and day. Lugo and Vicario, take Consuela and go to American University. Didn't you guys go to American University?" All four guys nodded yes. "See if you can find her. Report to me tomorrow night. For some reason, we don't have a picture of Flores's son. Maybe it's coming. That will be more difficult. Once you find where Consuela lives, you'll have found where the boy and Lucia are living, too. Very simple, right?"

Dario felt all the college men had mastered surveillance techniques and were ready to go.

* * *

Cabrera and Iglesias pulled their ordinary-looking, gray Ford Fiesta down the block from Sydney's building on Nebraska Ave. They waited for a while. They didn't want to cause anyone to get suspicious. So, Cabrera got out of the car and walked down the street. Iglesias drove around the block a few times. He found another parking spot and pulled in. Iglesias took his cell phone and called Cabrera and asked, "Did she come out?"

"No, I don't think so."

"What do you mean you don't think so? You either saw her or you didn't," replied Iglesias. "So, what is it?"

"I didn't see her, yet. Where are you? I don't see you," responded Cabrera.

"I'm right down the block from you. On the other side of the street. Do you see me now?" asked Iglesias.

"I see you. Yeah, I've got the car in my sight," answered Cabrera. "I'm coming to you."

As Cabrera was approaching the car, a motorcade was getting ready to come out of the complex. He looked to see if it belonged to Sydney. He couldn't believe he saw her. He quickened his pace and got to Iglesias. He got in and said, "I see her. She's getting into a black SUV. I think she's traveling in a motorcade. So, we've got to be sure which car she's in."

"How do we do that?" asked Iglesias.

"I'm not sure."

Suddenly, one black SUV came out onto the street. Cabrera said, "Let's follow that SUV."

"Are you sure?"

"No, I'm not sure. But it's the best thing we've got. So, go."

Iglesias started the car and pulled into traffic. He got three car lengths behind the SUV that was hopefully driving Sydney. The SUV went to a Georgetown restaurant.

It dropped someone off. It wasn't Sydney Alvarez, the secretary of the Department of Homeland Security. It was a man. Cabrera and Iglesias couldn't identify him.

"What do we do now?" asked Iglesias.

"All we can do is call back to Dario. We'll tell him what happened. He knew we had just a slim chance to spot this woman," answered Cabrera.

"Yeah, I guess you're right," replied Iglesias.

Cabrera made the call and related to Dario what transpired.

"Well, you did as you were ordered. No one can blame you for that. Tomorrow is another day. You try again. Now go home and get some rest."

As Cabrera and Iglesias were driving back to where they lived, Cabrera said, "Let's go back to Nebraska Ave. We may get lucky."

"I don't know about that. Dario said to go home and get some rest," responded Iglesias

"So what? If we go back and find this woman, Dario will be satisfied. He'll be thrilled. Don't you think? If we find nothing, he's none the wiser. Right?" asked Cabrera.

"When you put it that way, I can't disagree," answered Iglesias.

When Cabrera and Iglesias got to Nebraska Ave., it was about seven in the evening. They parked the car. This time, Iglesias got out and took a walk. Cabrera stayed with the car. Iglesias walked past the building Sydney was supposedly working in. He stopped and looked. He thought he'd seen a woman who looked like the picture of Sydney Alvarez walk out with a group of people. She got into a black SUV.

Iglesias immediately call Cabrera. "Do you see me?" asked Iglesias.

"Yeah, I see you."

"I think I saw Alvarez get in a black SUV. Get over here, now!" exclaimed Iglesias.

Cabrera started the car and pulled out of the parking place. He picked up Iglesias.

Iglesias said, "The SUV just pulled out. It's just up the street. Do you see it?"

"Yeah, I see it. I'll get a few cars behind it," replied Cabrera.

Cabrera and Iglesias followed the SUV to a Georgetown neighborhood. The SUV stopped in front of a townhouse and Sydney Alvarez got out. As Sydney went into her home, she waved to the CIA detail as it left. There would be two other agents in place for the night. Dick Henderson and Joe Bandy were the agents. Mario Biscotti was the CIA supervisor who made the assignment for Henderson and Bandy to keep watch over Sydney that night.

As Cabrera drove past Sydney's townhouse, Iglesias said, "Slow down, I want to try to get the address."

* * *

"Did you see that car slow down in front of the secretary's place?" asked Henderson.

"Yes, I did. When the brake lights went on, I was able to get the license plate number," answered Bandy.

"Great. The car just pulled into a parking spot down the street a block away."

"That's interesting. Maybe the people in the car are looking for someone. Just because they slowed down in front of the secretary's place doesn't necessarily mean they're following her," responded Bandy.

"You should run a check on the plate, just to check it out," said Henderson.

Bandy made the call. "It's a rented car. It's got Carlito Dario as the lessee."

"That name sounds familiar to me. Why don't you run it?" asked Henderson.

Bandy ran the name through his computer. "It says here that he's a member of MS-13. He's the leader of the gang in DC."

"I knew I heard that name somewhere. We'd better call Biscotti and report this. He may want us to pick up whoever is in the car," said Henderson.

Henderson called Biscotti.

"This is Biscotti, Henderson. What do you have?"

"Well, sir, we just caught a glimpse of a car and ran its plates. We think the car followed Secretary Alvarez home," reported Henderson.

"I'm listening," replied Biscotti.

"We ran the plates and it turns out the car is a rental. The name on the rental is Carlito Dario," continued Henderson.

Biscotti thought for a second and said, "For some reason that name rings a bell, Henderson."

"It did to us, too, sir. It appears Carlito Dario is the lessee and an MS-13 thug. We want to know if we should pick up whoever's in the car. Or do you want to send someone over to pick Dario up at his place? We've got his address," replied Henderson.

Biscotti thought for a moment and said, "No, I don't want you to pick anyone up. Not yet. If indeed they are surveilling the secretary's house, they'll come back. When they come back, I'll think about having you pick them up then. This must be considered a serious threat to the secretary. These fellas are the small fish. I want the people behind it. Dario may be part of it. He's not the big guy. The big guy is Benito Flores. I think there's another guy between Dario and Flores. I'd like to get that guy, too. Flores has said all along he wants revenge. So, I think we let this play out. At least for the time being. See where it goes. We don't to move too fast. I'll pass this information along to Director Yanelli. At the same time, I'll ask him to beef up the security for the secretary, the Martinez family, the Hernández women, and her family, with more agents."

"Roger that, sir," said Henderson.

* * *

Cabrera and Iglesias sat in the car for a while. Cabrera said, "Maybe we should call Dario and report what we've found. He should be very happy." Cabrera made the call and reported what they had seen and done.

"So, you took it on yourselves to go back and try to find the secretary," was the first thing out of Dario's mouth.

Cabrera thought this was not going to turn out good. He thought, *why not go for it.* He said, "We thought we'd take a shot. That's all. We thought you'd be glad."

"Are you kidding me? I'm very happy. You fellas used your common sense. Your initiative. There aren't many who would do that. You men have done a very good job. I'll tell Lenny. He'll be very happy to send this up to Flores. Now go home and get some rest. You'll need it. You'll stake out that house in the morning."

"Count on us," said Cabrera.

Iglesias heard the conversation and said, "We did the right thing. Let's get going. We have to be here early tomorrow morning."

"It's probably a good idea to check on the back of her house," stated Cabrera.

"Why?"

"It may come in handy sometime. You never

know."

"You're right. We'll do it the first chance we get."

Iglesias started the car and slowly headed down the street. Henderson and Bandy watched it go.

* * *

The next morning, Cabrera and Iglesias got to Sydney's house at five in the morning. Henderson and Bandy were still on duty. They'd been in front of Sydney's since seven o'clock last night. Henderson said, "I think the same car is back. What do you want to do?"

"Let's call Biscotti for direction," answered Bandy.

Henderson made the call. Biscotti, aroused from sleep, answered and listened to Henderson and said, "Well, we know for sure someone is surveilling the secretary. Just sit tight and whatever you do, protect the secretary. Don't let whoever is in the car know you've made them."

"Yes, sir."

When Sydney came out of her townhouse with a man, her CIA detail was waiting.

Cabrera said, "That may be Vince Gonzales. He must have come after we left last night. What do you think, Iglesias?"

That's exactly what happened. Gonzales came shortly after Cabrera and Iglesias left.

"Could be. We just don't know. We have a picture of the woman, but nothing of her man friend. We wait and see."

Sydney gave Gonzales a peck on the cheek and got into a black SUV. The CIA detail drove her to her next destination. Gonzales got into his car and drove off in the same direction as Sydney's vehicle. "That's got to be her man friend. He must have stayed with her overnight," said

Cabrera.

Iglesias said, "You may be right. But just because a man came out of the house with her doesn't make him a man friend."

"Yeah, she kissed him on the cheek, though. That means something to me!" retorted Cabrera.

"You're probably right. Let's wait and see before we make any judgments. We'd better get in behind them and see where they go."

"Yeah, we've stumbled on some good information," said Iglesias.

Iglesias pulled the rented Ford Fiesta out of the parking space and stayed three to four car lengths behind Gonzales. Sydney's vehicle pulled into the National Cathedral. Gonzales did the same. Sydney and Vince went into the cathedral together. The CIA was right behind. The CIA detail didn't miss the Ford Fiesta.

Iglesias pulled into the cathedral parking lot and turned the opposite direction and parked down from where Sydney was parked. They stayed in the car. It didn't look like they'd been spotted. The CIA detail didn't miss Iglesias parking opposite from them.

Iglesias said, "Are they going to Mass? Can you believe it?"

"I think they may be going to Mass, Iglesias. Why else would they come to a cathedral? It makes sense. They are Mexican. Why not Catholic? Most Mexicans are Catholic. I'm Catholic. Are you?" asked Cabrera.

"I was raised Catholic. I haven't been to Mass or received the Eucharist in years. How about you?" asked Iglesias.

"Like you, I was raised Catholic, and like you, I haven't been to church since my parents died. Now, we sit and wait for them to come out. A weekday Mass usually takes about thirty to forty minutes." Iglesias nodded his head in agreement.

Thirty-five minutes later, Sydney, Gonzales, and the CIA detail came out. The CIA and Sydney got into their vehicle and drove off. Gonzales followed. Cabrera and Iglesias waited for their vehicles to get out of the parking lot before following them. The traffic was light for DC at that early morning hour. So, it didn't take much to keep Gonzales in their sights. Sydney's vehicle stopped at a little restaurant. Sydney got out, as did the CIA. Gonzales pulled in right behind Sydney's vehicle, got out, and followed Sydney into the breakfast place. Henderson and Bandy were aware that they'd been tailed by Cabrera and Iglesias.

"This is very interesting, Iglesias. I wouldn't have figured this kind of a start. I'll drive around the block and park as far away as possible without losing sight of them when they come out."

An hour later, they came out of the restaurant. Sydney gave Gonzales another peck on the cheek, got in her vehicle, and drove off. Gonzales got in his car and drove off in another direction. Cabrera took his phone out and took a picture of Gonzales before he drove off. "Now we have a picture to show Dario."

Iglesias said, "I'm following the woman."

"That's what they're paying us for. Let's see where she goes."

Sydney's CIA detail drove to Nebraska Ave.

Iglesias said, "We should find a place to park as close by as possible. She may be here for an hour or the day. We know she works here. Here's a space; I've got some change for the meter. Do you have any, Cabrera?"

"I've got a little, but not enough for a few hours or the day. We may need twenty dollars' worth of quarters," answered Cabrera.

"Well, maybe you should go get some more at one of the stores."

"Okay, I'll go see what I can get."

Cabrera got out of the car and walked to a restaurant down the street. He walked in and asked the cashier, "Do you have twenty dollars' worth of quarters?"

She looked at him and asked, "What for?"

"The parking meter," answered Cabrera.

She said, "It would be a lot easier to use a credit card."

"Listen, do you have twenty dollars' worth of quarters or not?" retorted Cabrera.

"I'm not supposed to give that kind of change out. My manager wouldn't like it. So, no, I don't have twenty dollars' worth of quarters. Use your credit card," said the cashier.

Cabrera said, "Forget it," and walked out in a huff.

The cashier called her manager over and told her about the conversation she'd just had with a good-looking Latino guy.

The manager got suspicious and asked, "After he left the store, did you see which direction he went?"

"Well, you know, I thought the guy wasn't telling me the truth. So, I watched which way he turned. He turned left. I casually walked over to the window to watch him. He walked down the street to his car. He put some money in the meter before he got into a gray Ford. Why would he need twenty dollars' worth of quarters?"

The manager said, "I don't know. It doesn't sound right to me. I'm calling the DC police. After what happened in Chicago, we can't be too careful. Better safe than sorry."

The manager called the police and explained what she and the cashier had seen. A DC black-and-white arrived a few moments later. Cabrera and Iglesias noticed the cop car stop in front of the restaurant. One officer got out. The other stayed in the car. The officer went into the restaurant and heard the story from the cashier and the manager. He stepped out of the restaurant, walked over to his partner, and explained the situation.

"There's no law against parking on the street or asking for change for a parking meter," said the officer to his partner. "This does look a little suspicious, though. Who needs twenty dollars' worth of quarters for the meter? Why not use a credit card? Let's go over and ask a few questions."

Cabrera and Iglesias were starting their car. The police officer tapped on the passenger's-side window. Cabrera rolled the window down. "Is there a problem, officer?" asked Cabrera.

"What are you guys doing? You've been sitting here for at least an hour."

Cabrera answered, "We're just talking."

"You need twenty dollars' worth of quarters for the meter just to sit here and talk?" In the meantime, the other officer ran the plates on the gray Ford Fiesta. The officers were mic'd up. The officer said into his mic, "Hey, Joe, the car is a rental. It's in the name of Carlito Dario." Cabrera had begun to think of a reason for him and Iglesias being there.

The officer asked Cabrera, "May I see both of your driver's licenses?"

Both Cabrera and Iglesias said, "Yes, sir."

Cabrera and Iglesias fumbled with the seat belts to get their wallets out of their pockets. They gave them to the officer.

The officer looked them over and said, "I'm going to run this license for any warrants." The officer went back to the car and put the necessary information into the computer. Iglesias and Cabrera waited patiently, trying not to show any sign of emotion. The check came back to the officer's computer. It was negative. The officer did run the plates on the car. It was a rental in the name of Carlito Dario. Neither Cabrera nor Iglesias had warrants. The officer went back to Iglesias and Cabrera. He gave the license back to Iglesias and said, "We have no reason to hold either of you. I have to ask what you're doing sitting in this car."

"Officer, we're new to DC and looking for jobs," offered Cabrera.

"What kind of jobs?"

"We're Political Science majors and recently graduated from American University. We're looking for jobs in our field. We were just sitting here discussing where to look. We were thinking of some lobbying group."

"Isn't American University in DC?"

"Yes, it is, officer."

"Why would you say you're not familiar with DC? You went to school here."

"We never got to this part of town," answered Cabrera.

"Okay. But why not use a credit card?" asked the officer.

"We don't have one, officer. We don't even have jobs."

"Okay, okay, that's enough. Now, get out of here."

"We were just on our way, officer, thank you." With that, Iglesias pulled out into traffic, very carefully. The officers' body cameras were on and recorded the whole incident. As soon as the officer got back to his black-and-white, the officer who had stayed in the car said, "We'd better call this in. We can pick those guys up at any time.

Carlito Dario is MS-13." The officer made the call and reported to his superior.

* * *

Once on the street, Cabrera said, "That was not good. We must be more careful. We can't let that happen again."

"No kidding. What are we going to do now?"

Cabrera answered, "We drive around the block. We may miss her or we may get lucky like last night and catch her as she leaves."

Iglesias drove around the block and asked, "What are we going to tell Dario? That story you told the cops was good thinking."

"We tell him everything. Including the run-in with the police. We followed the woman to the cathedral, to the restaurant, and this building. We have a picture of a man who may be Vince Gonzales. That's not a bad day's work. Let's get back and report to Dario. What I said to the cops was not a story. You should know that. It's the truth. We're Political Science majors who are looking for a job," said Cabrera.

* * *

Chaco Lugo and Edwardo Vicario had a much different experience following Consuela Hernández. The night before, Lugo said, "I'm going to look on the internet and find American University's website. The site may give information."

"What kind of information?" asked Vicario.

"The site may have a class schedule. We'd get a head start if the site had when the Political Science classes were scheduled," answered Lugo.

"I never thought of that. What a good idea," replied

Vicario.

Lugo looked up the American University's website. He looked for the Political Science schedule.

Lugo said, "Here it is. The first introductory class starts at ten o'clock tomorrow morning at Kerwin Hall. What a break! That's where we took our Intro to Political Science class. That's where should start."

The next morning, Lugo and Vicario were on American University's campus at nine o'clock. Since they had graduated from American University, they were very familiar with the campus.

Vicario said, "I think we can do better by splitting up."

"What would you suggest?" asked Lugo.

"I think one of us should sit in front of the building and the other should sit in the back. That way, we can cover the whole building. I'll take the front. You take the back," answered Vicario

"Vicario, I never knew you were so sinister," replied Lugo.

"I'm really into this cloak-and-dagger stuff," responded Vicario.

Lugo opened his backpack and took out a Political Science book. "Take one. I brought these for us to browse through as we wait. It should make us blend in better."

"Great idea. It's nine thirty. A half-hour before the class starts. We'd better get to our places," responded Vicario.

Each man settled into a good spot to carry out surveillance on the building, each hoping one of them would pick up Consuela. They didn't have to wait too long. A black SUV pulled up in front of Kerwin Hall.

Vicario noticed the black SUV first. When it stopped in front of Kerwin Hall, Consuela got out...or at least, it looked like her. Vicario pulled out his cell and speed-dialed Lugo.

"I think I've got her. It has to be her," said Vicario.

"Why does it have to be her? It could be one of a thousand students," replied Lugo.

"How many students arrive at a university in a black SUV with three men in it? One of the men got out and followed the woman student into the building. The other two parked the SUV in a student parking lot. They're sitting there right now," said Vicario.

"That's got to be our lady," replied Lugo. "Good work. Let's just sit tight and wait. Classes normally last about one hour. If I remember right, that's what the class schedule said last night. When I checked the schedule, the class was from ten to eleven. We should be ready when they come out. I'll wait until ten minutes to eleven. I'll get the car and bring it around. She should come out a little after eleven."

Just like clockwork, Consuela came out of the building at ten minutes past eleven. She came out with a CIA agent following her. She and the agent went directly to the waiting SUV, which had just pulled in front of Kerwin Hall. The SUV left the American University campus. Lugo had driven his Ford into the university's parking lot right next to Kerwin Hall. Vicario jumped in. They were in traffic immediately and were just a few car lengths behind Consuela's SUV.

"We did it, we did it!" said Vicario.

"Now, we follow them. Maybe she's going home," said Lugo.

The SUV carrying Consuela didn't go to her home. It went to her job at the State Department. Consuela was dropped at the front door. A CIA agent got out with her. He and Consuela went into the building together. The other two agents parked the SUV and went into the building, too.

"I wonder what they're doing here. This is the State Department building. Why would she come here? What should we do? Should we wait here and see when they come out?" asked Vicario.

"Let's call Dario and tell him what we've seen so far. I'll call," answered Lugo.

Lugo made the call. "That's very interesting," said Dario. "You're sure she went into the State Department?"

"No doubt about it," replied Lugo. "What should we do?"

"Stay there. When they come out, you follow them," responded Dario. "Maybe one of you can go into the building, nose around, and maybe pick up something."

"Okay," responded Lugo. He hung up and turned to Vicario. "Dario wants us to stay here. He said one of us should go into the building and try to pick something up. I'll stay in the car. You go in."

Vicario went in. Lugo found a place to park the car and stayed with it. A couple of hours passed. Lugo's phone rang. "Lugo, they're coming out. Get ready to pick me up on the street. I'm out the door now. Do you see me?" asked Vicario.

"Yeah, I see you. I'm coming now. Do you see me?" asked Lugo.

"Yeah, I see you. They're right behind me."

Lugo got the car out onto the street just as Vicario got there. Vicario jumped in and turned to see which way the SUV was headed. The SUV went in the opposite direction.

"They're heading away from us. Turn around somewhere. I'll keep my eye on them!" exclaimed Vicario.

Fortunately, Lugo found a place to turn around. Vicario asked, "Do you see them?"

"Yeah, I've got them. I'll fall three cars behind them. Let's see where they take us now."

The SUV drove to Georgetown, to a residential area. It stopped at Consuela's townhouse. She got out of the SUV and went in.

Vicario said, "This must be where she lives. It's a pretty nice place."

"Did you see the SUV pull into that reserved parking spot?" asked Lugo.

"Yeah, I did. Call Dario and tell him what we've got."

Lugo drove down the street and found a place to park. It was two blocks away. A place where they could set up surveillance for a while.

Lugo made the call and related what he and Vicario had discovered. "You stay where you are. Did you get the address?" was Dario's reply.

"No, we didn't have a chance to take a look," answered Lugo.

"You sit there and write down on paper what you see. This way, you won't forget anything. Call me if anything develops," responded Dario.

"Okay. We're on it," said Lugo.

Vicario heard the conversation. He said, "Well, it looks like we're here for a while. Do you think the CIA spotted us?"

"No, I'm not sure," answered Lugo.

"Maybe we should call Dario back and ask him if we can go get something to eat. I'll call this time," answered Vicario.

Vicario made the call and gave Dario an update. He finished his update with, "Do you mind if we get something to eat? We haven't eaten since this morning."

"Do I mind? Sure, I mind. You stay there until I

say you can go," answered Dario. "She may come out and go somewhere. Or someone might come in for a visit. You stay put, for now."

"Sure, we can do that. You're the boss," replied Vicario. "It's a good bet she's done with class today."

Dario thought for a second and responded, "You wait there for another hour. If she doesn't come out, let me know."

"Will do," said Vicario.

Vicario and Lugo waited an hour. Consuela didn't come out. Vicario said, "Look, it's five o'clock in the afternoon. All we can do is wait for her to make a move... if she does make a move."

Another half-hour passed, when Bob Chavez showed up. He talked with the CIA before entering Consuela's home.

"That may be her man friend, Chavez. Get a picture of him," said Vicario.

"I'll try to get one, but it's getting late." He quickly took a cell phone picture. "I've got him. Let's call Dario," said Lugo. Vicario nodded his head in agreement.

After Vicario called Dario and told him they may have a picture of Consuela's man friend, Dario said, "That's great work. Well done. You guys send me the picture. You can go home for the night. If this picture turns out to be Consuela's man friend, Flores will be very happy with you guys."

* * *

The four surveillance specialists—Vicario, Lugo, Cabrera, and Iglesias—got back to Dario a few minutes apart. Each team submitted its report. Dario said, "That's not bad, not bad at all. I'll send this report and the pictures up the ladder. El Gato should be happy."

Chapter 25

Covert Bravo were at their place in Virginia. They were in the big house. Sanchez was preparing dinner for them. He had roasted beef tenderloin with mashed potatoes and broccoli.

As they sat down to eat Ramirez said, "Sanchez, you should have been a chef."

"Yeah, yeah," said Sanchez.

Gonzales had other ideas. He wanted to discuss what President Rivera had said. "You know what the president wants from us. Do any of you have any ideas?"

Bob Chavez spoke first. "I think we go up to the Mohawk Casino and ask Roberts for work. We should take whatever he gives us. You never know."

Manny Sanchez said, "We've got to start somewhere. If we want to get some intelligence on how drugs and human trafficking are coming into the country. Roberts may be the key. I think he is the key. He's got to be in it up to his neck. He may be desperate for Latinos— or Mexicans, as he called us—to work for him. Desperate might be a little strong. He might need some guys like us to work for him."

Gonzales looked to Gomez and Ramirez and asked, "You guys have any thoughts?"

Ramirez said, "That sounds right to me. We're Mexican men, Latino. We may be just what he's looking for. Why hide it? We need work. He offered us jobs."

"That's exactly what we'll do. Okay then," said Gonzales, "I'll set up a meeting with the president. We'll tell him then. I think it's the best way to get started, too.

We agree, then."

"Yes," came back from Covert Bravo.

"I'll call the president now."

* * *

"Mr. President, how are you?" queried Gonzales.

"I'm fine. Thanks for asking. I hope this isn't just a how are you call, Captain."

"No, sir, it isn't. You don't pay us for those kinds of calls, do you."

"No, I don't. I didn't mean to offend. Just being a little facetious."

"No offense taken, sir."

"Good. How are you fellas doing out on the farm?" asked the president. "Have you given any thought to what we talked about yesterday?"

"That's why I'm calling, sir. We've decided on how to get started. We'd like to meet with you at your convenience, sir."

"I can't do anything the rest of today or tomorrow morning. How about Wednesday. That's two days from now, say about four o'clock? We'll get Secretary Alvarez, Reynolds, Yanelli, and Madden here, too."

"Sounds good, Mr. President. We'll be there."

Gonzales said to Covert Bravo, "Well, here we go, guys. We meet with the president Wednesday at four o'clock."

Chapter 26

That night, Gonzales met Sydney at her townhouse. As they left for dinner, she told her CIA detail to stand down. The detail would not need to be on hand when she and Gonzales had dinner at a DC restaurant: Ocean Prime. However, the detail would disregard her order. They followed them to the restaurant and waited outside.

After they were seated, the waiter came and asked, "May I take a drink order?"

Syd looked at Gonzales and said, "Do you want anything to drink. Maybe a glass of wine or a cocktail?"

"I think I'll pass on a drink tonight. But you go ahead, if you'd like."

"I think I'll pass, too. Let's just order dinner."

Sydney ordered. "I'll have a shrimp cocktail as an appetizer, filet mignon with a side of asparagus spears, and a dollop of whipped potatoes. Medium rare on the filet."

The waiter said, "Very well, Madam Secretary." Sydney was a frequent visitor at the Ocean Prime.

Gonzales looked over the menu and said, "I'll have the same thing, and the same way on the filet."

"Very well, sir."

Dinner came and they made small talk. "What should we do this weekend?" asked Gonzales.

"To start, I thought we'd take a ride into Falls Church, Virginia, on Saturday morning. They've got a good farmers' market there. Then I thought we'd have lunch. After lunch, I thought we'd go back to my place and have dinner. I have one of your favorite Mexican dishes planned for you. After dinner, I have tickets to the National

Symphony at the Kennedy Center," replied Sydney.

"All I can say is, you're the best, Syd. I'm in on all parts of the day."

When they finished dinner, Gonzales drove back to Sydney's place.

The CIA security detail followed. She gave them a wave, which they returned.

Once they were settled, Sydney asked, "Do you have an idea on how you're going to approach this Chief Roberts?"

"We thought we'd ask Roberts for work. He knows we need work and has offered us jobs."

"I want to know where and when you're going and when you're coming back. Not because I'm the secretary of the Department of Homeland Security—"

Before she could finish, it was Gonzales who interrupted. "Hold up a minute, Madam Secretary." Gonzales used Sydney's title when he wanted to get her attention—and her goat. "You know when we're going. Currently, I'm not sure when we'll be back. I suppose it'll depend on how long it takes to get the information the president wants. If I had to guess, it might be six to eight weeks."

This got Sydney's dander up. Her eyes were filled with hurt and pain, but mostly fear. She began to tear up. "I want to know because I care about you, Gonzales. I do. I don't want you to get hurt, or I dread the thought, get killed."

Gonzales knew he'd gone too far and immediately turned down his rhetoric. "None of us are going to get hurt or killed. Believe me, we've been in situations much worse. I want to say I care about you, too, Syd."

As soon as Sydney heard what Gonzales said, she burst into tears. She was standing in her kitchen and ran to him, burrowing her face into his chest and began to sob uncontrollably. All Gonzales could think to do was hold her tight. "Now, now, honey." When he called her honey, she sobbed all the harder. "Syd, please get a hold of yourself. Come on, honey. Settle down." With that said, Sydney started to settle down and stopped sobbing.

When she caught her breath, she said, "Okay, Gonzales, I'm...I'm okay. Let's sit on the couch for a minute."

"Sure, sure," was Gonzales's response. They sat for a few moments. Sydney clung to Gonzales tightly, as if she'd never get another chance. Gonzales held her tenderly until she stopped weeping.

"Okay, now. If you remember, this was your idea in the first place. It was you who told the president we should go back there," said Gonzales.

"I know what I said. As soon as I said it, I immediately regretted it. I don't want you to go. Can't Covert Bravo do this on their own?"

"I can't leave my men. We talked about this one of the first times we were together. I told you, I'm an Army Ranger. You said you'd be okay with that."

"I know. I know. But I wasn't as fond of you then as I am now. I wonder what Consuela will say to Bob Chavez when she finds out? I think she'll feel the same way."

"That's between them. Isn't it? We must deal with this. Don't we? I don't think we'll be in any danger."

"Really. Are you taking your weapon? You must be taking something."

"Of course, we're taking our guns. We go anywhere with a Glock. I've got one behind my back right now. You now that."

"Yes, I know you carry when we are together. Don't you think you should have other weapons?" asked Sydney.

"What other weapons?"

"I don't know. The weapons used for other fighting. M16s. I know you use them," answered Sydney.

"We can't take those with us. Someone might see them in our vehicle. There's no place to hide them," responded Gonzales.

"You let me worry about that."

"Okay. I still don't understand the concern. You're going to be safe. You've got the best security in the world."

"I do feel safe, but not as safe as when I'm with you, Vince. I think I don't want to be away from you. I'm afraid for you and me."

"Let's not get ahead of ourselves. Don't forget you're the secretary of the Department of Homeland Security."

* * *

Gonzales and Covert Bravo were at the White House Wednesday at 3:30 p.m. Pattie Hayes was there to greet them. They were thirty minutes early.

"You're early, as usual, Captain Gonzales."

"We never want President Rivera waiting for us. It's better if we wait for him."

Pattie directed them to the Oval Office and said, "The president appreciates your timeliness." She made the usual offer of coffee, tea, and/or juice. Gonzales looked at Covert Bravo for an answer. All declined.

"I guess we'll pass this time, Pattie."

Pattie said, "The president will be in shortly. Take a seat and make yourselves comfortable." As Pattie Hayes left the room, she gave Sanchez a good look.

A few minutes later, President Rivera came into the Oval Office followed by Sydney Alvarez, Bob Reynolds,

Frank Yanelli, and Joe Madden.

"You're here early, aren't you, Captain?"

"No more than usual, Mr. President."

"Well, let's go to the Situation Room. We can begin our discussion there."

Once all were seated in the Situation Room, the president said, "I take it, Gonzales, you and your men have made a decision on how to approach the Mohawk Reservation and the drugs and human trafficking that flows through it."

"Mr. President, we talked about this at the farm last night. The consensus is we should go to the casino and ask Roberts for a job. Any job. We think, like everyone in this room does, Roberts is key to getting access to any information on drug and human trafficking, sir. If we gain his trust, he may give us more responsibility, just like Flores did in Mexico. So, if it's all right with you and this committee, we'd like to take a few days to get ready to go back to the reservation."

The president looked to the others in the meeting and asked, "What do you think about this idea?"

Reynolds spoke first. "I think the idea has some merit. Covert Bravo may be able to get in with the people who're involved with smuggling drugs and human trafficking. We should give this some real consideration, Mr. President."

"Joe, what do you think?"

"I concur. I think the idea is really good and we should consider it."

The president looked at Sydney. "What're your thoughts, Sydney?"

"Speaking as the secretary of the Department of Homeland Security, I think the idea has merit, too. Captain Gonzales will put himself, and perhaps Covert Bravo, in harm's way. They've been there before and will be again. It's what they signed up for, Mr. President." She glanced at Gonzales. She gave him a look. It didn't go unnoticed by anyone in the room.

"Okay then, we'll proceed with this idea. Gonzales, let us know what you'll need and when you'll need it."

"Mr. President, we've talked this over. We're sure we'll need our Glocks. We'll take them. I'll make a list of things we'll need. We should take our rifles, with plenty of ammo. I don't know where we will put them. Like I said, I'll make a list, sir. We'll need a day or two to get ready, Mr. President. We need to talk about this a little more."

"We thought you should have your rifles, too. A mechanic is building a case for your rifles in the rear seat of the Buick SUV that you'll be using. It will house five M16s and plenty of ammunition, plus Glocks and ammo. The seat won't pull up with the standard pull. If someone tries to open it, it'll appear broken. There's a place under the rear floor mat where you can open it up. It's very clever.

"Okay, then, let's see, today is Friday. You and Covert Bravo can take the weekend off, Captain. So, you'll start on Tuesday of next week," said President Rivera.

"Yes, sir," said Gonzales. "Thanks for thinking about our rifles. Hopefully, we won't need them," responded Gonzales.

The president nodded and looked around the room. "This meeting is adjourned."

Pattie Hayes showed Gonzales and Covert Bravo out of the White House. She gave Sanchez the look again. Sanchez gave her a smile. But he blushed. She smiled back. The others didn't mis it.

When Gonzales and Covert Bravo left, the president motioned for Sydney, Reynolds, Yanelli, and Madden to sit still. "Madam Secretary, do you have some misgivings about the operation? None of us, including Gonzales and Covert Bravo, missed the expression on your face. We all know you are seeing Gonzales on a social basis. I don't mean to meddle into your private affairs. But if this relationship is going to interfere with this operation, let us know now."

Sydney was caught off guard, but quickly regained her composure and said, "My relationship with Gonzales will not affect my ability to do my job. I was the one who suggested it. Gonzales wouldn't stand for it, either. We talked about this when we first started seeing each other. He said he's an Army Ranger and will always be an Army Ranger. I would have to deal with that."

"And?" asked the president.

"I thought I answered it, sir. I said it's not a problem, Mr. President. And it won't be, sir."

President Rivera looked at Reynolds, Yanelli, and Madden. They all nodded their heads affirmatively. "Okay, then it's a go for Tuesday," finalized President Rivera.

Chapter 27

As soon as Covert Bravo got back to the farm training facility, Gonzales's cell phone rang. He didn't have to look at caller ID to know who was calling him. Sydney Alvarez.

"Hi, Syd, what can I do for you?"

"You can start by coming over to my place," answered Sydney.

"That's easy. Count on me, honey. Do you have anything special planned?"

"You'll have to come and see for yourself," answered Sydney in her best coquettish voice.

"Like I said, count on me."

* * *

Bob Chavez thought he ought to tell Consuela what he was going to be doing next week.

He made the call. "Hi, Consuela, do you have any plans for this evening?"

Consuela answered, "Bob, I've got a test tomorrow. So, I've got to do more studying for it. What do you have in mind?"

"I thought we'd get something to eat. You know, go out for dinner."

"Well, Bob, you know I can't refuse an offer like that from you. Make it early, please."

"Great, I'll be right over."

It didn't take Chavez more than fifteen minutes to get to Consuela's Georgetown townhouse. As Chavez passed the CIA security detail, he waved to them, acknowledging their presence. She was ready when her doorbell rang.

"This is a surprise! Unexpected, but a good one!" exclaimed Consuela.

"I see you're ready, Connie. Let's get going."

They got to Chavez's car, where he opened the door for her and she got in. Chavez pulled into traffic. Consuela's CIA detail followed.

"I'm glad you were able to see me on such short notice. I have something to tell you over dinner," explained Chavez.

When the CIA security detail pulled out behind them, the MS-13 detail pulled out after the CIA. Their presence did not go unnoticed by the CIA.

"What is it, Bob? Tell me now. I want to know."

"I'll tell you as we eat dinner. How about some pizza? You know, the place we went to when we first went out in Georgetown. It's close by," said Chavez.

"Okay, Bob, I like that place. Then you'll tell me."

"That's what I said."

They ordered a pepperoni, mushroom, and cheese pizza. Chavez ordered a side of linguini with a marinara sauce with meatballs. The meatballs at this restaurant were legendary. They ordered a nice Chianti to go with their food.

They began to sip the Chianti. Consuela couldn't contain herself any longer.

"Okay, Bob, what is it, what is it?"

Chavez took a sip of Chianti and said, "Gonzales and Covert Bravo are being deployed."

Consuela's face turned white. "What do you mean deployed?"

Chavez thought he'd wouldn't say anything about working for Roberts. "We're going to a place near. We won't be that far away. We will to try to get some intelligence on the drug smuggling and human trafficking coming into the country. I can't say more than this. Very simple."

"Very simple. That's easy for you to say. What about me? I don't want you to go. Who's going to protect me? No, I don't like this, I'm sorry. I don't like this. No. I don't like this one bit."

"Consuela, honey, you knew I might have to go somewhere. I'm going to New York. It's just a little way. We're not being deployed to Afghanistan. If that were the case, you'd have something to worry about."

Consuela looked at Chavez. She was fighting off tears. "Who is going to protect me while you're gone? Who? I ask."

"You have the best people, the CIA, to protect you. I'm not going for a long time. They were right behind us as we drove over here. You've nothing to fear."

"When do you leave, and how long will you be gone?" pouted Consuela.

"We just found out about it this afternoon. We leave on Tuesday. It could be a week or as much as eight weeks."

"You call eight weeks not a long time!" exclaimed Consuela.

Their food came. "Now, let's try to enjoy this beautiful pizza," said Chavez, hoping to quell Consuela's fear.

They sat and ate their food without speaking another word. Consuela's eyes were filled with tears. Tears of fear and doubt. She'd known Chavez could and would be deployed eventually. She didn't know how she'd react to it. Now she knew.

After dinner, Chavez drove to Consuela's townhouse. He walked her to the door. "I'll call you tomorrow. I'll let you know. We leave on Tuesday. Things may change though. Like I said, I'll call as soon as I find out for sure." The CIA detail pulled into the designated parking spot that was reserved for them.

Consuela grabbed Chavez before he could walk away. "Please, Bob, come in with me."

"I thought you had to study for a test."

"I've already studied. I could use a little more, but this is more important to me. You are more important to me, Roberto."

"You haven't called me Roberto much since we left Mexico."

When Consuela called Chavez Roberto, his knees buckled. With that, Consuela put her arm through his and walked him into her townhouse.

* * *

Gonzales drove over to Sydney's townhouse. He didn't know what to expect, but thought of all the things they could do. Including lovemaking.

He saw the CIA detail parked in its reserved parking spot. The parking spot changed every few days, as did the car and the men in the car. He was forever grateful to President Rivera for beefing up Sydney's security.

Gonzales rang the doorbell and waited for Sydney to come and answer. She came to the door, opened it, but stayed back in the foyer. She had on a very tasteful robe. Underneath the robe was a sheer nightgown. It was the first time Gonzales saw her dressed this way. It took his breath away.

"Well, are you just going to stand there with your mouth open, or are you going to come in?"

Gonzales moved like lightning to get in the door. "What's this all about, Syd? That may be the dumbest thing I've ever said," laughed Gonzales.

"Yeah, it was dumb, Gonzales. I've got your favorite Mexican dinner in the oven. It's your mother's stuffed pork roast with all the trimmings. I've got our favorite Chablis on ice to get us started. How's that sound?" asked Sydney.

Gonzales, trying to recover from shock, said, "That sounds wonderful, Syd."

"Well, that's the response I was looking for."

During dinner, Sydney said, "I wish you weren't going to that reservation. I really mean, I wish you weren't. Vince, I've never been in love. Not like this. I love you like I've never loved anyone in my life. I am worried. Not necessarily about you. I'm worried more about us."

"What do you mean about us? Look, Madam Secretary"—the way he said it this time was with much love and respect—"I took this job because I thought Covert Bravo could make a difference. You know that, too, don't you?" Sydney nodded her head yes. Gonzales continued, "We've talked about this before. I told you I'm an Army Ranger. I'll always be an Army Ranger. This mission isn't like I'm going to Afghanistan or back to the cartels in Mexico. Is it?"

"I know. I know. That was before I fell in love with you. I'm not sure I can stand you being deployed anywhere, at any time. But I said I'd take you as you are. You're an Army Ranger. So that's what I'll do, Gonzales. I won't try to change you. I love you the way you are. Even the ugly part of being deployed to places no one else wants to go. This dinner is over. Are you ready for some dessert?" asked Sydney.

"I'll be fine, honey. You know how good Covert Bravo and I are at what we do. Before I forget—"

Before Gonzales could finish his thought, Sydney said, "Now what!"

"I love you, too, Madam Secretary."

Sydney burst into tears, and jumped up and into Gonzales's open arms. Gonzales said, "We can make this work, Syd." Sydney held him as tight as she could. He did the same.

The next morning, Gonzales woke up to the smell of bacon, eggs, pancakes, and grits. His favorite.

"We talked about doing something special on this day two nights ago. I'm still in. How about you?" said Gonzales as he was getting out of the shower.

Sydney answered, "I thought that night—and last night—were special."

"I thought last night was special, too. I meant, let's take that ride to Falls Church you suggested, check out the farmers' market, have lunch at a little restaurant, come back here, and have the special Mexican dinner you have in mind. Although, I can't imagine a better dinner than the one you had last night. After that, take in the symphony. You know, because of you, I'm becoming a fan of classical music. That about covers it."

"Sounds good. That's just the way I had it in my mind, Gonzales. Your love of music. That's one of the things that I love about you."

When they left, the CIA detail was changing. The night watch was leaving and the day watch was just coming on duty. Sydney told the CIA to stay where they were for the day.

The man in charge of the detail said, "Madam Secretary, you know we can't do that. We have orders from the president. When he found out you told us to take the night off and we did, he wasn't happy at all."

"I know! I know! I took a shot. Please stay as far away as possible."

"We'll do our best, Madam Secretary," replied the agent.

As Sydney and Gonzales drove to Falls Church, Sydney asked him, "Does Sanchez have a girlfriend?"

"Why do you ask?"

"Pattie asked if I'd find out."

"To answer your question, no, Sanchez doesn't have a girlfriend. From time to time he's had a lady friend. But nothing serious. You know, Pattie has been giving Sanchez the eye for a while. She gives him the eye every time she sees him. He sees her give it to him. We all see it. We think it's funny. Although he hasn't said so, I think Sanchez may have some interest in Pattie. He smiled at her the last time we were in Oval Office. He blushed when he did it. We've never seen him blush before."

"Really?"

"Yes, I think he does. We haven't talked about it, though."

"Why doesn't he call her?"

"It's very tough for guys like us to call classy ladies like you. I had a very hard time convincing myself to call you."

"I'm very glad you did."

"Not half as glad as I am, Madam Secretary."

When Sydney heard what Gonzales said, she stretched across her seat and gave Gonzales a big kiss on the cheek.

Gonzales responded to the kiss, "I'll talk with him. Listen Syd, I've got an idea. Before we go back to your place, there's something I'd like to show you."

"What's on your mind now Gonzales?"

"Have you ever shot a hand gun?"

"No. I've never felt the ne

"I think I need to teach you. I don't want to go away and feel like you can't protect yourself. You never know. There's a gun range on the way back. I've got my

Glock. How about a fast shooting lesson?"

"If you insist, I'll go."

"I'm not insisting you do anything. I would feel better knowing you will be able to defend yourself."

"Okay, Gonzales. I'll do it for you."

Gonzales stopped at the range and gave Sydney a shooting lesson. She was an easy teach.

As they pulled out, Chaco Lugo and Edwardo Vicario were two blocks down. Dario changed the teams. The two days before, Lugo and Vicario had followed Consuela. They casually pulled out and followed Sydney and Gonzales. The CIA detail picked up Lugo and Vicario immediately.

Lugo and Vicario followed Sydney and Gonzales to Falls Church. When Gonzales parked the car, Lugo and Vicario did the same, only two blocks away. They observed everything Gonzales and Sydney did that afternoon. When Sydney and Gonzales got back in the car to go back to Sydney's, they followed. Lugo and Vicario followed Sydney and Gonzales to the symphony. They ended their surveillance and made their report to Dario.

"You're telling me they went to Falls Church, went to the farmers' market, and had lunch. Then they drove back to her place. Later, they went to a symphony. That's all?" said Dario.

"Yeah, that's all. Some people do things like that. You know, nice things," responded Lugo.

"What do you mean by that? Are you saying I don't do nice things?" replied Dario. "If you are mocking me, you'll pay the price. If you think you're better than me, or any other MS-13 member because you are college boys. You *will* pay the price. You comprende?" said Dario.

This caught Lugo off guard. He regained his composure and said, "I meant no disrespect! None! I just said some people do those kinds of things. No more. No less. It has nothing to do with you or any other MS-13 member. We're MS-13," finished Lugo.

"Okay, but be more careful the next time. That's a good report. I'll send it up to Ortega."

Chapter 28

The next day, Gonzales stopped by Chavez's place. Chavez opened the door and said, "Come on in. I figured you'd stop by and see if I told Consuela about this."

"Yeah, that's what I wanted to know. I'll tell you; the secretary is not happy about this."

"No kidding. It was all over her face when you put your idea forward," said Chavez.

"So, you didn't miss the look either."

"I don't think anyone in the room missed it."

"I think you're right. Have you told Consuela?"

"Yeah, I did; last night. We went out to dinner. I told her as we ate dinner. She was not happy at all. She's afraid. She doesn't feel safe with me being gone. I assured her she had the best people in the world protecting her," answered Chavez. "How did Sydney take it?"

Gonzales answered, "Not very well. I told her we're just going to New York. Now, she knows we'll be gone for up to eight weeks. We don't know how long it will be. Do we?"

"No. We don't."

"By the way, how is Consuela doing at American University? How's Alejandro doing? Has he started school?"

"She's doing good. She's happy. That's all that's important to me. That she's happy. Alejandro is doing very good. He starts school in January. I guess it's when the next term starts. He's taking up where he left off in Mexico. I think he starts the second grade."

"Well, tell her Syd and I send our regards. Let's

get together tomorrow night. I know Syd thinks a lot of Consuela, and so do I. She's a terrific woman."

"That's a good idea. I'll ask her as soon as I can."

"That sounds good. Let me know what you're going to do about dinner."

"Okay. I'll do that. And thanks, Gonzales."

Gonzales went to see Sanchez.

"Hey, Gonzales. what's on your mind?"

"I talked with Secretary Alvarez last night. She said Pattie Hayes, you know, the president's secretary, wanted to know if you had a girlfriend."

Sanchez's face turned purple. "I know who Pattie Hayes is. She wants to know if I've got a girlfriend? Why would she want to know that?"

"Look, Sanchez, we all see her give you the look. You know it, too. I think you might be interested in her. At least that's my gut feeling."

"I am interested. How does a guy like me call a sophisticated lady like her? I don't know what I'd say."

"You know about the secretary and me, don't you?"

"Of course, we all know about it. So, what's that got to do with me?"

"Sanchez, as smart as you are, you are as dumb as a rock sometimes. How do you think I felt when I first called the secretary? You're as courageous a man as I've ever known. We've put our lives in each other's hand's many times. If you want to, you call Pattie. She wants to hear from you."

"Okay. I hope you're right."

* * *

Pattie Hayes had been President Rivera's secretary from his first day in office. She worked on his presidential campaign. She showed excellent organizational abilities. After the election was won, she was out of a job. The newly elected president knew her circumstances. After a meeting concerning his cabinet, President Rivera walked up to Pattie and asked, knowing the answer, "Do you have any plans now, Pattie?"

"No, Mr. President, not really."

"Would you consider working for me in the White House?"

The shock on Pattie Hayes's face was evident. She tried to recover and answered, "It would be my privilege, sir. What would I be doing?"

"What would you say if I told you, you would be my secretary?"

"I can do that, sir. I'm sure of it. I'll not let you down. What'll I be doing?"

"Talk with my chief of staff, Tom Magill. He'll fill you in on the details. I'm certain you're up to the task," finished the president with a chuckle.

* * *

Sanchez screwed up his courage and called Pattie Hayes.

Pattie answered, "What can I do for you, Ranger Manny Sanchez?"

This shook Sanchez. "Miss Hayes, I'm, uh, I'm calling you to see if you'd have dinner with me."

"When?"

"I was hoping tonight."

"Of course, I'll have dinner with you. How about being at my place at six this evening?"

"I can do that. Give me the directions, please."

Sanchez arrived at Pattie Hayes's at 6:00 p.m. sharp. She met him as he knocked on her door.

Sanchez, still feeling a little uneasy, blurted, "Hi, Miss Hayes."

Sensing Sanchez's uneasiness, she replied, "Hi, back at you, Manny. Where would like to have dinner?"

"You pick. You know, I'm not very good at that sort of thing."

"I know just the place for good Mexican food. It's a mom-and-pop place," responded Pattie. "I went there all the time when I first came to Washington. I like the food there."

"Wait a minute. What's a mom-and-pop place?" asked Sanchez.

"It's a place where the people who own it do the food preparation and most of the work. Like scrubbing floors. If you go to any small business, you will always see the owner working. Along with the family. They do the work. It's not a chain restaurant," answered Pattie.

"Oh, okay, I'm in for that," said Sanchez. "I need directions."

"Of course, I'll give them as you drive."

Sanchez followed Pattie's directions. It was about half an hours' drive. During the drive to the restaurant, Sanchez asked Pattie, "If you don't mind, Miss Hayes, I like to be called Sanchez if you don't mind."

"I don't mind calling you Sanchez if you don't mind calling me Pattie." They both got a little laugh at that. The ice was broken for Sanchez and Pattie.

* * *

They were seated at a table by the hostess, who was the daughter of the couple who owned the place.

"It's nice to see you again, Miss Hayes," said the hostess while seating Pattie and Sanchez. At the same time, she gave them a big smile.

"It's good to see you, too, Maria. How're your mom and dad?"

"They're fine. Working too hard. They're getting older and I worry about them. My brothers help as much as they can. They have other jobs, too. They worry, too. So, it's hard."

"I'm sure your family will work it out," said Pattie.

Maria left the menus and said, "Thank you for asking. Your server will be with you shortly."

"You like Mexican food?" asked Sanchez.

"I certainly do," answered Pattie. "Let's look over the menu. Do you see something that interests you, Sanchez?"

"I like the Enfrijoladas. My mother made them when I was a little boy. And, when I came home on leave," answered Sanchez.

"I've never had one. I've always had tacos. But on your recommendation, I'll try an Enfrijoladas."

The server came. They ordered Enfrijoladas. As the evening progressed, they began to talk. Pattie asked, "Do you get home to see your parents very often?"

"Not anymore."

"Why is that?"

"My parents died a few years ago. The army is my family now."

"You don't have any other family members, you know, that you keep in touch with?"

"I've got a brother. He's in prison."

"Oh, my goodness. What happened?"

"I came from a tough Latino neighborhood. Lots of bad stuff went on there. My brother got caught distributing drugs. He became a guy selling drugs on the corner. He got caught," answered Sanchez.

"How did you avoid getting involved in that sort of thing?"

"I was lucky. I knew I didn't want any part of that life. I saw my best friend shot dead, right in front of me. One day in high school, a teacher told me about the army. He told me where the army recruiter's office was located. I told him about my older brother. He said, 'The army could be your ride out of here.' I took his advice, and as you say, the rest is history."

"That's quite a story," was all Pattie could say. After that, they ate in silence.

On the way home, Pattie asked, "When are you going to New York to the Mohawk Casino?"

"How do know about that?"

"I took a guess. I knew something was going down. So, when do you leave?"

"In a few days. Why do you want to know?"

"Just curious, I guess. I want you to be careful, okay?"

"I'm always careful. I should say, *we're* always careful."

Sanchez dropped Pattie Hayes off at her place and walked her to the door. She kissed him and said, "Goodnight, Sanchez. Call me tomorrow."

"Are you sure, Pattie?"

"I wouldn't have asked if I didn't mean it, Sanchez."

"Okay. I'll call tomorrow afternoon."

* * *

The next morning, Gonzales asked Sanchez if he'd called Pattie. "Yes. I called her. We went out to dinner last night."

"You don't waste time, Sanchez."

Sanchez turned purple again. "We had a nice time.

She took me to a nice mom-and-pop Mexican restaurant. When I dropped her off, she asked me to call her today. I said I'd call her this afternoon."

"That's great. Syd and I are going out with Chavez and Consuela tonight. Would you and Pattie like to join us?" asked Gonzales.

"When I call, I'll ask her, but I don't see any problem. I'll let you know."

"Good enough."

* * *

That night, Gonzales and Sydney picked up Chavez, Consuela, Sanchez, and Pattie, and took them to dinner at the pizza place. Sydney and Consuela had their security details with them. The details parked down the street. One man from each detail went into the restaurant with the couples. They sat in a booth on the other side of the restaurant. The security detail didn't miss they were followed by the same cars that had been at the secretary and Consuela's.

Sydney said, "The president found out I dismissed my security detail a few times. He didn't like it. So, I'm sorry, Consuela and Pattie, for our lack of privacy."

"I don't worry, Madam Secretary; they don't bother me," said Consuela.

"They don't bother me, either," said Pattie.

"Consuela, I've asked you before to please call me Syd. You're my friend. We're friends. When we meet socially, Pattie, that goes for you, too. We should keep some decorum when we are together professionally."

"Of course, Madam Secretary," replied Pattie. "I'm just happy to be here with all of you. Thank you for including me and Sanchez."

"I'm sorry, Syd. I'll try to remember. From now on, I'll call you Syd," said Consuela with a beaming smile on her face.

"Okay, that's good. Let's order," replied Sydney. "Since this is one of your favorite places, what's good?"

Chavez said, "We always get a pepperoni and mushroom pizza. I get an order of linguini and meatballs. The meatballs are outstanding, guys."

Gonzales looked at Sydney and asked, "How about a pepperoni and mushroom pizza? Do you care for some spaghetti or linguini with meatballs?"

Sydney answered, "I'll have the pizza. You can have the pasta and meatballs, along with the pizza."

Sanchez looked at Pattie. She said, "I'm good with pizza, Sanchez. You order what you want."

Chavez called the waiter over. "I think we're ready to order."

Everyone gave the waiter a food order. Chavez, Gonzales, and Sanchez ordered linguini with meat sauce and meatballs along with the pizza. Before the waiter moved away to put the food order in, Chavez added, "We need a bottle of your best Chianti."

The waiter answered, "Very good, sir. I'll put the order in before your dinners come out."

"Thank you."

The Chianti came and the six of them had a glass. The bottle was gone before their dinners came. Chavez gave a wave to the waiter. "I think we'll need another bottle with dinner." Dinner came, along with another bottle of Chianti.

Sydney started the conversation. "Consuela, do you know what Gonzales and Chavez are about to do?"

"Yes, I do. Bob told me."

"How do you feel about them going on this job?"

asked Sydney. She was vague, and didn't mention the job specifically.

"I told Bob I don't like it...not one bit. I don't want him to go. He said he would not be in any danger. I have to respect that...even though I still don't like it."

"I feel the same way, Consuela. I don't like it either. But they are doing what they said they'd do. Like you, I must respect it."

"I take it you know what we're talking about, Pattie. How do you feel about Sanchez going?"

"I've told him to be careful. I don't want to see him get hurt...that's for sure. As you know, we aren't very far in our relationship. This is only our second date. I'm hoping it won't be the last."

When Pattie said this, Sanchez's face turned purple. He couldn't help himself.

After a little chuckle, Sydney said, "Now, let's eat this beautiful pizza. You guys can eat pasta and meatballs with the pizza. I don't know where you put it, guys." They ate and drank Chianti and had a fun time. The air was cleared.

Chapter 29

Tuesday came, and Gonzales and Covert Bravo packed their bags and were on their way to the Akwesasne Mohawk Reservation's gambling casino in Hogansburg, New York. They drove the Buick SUV provided by President Rivera. Although they wouldn't need them, they had passports. They also carried driver's licenses, cash, and credit cards in their names. These were necessary for identification. Just in case. Chavez drove the Buick SUV to the casino. He parked in the casino's parking lot.

"It's five o'clock right now. Let's check in to our rooms. We can clean up, grab something to eat, and look for Roberts," said Gonzales.

After checking in at the casino's front desk, Gonzales and Covert Bravo went to their rooms and cleaned up. They met at the casino's restaurant. Chavez said, "The food on the menu looks okay. The all you can eat buffet was great last time. Let's ask our server."

The server came. It was the same Latina lady they had the last time they were there. She said, "Welcome back, gentlemen. What can I get for you to drink? I think you all had coffee the last time...black."

Gonzales said, "You've got a great memory, young lady. You're correct about the coffee. How about it, guys?"

"I'm good with coffee," chimed in Gomez.

"Bring the pot and keep it coming," said Gonzales.

The Latina brought the coffee and said, "You had the buffet last time. You ate like you hadn't eaten in a week. Will you be having the buffet tonight?"

Gonzales had a chance to look at her name tag.

"You're really good, Francesca. You remember all of your customers like you do us?"

"Only the nice, handsome ones. You men are both," replied Francesca.

"You know that's the nicest thing anyone has said to us, Francesca," responded Gonzales. "We thank you for saying that."

Covert Bravo was smiling at this lovely, young Latina girl, Francesca. In unison, they said, "Thank you."

"Thank you, too," said Francesca. "So, what will it be tonight? Are you going to order off the menu or are you going to have the buffet?"

Gonzales said, "I'm going to hit the buffet. You guys can do what you want."

As soon as Gonzales got up, Covert Bravo followed. Francesca kept the coffee coming. The dining room was busier than the last time. When Gonzales and Covert Bravo had finished eating from the buffet, they asked about the dessert table. They couldn't see it from where they were sitting.

"Yes, of course, the dessert table is there for your pleasure," answered Francesca. "It is included in the price. I bet you remember that." Gonzales and Covert Bravo just got a chuckle out of that remark.

"Let's go, guys," said Gonzales.

After dinner, Gonzales asked, "Francesca, if you have time, we'd like the check. Put it all on one, please."

"Yes, sir. I'll bring it right now." Francesca brought the check and said, "Have a nice stay with us, and good luck if you're going to the tables."

"Thank you, Francesca. I hope all of your dreams come true," said Gonzales.

"Thank you. That's the nicest thing anyone has said to me," replied Francesca.

She left them. Gonzales was pleased with Francesca, her attitude and service. He left a 30 percent tip. After paying the check with cash, Gonzales said, "Let's hit the tables, guys. Hopefully, Roberts will see us."

Chief Jimmy Roberts knew Gonzales and his friend were in the hotel. Roberts had access to the casino's reservations. He checked the reservations daily. As Gonzales gambled at the blackjack table, Roberts watched from a camera in a booth. Like all casinos, the Mohawk Casino had cameras in a booth looking down at all the tables. The cameras were there to catch a gambler who was cheating or an employee who was stealing. Roberts observed Gonzales and Chavez especially. As far as he was concerned, Gonzales was the leader of the group. Chavez was the man who got upset with Roberts's comments. Comments he thought were not meant to be harmful or hurtful. When he'd seen enough, he left the booth and walked casually around the casino floor.

Gonzales looked up and he was face-to-face with Roberts. "How're you doing, mister?" Chief Roberts said. "If I remember right, I think your name is Gonzales."

"You've got a great memory, Jimmy," responded Gonzales.

"It's my job to remember people and their names. I saw your friends around the casino. I figured you'd be here, too," replied Roberts.

"If you'd like to see them, I can send them a text."

"Of course, I'd like to say hi. Send them a text. When I was walking around, I didn't see Chavez. Is he here?"

Gonzales sent the text and said, "Chavez is here somewhere. He'll be here in a minute. Speak of the devil. Here he is. Hey, Chavez. You remember Jimmy, don't you?"

The rest of Covert Bravo showed up a second or two after Chavez.

"Sure, I remember Jimmy. How're you doing, Jimmy?"

"I'm doing just fine, Chavez. How're you and the rest of you guys?" answered Roberts.

"Well, that depends on one's perspective," answered Chavez.

"How so?"

"I've just retired from the army. All of us have. It's very hard for Mexicans, like us—that's what you called us—to land any kind of job that pays according to our skills."

"Now look, Chavez, I meant no offense when I called you Mexicans. As far as you not getting jobs that pay well, I told you the last time you were here I might be able to help. Didn't I?"

"We heard you, Jimmy," replied Gonzales. "We have skills that may interest you."

"Is that so. What skills would that include? What was your MOS?" asked Roberts, wondering about their Military Occupational Specialty.

"We were all Army Rangers. We're all combat veterans. We can do anything," answered Gonzales.

When Roberts heard this, his eyes lit up like the sun. "That's pretty impressive. You said you were combat vets. Were you in Afghanistan?"

"Yes. We were. We've all had Purple Hearts and received other citations for bravery."

Chief Jimmy Roberts let out a big breath and said nothing for a few moments. He was thinking. "That's even more impressive. You guys just might have the right skills I'm looking for in my men. If you don't mind going on the shady side of the law."

Gonzales looked at Chavez. It was Gonzales's time to think for a moment. "What do you mean by the shady side of the law? You're either on the side of the law or you're not. There is no shady side."

"Like I said, if you're interested in a job that pays according to your qualifications, you can work for me," responded Roberts.

"What would you have us do?" asked Chavez.

"If I tell you, you'll be in. That's the best I can do right now."

Gonzales responded, "Why don't you let us think about this, Jimmy. We'll have an answer tomorrow morning."

"Sure. Take all the time you want. It's you who need jobs. I'm a vet. I'm not a combat vet, but I know where you're coming from. I was in the same place a few years back. I was looking for a job," said Roberts.

Chapter 30

Later, Covert Bravo met in Gonzales's room. Gonzales said, "Let's go for a walk." He put his fingers to his lips and indicated, *shush*.

Once outside and walking, Gonzales said, "I may be a little paranoid. I think we should be careful when speaking about what we're really doing here. Director Reynolds gave me his private cell phone number. He said to call him with any news. He'll deliver any message we have to the president. President Rivera is very busy. He's got a lot on his table."

"He's just the president of the United States. Why would he be busy?" joked Ramirez.

Gonzales used his cell phone to call Director Reynolds. Reynolds answered, "Hello, Gonzales. What can I do for you?"

Gonzales told the story of Chief Jimmy Roberts.

"It happened that soon?" asked Reynolds.

"Well, sir, we had our story set up beforehand. We ambushed him. Chavez gave an unbelievable performance. He had the rest of us believing what he was saying. Pass this on to President Rivera, sir."

"Will do. And Gonzales, keep yourselves safe."

"Not to worry, sir. We can take care of ourselves."

* * *

The next morning, the team hit the breakfast buffet. As they ate, Gonzales said, "I wonder where Roberts is. I have a feeling we're being watched. It unsettles me."

"Don't look now...but here comes Roberts," said Chavez.

Gonzales and his men looked up. Roberts was next to their table. "Did you guys have a good sleep?" asked Roberts.

"Yeah, we did," answered Gonzales.

"Did you have a chance to consider my offer?"

"We did. We're going to accept whatever work you give us. We want to work for you," responded Gonzales.

"That's great. I thought you would," replied Roberts.

"When do we start?" asked Chavez.

"Right now, if you want."

"We'll do whatever you ask," said Gonzales.

"After you finish your breakfast, come outside. I'll be waiting. Once I tell you what your jobs are, there's no way out. You got that straight?"

"What do mean there's no way out. Is this a threat?" asked Gonzales.

"You could call it a threat. All I'm saying is, what I'm offering you is important work. It pays very good money. If you accept my offer, you're in for good. Once you accept my offer, it won't matter. You'll see," responded Roberts.

"Yeah, we know, Jimmy. It's illegal. We know that," said Gonzales.

"I'll see you outside."

"Okay. Let's go," responded Gonzales.

Outside, Roberts walked out of earshot of anyone else. "I can't be too careful. Okay?"

Gonzales nodded his head yes.

"I can offer you jobs running drugs across the border. Then back again. So, it's transporting drugs in both directions," said Roberts.

"We thought that's what it would be. We're okay with it. We need jobs. Jobs that pay a lot of money," responded Gonzales. "When can we start, and where will we live, you know, where will we bunk? Most importantly, how much money does it pay?"

"First, you have to learn to use a snowmobile and a hovercraft. Once I'm satisfied you can operate them, I'll give you a test run," replied Roberts.

Ranger cold weather operations training didn't include snowmobile operation and hovercraft was not included in water operations. Gonzales took a chance. He knew he and his team could operate those machines. They learned when they went on leave.

"We can operate those machines. We don't need training, if that's what you were referring to," said Gonzales. "We were trained to use snowmobiles during Ranger cold weather operations training and hovercraft during water training."

"Really? That's great. This is what I'll do. You won't need to be trained. I need to see you in action. You know, I need to see you drive the machines just to satisfy my professional curiosity. You meet me later today in the casino's lobby, say about six. It'll be a little dark. I'll let you take both of the machines out on the ice."

Although Gonzales knew what ice Roberts was speaking about—the St. Lawrence River—he asked, "What ice are you talking about?"

Roberts replied, "The St. Lawrence River. I hope you can operate those machines better than you know your geography. Like I said, I want you in the casino's lobby at six."

"Okay. We'll be there. You didn't tell us where we'd be bunking."

"I know. Just be there at six. For now, you can stay

in the hotel, eat there, and not pay. That's a start."

* * *

Covert Bravo went back to the casino's lobby. Gonzales said, "I still don't think we should talk freely here. Let's take a walk."

Once back outside, Gonzales felt safe talking. "I can't help feeling we're being watched inside. I thought we'd come outside to talk," said Gonzales. "We knew Roberts was probably going to offer us jobs in illegal drugs. We just have to keep our eyes and ears open, and gather all the information we can. Then get it back to President Rivera."

* * *

Roberts made a call to Ernesto Fuentes. Fuentes oversaw the Latino group who got the drugs across the border. "Ernesto, we've been looking for men for a while now. I've got five good men."

"Is that right? What makes you think they'll be what we need?" asked Fuentes.

"They're all Latino, and are all retired United States Army Rangers—and don't need training to operate snowmobiles or hovercraft. The army trained them. They need work and can't find any that pays any good. I was in that position ten years ago. You remember that. Don't you?" answered Roberts.

"Yeah, I remember when we found you, Jimmy. They do sound promising. When can I meet them?"

"How does six this evening sound? They say they can operate snowmobiles and hovercraft. They said they trained with those machines. I looked on the internet for Army Ranger training. It said nothing about training with the machines we use. I'll call them on that. I told them to meet me at six this evening. They said they'd be there. Are you in?" answered Roberts.

"Yeah, I want to meet and see them. If they're half as good as you say, they will more than fit our needs even if we must train them," responded Fuentes.

"I doubt they'll need training. I think these guys are the real deal. I'll see you at six," replied Roberts.

Gonzales and Covert Bravo were in the casino's lobby at six that evening. Roberts was there at five minutes past six with Fuentes.

"I'd like you to meet Ernesto Fuentes. He'll be your supervisor," said Roberts.

"It's nice to meet you," said Gonzales.

Fuentes didn't say anything. He just looked at Gonzales and Covert Bravo. Gonzales just shrugged his shoulders and said nothing else. The snub, if that's what it was, from Fuentes, didn't faze Gonzales in the least. Gonzales's reaction didn't go unnoticed by Fuentes or Roberts.

"I looked on the internet for Army Ranger training," said Roberts.

"Oh yeah? What did you find?" asked Gonzales.

"For starters, it said Rangers are trained in cold weather operations. It didn't say Rangers were trained to operate snowmobiles during cold weather training. I didn't see where Rangers are were trained in hovercraft operations during water training," answered Roberts.

Gonzales knew these things to be true. He was ready for Roberts. "The things on the internet don't include all Ranger training. I don't think snowmobile and hovercraft training would be there. Some things are left out," countered Gonzales.

Gonzales could see Roberts trying to process this

information. Roberts looked at Fuentes. They nodded their heads in what Gonzales thought was agreement. "Okay. I'm going to give you guys a trial run tonight. You'll operate both machines. If you satisfy me, I'll get you working tomorrow night," said Roberts.

"Great. We won't disappoint you. We want to work for you, Chief," replied Gonzales.

Roberts said, "The nighttime runs will require you to use night vision goggles. Here is a set. Have you ever seen this type of equipment?"

"Sure, we used NVG in Afghanistan," answered Gonzales. "These look a little different than the ones we used, though."

"They don't have to be like the ones you used in the military. Put these on and get used to them before you start," said Roberts. "You must know how to use a radio."

"Right, again."

"Okay then. We have spotters out there. You won't see them, but they'll be there. When the spotter sees the Border Patrol or the Mohawk Police, they'll send a radio message. You can take action to avoid being caught. The spotter will give you an edge," said Roberts.

"All right, let's see what you can do. Get in my car. I'll drive you to the river."

Fuentes followed in his car.

Once at the river, Roberts said, "You can show me how you handle snowmobiles loaded up with my product. Each snowmobile will have a sled behind it. You'll be pulling the sled. It'll be loaded, too. You'll take the machine and drive across the river through that island and to the other shore beyond and back again. You can't tip it over. You got that? You can do this, right?" instructed Roberts.

Gonzales looked at Covert Bravo, who nodded their heads yes. "Sure thing. We've got this. Let's give Jimmy a sample of what we can do, guys," replied Gonzales.

Gonzales and Covert Bravo each took a snowmobile, started it, and drove it through the island and back to Roberts.

Fuentes and Roberts waited. Fuentes said, "If they get across without tipping over, I'll be very surprised."

A short time later, Gonzales and his crew were back. "How'd we do?" asked Gonzales.

Fuentes stood with his mouth open in total disbelief. "I don't know how you guys did this in so short a time. You were very fast, and you didn't lose any product. I sent you through some rough terrain. You were successful. You guys are very good. Now, I want you to try the hovercraft."

The team performed the same way with the hovercraft. Roberts knew he had five good men. He knew Army Rangers were among the best military in the world.

"You guys have satisfied me. You passed my test with flying colors. What do you think, Fuentes?"

"You guys look good. I'll wait to see how you do when it counts; when you are transporting the real deal. Our drugs. You can start you tomorrow night. You can take off until then. Be ready at eight in the evening."

"Would it be all right for us to take the snowmobiles and use them to study the islands, Jimmy? You know, take a dry run. We should get as familiar with them as we can," remarked Gonzales.

Roberts looked at Fuentes, who had a surprised look on his face. Fuentes nodded his head in agreement.

"I've never had anyone ask that question, Gonzales. I don't see why not. It's a very good idea," responded Roberts.

"What island will be we using tomorrow night?"

"The same one you used tonight. Since you'll start on the Canadian side of the river, we have a place for you to stay there. Fuentes will set you up tomorrow morning. You can drive your snowmobiles over and meet him. What time do want them, Fuentes?"

"Since they want to practice tomorrow, they should meet me at nine a.m. Chief Roberts will drop you off at the casino. You can have dinner there tonight. I'll see you guys at nine tomorrow morning."

"Great, we'll be there at nine," responded Gonzales.

After Roberts dropped Covert Bravo off at the casino's hotel, they went to the casino's restaurant. "You heard the man. We haven't eaten dinner. Let's hit the buffet."

After dinner, they went to Gonzales's room. "I think Roberts and Fuentes bought into us tonight," he remarked.

"Yeah, they did," said Sanchez. "I think this will be a very productive operation."

"Me too," Chavez agreed.

"Anyone have anything to add?" asked Gonzales. Ramirez and Gomez didn't say a word, just nodded their heads. "Okay. It looks like we're good to go tomorrow night. Let's take advantage of our time off and get some rest. We want to be ready. Let's not get cocky. We can talk more about tomorrow; what we can expect, and what we can do to help ourselves stand out. Like getting all of Roberts's drugs through. Just like good mules do. Let's take a look at the maps Roberts gave us. We should study them. We can get a head start on tomorrow's practice runs."

The next day, Gonzales and his men got on the frozen St. Lawrence River. "Okay, guys. We're just out to have some fun. Or pretend to be having fun. Since we don't have any drugs on us, we have nothing to worry about. If anyone stops us, we just tell them we're on a joyride. We meet Fuentes at nine. Let's be a few minutes early. Let's go."

When Gonzales and his team showed up a few minutes early, Fuentes was there waiting. "You guys are ten minutes early. I like that. I'll take you to your place. I brought two SUVs. We can't all fit in one. Gonzales and Chavez, ride with me. You other guys, ride in the other SUV."

Fuentes led the way. He drove through the forest until he came to a group of houses. He pulled into the driveway of one them. The other SUV pulled in behind Fuentes. Fuentes got out. The others did the same. "This will be your home while you are with us," said Fuentes.

"It looks good to me," said Gonzales. "Let's go inside."

Fuentes took them inside. "There are five bedrooms and three bathrooms. There is a great room and a full kitchen. The kitchen is fully stocked. This will have to do."

"We've slept in much worse places," remarked Chavez.

"He's right. We've been in a lot of worse places," responded Gonzales.

"Okay. You guys are free until tonight. I'll see you then. Any questions?"

Sanchez held up his hand. "We drove by a big mansion down the road. Who lives there?"

"That place is mine. I live there with my family. You brought snowmobiles with you. You will use them tonight. No one has ever asked to study maps or to practice runs. Except you guys."

"We want to prove ourselves to you and Jimmy."

"We'll see what happens tonight."

"One more thing, if you don't mind.

"What is it, Gonzales?".

"Would it be all right if I sent one of my guys to get our SUV. I don't like it parked in the casinos parking lot?"

"Sure. Go get it," answered Fuentes.

After Fuentes left, Francesca, the Latina girl who had waited on them in the casino, came out of her little house. She lived down the street. She immediately recognized Gonzales and his men. She walked over to them.

Gonzales looked up and saw her coming. He couldn't believe his eyes. "What are you doing here?" asked Gonzales.

"I live down the street a few houses away. I saw some commotion out here. I looked out my window and saw you guys. I thought I'd come out and see what was going on. My name is Francesca. Do you remember me?"

Gonzales was completely caught off guard. He struggled to keep his composure. He finally did. He did not want the Latina to get any ideas. Ideas that may put her in danger.

"Of course, I remember you, Francesca. You took care of us when we had dinner at the casino. You live on the Canadian side of the reservation. Why?"

"It's a lot cheaper for me. The Latino community is small. But these are my people. What brings you over here?

"It looks like we're going to be neighbors, Francesca. We took jobs at the casino."

"You took jobs at the casino? Why?"

"It's the best we can do right now."

"I should see you more often then."

"I would bet on it."

Chapter 31

Benito Flores and Dize Cruz had moved from the safe house they occupied and moved to a house on the Usumacinta River. Flores felt safe there. Flores built his semisubmersibles there. The jungle was mostly impenetrable. It surrounded the Lacandon village where Flores had a house. It wasn't anything fancy. He didn't need anything fancy. He needed a functional place. This house was functional. Flores brought Baha el Din along.

The Usumacinta River is the largest river in Mexico, the seventh-largest in the world based on water volume, and serves as the modern border between Mexico and Guatemala. The river is in the Lacandon Jungle, which contains the largest rain forest in North America and stretches from the Mexican state of Chiapas into northern Guatemala and to the southern part of the Yucatan Peninsula. The Montes Azules Biosphere Reserve is in Chiapas near the border of Guatemala. It is where the heart of the rain forest is located.

The people who inhabit the area are subsistence peasants who migrated there during the early part of the twentieth century and are referred to as Lacandon. They farm the land and practice agroforestry, a method of farming that rotates farmed areas. This method of farming lets areas not farmed lay fallow to regenerate.

The Lacandon are among the most isolated and culturally conservative people living in Mexico. Some of the Lacandon people still wear traditional clothing; an undyed tunic called a *xikul*. Other Lacandon people have gone to modern clothes and use modern conveniences.

Although modern shelters are used more and more by Lacandon, some still prefer the traditional structure, which are huts made from fronds and wood that cover an earthen floor. Some Lacandon people will never give in to modern technology, like a modern shelter. They cling to the old ways.

Flores thought the Lacandon jungle rain forest a good place to build his semisubmersibles. When he made the deal with ISIS, he thought the Lacandon jungle the perfect place to store the heroin coming from Afghanistan. It was remote, and was unlikely to be found by anyone. Plus, it had the Usumacinta River to transport the product out for distribution. Flores took five hundred acres there. There were Lacandon people there to do the work for him. As always, Flores took good care of them.

"You've been here once before, Dize. I was just setting up the construction of the semisubmersibles. What do you think of this place?"

"For sure, it's hard to find. I'm not sure anyone would come here for any reason...not even the police. This is a very tough place, Benito, very tough. I don't think the Mexican Special Forces would want to come here," answered Dize.

"I knew you'd like it. The people who live here, love me. They're the ones who build my semisubmersibles. I pay them a little money and give them the things they need. Simple things, like better tools for farming. They will work for me. Some of them still live in traditional frond and wood huts. I'll make it easy for them to get into better shelter. They are loyal to themselves and me. If anyone comes snooping around, I'll be the first to know it," said Flores.

"You're very ambitious, as usual, Benito. I think you're right about this place. I think it's everything you say it is. When are you going to start building housing to store the heroin?" asked Cruz.

"The ship carrying the heroin from Afghanistan will make port in Venezuela in a day or two. It should be here next week. The heroin is on a North Korea ship and is in crates labeled FURNITURE. I've got building material for the heroin shelters coming tomorrow. The Lacandon people will build the buildings we need to store our product."

"Is there a problem storing heroin?" asked Cruz.

"No problem. Heroin has a long shelf life. This is the perfect place to store and distribute this product. I've got the heroin coming through Guatemala. It'll cross the Usumacinta here. We'll receive it where I've got my speedboat docked. As you said, this is a tough place. We have our semisubmersibles being built down on the Usumacinta River. I will use them to get the product to other distribution points in Mexico. I'll have the US market locked up and be the biggest supplier of cocaine and heroin in this hemisphere. No one in this part of the world will have the supply I have. The Columbians may complain a little, because they make heroin. But I'll take theirs and distribute it, too. Just like I do now. So, why would they have a problem?"

"I don't think the Columbians would have a problem, either," answered Cruz.

"I think we should stay here for the time being, Dize. It's safe, and no one is going to come here looking for us," said Flores. "I had that communication tower built so we can have phone service here. We can keep in touch with our people here. My biggest semisubmersible is just being finished. Once the heroin gets here, we'll supervise loading the first load of heroin that'll go out on it," said Flores.

"That sounds good to me," replied Cruz.

Cruz's cell phone rang. "Well, we know the tower works," said Flores.

"This is call is from Washington, DC. It's Ortega," said Cruz. "This is Dize Cruz. What's up, Lenny?"

"I've got two photographs taken by my men. We think they are Vince Gonzales and Bob Chavez. I'll send them. They're a little grainy. They were taken from a pretty good distance. Do you know what these guys look like? One of my teams noticed the man the secretary hangs out with had been gone for a few days. He may be Gonzales. Then he suddenly appeared the other night. They have no idea where he's been. I just thought you'd be interested in the information."

"Yeah, I know what those guys look like," answered Cruz. Cruz motioned to Flores, who was already looking at him with anticipation. "Send them now. Benito is with me." The pictures were sent and received by Cruz.

"Look at these, Benito. What do you think? The pictures aren't very good. But I think that's Gonzales and Chavez," said Cruz. "Ortega said his men noticed that Gonzales—or this guy they think is Gonzales—was gone for a few days. Then he suddenly appeared the other night."

"Give me the phone, Dize."

Flores said, "It's them, all right, Lenny. Where were the pictures taken? I wonder where this guy was for those few days. It doesn't make sense to me. You keep watching the secretary and Consuela. What about my son, Alejandro? Do they have anything on him?"

The answer came back, "Both pictures were taken outside of the places where Sydney Alvarez and Consuela Hernández live. They haven't seen Alejandro yet. They're watching for him."

"Good work, Lenny. Keep your men doing what

they're doing. You can expect a bonus for you and your men. I want information about my son. I want my son back!"

Chapter 32

Carlito Dario sent out two of his men to surveil Secretary Alvarez and two more to surveil Consuela Hernández. "Cabrera and Guerrero, you'll take the secretary. Lugo and Iglesias will watch the Hernández woman," ordered Dario. "Since you've never worked with each other, it will be harder for the security to notice."

"We won't disappoint you," each team said as they left for their assignments.

Cabrera was driving a nondescript Ford Fusion. Guerrero said, "I see a parking place behind an SUV. It's about two blocks from the secretary's place. The SUV will give us some cover pull in behind it."

"The security is not in the same place this time. We'll have to keep our eyes open. We need to find them," said Cabrera.

* * *

Dave Henderson and Dick Osborne were the CIA detail for Secretary Alvarez this morning. Henderson spotted the Ford Fusion as soon as Cabrera parallel parked and said, "I think we have company this morning, Osborne."

"I see it. Biscotti said we should call him if we saw anyone who may be surveilling the secretary."

"You make the call," replied Henderson.

Osborne made the call to Biscotti and related what he and Henderson had observed. "Okay, keep them in your sights. I'll send Joe Bandy and John Evans out to follow these fellas when they leave," responded Biscotti.

* * *

"The secretary is coming out of her place. She's alone," said Guerrero.

"Does that seem suspicious to you?" asked Cabrera.

"More often than not, she does come out with that guy we know is Vince Gonzales. He was gone for a few days the last time the secretary was surveilled," answered Guerrero.

"That doesn't mean Gonzales is gone this time. Does it? We should put this in our report to Dario," replied Cabrera.

When the secretary left, Cabrera and Guerrero slipped in three cars behind her car. CIA agents Bandy and Evans were the same distance behind them.

Cabrera said, "We'll follow her today—or as long as we think is necessary."

The secretary's CIA detail escort drove her to her office, prompting Guerrero to say, "This is the building. It's the same building she came to the other times Dario had her watched. She must have her office here."

Cabrera agreed, "This is the same building. I was with Iglesias that day. It was the first time Dario sent a team to watch her. Iglesias and I waited for her to come out. She never did. We got tired of waiting for her. So, we called Dario for instructions. He said to stay a while. If she didn't come out, we should go back to her place at about six o'clock and wait there until she came home. Or she may be home already. We did that, and she was home. She must have used a different exit out of the building. We should be aware of that this time."

Guerrero interrupted and said, "How did you know she was home when you got there?"

"There were lights on in her place. Vince Gonzales

opened the door her. He didn't come out until the next morning. They went out to breakfast and then to morning Mass at the cathedral," answered Cabrera.

"What do you think we should do now?" asked Guerrero.

"I'll call Dario and tell him what's going on. I think he'll tell us to do the same thing this time," answered Cabrera. Cabrera made the call.

"Well?" asked Guerrero.

"Dario said, do the same thing you did the last time. We go to her place and wait until she gets there."

Cabrera drove to the secretary's place. They spotted the CIA and parked two blocks away from them. The CIA spotted Cabrera and Guerrero, too. They waited for the secretary to come home. They didn't have to wait long.

* * *

Henderson said, "Here are our boys. They pulled in about two blocks up the street."

"Yeah, I see them," responded Osborne.

"There go Bandy and Evans. They're taking a place a block behind our boys. Those guys have no idea they've been spotted," noted Henderson.

* * *

"Here she is," said Cabrera. Sydney parked in her designated parking place and was greeted by the CIA detail that was there.

"I wonder if that Gonzales guy will show up tonight," said Guerrero.

"All we can do is wait and see."

Vince Gonzales never showed. Although Guerrero and Cabrera didn't know Gonzales and Chavez would be away for more than a few weeks, they reported what they saw to Dario.

Chapter 33

Dize Cruz was walking around the buildings Flores was building to shelter the heroin. He thought the construction was slow. He looked for Flores.

"Benito, are these Lacandon men keeping up with the construction of these buildings? It doesn't look like it to me," remarked Dize Cruz.

"What do you mean, Dize?"

"I thought they'd be further along than this by now. Your first shipment of heroin is coming in two days, isn't it?"

"All we need are the buildings that are built now. These buildings will provide enough shelter for the heroin coming in the first shipment. The next shipment won't be here for another week. That's what el Din told me. He'd better be right, or else, and he knows it. I won't kill him. I'll make sure the Americans pick him up. I'll deliver him to the Americans. I've told him that. He's told his people in Afghanistan what I'll do to him. They don't want that either. They know I mean business, too. If the Americans get a hold of el Din, they will get everything he knows about ISIS. He knows that, and so do his people in Afghanistan," responded Flores.

"You're right, Benito," said Cruz.

Cruz's phone buzzed, which prompted him to say, "Your cell tower is still working fine. It's Dario."

He answered, "Dario, I hope you've got some news for me."

"I've do have news, Dize."

"I'm listening."

"The secretary goes to work at the same building every day. She comes out occasionally to go to another building."

Cruz interrupted Dario, "Do you know the name of the buildings?"

Dario thought about what to say. He thought it wise to tell the truth. "No, my men didn't think to look for the building's name."

"What? They didn't think to look at the building's name? Aren't these guys supposed to be college-educated? Haven't they been trained in surveillance?"

"Yeah, yeah, what you say is right, Dize. There is more."

"Okay. What do you have for me?"

"That Gonzales guy hasn't been around for a few days and neither has Chavez. It's the same as last time. Both of those guys disappear for a few days. We don't know where they go."

Cruz thought about what he'd heard. "That's good intelligence. I'll tell Benito. He's right here." Cruz related what Dario had to say.

Flores thought for a moment and said, "Tell Dario to keep watching the women and my son. It makes me a little suspicious that Gonzales and Chavez aren't around for days. But my real interest is in those women and my son. Tell them to keep watching those women every few days. When we have them, Gonzales and Chavez will come to us. So will the rest of, what does Gonzales call them? Covert Bravo."

Cruz told Dario what Flores said. Dario said, "Okay, Dize. We'll keep watching the women and try to find a weak spot in their security. There doesn't seem to be one right now." The call ended.

"Dize, I want you to send the pictures of Gonzales

and Chavez to all of our people. Someone may recognize them. I wonder where they go. You send the pictures," said Flores.

"I'll do it right now."

Chapter 34

Chief Jimmy Roberts was satisfied with how Gonzales and Covert Bravo handled the snowmobile and hovercraft. He was eager to see how Ernesto Fuentes felt about them.

"Ernesto, what do you think of Gonzales and his friends? I'm impressed. They must be very tough men to be Army Rangers. They're combat veterans. They are all Purple Heart recipients. They're all disappointed in the opportunities offered to them as civilians. I think they'd make good mules. They're in the same place I was in ten years ago. I'd just got out of the Marines and couldn't find a job. A job that could sustain me and my family."

"It looks like they would be a good fit for us, Jimmy. I'll hold my judgment until I see what they produce. You said you'd give them a job tomorrow night. We'll see then," responded Ernesto Fuentes.

* * *

After what Gonzales thought was a successful tryout, he said, "Let's take a walk." There was a walkway outside the casino. Gonzales led them there. He had scoped it out when they waited for Roberts. "I think that went very well. I'm convinced they bought it. Does anyone have any ideas or feelings about it?"

"I would agree with you, Gonzales. That Fuentes guy just doesn't sit well with me, though. I didn't like the way he fluffed you off. He didn't recognize you when Roberts introduced you to him. You played it well, though. You didn't give him the satisfaction of letting him know your feelings. Other than that, I thought Roberts, like you just said, bought it. Even though he didn't say anything, I do think Fuentes was impressed. He had to be. How many men work for him and can operate those machines like we did? He's impressed all right. He just won't admit it now. When he sees what we can do for him, he'll change his mind," said Chavez.

"I feel the same way about Fuentes," said Gomez. "We should keep an eye open for him. He's the link to the Latino community here. He must have some of them working for him, and probably some Mohawks. Roberts is one of them."

"You might be right, Gomez," said Sanchez.

Ramirez just nodded his head in agreement.

"Okay," said Gonzales. "I agree with you concerning Fuentes. I was hoping I'd get that response from you. I guess we're free until tomorrow night. Let's get some rest and meet for breakfast tomorrow morning. I'm going to call Reynolds and fill him in on our progress."

Gonzales made the call. Reynolds answered. "Hello, Gonzales. What do you have?"

Gonzales related what they had done for Roberts. They were hired by him to run drugs across the St. Lawrence River.

Reynolds's response was, "That's good work, Gonzales. I'll pass this along to the president. Keep me informed."

"Thank you, sir. I'll let you know if anything new comes up."

Chapter 35

Benito Flores received the first shipment of heroin from Afghanistan. When Flores took the shipment, Baha el Din was there. To say el Din was relieved would have been an understatement.

"I told you. Didn't I? I said I'd get the heroin to you. I guaranteed it. Didn't I? Now I want you to release me. I want to go home!" exclaimed el Din to Flores. Dize Cruz was present.

Flores looked at Cruz and said, "We'll see. We'll see."

"What do you mean, we'll see? You said you'd let me go home when you got the heroin," replied el Din. "You've got it. Haven't you?"

"You don't have to tell me what I said. I know what I said. I've got one shipment. That's all. We'll see if more is coming," said Flores.

"So now you say I'll be held indefinitely," said el Din. "That's what you mean by we'll see."

"You could take it that way," replied Flores.

"What if I tell my people in Afghanistan to stop sending you heroin?" countered el Din.

"If you do that, I think you know what would happen."

Baha el Din let out a big breath and said, "Yes, I suppose I do. You'll make sure the Americans get me. If you do that, you won't get any heroin. So, where does that leave us?"

"That's right. I'll make sure the Americans get you. I'll deliver you to them. They will get everything you know about ISIS. Think about that. Tell your friends in ISIS that! I'll tell them! See what they say!"

Baha el Din stood with a shocked look on his face. He said nothing for a moment. He mustered up his courage and said, "So, Benito, you hold me against my will for an indefinite period?"

"That's exactly what I'm saying."

"You lied to me. Didn't you. You never intended to let me go. Did you?"

"Yes, I lied to you. And yes, I never intended to let you go."

"What're you going to do to me?" asked el Din.

"Nothing—if the heroin keeps coming," answered Flores. "If the heroin stops, I will deliver you to the Americans."

"I've got a wife and family back there. Who's going to provide for them? What will become of them?"

Flores answered, "You have friends in high places back there. You're one of the top people in ISIS. Aren't you? Tell them to take care of your family."

El Din dropped his head in utter defeat. He took a walk around the compound. He thought, *I've got to think about a way out of here. How can I help myself? I've got to get out of here.* These thoughts consumed him.

The Lacandon elder and a well-respected leader, Chan K'in Viejo, was in the same area as el Din was walking. Viejo stopped and just looked at el Din and shook his head with a look of utter contempt on his face. El Din saw Viejo's look. It shook him to his core. He screwed up his courage and walked over to Viejo and asked, "Do you speak English?"

Viejo nodded his head yes with the same contemptuous look on his face but said nothing else. Continuing to look el Din in the eye Viejo finally said, "I don't like what you're doing here. You are not doing right by me or my people. Some of our young people want what you and the man, Flores, bring here. You bring bad things to them."

"I don't bring anything here. Flores does," responded el Din.

"You bring drugs. I know you do that; I know. I want you to leave me and my people. Leave, go back to where you came from," replied Viejo.

"I bring drugs to Flores not to your people. Flores gives the drugs to some of your people as payment for their work," said el Din. "I'm a prisoner here. Flores won't let me leave. I don't want to be here. I've got a family in my country. I want to go back to them. Flores won't let me leave."

The old Lacandon, Viejo, showing no fear, looked el Din in the eye and asked, "Why?"

"He's afraid if I go back to my country, he won't get any more drugs. He thinks as long as I'm here, the drugs will keep coming," answered el Din. "If the drugs stop coming, he tells me he'll turn me over to the Americans. He figures if the Americans get a hold of me, they'll get all the information I've got inside my head," answered el Din. El Din was still limping. His knee had not completely healed. "Do you see how I'm limping around?"

Viejo nodded his head yes and asked, "Who did this to you?"

"The Americans. A man named Vince Gonzales shot me in the knee," answered el Din.

Viejo said, "That's too bad. Are you the one who caused the explosion in Chicago?"

"I didn't make the explosion happen. Flores did that. I helped get the bomb into the United States," answered el Din.

Viejo thought for a moment, "You brought the bomb to the United States. You're just as guilty as Flores. You're a terrorist. You're afraid of Flores and what he'll do to you. Send you to the Americans. You're afraid of the Americans because you think they'll get information from you. How will they do that?"

"They have ways of making a man talk. To say things, he doesn't want to say," answered el Din. "Vince Gonzales shot me in the knee. My knee will never be the same. I'm lucky to be able to walk. If the Americans get me, they will use certain methods to make me talk."

"You mean the Americans will torture you. You are afraid of that," responded Viejo.

"Yes."

"You don't want to be here with Flores. You're afraid the Americans will torture you. I think you're in a bad place. Would you consider going to the Americans?"

"No, no. Once they get the information from me, they'll probably put me to death or put me in prison for the rest of my life," responded el Din.

"Because of your involvement with the bomb," said Viejo.

"Yes."

Chapter 36

Sydney called Consuela. "Hi, Consuela. It's me, Syd Alvarez."

"Hi, Syd, how are you?"

"I'm fine. And you?"

"All things considered, I'm as good as can be expected. I miss Bob very much. I know we said he and Gonzales should do their jobs. They told us before we started seeing them that they were in the army; would stay in the army and be Army Rangers."

"I know, Consuela, I know. I think it's just as hard for them to be away from us as it is for us to be away from them. I miss Gonzales very much, too. I thought you and I could get together for dinner tonight."

"I'd love that, I really would. Do you have any suggestions? Where would we go?"

"Why don't you come here, to my place? I've got dinner in the oven. It's one of Gonzales's Mexican favorites. I can have my security detail pick you up. There are always four CIA men in two cars outside my place. I don't like that many, but that's what the president ordered. Gonzales made sure of that. I think Gonzales made sure the president did the same for you."

"Why yes, yes, he did. I have the same thing and for Alejandro. Four men in two cars. I'd love to come to your place. When do you want me there? I can be ready anytime."

"If you're ready, I'll send them right now."

"I'll be waiting," said Consuela.

Consuela was ready when Sydney's CIA detail

came for her. The CIA detail informed Consuela's detail about what was going to take place. One of Consuela's detail said they would follow her to Sydney's place. The other stayed in place.

Since security was doubled for Sydney and Consuela, two teams were watching both women. When Consuela and her retinue pulled away, so did Lugo and Iglesias. The security detail assigned to Consuela saw them. They called Biscotti and reported it. Biscotti said, "Stay with Consuela. I've been told she's going to the secretary's for dinner."

When Consuela got to Sydney's door, she was waiting. "Hi, Consuela. I'm so glad you could come."

"Thank you for inviting me. It's good to see you."

"I'm glad to see you, too. Please come in," said Sydney.

They went into the living room. "Dinner's almost ready. Please sit down. Have you heard from Chavez?"

"No, I haven't."

"I've got something to tell you."

"What is it? Is it about Bob? Has anything happened to him? Please tell me!" said Consuela.

"Now, let's not get ahead of ourselves, Consuela. Nothing has happened to Chavez. I mean Bob. I just heard from the president. Our guys aren't coming back for a few months."

When Consuela heard this, she burst into tears. She said, "I knew it! I knew something bad would come from this business!" exclaimed Consuela.

"Now, now. Nothing bad has happened, has it? Our guys are okay. They haven't been hurt," responded Sydney.

"Why do they have to stay there at the casino for more time? You just said a few months. Bob said a few weeks. Now it's a few months. I don't like it. I told Bob I didn't like it."

"I know. I know, Consuela. I don't like it either. I told Gonzales that I didn't like it, either. But we agreed to the fact that they're in the army. They're Army Rangers. They can and will take care of themselves," said Sydney.

"Yes, I know what they do and why they do it. They're protecting us. I know that. What you say is right. They can take care of themselves. When Bob isn't with me, I don't feel safe. Bob told me I've got the best protection in the world. They're with me night and day. I do feel safe with their protection. But not as safe as when Bob is around and with me. Bob, Gonzales, and the others, saved us. They saved my son, Alejandro, and Lucia. If not for them, I wouldn't be here. How long exactly will they be away?" asked Consuela.

"Maybe three months. I don't know. That's what the president told me. That's why I said we'd have dinner here. I can talk without being overheard," answered Sydney.

"Do you know why they've got to stay longer?" asked Consuela.

"Yes, I do. It's nothing we didn't know. They got jobs running drugs across the St. Lawrence River between the Mohawk Reservation. The river separates the reservation. That's all I know. We knew they were going to do that. Didn't we?"

"Yes, we knew that. But I don't like it."

"Gonzales let Chief Roberts know he and Covert Bravo would take any job that paid big money. Legal or illegal. They didn't care. Roberts is a man who supervises bringing drugs into the country. Roberts offered Gonzales and Covert Bravo, including Chavez, a job. This fella, Chief Roberts, thinks Gonzales, Chavez, and the rest of Covert Bravo would do a good job for him. They will bring drugs from the Canadian side to the American side. Then go back to the Canadian side with another load of drugs," said Sydney.

"I see," said Consuela. "Three months is a long time for me to be alone, without Bob," said Consuela. "I don't know what I'm going to do."

"That's a long time for me to be alone, too," said Sydney. "The first thing is, we don't have to be alone. You can stay with me the whole time. That is, if you want to. We'll have double-double security. We can get through this together."

"Thank you, Syd, that's very thoughtful of you. I'll think about it. I don't want to be an imposition."

"Hold it right there. You'll never be an imposition. Don't think that way. You think about it. Let me know as soon as you decide."

"Why didn't Bob call and tell me himself? Why did he have you do it?"

"Consuela, Chavez is worried about you. He didn't want you to be alone when you found out. Gonzales asked me to do it. Chavez will call you soon. Maybe tomorrow morning. He'll tell you then. He doesn't want you to worry. He knows you will."

"Thank you, Syd. I appreciate your concern. Maybe we can help each other get through this. I know it'll be hard for me and, maybe, for you, too."

"I knew you'd understand. And yes, I could use your help, too. I'm not too sure about myself, either. Chavez will call you tomorrow morning. At least that's what Gonzales told me. I should clear this with President Rivera. Though, I don't see why he'd object to us bunking together until our guys get back. I'll see him tomorrow morning. I'll ask him then. How does that sound?" said Sydney.

"That sounds very good to me. I hope Bob will call tomorrow morning. I'll be waiting for it," responded Consuela. "I hope Alejandro and Lucia are included. If not, I won't do it," replied Consuela.

"Yes, of course, Alejandro and Lucia are included. I'd never leave them out," said Sydney.

"Okay, you ask the president. Like you say, why would he care where I stay? As long as we're safe. And we'll have more security this way," responded Consuela.

"Good, now let's have dinner. I think you'll like this. It's one of Gonzales's favorites," said Sydney. "He said his mother made this stuffed pork roast for him. He loves it."

Sydney and Consuela spent the rest of the evening eating and talking. After they finished, Consuela said, "I'm getting a little tired. Could you ask your security to take me home, please?"

"Of course, of course, my security will take you home."

When they got to the door, they hugged each other. Sydney said, "Don't forget my offer, Consuela. Don't ever feel you'd be imposing. I made the offer because I need you as much as you need me."

"Thank you, Syd. I want to talk to Bob first. I know what he's going to say," said Consuela.

"You ask Bob about it. I know the answer, too," responded Sydney.

Once Consuela was home, she got ready for bed. She spent the first hour in bed thinking of Bob Chavez and anticipating his call the next morning. She thought the offer Sydney made was good. She thought she'd wait to decide until she talked to Chavez. Although, she knew what he'd ask of her. She knew he'd say stay with Syd.

Her phone rang at about 7:00 a.m.

"Hello, Bob," answered Consuela.

"How are you, Connie?" asked Chavez.

"I'm okay."

"Just okay?"

"What do you want me to say? You're going to be away for three months. You said three weeks. Now for three months."

"I'm sorry, Connie. It's the way things worked out. There's nothing I can do about it now. I've got to finish this."

"You could leave right now if you wanted. Couldn't you?"

"You know I can't do that, Connie; you know that. I can't get up and leave. That would put the other guys in danger. No danger, but in a bad position."

"I know, Bob, I know. Sydney called me late yesterday afternoon. She asked me to come to her place for dinner," said Consuela.

"That was thoughtful of her."

"Yes, yes, it was very thoughtful. We talked for a while about how we were going to handle this situation. We decided we needed each other to get through this. She asked me to stay with her in her home until this is over. I can bring Alejandro and Lucia. I told her I appreciated the offer, but I'd have to talk to you first. How do you feel about that?" asked Consuela.

"I think that's a very good idea. It might be good for Syd, too."

"I thought you'd say that. So, did she."

"Well, then it's decided. You and Syd will bunk together till Gonzales and I get back. I'll call you every chance I get. Try not to worry. I'll be back."

* * *

When Sydney met with President Rivera the next day, she told him what she and Consuela had discussed. He said, "What a good idea. I have no objection. None."

"Thank you, sir. Consuela will be thrilled. So am I. Thank you again, Mr. President."

Chapter 37

The next day, Gonzales and Covert Bravo gathered in the living room of the house they'd just moved into. Gonzales said, "Let's take a walk."

Once outside Gonzales said, "We don't have any bug detecting equipment with us. I think we should take a walk when we want to talk about our mission."

Sanchez asked, "What's on your mind, Gonzales?"

"I've been thinking. I think we should take our communication equipment. The earbuds can't be seen when we have our parka hoods over our heads. The mic can easily be hidden inside our parka zippers. We can communicate without Roberts listening."

Chavez concurred. "You may be on to something, Gonzales. We should be prepared for anything."

"Okay, then, we use our comms equipment," finalized Gonzales.

* * *

After a little more preparation, Gonzales announced, "Okay, guys, it's time to go. This is our night."

Fuentes met them outside of the house. "You guys ready?"

"Let's get this show on the road," answered Gonzales.

Fuentes loaded them into two SUVs and took them to the snowmobiles. "Well, this is it, guys."

Gonzales said, "We're ready. We will be successful." The snowmobiles were loaded with hockey bags full of marijuana. "These snowmobiles are loaded with more weight than we trained with. They look top-heavy. How come?"

"We want to see if you're as good as you appear. This is the real deal. Okay, get your machines on the ice and get going," ordered Fuentes.

Gonzales spoke quietly into his mic. "They may have us run into a situation we're not familiar with. Let's show these guys we mean business."

In unison, Covert Bravo replied just as quietly into each mic, "Roger."

Gonzales led the way. They operated their machines without lights. Instead, they used the night vision equipment they were given. These snowmobiles were customized to run very quietly, with beefed-up mufflers to further suppress the engine's roaring sound. Fuentes didn't notice Gonzales and Covert Bravo were wearing earbuds and a mic.

The team delivered the load on time and to the right place. The place was on the New York side of the border. They were met by Jimmy Roberts, who looked surprised to see them.

"How did you get here so fast?" asked Roberts.

Gonzales answered, "We took another route, Jimmy. We used our initiative and thinking."

"Why would you take another route to get here?"

"I don't know. Just gut instinct. I've always relied on it especially in combat situations. I think we did a good job. We weren't caught by anyone...either by the Border Patrol or the Mohawk Police. We saw some Border Patrol, but were able to hide in the islands...you know, until it was good to go. We got our loads here, didn't we?"

"I give you credit, Gonzales. You thought this through and used leadership skills."

"Yeah, we did. When can we go again? This was kind of fun."

"I'm going to let you go tomorrow night...be ready. You guys were great tonight. I'll tell Fuentes to have a big load of the high-potency wacky tobacky for you. First, you have to get back to the Canadian side with another load of product."

"We're ready for anything, Jimmy. You just give us a chance," answered Gonzales.

Roberts had his men load the snowmobiles with the product. "You'll double your pay. That should incentivize you. Okay, now get going before the authorities get a whiff of what we're doing."

"Okay. We won't let you down."

Gonzales led the way. He said into his mic, "I think we should take another route. Not close to the one they gave us or the one we took to get here. We know this area pretty good from studying our maps and our practice runs. Follow me."

Gonzales headed north to St. Regis Island. He'd followed a westerly route around the island, coming to the south side of the reservation. Roberts's suggested route was easterly around the island. Gonzales spoke into his mic and said, "I think we'll cut through the middle of the island this time. We've been all over the island in our practice, and know how to get through its many trails."

Just as they got on the island, they heard a snowmobile go by.

Chavez asked, "Did you hear that? Did anyone see it?"

Gomez was in the rear and answered, "I heard it and saw just a little as it passed by us."

Gonzales asked, "Gomez, do you think they spotted us?"

"They didn't slow down. So, I don't think they saw us. But that doesn't mean they didn't see us. We don't know who it was. It could be kids out for a ride. We should be careful."

"I agree. Okay, let's keep our eyes open. I'm going to slow the pace down. If someone has seen us, they may be looking to double back, either on the river or through the island."

Gonzales slowed his snowmobile down to one-quarter speed. They moved slowly through the trail. Finally, they punched through to the other side of the island. They were back on the ice of the St. Lawrence River.

"I guess that snowmobile wasn't looking for us," said Gonzales. "Let's finish this job. We're more than halfway back. Follow me."

When they got back to the Canadian side, Fuentes was waiting. "You fellas are fast. How'd you get here so fast?"

"We took a short cut," answered Gonzales.

"Short cut? What short cut?"

"We went through the middle of an island. We knew we could get through it. We knew it would cut the time down because we went north instead of west or east on the river," answered Gonzales.

"Well, you fellas did good tonight. I'll tell Roberts. He'll be very happy—and surprised. I know I'm happy. By the way, how did you know the short cut?" asked Fuentes.

"We found it on a training exercise," answered Gonzales.

"You know, no one else who works for us found this way. You are the only ones."

"That's great. I guarantee you we'll be ready, and we won't fail. You can take that to the bank."

"That's the whole idea, Gonzales. Take it to the

bank."

* * *

Covert Bravo got back to their new digs. Gonzales said, "Let's take a walk." Once outside, he said, "I think we fooled them good tonight. I'm going to call Reynolds and let him know we're in good stead with Roberts and Fuentes." Covert Bravo nodded their heads in agreement. When Gonzales made the call, Covert Bravo was there and listened.

Reynolds's phone rang. He picked up the phone and said, "Gonzales, it's good to hear from you. What's happening at the casino? Do you have anything to report?"

"Sir, I think we've gained the trust of Roberts," answered Gonzales.

"What makes you so sure?"

"Well, sir, Fuentes set us up with living quarters on the Canadian side. For this to work, we had to get started on the Canadian side of the border. We delivered a load of marijuana, which was in big hockey bags, to the New York side. Roberts was waiting. He unloaded our sleds and reloaded them with more drugs. We brought the load back to the Canadian side. Fuentes was waiting. We were successful. We decided to take another route to the Canadian side. We saw a sled but were able to hide in the islands and had no problem getting to our destination. Fuentes was waiting for us. I think he was a little shocked to see us so soon. He said we'd make more money doing it if we did a return trip with the product. That was the deal in the first place. I think cocaine and/or heroin were the products we brought back."

"That's great work, Gonzales...just great. Is there more?"

"Yes, sir, there is. We are to deliver a big load of the high-potency marijuana tomorrow night. If we're successful, I think we'll get to transport Ecstasy the next trip. Neither Roberts nor Fuentes ever mentioned Ecstasy. All he's said is if we're successful bringing marijuana across, we'd get better drugs to take across the St. Lawrence. That's what we're after, aren't we, sir?"

"That's exactly right. Be careful, Gonzales. Keep me abreast of how you're doing. I'll pass this information to the president."

"Roger that, sir."

Chapter 38

The next morning, Fuentes met Covert Bravo outside of their new digs. "I've got a big shipment of high-potency marijuana for you to take tonight."

"Thanks," said Gonzales. "We're ready to go."

"No need to thank me. You fellas deserve this opportunity. You fooled everyone last night. You'll meet me tonight at the same spot we met last night. I know you're anxious to do this. Let's go. I'll introduce you to some of the other mules."

Fuentes took Covert Bravo to meet the Latino community that lived on the Canadian side of the Mohawk Reservation. The men they met were MS-13. There were just eight of them. Gonzales and his team shook hands with the MS-13 guys. The Ms-13 guys were not very friendly.

After they broke up the introductions, Gonzales asked Fuentes, "Are there other people living here besides the guys we just met?"

"Sure. There are Latinos and Mohawk Indians living here, too."

"Those people have nothing to do with the drug business?"

"No. Some work at the casino. Why do you ask?"

"We just want to know who we have to be careful with; you know, who is on our side."

"You guys are something else. First you want to study maps and take practice runs. Now you want to know who you can talk to and what you should or shouldn't say."

The afternoon before the drug mission, Gonzales and Covert Bravo met to discuss what might happen.

Gonzales motioned them outside. Once outside and a good distance from the house, Gonzales said, "Okay, we all know the islands that may come into play tonight. Roberts gave us maps to study. We've checked them out and have been all over them on our practice runs. The maps indicate the big islands would be a good place to hide. Anyone have any other ideas?"

Covert Bravo answered in unison, "No."

"Then we study the trails on the maps. We are familiar with these islands and the trails, because of our practice runs. So, we should have an edge on whoever may be chasing us. Border Patrol, local police, and Mohawk Police will have the same knowledge of the islands and the trails. The Mohawk Police will have native knowledge. I doubt they would need to study maps. I'm sure Roberts has given these maps to other mules. I doubt they'll study them like we have. We'll be more ready than any of the others," said Gonzales.

Just as nightfall was approaching, Fuentes came for them. "It's showtime, fellas. I'll take you to your snowmobiles. Like last time, we have night vision goggles for you to use. Are you comfortable using them?" asked Fuentes.

"Why would we have trouble with night vision goggles? Of course, we're comfortable with them. If we weren't, we'd say something. We wouldn't want to screw up a run," answered Gonzales.

"Good. I'm glad to hear that."

By the time Fuentes got them to their snowmobiles, it was dark out. "You'll be driving the same machines you did last night. This is a serious business. There's no room for mistakes tonight. If you get caught by the Border Patrol, you'll be on your own. Keep your radios on. You may get some help from our spotters. You've got to pay attention to what's around you. Good luck," said Fuentes.

After Fuentes left, Gonzales said, "Let's check our communication system. Everyone checks in with me and with each other." They checked with each other and Gonzales. The check went perfectly, as expected. Gonzales said, "Let's check our radios for frequency. We need to hear anything the spotters say and what we say to each other." The frequency check was perfect. Gonzales led the way.

The sky was cloudy. The night was darker than dark. As they got onto the ice of the St. Lawrence, Gonzales said into his mic and away from the radio, "You guys follow me in single file. Chavez, you follow me. Sanchez, get behind him. Ramirez, you get behind Sanchez and Gomez, you get behind Ramirez. Everyone good with that?"

In unison, he heard them say, "Roger."

"Okay, here we go." He started slowly. The snowmobiles ran very quietly. Gonzales knew the route he wanted to take. It was a little different from the one Fuentes suggested. He headed toward an island in the river.

Suddenly, Gonzales heard his radio squawk. The spotter said, "Gonzales, there's Border Patrol in your area. Get into cover on the island."

"Roger that," responded Gonzales. Gonzales said into his mic, "Did you guys hear that?"

He got a yes from Covert Bravo. "Follow me."

Covert Bravo followed Gonzales. He took them into the security of the trees on the island.

"Gomez, did you see anything or anyone come onto the island?" asked Gonzales into his mic.

"No," answered Gomez.

Then, over the radio, Covert Bravo heard, "There's a Border Patrol snowmobile coming toward your location."

"Okay," was Gonzales's response. Gonzales said

into his mic, "We studied our maps this afternoon. Each of us knows what to do."

Gonzales and Covert Bravo went their separate ways. Each man took a different route to the New York side of the border. None of them heard from the spotter, nor did they encounter the Border Patrol or the Mohawk Police.

When Gonzales and Covert Bravo got to the New York side of the border, Roberts was there waiting. Gonzales said, "It looks like we all made it. Our plan worked."

This caused Roberts to say, "What plan, Gonzales?"

Gonzales answered, "We talked things over this afternoon. We were ready for anything that might come up. We studied the maps you gave us. So, we knew where to go and what to do. As soon as we got the call from our spotter, we split up. Our thinking was, the Border Patrol couldn't track all of us. We thought the Border Patrol may get confused. I don't know what happened to them. We got the product here and are ready to pick up whatever you have for us to take back to Fuentes."

"Gonzales, I don't know what to think of you and your men. You seem to be ahead of everyone, including me. I'm not sure about this...what you did tonight. I should be happy you got through with all this high-grade marijuana...wacky tobacky. And I'm very happy you got this load through. We can talk about this some other time. We'll load you up with more of our product to take back with you."

Roberts had his men load each snowmobile with cocaine and heroin. The cocaine and heroin were stored in big hockey bags, just like the marijuana.

The team had an uneventful trip back. They delivered a load of cocaine and heroin to Fuentes, who was happy to see them.

"You fellas were very good tonight...very good. Roberts should be very happy. You got his high-octane wacky tobacky over to him," said Fuentes.

When Gonzales and Covert Bravo got back to the house where they were staying, Gonzales said, "Let's take a walk."

As Gonzales and Covert Bravo were walking, he said, "We did really good tonight. I think Fuentes may have been a little doubtful about us. We all had some misgivings about him. I think between our audition run, last night, and tonight, he's convinced about us."

Sanchez said, "What we did tonight should convince Roberts and Fuentes we're for real."

"I'm going to call the Reynolds."

Covert Bravo walked with Gonzales as he made the call. They heard every word. "Director Reynolds, we made our second trip across the St. Lawrence tonight. The spotter radioed us about seeing a Border Patrol agent in our vicinity. We went into the woods on the island and followed the procedure we worked out this afternoon. It worked like a charm, sir. Roberts and Fuentes bought it."

"Well, Gonzales, I'm glad for your and Covert Bravo's success. We know exactly where that high-potency marijuana is right now. We'll follow it up. Probably won't intercept this time; probably not the second time you're involved with a crossing. We want Roberts and Fuentes to trust you. I'll pass this along to the president. Is there anything else, Gonzales?" asked Reynolds.

"No, sir. We're good right now. I'll let you know when we try again."

"Have you heard where the lab is? The lab where they make the Ecstasy?" asked the director.

"No, sir. We haven't heard a thing about that.

I think we've got to wait a while before we can get that information. It may be coming sooner rather than later," answered Gonzales.

"Keep your ears and eyes open, Gonzales. And good luck."

"We'll do that, sir. And thank you." The call was disconnected.

Chapter 39

After taking the walk and calling the director, Gonzales and Covert Bravo went back to their house. Roberts was waiting. "I've been waiting for a half-hour. Where have you guys been?"

"We took a walk. Is there something wrong with that?" answered Gonzales.

"No, there's nothing wrong with that," answered Fuentes. "I wasn't expecting you to be gone...especially on a walk. Especially after you just got back from a crossing. It's cold out here. Aren't you guys cold?"

"Yeah, we're cold. But we're full of adrenalin. So, we thought we'd walk it off. You know that was an amazing trip. What a rush!" said Gonzales.

"Look, you guys are going tomorrow night. I just wanted to let you know. You need to get some rest. I just talked to Roberts. He's impressed with how you outwitted the Border Patrol tonight. He normally has a team rest a day or two before sending them out again. I think he's got a special cargo for you tomorrow night. I think it's Ecstasy. I'm not sure. You okay with that?"

"Sure, we're okay with that. This trip should pay more money. You said it would."

"I think it'll pay double what you made tonight. By the way, here's your money for tonight. Two thousand each." Roberts passed two thousand dollars to each man.

"Thanks for bringing our money to us," said Gonzales. "You say tomorrow night we'll each get four grand?"

"That's right, Gonzales...four grand each."

"We'll be ready."

"That's what Roberts likes about you fellas. You're always ready. I'll be back tomorrow afternoon. Okay. Now get some rest," said Roberts as he turned to leave.

"Will we be leaving from the same place as tonight?" asked Gonzales.

"Why do you need to know?"

"No reason. I just thought it might be handy information. We can study our maps. That's all. If you don't want to say, that's okay," answered Gonzales.

As Fuentes looked Gonzales in the eye, he thought for a moment. He finally made up his mind and said, "You guys look good to me. I'm not supposed to give this information to anyone. But I'll make an exception with you. You'll leave from another area. It'll be just east of where you left tonight."

"How far east? Will we need to study another island?"

"It's far enough east that you'll need to study the islands in that area. The only reason I'm telling you this is because you have always been thorough. We appreciate that. No one else has taken the time to study. They just go. And hope. Now, get some rest."

* * *

As Gonzales and Covert Bravo made their way back to the house they were using, Gonzales said, "I've got to call Reynolds and fill him in on what we've just found out. He should be very happy about this news. It's still a decent hour. Director Reynolds, I hope I'm not interrupting anything important."

"Well, Gonzales, I'm in a meeting now with the

president and Secretary Alvarez. We were just talking about your crossing tonight. What's on your mind?" asked the director. "I'll put you on speaker so President Rivera and the secretary can hear our conversation, too."

"That's fine with me, sir. I'm calling about tomorrow night. We'll be making another crossing. This time, we will bring Ecstasy."

The president motioned Reynolds off and said, "This is the president, Gonzales. Are you sure it's Ecstasy?"

"That's what Roberts told us, sir."

"We'll follow that load of Ecstasy. But won't intercept it. I think we should let that load get through and maybe the next two or three. As I said in the past, we want Roberts and Fuentes to get comfortable with you and Covert Bravo," replied the president.

"That's a good idea, sir. We don't want to raise any suspicion," responded Gonzales.

"That's right, Gonzales. Let me know how things go tomorrow night. And good luck," said President Rivera.

* * *

Gonzales and Covert Bravo went to bed that night feeling good about the crossing the next night.

The next night, Fuentes met Covert Bravo. "You look rested and ready to go," said Fuentes. "Roberts told me the Mohawk Police won't be on duty tonight...neither will the Border Patrol. When they stand down, the Border Patrol do too...most of the time. Sometimes they don't have enough border officers to fill the gap. The area tonight is considered a gap. But be careful anyway. Always be alert. We've got to get this shipment across the border. I asked Roberts if we should use a more experienced team. He said no...you guys were the best he had. He's the boss and knows what he's doing. Okay. Now my men will load your hovercraft with our product...Ecstasy. The hovercraft can carry a bigger payload."

"You tell Roberts he picked the right team. We won't let him down. After we deliver this load of Ecstasy, will we be bringing another load back here? You know, like we did the other nights?" said Gonzales.

"Yeah, you'll be bringing a load of cocaine and heroin back. Be alert, be alert. We never know if our information is good. Even though we know the Mohawk Police and the Border Patrol won't be out there tonight, our spotters will be out watching for you. If you get something from a spotter, take it seriously," replied Fuentes.

"No worries. We're always alert. We've studied the islands. And we're good with all the routes we could use to confuse the Border Patrol," said Gonzales. "We'll be back before you know it."

"I'll be waiting here," responded Fuentes. Gonzales and Covert Bravo were off.

As soon as the team were on the frozen St. Lawrence, Gonzales said into the mic that was buried in the fur of the parka he wore, "According to Fuentes, Roberts has the Mohawk Police standing down tonight. That's interesting. That just leaves the Border Patrol for us to deal with...maybe not them, either. Roberts said if the Mohawks are standing down, the Border Patrol probably will be doing the same."

Suddenly, the spotter came over Gonzales's radio. "There's someone on your left. He's running very quiet and without lights. Get into the islands as soon as possible."

"Is it the Border Patrol?" asked Gonzales.

"No, there aren't any markings on the snowmobile. I don't know who that is. You fellas better get in the woods and ditch this guy," was the response from the spotter.

"Let's go, guys," said Gonzales into his mic. "You know what to do."

Gonzales and Covert Bravo disappeared into the woods of one of the islands. They were running silent and without lights, and were using night vision goggles, too.

"Let's wait here," said Gonzales.

Gonzales heard a faint noise. "Anyone hear what I'm hearing?"

"Yeah, I hear a faint sound of a machine," answered Gomez, who was in the rear.

Sanchez said, "I hear it, too. It's moving slowly, though."

"Okay. The Mohawks are standing down tonight. It's probably not the Border Patrol. This guy has no markings on his snowmobile. Let's see what he's up to. Everyone off your hovercraft. Hide them in the trees. Whoever it is, it's moving very slow. Let's set up an ambush. We'll take him. Sanchez, you and Chavez on the left side of the trail, Ramirez and Gomez on the right side. I'll take the center. Pick up something to throw at him...anything; a stick, stone or snowball. If he comes this way, we'll jump up on my command and throw whatever we've got. That should startle him. We can jump him then. We've got him outnumbered and have surprise on our side. He may have a weapon. I doubt if he'll have a weapon out while he's driving. Okay, be alert...is everyone in position?" asked Gonzales.

"Roger, that," came back from Covert Bravo.

They all hid their hovercraft in the trees. They found good cover in which to hide. They found things to throw and had them ready. They waited in silence.

A few minutes passed. Still, no one came. Then they heard a muffled snowmobile. It moved slowly. As the snowmobile came close to Gonzales, he said into his mic,

"Now!"

He jumped up in front of the snowmobile and threw a chunk of dead wood right at the driver. It hit him in the arm. The driver let out a yelp. The snowmobile came to a halt. Covert Bravo threw hard-packed snowballs and chunks of deadwood. The startled driver stopped in his tracks. Gonzales was the first to reach the driver. He was able to knock the driver off the snowmobile. Covert Bravo was on the driver before he knew what happened.

After the scuffle, Gonzales grabbed the driver's parka hood and tore it off the driver's head. Gonzales asked, "I know you. What are you doing following us?"

Gonzales recognized the person as soon as he saw his face. He was a bartender in the casino.

"Okay, guys. Stop right now. I know this guy. He's the Asian bartender who works in the casino. What are you doing? Are you following us? What's this all about? We'll see about this. Get on your snowmobile and get in the middle of our formation," said Gonzales. The Asian showed his contempt by trying to wiggle free. "He defiantly said, "You won't get anything from me."

"We'll see about that, Mr. Bartender. Okay, guys let's get going," ordered Gonzales.

Gonzales, Covert Bravo, and the bartender formed up. The bartender was in the middle of the formation. They made their way across the St. Lawrence to where Roberts was waiting.

The Asian made a break to get away. Ramirez was right behind him. Ramirez said into his mic, "He's trying to get away. I've got him."

"You get him, Ramirez," barked Gonzales. "Gomez and Sanchez, you help."

Ramirez, Gomez, and Sanchez took off. Ramirez said, "I'll get in front of him and try to stop him or slow him down. Gomez and Sanchez, bring your hovercraft alongside him...one on each side. We can box him in and jump him."

"Roger that," said Gomez.

Ramirez got in front of the Asian and slowed him down considerably. This gave Gomez and Sanchez a chance to drive their hovercraft up alongside the snowmobile. The Asian man was boxed in and had little chance of getting away. He stopped completely. The plan worked perfectly. They had the Asian. "All right, let's get this guy back in line," said Ramirez.

* * *

Roberts saw Gonzales had an extra snowmobile with him. "What did you pick up out there, Gonzales?"

"We don't know. We got an alert from our spotter. He said we were being tailed. So, we went into the woods on the island and waited. Fuentes told us not to worry about Mohawk Police...and that the Border Patrol probably wouldn't be out either. He said when the Mohawks stand down, the Border Patrol usually stands down, too. We knew we weren't being chased by them. We weren't sure he'd come our way. We waited anyway. We heard him moving slowly and quietly and when he passed us, we jumped him. He hasn't said a word. I know him from the casino. He's the Asian bartender."

"Well, you guys are never cease to amaze me. I know him, too. I've been waiting for him to do something like this. He works for a competing gang. Asian gangs are competing for a piece of the pie. They supply the pill-making machines and the MDMA and the other components for making Ecstasy. They're ruthless. They sent this guy to spy on us; to see how we operate on the river at night. That's my gut feeling. Transnational gangs are trying to cut in on our trade. I thought we had it worked out with them; I guess I was wrong. I'll call a parley with them and try to find out what this is all about. Like I said, you guys are very good. You proved it again tonight." He paused to survey the scene. "Enough of this. You take this load of cocaine and heroin back. My men will unload what you brought and reload. Good luck," responded Roberts.

"We've never let you down. We won't this time either," said Gonzales.

When Gonzales and Covert Bravo were safely back on the Canadian side of the reservation, Fuentes was waiting for them and said, "How did it go?"

"It went pretty good—"

Before Gonzales could say another word, Fuentes interrupted and said, "What's pretty good? You didn't have any trouble, did you?"

"Let me finish. I just said pretty good because we didn't run into any Mohawk Police. The spotter alerted us to a snowmobile that was following us. I asked him if it was Border Patrol. He said no. So, we set up an ambush and got the guy. He's the Asian bartender who works at the casino. He was trying to follow us. We caught him and delivered the Ecstasy, along with the Asian. Can you believe that?"

Fuentes remarked, "What do you mean an Asian man was following you?"

"Like I said, he is Asian. Roberts has him now. I recognized him from the casino. He's a bartender there. You told us the Mohawk Police were standing down tonight and the Border Patrol would probably do the same. When we got a radio message from the spotter, he said there was someone following us. He told us to get on the island and hide. We did that. I thought, this can't be the Mohawk Police. The spotter said the snowmobile didn't have markings on it. So, it wasn't the Border Patrol. So, why not try to catch this guy? We thought he might come our way. So, we set up an ambush and picked up whatever there was lying on the ground...chunks of dead wood, rocks, and snowballs. He had a snowmobile with a bumped-up muffler...like ours. He ran slow and quiet. When he came by our position, we jumped up and threw what we had in our hands. It startled him. Then we jumped him and delivered him, along with the Ecstasy, to Roberts."

"That's some story all right, Gonzales. You did a good job tonight. I'm very happy. Roberts should be too. I'm just as surprised as you are. As far as I'm concerned, you guys have done good work. You learn fast and are intelligent about it. You study maps and learn where to go. Okay, let's get you guys paid. You earned double the money tonight...four grand each. Now go back to your place and get some rest."

"Will do."

When Gonzales and Covert Bravo got back to their place, they took a walk, despite the cold night. "Let's take a walk. I'm not quite sure about what happened tonight," said Gonzales.

"What're you uneasy about, Gonzales?" asked Chavez.

"How did Roberts know the Mohawk Police were going to stand down? There must be someone on the Mohawk Police force that's tied in with him.

"Someone on the Canadian side is working with him. I'm calling the director first thing in the morning. It's a little late tonight. This can wait. We need to get some rest. So, let's go back to the house."

* * *

The next morning, Gonzales and Covert Bravo got up. Sanchez had breakfast going...the usual...bacon, eggs, flapjacks, grits, toast, and coffee. Gonzales and Covert Bravo came into the kitchen. Sanchez said, "Get it while it's hot." The men ate like they hadn't eaten in weeks. "The cold must make you guys hungry. You haven't eaten like this since I can't remember!" exclaimed Sanchez. After eating his fill, Gonzales called Director Reynolds.

"Good morning, Director Reynolds."

"Good morning, Gonzales. What do you have for me?"

"Sir, as you know, we made a crossing last night. It didn't go exactly as we thought. Fuentes told us the Mohawk Police would stand down. And the Border Patrol would probably not be present either. There weren't any Border Patrol or Mohawk Police around. The question is, how did he know? We're the only people in the loop. And none of us told him. I'm certain no one on our committee said anything. I think there must be a leak on the Canadian side. Someone knew and gave the information to Roberts. I wonder if someone is working for Roberts. Or maybe Roberts is working for them. Maybe there's someone else who oversees the whole operation...and not Roberts...like we've been thinking. It would be a big advantage to have that knowledge. They may have been operating with this information all along, sir," said Gonzales.

Reynolds listened carefully as Gonzales made his report and said, "That's entirely possible. You're right about operating with a big advantage. I think you should keep your eyes and ears open...get any information you can regarding this. I'll pass this along to the president."

"Yes, sir. I was just thinking the same thing. I've got more to report."

"Go on, Gonzales."

"We were told by our spotter that someone was following us. We got into the trees on a small island and waited. Because Roberts said the Mohawks were standing down and the Border Patrol probably would be standing down too, we thought we'd try to grab the guy. We set up an ambush, so to speak, and grabbed him. We took the guy and delivered him to Roberts, along with the Ecstasy. Roberts said the man, who is Asian, was part of an Asian transnational gang. I recognized him. He works at the casino as a bartender. He said the Asians supply the pill-making machines and the MDMA to make Ecstasy. Now the transnationals want a piece of the retail sales."

"I'll look into that question immediately. We've known the Asians are behind getting pill-making machines and MDMA into Canada. As far as the Asians getting into the retail side of the business, this is new to me. It sounds like a good piece of information. Information that needs further investigation. See what you can find out. Is there anything else?"

"No, sir. That's what happened last night. I think Roberts and Fuentes think we're good men. I think they trust us and will give us more responsibility. We make them money. We're here to gather as much intelligence as possible, sir. That's what we intend to do."

"Do you know what happened to the Asian man you captured?"

"No, sir. We left him with Roberts on the New York side. We'll try to find out. I'll let you know when we've got that intelligence, if there's any more to gather."

"Good luck, Gonzales. And be safe."

"Thank you, sir."

Chapter 40

The day after Sydney asked Consuela to move in with her, she called Consuela, "Hi, Consuela. I thought I'd call to see if you have time to have dinner tonight. Why don't you bring Alejandro and Lucia with you?" asked Sydney.

"I just got back from my job at the State Department. I don't have anything planned for dinner. I'd love to come for dinner...thank you for inviting Alejandro and Lucia, too. I'm sure they'd love to come along. Is there something on your mind? Does it have something to do with Chavez and Gonzales?" asked Consuela.

Not wanting to lie, Sydney answered, "Yes, it does."

"Are they in any danger?"

"No. No more than they have been since they got to the reservation. We've found out something that may be of help in their investigation. It's nothing. I thought you'd like to know. That's all. I'll send my security to pick you up. Does five o'clock sound good?"

"I don't like the sound of this. They're in trouble. I know it," responded Consuela.

"Hold on, Consuela. Just hold on a minute. I didn't say any such thing, did I? I've got some news from them. That's all. Don't read anything more into it. Okay?"

"Okay, if you say so, Syd. We'll be ready. And thank you."

* * *

Sydney met Consuela, Alejandro, and Lucia at her front

door. "It's so good to see all of you, Consuela...please come in."

"Thank you, Syd. It's always nice to see you."

Sydney led them into her front room. She didn't want to upset Alejandro, so, she said to Lucia, "Would you take Alejandro in the other room? There are some things there that he may find amusing."

Lucia took the hint and said, "Yes. Yes, of course. Let's go, Alejandro. We can play in the other room."

"I don't want to go. I want to stay here," objected Alejandro.

Lucia would have none of that. "Let's go now. Your mother and Miss Alvarez have business to discuss."

Alejandro looked at his mother, then at Lucia. He decided from the look on his mother's face he'd better go with Lucia, so off he went.

Once Lucia had Alejandro in the other room, Sydney said, "The president is very much in favor of you and your family staying with me. I knew he would approve. I met with him this morning."

"That makes me very happy!" exclaimed Consuela.

"Did Chavez call you this morning?" asked Sydney.

"Yes, he did."

"Did you tell him about my asking you to stay with me until he, Gonzales, and the rest of Covert Bravo get back?"

"Yes, I did tell him. He thought it was a good idea. I agree with him. I need you to help me get through this. I think you need me, too."

Sydney's face beamed with a dazzling smile. She said, "That's wonderful, Consuela. I cleared it with the president. He's all for it. When can you come?"

"Well, I hope I'm not being too forward, Syd. But I brought some things for me and Alejandro for tonight.

Lucia brought a few things, too," answered Consuela.

"That's great...just terrific. I was hoping you'd start tonight. Now, let's have dinner. It should be ready. Lucia, dinner is ready," called Sydney. They all sat down, ate dinner together, and talked. After dinner, Lucia took Alejandro and put him to bed. She retired for the night as well. Sydney and Consuela were free to talk.

Sydney asked, "Where are you and Chavez headed?"

"You mean our relationship?" answered Consuela.

"Yes," said Sydney.

"We've talked a little...not much. Bob knows I don't like him going away. I know there is little danger where he is now. But what happens when the president sends him, Gonzales, and the others to Afghanistan or some other dangerous place? He's told me he loves me. I believe him. I've told him I love him. He said he's thinking about retiring from the army."

"Chavez told you he was considering retiring from the army?" responded Sydney. "Why?"

"For sure, he told me that. He knows he's getting older. Not that he's old, old...just old for being an Army Ranger. He thinks he's slowing down...as he says...a step or two. He feels he may not be able to hold up his part," replied Consuela.

"What would he do after his retirement?" asked Sydney.

"He said he's thinking about going into the security business. You know, working for important people and providing them with professional protection. That's about it," said Consuela.

"There are many good jobs out there for people with Chavez's skills. They pay good, too," responded Sydney.

"That's what Bob said. The pay was good. I asked him if he would be gone for any reason," replied Consuela.

"What did he say?"

"He said it was possible. He wasn't sure...but it was possible."

"If he does retire from the army, maybe he could get a job with the Secret Service. If he'd like, I'd be happy to recommend him to the president. Although, I doubt he'd need my recommendation. The president would see to it himself...once he knew Chavez was interested. We don't even know that he'd be interested. You could ask him if he was interested," replied Sydney.

"Would that mean he wouldn't have to go away? You would do that for him?" asked Consuela.

"Absolutely, without a doubt. Sometimes, Secret Service must...as you put it...go away. But not always. Maybe I could put a bug in the president's ear concerning that. Maybe the president could put Chavez in a permanent position so he wouldn't have to go away," answered Sydney.

"You would do that for Bob and me?" asked Consuela again.

"Of course, I would. Don't be silly, Consuela," answered Sydney.

"Thank you. Saying thank you seems...how to say this...not enough, inadequate. You've done so many good things for me...you've been such a good friend. Especially now. Thank you so much," said Consuela.

"You're welcome," replied Sydney.

"Now tell me about you and Gonzales. Where do you see you and Gonzales going?" asked Consuela.

"That's a good question, Consuela. We've talked about us for some time...more so lately. Gonzales is an Army Ranger. I've got to learn to handle that. He won't retire. I'm sure of that. It does scare me that he may be deployed to a more dangerous place. Right now, things are quiet, despite the catastrophe in Chicago. Our nation isn't at war with anyone right now. Beyond that...he's told me he loves me."

"He told you that, Syd? That's wonderful. I know you love him. When you're with him, I can see it in your eyes and face," responded Consuela.

"Is it that obvious?" asked Sydney.

"It is to me. I doubt anyone else is looking for what I look for," answered Consuela.

"Well, I do love him. As you know; that's the easy part," replied Sydney.

"Yes, I know that's the easy part."

"I don't know what I'd do if Gonzales was sent into harm's way again. He's very good at what he does, as is Chavez and the rest of Covert Bravo, but sometime...I don't like saying or even thinking this...their luck may run out," said Sydney, bursting into tears. Consuela immediately jumped up and ran to Sydney, sat beside her, and held her as Sydney cried her eyes out.

"I know. I know. That's exactly how I feel, Syd."

Sydney regained her composure. "I'm sorry, Consuela. I didn't mean to break down like this. It's just...I'm as afraid as you are. I think we need each other until our guys get back. I hope Chavez is seriously considering retiring for your sake and his, too. I don't know about Gonzales. He's getting older. Again, as you say, not old, old, but older for what he's doing. When Gonzales and Chavez get back, maybe you could have Chavez say something to him."

"When Bob gets back, I will talk to him. I think Bob is serious about retiring. He's been in for over twenty years. So, he would get his military pension. If he gets into the security business, as he says, we'll be able to start a life together. I want that; I want it very much," responded Consuela.

Chapter 41

Benito Flores was at the construction site of his semisubmersibles and admiring the newest and biggest one. It had just come off the assembly line.

"Dize, what do you think of my new semisubmersible? It's twice as big as the older ones. They're built of fiberglass and lead. Because of these construction components, they're virtually undetectable by infrared. Radar and sonar can't pick them up because they sit low to the water. This one can carry twenty tons of heroin and cocaine. What do you think, Dize?"

"I think this is a masterful work of shipbuilding, Benito."

"It is. I've got the best shipbuilders in Mexico overseeing this construction. Where is el Din? He should see this boat."

El Din was walking toward Flores and Cruz. Flores motioned for him to come and see his newest and biggest. "What do you think, Baha?" asked Flores.

"I think you should send me home. I've completed my task," answered el Din.

"I didn't ask you that. I asked you what you think of my new boat."

"I think it's very good. Maybe the best idea you've had for getting your drugs into the United States. Now, when do I go home? I have a family that's waiting for me."

"I told you, you'll go home when I say! Now that's enough! You have everything you could ask for here... good food, good shelter, and a good woman. What more could you ask for?" exclaimed Flores.

Baha el Din said nothing. He listened to what Flores said next.

"Dize, we have the complete shipment of heroin from Afghanistan. This new boat will transport my new product, heroin, to the United States. Okay now, we go back to our place. Let's go, el Din, let's go." El Din had little choice. He did as he was told and went with Flores.

When they got back to the village, el Din went to his hut. The hut was in the traditional style of the Lacandon. El Din had lived in worse places during the war years...mostly caves in Afghanistan. This place happened to be the place where Flores decided to build his heroin reception and distribution center. El Din decided to take a walk and try to figure a way out of the mess he was in.

Chan K'in Viejo walked up to el Din and said, "You know how I feel about what you and Flores are doing here."

"I don't like being kept here against my will, either," responded el Din.

"I don't like Benito Flores coming into my village with his drugs and corrupting my people. They call him 'el Gato.' It means 'the cat.' I know this name. I don't like him building those ships here in my village. A few young people are using these drugs now. This isn't good for them or the Lacandon people. I'll fight him on this. He's very strong and has many men with guns. I have men without guns. They are brave. I'm not stupid enough to send my men to fight men with guns. They'll all be killed. I'll probably be killed."

"If I could help you, I would," said el Din. "What can I do? I can't even help myself. My family and friends are waiting for me. I may never see them again." The village elder just looked at him, shrugged his shoulders and walked away.

Chapter 42

Dize Cruz's cell phone buzzed. The caller ID said it was Little Lenny Ortega. Cruz answered and said, "Hello, Ortega. I hope this isn't a courtesy call."

"What's a courtesy call?" asked Ortega.

"Never mind. Do you have anything to report?"

"I've had my men watching both women," answered Ortega.

"And?"

"Gonzales and Chavez have not been around for a couple of weeks. I don't know what to make of it. My men report the security details have doubled. It looks like Hernández has moved in with the Alvarez woman. I thought I'd pass the information along to you. That's all I've got," responded Ortega.

"Are you sure about Gonzales and Chavez being gone for that long? What makes you think Hernández moved in with the Alvarez woman?" asked Cruz.

"I'm positive about Gonzales and Chavez. They're gone. Even though we watch those women only three to four times a week, my men haven't seen them in two to three weeks. I know Consuela moved her family in with Alvarez because my men saw her and her family go into the Alvarez woman's place the other night. They didn't come out until the next morning. Hernández went to school. When she got out of school, she went to the State Department. Then she went back to her place. When she came out, she had two big Secret Service guys carrying suitcases in their hands. She's been at Alvarez's since then. My men say she's not gone back to her place. She hasn't been to her place for the last three nights. So, yes, Hernández has moved in with the Alvarez woman with her son and Lucia," concluded Ortega.

"That's very interesting. I wonder where Gonzales and Chavez could be. I wonder why security has been doubled. The fact that Consuela, her son, and Lucia have moved in with Alvarez is strange. Something's not right. I'll tell Flores. Keep your men on the women. Anything on Alejandro?"

"He's going to school every day; we watch for him. His security has doubled, too. We don't watch the women or the boy every day like you ordered. Maybe we should increase our surveillance to maybe five days, including Saturday. Hernández takes her son to the swim club on Saturday."

"I'll talk to Flores about increasing the days you watch the women. This is good information. Continue to do what you've been doing. I'll tell Flores."

"Okay. I hope this helps. I'll keep my men working just like you want," said Ortega.

"You do that. And let me know what is happening there. Those guys are gone for a reason," said Cruz. "Maybe you can find out why."

Ortega asked, "How am I gonna find that out?"

"I don't know. You may hear something or see something that may shed some light on this. Okay, Lenny. You do your job."

"I'll do my best. That's all I can promise."

Cruz disconnected the call and went to find Flores. He was outside the village at the heroin storage buildings.

"Benito, I've got some news from Ortega."

"Let's have it."

Cruz related the story Ortega gave him. "Gonzales

and Chavez haven't been seen for two weeks. Consuela, Alejandro, and Lucia moved in with the Alvarez woman. I wonder what they're up to?"

"That's a good question. I wonder why security has been doubled. Unless Gonzales and Chavez are on another mission. I'll bet the rest of his men are gone, too. They may be expecting something to happen in the world. That's why Gonzales and Chavez are gone. I wonder how long they'll be gone. I'll bet Consuela has moved in with Alvarez because she feels safer there," said Flores.

"Ortega suggested he put another day of surveillance on both of the women. I told him I'd check with you. I told Ortega to keep his men on the Alvarez woman and Consuela, as you ordered, for now," replied Cruz.

"Did Ortega have anything to report on my son?" asked Flores.

"The boy is going to school. He must be learning how to swim. His mother takes him to a swim club on Saturday mornings. I told them to keep a watch on him, too, just like you ordered. A few times a week," responded Cruz. "Maybe we should increase his surveillance days, too."

"I think we should increase our surveillance to six days a week, for now. Or until Gonzales and Chavez return. Maybe I should rethink my position on when I try to make my move, Dize. At first, I thought I'd wait for six months before I gave the order to make my move. Since Gonzales and Chavez are out of the area, now may be the time," said Flores.

"I'll call Ortega right now and give him your new orders," responded Cruz.

* * *

CIA Director Yanelli called Biscotti and filled him in on Consuela's move to Sydney's. "I think it's a good move. The women will be together most of the time," said Yanelli.

"I do, too. Do you think we should cut the security detail?" asked Biscotti.

"I was just thinking of that. If we don't cut it, we'd have double-double security. I think we cut it to just double. That's two men in two cars, all the time, for the secretary and Consuela," answered Yanelli. "We don't want overkill. That will free your agents up for other duties. I think we should go with this plan until Gonzales and Chavez get back," answered Yanelli.

"I agree. When do you want us to pick these guys up?"

"Let's give it another day, Biscotti. I want to speak to the president about what you've just related to me. He knows all about what's going on with these guys. You know, some of the MS-13 thugs don't wear tattoos. However, we know these guys report to Carlito Dario, who is MS-13. The guys who're staking out the secretary and Consuela must be MS-13," answered Yanelli.

"Yes, sir, we're aware of that fact. So, you want my men to do as they've been doing? We won't make a move until we hear from you or unless they make a move on the secretary, Ms. Hernández, or her son or his nanny," responded Biscotti.

"That's right. You sit tight and keep those guys in your sight. Stay put unless they make a move. We know the only reason they stake out the secretary and Ms. Hernández is to execute a kidnapping. Because of that threat, we've doubled our protection on the orders of President Rivera. We'd like to get the big fish who's behind this. We know it's Benito Flores, who's hiding in Mexico. We're trying to get a fix on Flores's location now. We think someone is directing Carlito Dario. We'd like to get him along with these other guys," replied Yanelli.

"Okay, sir. We'll be waiting for your order," responded Biscotti.

After Biscotti disconnected his call with Yanelli, he called the men who were keeping surveillance on Sydney and Consuela. Dick Henderson and Joe Bandy had Sydney. Dave Osborne and John Evans had Consuela. Biscotti put a conference call to Henderson and Osborne.

"Are the guys watching the secretary and Consuela there?" asked Biscotti.

Henderson answered first. "Yeah, they're in front of us a couple of blocks. They may not be the same fellas... but there are two men up the street. And they're watching the secretary's place."

"The guys who've been tailing and watching Consuela have just turned up. They parked down the street from us...probably a couple of blocks. I think they figured out that she and her family are staying with the secretary. She's been staying with the secretary for the last three nights. They just parked down the street a couple of blocks," reported Osborne.

"Yeah, I'd agree with that. Consuela hasn't been at her place for the last two days and three nights," remarked Biscotti.

"It's the same routine every time. They aren't here every day. We see them three days a week...four at the most. They watch either the secretary or Consuela. We know they report to Dario and go back to their place. They've been tailed to Dario's place from time to time. Why would they not do it now? The next morning or afternoon, they go to work in DC at a building full of lobbying firms," responded Evans.

"We should find out which firm they work for and

ask some questions. It's been that way for longer than three weeks. I wonder when they plan to make their move," replied Osborne.

"Yanelli wants us to keep doing what we've been doing for at least another day. He said not to move on the men watching the secretary, Consuela, or Alejandro and his nanny. He'll tell us when to pick them up. Unless they make a move," responded Biscotti.

* * *

Yanelli called President Rivera and related the conversation he'd just had with Biscotti. The president responded, "What do you think we ought to do? Should we wait to pick those fellas up?

"Sir, my feeling is to wait another day or so before we pick them up," answered Yanelli.

"You're the expert. I'll go with your judgment," responded the president.

"I'll wait until I feel the time is right. The situation is fluid, and may change from hour to hour or minute to minute. As I said, my men are not going to make a move until I say or unless those guys make a move against the secretary, Consuela, or Alejandro and his nanny," replied Director Yanelli.

Chapter 43

Gonzales and Covert Bravo had crossed the St. Lawrence several times over the past couple of weeks with Ecstasy. On the return trip to the Canadian side, they brought back cocaine and heroin. They were always successful. This time was no different. Fuentes said the Mohawk Police would not be in the area and the Border Patrol would probably not be there either, guaranteeing their success. Fuentes went to the New York side of the reservation this night. Roberts would be on the Canadian side. Remus Escobedo, Fuentes's connection in New York, was there to personally take the shipment of Ecstasy on the New York side. Escobedo wanted Fuentes there. Escobedo was involved with receiving the shipment. He stayed by his vehicle, and never laid eyes on Gonzales.

When the team made the delivery to Fuentes, he said, "You guys must live a charmed life."

"Why do you say that?" asked Gonzales.

"Because there never seems to be any Border Patrol around when you fellas make a crossing. You must have the spirits on your side. You've made a dozen crossings. Our spotters have seen a few Border Patrols. But those Border Patrol don't seem to be in your area. The ones you do encounter, you lose on the islands."

"So what? You tell us not to worry, the Mohawk Police are standing down. When they do, the Border Patrol seems to do the same. As far as us not encountering the Mohawk Police or the Border Patrol, we know those islands better than they do, or at least as well as they do. We study our maps and make practice runs," said Gonzales in self-defense.

"What're you so jumpy about, Gonzales?" Fuentes cut in. "That's not like you. I know I tell you about the Mohawk Police not covering for this or that night. But I tell you that fifty percent of the time. The other fifty percent you must deal with the Border Patrol and the Mohawk Police. You've had some brushes with those guys. But you've always been able to ditch them. I just said you must live charmed lives. You've done good work for me. I know that. I'm very happy you fellas have been able to outwit the Mohawk Police," replied Fuentes. "You made a good run tonight. Now go back with this load of cocaine. I'll see you tomorrow sometime."

"Okay. I'll look for you tomorrow."

As the snowmobiles and sleds were being unloaded and reloaded, Fuentes and Escobedo began talking. Gonzales noticed they were beginning to talk about something. He casually moved closer to them, hoping to hear some of what they said. Neither of them noticed Gonzales and didn't try to hide what they were saying or doing. Gonzales pretended to be adjusting something on his gear. He tried to keep his back to them and his parka hood up around his head. Especially Escobedo. He and Covert Bravo had been waiting for an opportunity like this.

Escobedo said, "Ernesto, our business is booming. We can't keep up with the demand. When do you think the new pill press will be available for production?"

Fuentes answered, "The press will be here tomorrow morning. The building is just about ready. Maybe in a day or two, the new lab will be up and running."

"So maybe two days from now we can expect a double shipment of pills?"

"That's about right. It may take three days at the longest. Don't worry, I'll let you know."

"Before I go, I want you to look at these pictures," said Escobedo.

"Pictures, what pictures?"

"Little Lenny Ortega got them from Flores.

Flores sent them to me. He said they're pictures of men Flores wants all his people to look at. These guys are important to Flores. Both were in on the rescue of the secretary of the Department of Homeland Security for the United States and Consuela Hernández, Flores's girlfriend and the mother of his son. If we see these men, Flores said to capture them and hold them. Flores will decide what to do with them."

"I doubt we'll see them around here; who would come up here?"

Escobedo laughed. "True. I've got their pictures on my cell phone but my phone is out of charge. I'll have to text them to you."

"Okay. But like I said, who would be up here hiding? Especially those guys. I'll look at them after you send the text. And after I get out of a warm shower. I've got to get out of this weather first, before I do anything. I'm freezing my balls off. I remember that those women were rescued by someone. It had to do with the bomb explosion in Chicago," replied Fuentes. The forecasted snow had begun in earnest.

"That's right, that's right. You look at them when you get out of this weather."

Escobedo's trucks had been loaded with pills. He got in on the passenger side of one of them and left for New York City.

Gonzales heard the whole conversation between Roberts and Escobedo. He casually walked over to where Covert Bravo was standing. The snowmobiles were loaded and ready to go. Gonzales said, "Let's get this load back to

Roberts. I'm sure he'll be waiting."

* * *

Roberts was on the Canadian side this time. Gonzales and Covert Bravo delivered the cocaine and heroin to Roberts. He was waiting for their return.

"You fellas made another successful crossing. Good for you. Fuentes has to be happy."

Gonzales said, "He seemed pretty happy that we got another load of Ecstasy pills across and delivered another load of cocaine and heroin back to you."

"He should be happy. You guys have delivered... better than I even thought. I thought you'd be top men. You sure have proven yourselves."

"Yeah, we've been pretty lucky. We haven't had to dodge the Mohawk Police. Like I said, we've been lucky. I doubt this will go on forever. But we aren't afraid of the Mohawk Police. We've done our homework. We know the islands and the escape trails as well as anyone does... maybe better."

"You're probably right about that, Gonzales. Okay, let's get this load of cocaine off your snowmobiles...and get you paid."

"That's the part we like to hear," said Gonzales.

"Which part do you like to hear?" asked Roberts.

"The part about getting paid."

When Gonzales said this, Roberts just smiled.

Chapter 44

After Gonzales and Covert Bravo got back from the night's drug delivery, they went for a walk. When they wanted a private conversation, they always went for a walk. This night called for a walk.

Gonzales said, "Listen up, guys. I don't know if you knew Fuentes and that other fella had a conversation. I think the other guy's name is Escobedo. I heard Fuentes call him by that name." Covert Bravo looked at each other and shrugged their shoulders as if to say, not really. Gonzales explained, "We may be in trouble. I think Escobedo gave Fuentes pictures of me and Chavez."

Chavez said, "How could they get pictures of us? That's impossible."

"Not so fast, Chavez. One of the guys who's been surveilling Syd and Consuela could've gotten a picture with a cell phone. He could have gotten a cell phone picture when we were going or coming from their places. The pictures probably aren't good ones, but good enough for Flores to recognize us. Escobar's phone battery died, but he's going to text them over to Fuentes as soon as it's charged. He said he'd look when he got out of the weather.

"I also heard Fuentes tell Escobedo that the new pill press was coming in tomorrow morning and that the new lab would be working in no more than three days... no longer. When the new lab gets up and running, Fuentes will let Escobedo know so he can get ready to receive more pills to fill the demand. Escobedo said the demand was great and the supply right now hasn't covered it. He's chomping at the bit to satisfy the demand."

"If the pictures Fuentes receives from Escobedo are of Gonzales and me, we've got bigger problems," responded Chavez.

"You're right, Chavez. If the pictures are of us and Fuentes recognizes us, I think we should start carrying our Glocks. When we get back to the house, Ramirez, you go and get them out of the Buick. We may have to fight our way out of here," said Gonzales. Gonzales looked at his watch and said, "I'm calling the president. I still have his number. I think he'd want to know about this development. He said any time, night or day. Well, it's eleven p.m. in DC. That may be late, but this takes precedence."

Gonzales dialed the number and waited for the president to answer. "Hello, Gonzales. It must be very important. If this were not, you wouldn't be bypassing Director Reynolds and calling me at this hour," said the president.

When Gonzales made the call to the president, he and Covert Bravo were still on a trail in the woods and out of sight. "Mr. President, once you hear what I have to say, I think you'll agree it's very important."

"What's on your mind, Gonzales?" asked the president.

Gonzales related the night's events.

"So, you think this Fuentes has pictures of you and Chavez?" said the president.

"Well, this Escobedo fella knew the story behind us. So, I think it's safe to say he has the pictures. I don't know how good the pictures are. They may be too grainy to make an identification," responded Gonzales.

"That makes sense. You've said Fuentes says he knows when the Mohawk Police will be standing down on certain nights. He must be getting his information from someone in or close to the Mohawk Police Department.

I'm certain the leak is on the Canadian side. This has been a very tight operation. No one on our side would have leaked this to anyone. If you and Chavez are recognized, the party's over. You and Covert Bravo may have to get out of there fast. Let me get back to you in, say, one hour. I'll call the others and fill them in. Sit tight," responded President Rivera. The president disconnected the call.

"The president said he'd get back to us...and to sit tight."

They waited for the call. It came exactly one hour later. When the president called back, he had Sydney, Reynolds, Yanelli, and Madden on the speakerphone.

Gonzales filled them in on what he had.

The president said, "We think you should get out of there right now. We don't want a shoot-out there. I'm having the Mohawk Police come to you. They will escort off the reservation. I've made the call to the Mohawk Police Department...so be ready when they get there."

"Yes, sir. We're at the house where we've been quartered. Will be ready when the Mohawk Police arrive." The call disconnected.

"Okay, guys, you heard the man; let's get our stuff and wait for the Mohawk Police."

* * *

Ernesto Fuentes got back to the casino, where he had a suite of rooms. It felt good to be in a warm building again. He took off his parka and hung it up. He wanted a warm shower. He undressed and climbed in the shower and adjusted the water temperature to his liking. He stood in the warm shower and felt his body warm. After a long, hot shower, he got out and toweled himself dry and got dressed. He remembered the pictures Escobedo was planning to send to him. He wondered if Escobedo sent the text. He opened his phone. Sure enough, the text was there. He opened the text, thinking, *I can't believe those guys would be anywhere around here.*

The pictures came up on his phone. He wasn't expecting what he saw. The pictures were grainy, but clear enough to recognize Vince Gonzales and Bob Chavez. It hit him like a sledgehammer. He knew he'd been had. He immediately used his cell phone to call Roberts. "Jimmy, we've got a problem...a big problem."

"What's the matter, Ernesto? What kind of a big problem are you talking about?" asked Roberts.

"I've just looked at pictures of Gonzales and Chavez. Escobedo sent me a text. He wanted me to see them when Gonzales and his guys dropped off the load of marijuana. But his phone was dead. He said he'd text them to me. I just looked at them," answered Fuentes hurriedly.

"So, what's the big deal?" asked Roberts.

"I'll tell you what's the big deal! I'll tell you! These guys aren't who they say they are. That's the big deal!" shouted Fuentes.

"Hold on a minute. What guys are you talking about?"

"Gonzales and Chavez. Probably the others, too," answered Fuentes.

"I don't understand this. You say that Gonzales and Chavez aren't who they say they are. If they aren't, who are they?"

"They are the guys who rescued the secretary of the Department of Homeland Security and Consuela Hernández, Benito Flores's girlfriend. Flores wants these guys. Escobedo said if we see these guys, we should grab them and hold them until we hear from him. Who would think they'd be right in front of us all along? I should have caught on right away. I can't believe I've been duped!" said Fuentes.

"Okay, okay, Fuentes. What do you want me to do?" asked Roberts.

"You take some men. Don't forget, there're five of them. The others must be in on whatever they're doing. Take as many as you can get together. They don't know we know. So, you can surprise them. Don't go with less than five...better seven or more...if you can find that many. When you find them, take them to the pill manufacturing plant. Just capture them and hold them somewhere. Let me know you have them. I'll tell what to do," answered Fuentes.

"Okay. I'm on it. I can't believe it either. I knew those guys were good. But not that good. Who would've thought?" replied Roberts.

Chapter 45

When Gonzales and Covert Bravo got back to the house, Chavez went to get the Glocks, extra ammo. He found the latch under the floor mat in front of the seat. He pulled it and the seat came up, just like the president said. Chavez brought the Glocks and ammo. He left the M16s in the seat of the Buick.

"Let's get our stuff and get out of here," said Gonzales. "Chavez, give everyone a Glock and extra ammo."

Chavez gave everyone a Glock and ammo. Gonzales and the rest of Covert Bravo put the Glocks in the small of their backs.

Just then, Roberts drove up. He pulled up next to Gonzales and said, "Let's take a ride."

"Take a ride? Why? Is there something wrong?"

"Fuentes wants you guys to see his pill-making operation."

Gonzales looked at Covert Bravo: a look of, let's be ready. "Why does he want us to see his pill-making operation?"

"I don't know. He said to take you there. It isn't very far."

Gonzales didn't know what to think of the situation. Had Fuentes recognized him and Chavez? Did Fuentes call Roberts and tell him? "Is this really necessary?"

"Yes, this is necessary. Fuentes wants me to show you the pill lab. The place where he manufactures his pills," answered Roberts, like he was reading a script.

Gonzales saw a couple of men come out of the

house next door. Men he'd seen and met on the New York side of the reservation. They all had MS-13 tattoos identifying them. They just watched Roberts give his speech to Gonzales and Covert Bravo. Gonzales thought the men were there to back up Roberts. He didn't want to start a gunfight around the houses. He knew young children were around. He didn't want to take a chance of one of them getting hit by a stray round. He thought, *We'll get our chance at these guys, if in fact they're here to take us. If not, nothing will come of it. Maybe he really means Fuentes wants us to see his lab. Maybe he didn't recognize us. Maybe this is a break for us.* Gonzales said, "Okay, let's go."

Roberts said, "Get in my SUV. Two of you will have to squeeze in the back seat."

This caused Gonzales to say, "Wait a minute. Why can't I drive my Buick and follow you?"

Roberts answered, "Because Fuentes doesn't want you to drive. He specifically said you were to come with me."

"Okay," responded Gonzales. He thought, *This is not good.*

"Ramirez and Gomez, get in the back seat. Sanchez and Chavez, get in the middle. I ride up front," ordered Gonzales. As soon as everyone was situated, Roberts drove off.

"This is very unusual. Fuentes never lets one of his mules see his drug-making operation. This is an honor. He must have big plans for you guys. You guys must be ready to be moved up in the operation," said Roberts as casually as possible. He didn't want to give himself away.

"We're honored. We know Fuentes is very careful with whom he shares any information...especially this," responded Gonzales.

"I've never known him to show the place to any other mule. I'm shocked. He must really have faith in you fellas," responded Roberts as he drove off to the pill lab.

Roberts drove for about ten or twelve miles, pulled off the main road, and drove up a trail. Gonzales noted the trail was barely visible from the main road. He would never have seen it driving by. Roberts drove as far as he could and said, "We walk from here." He led them down something that could hardly be called a trail to a small building. It was deep in the woods. Gonzales saw the building. It was made of cement block. It was sturdy-looking.

When they got inside, they discovered a laboratory... an Ecstasy lab. It was staffed with Asians and Latinos... men and women.

"Well, here it is. It's not much to look at. It does produce all the Ecstasy you guys and the other mules transport for Fuentes. You may or may not know a lot about Ecstasy," said Roberts.

Before he could go any further, Gonzales interrupted him and said, "We don't know anything about Ecstasy. I told you, we don't use drugs."

"I didn't think so. You're going to get a crash course on how to make Ecstasy. You can see how MDMA is mixed with other substances. How the pill machine spits out an Ecstasy pill."

Roberts shouted to the man in charge, "Hey, Woo, what substance are you mixing with the MDMA?"

Woo said, "Mercury for this batch."

Roberts turned his attention back to Gonzales and Covert Bravo and said, "I wanted to make sure what Woo was mixing before I told you fellas. We use other substances to mix with MDMA. The MDMA is the main ingredient. It can be mixed with formaldehyde and ammonia chloride. I wanted you to see how both substances are pressed together into a pill. MDMA seldom comes to the customer in its purest form. It comes cut with any number of substances, such as ketamine, aspirin, or caffeine. Millions of these pills are made here, and mules like you transport them to the other side of the reservation. Fuentes can't keep up with the demand. He is waiting for another pill press. He wanted to add on to this building; you know, make it bigger. You can see the new construction is almost finished."

Even though Gonzales and Covert Bravo knew about Ecstasy, they went along with Roberts.

"Where is the pill press coming from, Jimmy? How does it get here to the reservation?"

"I can't tell you that. This is all Fuentes told me to tell you. I don't know why he wants you to have this information. But he does. If he wants you to know anything else, he'll tell you himself. Okay. Now you know and have seen. Let's get back to your place.," said Roberts.

As Roberts led Gonzales and Covert Bravo outside, the two men who were watching the conversation in front of the house came out of the woods with four more men. Some of them had MS-13 tattoos showing on their faces. All of them walked toward Roberts and surrounded Gonzales and Covert Bravo. They had their hands in their jacket pockets.

Gonzales asked, "What's going on, Jimmy?"

"I'm not sure. Fuentes told me if I saw you, I'm supposed to hold you until I hear from him." He speed-dialed Fuentes. "Where do you want me to take them? Okay, I understand. Okay, I'll have my men check to see if they are carrying a weapon." After the call was disconnected, Roberts ordered one of his men, "Hey, Franko, frisk these guys."

"Hey, look what I found," said Franko. He found a Glock in the back of each of them.

The fact that Gonzales and Covert Bravo lost their Glocks didn't seem to faze them. Gonzales looked at Covert Bravo with a look of confidence on his face. Covert Bravo subtlety nodded their heads in agreement. They'd been in tougher situations. They had confident faces and showed no fear. Covert Bravo was waiting for Gonzales to make a move.

* * *

As Roberts left the house with Gonzales and Covert Bravo, some of the neighbors saw what took place. Most of the people who lived in that cluster of homes did not like what Fuentes and Roberts were doing with drugs. There were Latinos and Mohawks living there. They saw the other MS-13 men Roberts brought with him. They saw Roberts leave with Gonzales and Covert Bravo. The men Roberts brought followed the SUV Roberts drove away.

Roger Dylan, a Mohawk Indian, saw what took place. Dylan knew Roberts was a drug dealer. He didn't like what a few bad Mohawks did to the Mohawk Indian reputation. He thought it suspicious for Roberts to take Gonzales and Covert Bravo off like he did, especially with other men. The other men looked like they'd be willing to use force if necessary.

Dylan called the Mohawk Reservation Chief of Police, Chief John "Big Bear" Malone. Dylan related to Chief Malone what he'd seen. "We've had suspicions about Roberts for a while. I'll be right there with two men," said Chief Malone.

As soon as Chief Malone arrived at the address he was given, he talked with Dylan. "You're sure about what you saw?" asked Malone.

"I'm as sure as I can be, Chief," answered Dylan.

"The men with Roberts had tattoos...MS-13 tattoos. That's what raised my suspicion."

"Did you see what direction they went?" asked Malone.

"No, they left when I left my house to try to get a good look at what was taking place. I'm sorry," answered Dylan.

"I thought you said you got a good look at what was going on out here."

"I did, Chief. I saw what happened out my window. I had a clear view from there. I just lost them when I came outside. Maybe someone else saw something. Ask around."

Chief Malone interviewed all the people who were home. None of them saw anything. If they did, they were too scared to say.

The pretty Latina girl, Francesca, who'd served Gonzales and Covert Bravo the first time they went to the casino's restaurant on R & R, was there.

She also saw Gonzales and his friends leave with Roberts. She saw the other Latino men watching as Roberts, Gonzales, and his friends leave. When the other Latino men got into a SUV and followed, she thought something was not right. When Chief Malone began asking questions, she thought she should talk to Chief Malone.

"Excuse me, sir. Are you asking about the Latino men who drove away with Chief Roberts?" asked Francesca.

Chief Malone was caught by surprise by this and asked, "What's your name, young lady, and where are you from?"

"My name is Francesca Aguliar."

"Okay, Francesca. Do you know something about this?" asked Malone.

"Well, I saw them talking."

"You mean the Latino men and Roberts?" asked Malone.

"Yes."

"Go on, please."

"Well, I saw Roberts and the Latinos talking. Then they got into a SUV and drove off. While they were talking, I watched as some other Latino men were watching them. They had tattoos on their faces. I don't know much about tattoos, but I think the tattoos are gang-related," said Francesca.

"You mean you saw other Latino men watching Roberts talking to the Latinos?" clarified Malone.

"Yes, they were watching. When Roberts left with the Latino men, these other men got into a SUV and followed," said Francesca.

"Do you know what direction they headed? Or better yet, where they went?" asked Malone.

"They followed that road that goes into the woods."

"Do you know who the Latino men Roberts drove off with are?"

"Not really. I waited on them a month or so ago...and again when they came back for another visit. I remember them because they're like me...only men."

"You mean they're Latino, like you?"

"Yes. I've never seen Latinos come here to gamble. I think they are—or were—military...or something. They kept saying words like *chow* and *chow hall*. Those are military words, aren't they?"

"Yes, those are words people in the military use. Is there anything else you'd like to tell me? Anything you remember about this?" said Malone.

"I can't think of anything right now. I do know Roberts is in the drug business."

"Thank you, Francesca. You've been a big help,"

said Malone.

"You're welcome. I hope those Latinos aren't in trouble with the drug people. They didn't impress me as drug people."

"Well, thank you for coming forward, Francesca. It takes some courage to do what you've done," said Malone.

Malone called his deputies. "I think we just caught a break. Roberts was seen leaving with Gonzales and his men heading west. I think we should concentrate in that area. The road goes into the woods. We're all familiar with it."

* * *

Chief Malone and three deputies took the road west. They stopped when the paved road ended. It had snowed hard that day and was still snowing then. The dirt road they were on was probably not going to support two big Suburban SUVs.

Chief Malone said, "Okay, men, we go on foot from here. We don't really know what to expect. So, we expect the worst and prepare for it...take your side arm and an MP4 with extra ammo...one magazine in the rifle and six more magazines. Let's use our mics. Let's be as quiet as we can be...no noise...or as little as possible. Let's go."

* * *

Gonzales and Covert Bravo were being shoved into the new addition to the old lab building. Since they had their weapons taken from them, Roberts and his men felt safe. Gonzales and Covert Bravo had been disarmed. Roberts and his men were not paying too close attention to them. Gonzales made eye contact with Chavez, which meant, follow me. Chavez gave Gonzales a nod. Gonzales was close to Roberts and made his move. He felt Roberts behind him. As he put one foot on the step, he raised his elbow and swung it backwards. It landed directly on the side of Roberts's head. He went down. Roberts and his men were caught by surprise. Gonzales hollered, "Let's get 'em!"

At the same time, Chavez made a grab for one of the other men, who had a surprised look on his face. The rest of Covert Bravo went into action. Sanchez and Ramirez each took a man. The men were caught off guard. They could hardly respond to the assault made by Gonzales and Covert Bravo. Roberts was just getting up. Gonzales kicked him in the head. He went down again. One of Roberts's men went to his pocket for a weapon. Gonzales saw it and shouted and pointed, "Gun!" Gomez had just dispatched one of the men and was behind the man who went to his pocket. The man had a handgun in his hand. Gomez hit the man in the arm. The man's arm flew up and the gun fired a shot in the air. This gave Gomez time to spin him around and deliver a punch to the man's nose. The nose immediately gushed blood. The man went down. He was the last man to go down.

* * *

Malone and his men began walking slowly and quietly. All they heard was the rustling of the leafless trees and an occasional squirrel running up a tree. The snow was about a foot deep on the ground, which made the going a little hard and slow. Chief Malone said, "Did anyone hear that? That was a gunshot."

"Yeah, I heard it," came a response.

Chief Malone said, "It came from the north...follow me. Be ready."

Chief Malone and his deputies broke through the woods and came upon a group of men laying on the ground. It look like they had been beaten by five men who were still standing. Chief Malone pulled his handgun and fired one shot in the air and hollered, "Don't anyone make a move! Is there is a Vince Gonzales here? I want to know who he is. Who's Gonzales?"

"I'm Vince Gonzales. And who might you be?" answered Gonzales.

"I'm Police Chief Malone for the Mohawk Reservation and these men are my deputies. I heard you may need some assistance. It looks to me you may not have needed us after all," replied Malone.

"We just made our move, Chief. But we could've used a little help. Thank you very much. These fellas are drug people. This one is Chief Jimmy Roberts. The others are his men—and MS-13. You may want to talk with them when you get them back to your office. I think kidnapping and attempted murder would be a good place to start... not to mention drug trafficking, and possibly human trafficking, if you look in that lab over there. I think you should talk with Ernesto Fuentes, too. He's the boss, so to speak, of the drug business here on your reservation," said Gonzales. "I don't know how you found out who we are... or found us way out here. We're thankful."

"To answer your question, I got a call from President Rivera. He told me about your situation. He thought you might need some help. You men were handling the seven of them very well...five up against seven...you men are good! As far as how we found you, a Latina who waited on you and remembered you, Francesca, saw the whole thing. She came and reported what she saw to me. She told me you and the men who are with you were taken by Roberts in his SUV on a road that went west...and that five other men followed you. We knew that road was a dead end. We'd never have thought to look there. She really deserves all the credit.

"Well, now, let's get out of here. My folks will take Roberts and his crew back to my department and book them. Gonzales, I think you and your team can go. When these perps come to trial, I may need your testimony... just be aware of that. I doubt the trial will be soon. I think President Rivera wants you and your team back in Washington as soon as possible."

"Hey, Chief, look what we found," said one of the deputies.

"What have you got?"

The deputy showed five Glock handguns.

"Are these yours, Gonzales?" asked Malone.

"Let me have a look." After looking the Glocks over, Gonzales answered, "Yeah, they're ours. They took them from us." noted Gonzales.

"Here, don't leave them behind," said Chief Malone as he gave Gonzales the Glocks Roberts's men had taken.

"When you need our testimony, we're more than anxious to testify for you, Chief. I know our president wants us back as soon as possible. So, we'll head back now. Thanks for returning our Glocks," replied Gonzales. Gonzales and Covert Bravo were driven back to the house by one of Chief Malone's men after walking back to their SUVs.

"Okay, Chavez, bring the SUV up. We'll get our gear together. When you get it here, it'll be ready for loading. I've got to find Francesca and thank her for telling Chief Malone what happened to us."

When Gonzales and his men got back to the house, there were people milling around. Francesca wasn't among them. He knew where she lived. He walked over and knocked on the door. After a few seconds, the door swung open. Francesca was in front of him. She had that dazzling smile on her face.

Gonzales said, "Thank you, Francesca. When we left with that man, Roberts, I'm not sure how you knew what was happening."

"I wasn't sure. But when I saw those other men follow the SUV you were in, I thought I'd better tell Chief Malone. I guess everything worked out okay...right? I hope I did the right thing."

"You did more than the right thing, young lady. You probably saved our lives," responded Gonzales.

Francesca's smile beamed when she heard what Gonzales said. "I'm very happy it turned out okay for you." She hesitated. "I've got a question for you."

"What is it?" asked Gonzales.

"Are you and the other men some kind of military people? You know...like, soldiers?"

"Well, Francesca, I'm not supposed to tell anyone about us or what we do. But in your case, I'll make an exception," said Gonzales as he watched the look of anticipation appear on her face. "We are soldiers. But that's all I can say. Why do you ask?"

"Well, when you first came here, I don't know if you remember, I waited on you for dinner one night. It may have been your first night here. You kept saying things like *chow* and *chow hall*. I asked you about it then. You said yes, you had been soldiers...but weren't any more. I never said anything about it to anyone until tonight. I asked Chief Malone if those words *chow* and *chow hall* were army terms. He said they were. I knew you weren't drug people. I hate those people. All they do is bring misery to the Mohawks and the small Latino community here. I hope Roberts and the rest of them go to jail for a long time.

You know what? After meeting you, I am considering joining the army. Do you think you could help me?" said Francesca.

"Well, that answers a lot of my questions, Francesca. Except you joining the army. If you're serious about it, to answer your question, yes, I can help you join the army. Right now, my team and I have got to go. Here's one of my cards. If you ever need anything, and I mean anything, you call this number. I'll always answer your call. Especially if it concerns you and the army. The army is always looking for good people. You fit the bill on that point," replied Gonzales.

When Francesca heard this, she was speechless. She threw her arms around him and said, "Thank you." She had to look at the card to see Gonzales's name. She looked up at him and said, "Thank you, Mr. Gonzales; thank you."

"You're welcome. I've got to go now. Remember, call me for any reason. I mean it, really. Don't forget," said Gonzales.

"I won't," replied Francesca, already envisioning herself in her dress blues.

Chapter 46

Chavez drove all night. As they entered Washington, DC, Gonzales called the president. It was five thirty in the morning. "Mr. President."

"Yes, I've been expecting your call. I'm listening, Gonzales."

"We've just entered DC and could be at the White House in half an hour. That is, if you want us there this early," said Gonzales.

"Listen, Gonzales, why don't you and your men go to your place and get some rest. Then clean up and get something to eat. Be here at eleven this morning. It's five thirty right now. When you get here, I'll have the others here."

"That's what I was hoping you'd say, sir," Gonzales said with a smile. "We'll be there at eleven. Thank you, sir."

* * *

Pattie Hayes met Gonzales and Covert Bravo at the White House. She directed them to the Oval Office and offered the usual coffee and Danish. Gonzales looked around to check if anyone was so inclined. Since they were early, Sanchez said, "If it's not too much bother, I'd like some coffee."

"No bother. Do any of you gentlemen want anything?" replied Pattie.

"Coffee would be good," responded Gonzales.

Pattie brought the coffee and served it. She served

Sanchez last. When she did, she gave him the look. When she left them, Gonzales said, "Sanchez, that's the look."

They all began to chuckle.

Shortly, the president came in with Reynolds, Yanelli, and Madden. "It's good to have you back. I'm sorry Secretary Alvarez can't be with us. She has an important meeting with the Department of Homeland Security and FEMA. I talked with Chief Malone this morning. He said he had his men pick up Ernesto Fuentes, Chief Jimmy Roberts, and some other Latino and Mohawk men. He intercepted the new pill press, along with the old press and all the ingredients to make Ecstasy. You men shut down a very big drug operation. Good job."

"Thank you, sir," replied Gonzales. "Did you speak to Chief Malone about the leak that gave Fuentes the stand down information?"

"As a matter of fact, I did. He's very concerned and will look into it," answered the president. He continued, "You know, Gonzales, you and Covert Bravo have delivered a tremendous blow to the drug business coming through the Mohawk Reservation. We can't get complacent, though. It won't stop them from coming. Someone else will take the place of Roberts and the rest of them. At least we've shut them down for a time."

"You're right about the drug business coming back. We do have a good ally in Chief Malone. If our government can talk with him from time to time, we may be able to keep ahead of the drug business on the reservation," replied Gonzales.

The president said, "Let's keep things rolling. Yanelli, what have you heard from Biscotti concerning the surveillance of Sydney, Consuela, and her son and nanny?"

Yanelli answered, "Nothing new. Given what's happened, I think we should start to pick up those men who are surveilling the secretary, Consuela, and her son, and the men in Arizona who've been surveilling Governor Martinez and her family. We know where to find Carlito Dario and Lenny Ortega. It won't be hard to find Remus Escobedo. We don't want them to try a kidnapping. It would be better to pick them up now, sir."

"I think that's the right and prudent thing to do. Why don't you get the ball rolling on that?" replied the president.

"I'll call Biscotti now, sir. So, if you'll excuse me, I'll get things going."

"Go do what you have to do," said the president.

As soon as Yanelli left the room, Gonzales spoke. "Sir, if anything is going down concerning Madam Secretary, Consuela, and her son, I think we should be a part of it. I would like to be a part of it. I think Chavez feels the same way...and I'm sure Sanchez, Ramirez, and Gomez would want to be in on it, too. I'm certain none of us would like to see anything bad happen to the secretary, Consuela, or Governor Martinez and her family."

All the people in the room were aware of the relationship Gonzales had with the secretary, and the relationship between Chavez and Consuela.

Bob Chavez was bursting to say something, and he did. "If there is an operation going down concerning Consuela and Alejandro, I want in on it, sir. If I'm not included, I'll take it upon myself to get included...one way or another."

Yanelli had come back into the room. President Rivera looked around the room, especially at Yanelli, and said to him, "How do you feel about Gonzales and Covert Bravo being assigned to the operation?"

"Gonzales and Covert Bravo are experienced combat vets. When they executed the rescue of the secretary and the governor of Arizona, they proved they can handle anything. What they did on the Mohawk Reservation further proves their ability to act in a pressure situation. So, I'm good with it, sir. I've just thought of a way to get Gonzales and Chavez into the operation," responded Yanelli.

"We're listening," said the president.

"I listened to what Gonzales and Chavez said. I think the best way for Gonzales to get into the operation is for him to pick up the secretary after her meeting and stay with her...take her out to dinner tonight. I'll have my men securing her residence. They'll follow them to and from the restaurant. The security we've set up for her has not stopped them from continuing their surveillance, which leads me to believe they aren't aware that we've made them. I think the best time to pick these guys up is tomorrow morning...Saturday. Gonzales will stay with the secretary all night." Gonzales looked up for a second when he heard what Yanelli said. He thought better of saying anything.

Yanelli kept his explanation going. "Dick Henderson is the man in charge of the secretary's security detail. I think we should make our move when the guys make a shift change...usually around six a.m. We can get the team that's leaving and the relief team at the same time. Gonzales would be inside the secretary's townhouse...just in case," said Yanelli.

"In case of what?" asked the president.

"I don't know...just in case of any unforeseen situation that may arise. What do you think of that, Gonzales?" asked the CIA director.

"I like it. Secretary Alvarez will have triple security. Your two teams outside and me inside...just in case, as you said. I'm good with that, sir," answered Gonzales.

"That settles it, Gonzales. Now how do you get Chavez into Consuela's security?" asked the president.

"Well, sir, Miss Hernández, Consuela, as we know, has been staying with the secretary. She takes her son to a swim club every Saturday morning. This is Friday. I would like to set up the same scenario for Consuela. Since Chavez is back, he can take Consuela back to her place. Chavez stays there. If they guys surveilling Consuela follow form, they'll be ready for a shift change at about the same time as Secretary Alvarez. We'll get both teams at the same time... the one leaving and the relief. Chavez will be inside of Consuela's townhouse...just in case...just like Gonzales. What do you think of that, Chavez?" said Yanelli.

"I think that's a good way to approach the situation, sir," responded Chavez.

"I think Chavez should be with Consuela and her son when they leave for the swimming lesson. He should be in the car. How do you feel about that, Chavez?" asked Yanelli.

"That's exactly where I want to be...just in case," answered Chavez.

"I guess that settles it. Gonzales and Chavez will participate in any operation concerning Sydney and Consuela. Director Yanelli get things rolling," finalized the president.

Yanelli responded to the president, "Yes, sir. I'll call my man in the field, Biscotti, and fill him in on what's been decided.

Chapter 47

Chan K'in Viejo, the elder of the Lacandon village and its leader, called a meeting of all the tribal elders.

He said, "This has got to stop. We can't have these outsiders corrupting our culture any longer. They bring in new tools for farming and new housing. Our traditional huts are being abandoned by the young people. We'll lose our culture. Benito Flores has our people building his boats and buildings for this drug, heroin. We've got to stop this, now. Some of our young people are becoming addicts. The outside is taking our rain forest for lumber. We've been able to avoid them by going deeper into the rain forest. Now the outsiders have got us. Soon, there won't be any rain forests. We'll have no place to go."

Another elder stood up and said, "I agree with you. How do we stop a man like Flores? He has made improvements that young people want. They like the new farm equipment, the safer, more comfortable housing, and some get the addiction to his drugs, which is not a good thing."

"This is all true. There are only six hundred Lacandon who can speak our language. There are about one thousand Lacandons left. Unless we can stop Flores and his kind, we'll lose our culture and all we stand for. I've got an idea. We all know a man that is being kept against his will by Flores. He is a foreigner to me. He says he's a Middle Eastern man and wants to get away. If he doesn't cooperate with Flores, he's afraid Flores will not let him return to his homeland, or worse, turn him in to the United States government. He's done some bad thing. I think he may have something to do with the big explosion that took place in the United States. I'll talk to him. Try to find out some more about him. He may be looking for help to escape from Flores. This group will meet one week from now," said Viejo.

* * *

A few days passed. Viejo walked to where Flores had his heroin in storage. Flores had some of Viejo's Lacandon men working on building more buildings to store heroin. Viejo waited until he saw Baha el Din. He looked to see if Flores was anywhere around. When he was sure Flores was not in the area, he walked over to where el Din was standing.

"How are you?" asked Viejo.

"As good as I can be," answered el Din.

Viejo thought he'd get right to the point and asked, "Would you like to get out of here?"

"Sure, I would. If you were me, you'd want to get out of here, too. But how, is the question?" answered el Din. "Why do you ask?"

"I was just wondering. That's all. We talked about this before. You said you were being held here against your will, if I remember right."

"That's right, I do remember saying something like that. Are you going to tell Flores?"

"No. Nothing like that. I would never tell Flores anything about anything," answered Viejo.

"What's this all about, anyway? Why are you asking me these questions? Why do you care?" responded el Din.

"I thought it strange that Flores would hold you here. I'd like to know why," said Viejo.

"We've had this conversation. I've told you why Flores is keeping me here," snapped el Din.

"I'm just curious," replied Viejo.

"It's more than curiosity. Tell me now. Or I'll tell Flores you're snooping around asking questions," replied el Din.

"Okay. I may be able to help you."

When el Din heard this, he put up his hand and said, "How can you help me?"

"Maybe we can help each other. You know how I feel about Flores, don't you?" replied Viejo.

"Yeah, I remember you saying something like you didn't like him coming here. You don't like him bringing new tools for farming. And new housing. Even though these things are better than what you use now."

"That's right. I don't like those things because they are taking our culture from us. It's not just Flores. It's the lumber people who keep coming and taking our forest. They don't care about us. We want to live independently from the outside world. We keep moving further and further into the forest. Soon, there will be nowhere for us to go."

"What's this got to do with me?" asked el Din.

"Maybe we can help each other."

"What do you mean, we can help each other?"

"I can get you out of here, if you want my help," said Viejo.

El Din was surprised by what Viejo just said. "What do you want from me?"

"I want you to tell the outside authorities were Flores is. I want you to do that. I want Flores out of here. Out of my village," answered Viejo.

"If I take you up on this, I will have to turn myself in to those authorities, won't I," responded el Din.

"Well, you have to pick one or the other. You can stay here with Flores, with no chance of leaving this place. Or you can come with me and take your chances with the Mexican authorities. You pick," replied Viejo.

"It's not that easy. What will they do with me? If I can tell them where this place is, why can't you?" asked el Din.

"If I go to the authorities, Flores will know. I don't want him to know that. He won't know I'm the one who helped you escape," answered Viejo.

"How's that possible? If not you, who'll take me away?" asked el Din.

"You think about this. I'll come back to get your answer," said Viejo as he walked away, leaving el Din standing there.

El Din thought about Viejo's proposition and thought it had some merit. But again, it would mean he'd have to give himself up to the Mexican authorities. He thought the Mexican authorities would turn him over to the Americans; something he didn't want to happen. He knew if the Americans got hold of him, they would get all the information he had about ISIS and probably execute him...or put him in prison for the rest of his life. He simply couldn't let that happen. If he could get the Mexican authorities to guarantee his safety, he might be inclined to try Viejo's offer. How could he get that guarantee? That was the question. If he could get the Mexicans to find a way to get him back to his family, that would be the best-case scenario. He would have to think about it and talk with Viejo again.

Chapter 48

Flores asked Dize Cruz, "Dize, where's el Din?"

"I don't know. I haven't seen him," answered Cruz.

"You go find him and bring him to me," ordered Flores.

Cruz went out into the village looking for el Din. He saw him by his hut talking to Viejo.

Cruz walked up to el Din as he and Viejo were still discussing el Din's possible escape.

"If you go, you cannot use my name. If you do, you will never see your family again. You understand?"

A look of fear crossed El Din's face. He nodded his head yes.

As soon as Viejo saw Cruz coming, he stopped the discussion and walked away. Cruz heard nothing.

Cruz said, "Baha, Flores wants to talk with you."

"Why? What does he want?" asked el Din.

"I don't know. Now let's go. El Gato doesn't like being kept waiting," answered Cruz.

El din had a look of dejection and defeat on his face. He followed Cruz to a waiting Flores.

When Cruz brought el Din to Flores, he asked, "Where did you find him?"

"He was by his hut talking with the tribal elder, Viejo," answered Cruz.

"Is that so! What were you talking about with Viejo?" Flores asked el Din.

"Do I have to tell you everything I do and say?"

"I'm afraid you do, my friend," answered Flores. "Now tell me. If you don't, it won't be good for you or

Viejo. I know how he feels about me...I know. He doesn't like me bringing new things to his village. He thinks I'm corrupting the young people of his village. I know these things. So, are you going to tell me or not?"

El Din thought for a moment before answering. He wasn't sure if Flores knew about the things he and Viejo had been discussing. He had to take a chance and decide. "You know these things already. He told me the same thing. He doesn't like what you're doing to his village... that's all. He complains to me all the time about what you do here...building your boats and bringing in drugs. He's mad that some of the young people are using drugs."

"Are you sure that's all he says?" asked Flores.

"Of course, I'm sure. Why would I lie to you? He tells me these things. I answer, what can I do about it...I'm here against my will," answered el Din.

"You told Viejo that you were here against your will?" asked Flores.

"Yes, I did. What's wrong with that?"

"What did he say about that?" asked Flores.

El Din had to think fast. "He said, what do you want me to do about that...something like that."

Flores burst out laughing when he heard this. "So, you two can't do anything to help each other...what a predicament you two find yourselves in. Too bad. That's funny. He doesn't want me here and wants to escape from me. You can't escape from me. Everyone wants to escape. I'm the only one who escaped. I escaped from the Americans. That's funny. You can go, Baha. Everyone wants to escape. I'm the only one who escaped," he muttered, laughing to himself.

El Din left Flores and Cruz and went back to his hut. He didn't like sitting on the dirt floor. There was no other choice. He'd spent many days and nights in caves in

Afghanistan, not only sitting on the ground but sleeping on it as well. He thought he'd better get used to the ground again.

As night approached and darkness fell, Flores and Cruz were in the house. The house Flores had the Lacandon men build. El Din was just about to go to sleep when someone knocked on his door and came in, startling him. It was Viejo.

"What do you mean coming in here this way? What do you want now?" asked el Din.

"I came to tell you, if you want to get away, the time is now," answered Viejo.

"You mean if I want to get away, I have to leave now?"

"Yes, now!" exclaimed Viejo.

"I don't know what to do!" said el Din.

"I can get you out right now. I've got people ready to take you to the Mexican authorities. I might not have another chance for some time. The time is now...or you wait for I don't know how long. If you want out of here, now's the time. You can stay here forever or take your chances with the Mexican authorities," said Viejo.

If el Din took the opportunity Viejo offered him, he had to think about what he'd say to the Mexican authorities. He knew it was a gamble. He was hoping the Mexican authorities would cut a deal with him. He knew the chances were slim. But he knew it was the only chance. He was desperate to get back to his home.

"Okay, let's go. I'll tell the Mexican authorities where Flores is in exchange for safe passage to my country. I know I'll die here. I'm not sure if the Mexican authorities will turn me over to the Americans. It's worth the chance. At least I'm trying to help myself."

Viejo and el Din left the village in the dark of

night. As they left, Viejo was careful that no one saw them. Once el Din and Viejo were clear of the village, they went deep into the rain forest. They met a man. Viejo said to el Din, "This is the man who'll take you to the Mexican authorities."

"What's his name?" asked el Din.

"His name isn't important. He knows his job. You follow him...do as he says," answered Viejo.

El Din shrugged his shoulders as if to say, what choice do I have? He asked instead, "How far do we have to go?"

"It'll take tonight and tomorrow. We'll find the Mexicans tomorrow afternoon," said the man.

"Let's get going. I want out of here," said el Din.

The man said, "You follow me. I've got two mules. We'll ride them. Can you ride?" asked the man with no name.

El Din answered, "Of course I can ride. Okay? Now, can we get going? Thank you, Viejo," said el Din. Viejo just turned and left el Din standing there.

* * *

Baha el Din had not been on a saddled animal for years. The last time he could remember was in Afghanistan in 2016. Then, he was on a horse. This animal, a mule, was no different. He didn't like it then, and he didn't like now. That night in Afghanistan, he'd spent in a cave. At least they stopped that night so long ago in Afghanistan. Tonight, he'd traveled through most of the night without a break. "Hey, amigo," said el Din.

"What do you want?" asked the man without a name.

"Can we stop for a few minutes? I need to get off

this mule and relax my knee," responded el Din.

"We stop when I say we stop. When the animals get tired, we stop. They rest and we rest...when I say so," said the man with no name.

El Din shrugged his shoulders and stayed on his mule. He thought, *What else can I do?*

When they came to a little stream, the man with no name said, "We stop here for a few hours and rest. When I say we ride...we ride. We still have a long way to go. We've got to get to a certain place at a certain time tomorrow. If we miss the window of time, well, I can't say."

The man with no name pulled two hammocks out of the duffel bag he had and strung them up between the trees. He built a small fire and pull out a spear, which caught el Din's interest. El Din asked, "What's that for? Are you going to use it on me?"

The man with no name didn't bother to answer. He took the spear, went to the edge of the stream and, as silently as possible, waded into it. Standing perfectly still, he raised his spear and waited. His arm moved lightning-fast as he threw the spear. When he pulled the spear back, he had a nice-sized fish on the end of it.

He tried again and came up empty. He tried again. When he'd speared four fish, he cleaned them and put them on the fire to cook. El Din watched and was fascinated.

When the fish were cooked, the no-name man said, "Here, have some fish. You'll need it for the journey. After you eat, you sleep in the hammock for a while."

El Din could do little else but obey. He was hungry. The fish satisfied that hunger. When el Din finished eating, he gratefully climbed into the hammock no name hung for him and fell fast asleep.

A few hours later, the no-name man woke him and said, "Let's go. We have to get moving." Again, el Din did as he was told.

"Okay, amigo, okay, I'm coming," replied el Din.

No name just looked back at him with a blank face. El Din couldn't read it.

No name had the mules saddled and ready to go. They mounted and kept going, no name leading. They rode into the morning dawn. When they came to another stream and clearing, no name said, "We stop here and rest the animals." El Din thought, *To rest the animals?* "What about rest for me?" he replied. No name gave no answer.

No name went through the same ritual as he had earlier that morning. He started a fire, took his spear, and went fishing. When he had four nice-sized fish, he cleaned them and put them on the fire to cook. When the fish were done, no name brought the fish to el Din and said, "You need food. Eat this. When we finish eating, we go. Now eat." Once again, el Din found the fish very satisfying. His hunger was gone.

When they'd finished eating, no name said, "We go now." He saddled the mules.

El Din asked, "How far do we have to go, amigo?"

"Not so far. Maybe when the sun gets over there." No name pointed to a position of noon.

El Din said, "Maybe noon. We've got maybe three more hours."

"Yeah, yeah, we'll be there soon."

Three hours passed. They came to another big clearing. No name said, "This is the place. You get off. You stay here. Someone will come for you."

"What do you mean stay here? You mean stay here alone?" asked el Din.

"Yeah, someone will come for you. I go now." No name took the reins to el Din's mule and began to leave.

El Din said, "You can't just leave me here like

this!" No name kept moving farther and farther away until he disappeared into the rain forest.

Chapter 49

The next morning, Benito Flores asked Dize Cruz, "Have you heard from Lenny Ortega lately? The last time he called he said Gonzales and Chavez hadn't been around for ten days or so."

"No, I haven't. It's been a week since he's called; exactly a week ago. I'll call him now," answered Cruz.

At that moment, Cruz's phone rang. Cruz looked at the ID and said, "Speak of the devil. It's Ortega."

Flores listened as Cruz answered his phone. "Hey, Lenny, Benito and I were just talking about you."

"I hope nothing bad," responded Ortega.

"No, no, nothing like that. We were wondering about Gonzales and Chavez. The last time we talked, you said they hadn't been around for the past two weeks, or something like that. We were just wondering if they're back."

"No, they haven't been around. None of my guys have seen them for the last week. That means it's been about three weeks now," responded Ortega.

"That's about right...three weeks. We think that's very strange, you know? To be gone for that long. Has the security changed? They doubled it the last time you reported to us. Keep a careful watch. Let me know when something changes," replied Cruz.

"You know, Dize, I was talking with Dario. We thought the same thing. It's strange for those guys to be gone for so long. And yes, the security is still the same... doubled," responded Ortega.

Flores motioned for Cruz to stop his conversation

with the gesture of bringing a finger to his lips and whispering *shush*. This caused Cruz to say, "Hang on a minute. Benito wants to talk to me."

Flores said, "Ask him if he can grab the Alvarez woman, Consuela, or my son, without causing a big shoot-out."

Cruz posed the question to Ortega and got, "I doubt it. The security is very good. Especially with Hernández and her son. No one can get near them...especially since Chavez has been gone. With double security, it looks like it'll be impossible. If I tried to make a grab now, I might lose my men. Men you put through college," answered Ortega.

When Flores heard this, he slammed his fist on the table, knocking off everything on it. Flores said to Cruz, "Tell him to look for a weak spot. There's got to be one somewhere."

Cruz relayed the message. Ortega said, "I'll do my best. I can't promise anything."

Flores heard what Ortega said. He grabbed the phone from Cruz and said, "You listen to me. I want my son back. I don't care how many of your men you lose. I want my son back. You look for a place to grab my son... or something may happen to you. Do you understand me?"

Ortega's knees buckled when he heard the threat. He knew Flores was dead serious. "Okay, Mr. Flores, okay. I'll set something up maybe tomorrow or the day after. I think I know a place where I can surprise the security people guarding your son and Hernández. It's a long shot... but worth the try," said Ortega.

Flores had made a threat. Ortega didn't take it lightly.

Flores had a man on the way to DC. This man was a specialist. His specialty was kidnapping. Kidnapping high-profile people. Flores was tired of waiting for Ortega. He wanted action, and had a man was on his way to DC to facilitate the grab of Alejandro.

"That's better; that's what I want to hear. I tell you what I'm going to do for you, Little Lenny. I'm sending a specialist to you. His name is Juan Torres. His specialty is kidnapping. He'll be there tomorrow night. He's on a flight to DC as we speak. I'm tired of waiting. You tell him where you think the best place to kidnap my son is. He'll do the rest. He's bringing four men to help," said Flores.

"Thank you, Mr. Flores. I think having your man here will make a big difference," replied Little Lenny.

Chapter 50

Carlito Dario was to meet Juan Torres at the Ronald Reagan Washington National Airport. Torres was an educated man. He enjoyed the finer things in life. That's the reason he worked for Flores. The money Flores paid him provided him the lifestyle he enjoyed so much. He was polite to everyone.

Dario didn't know Torres by sight. He waited for Torres to deplane at Gate A-6. He was told Torres would find him. Dario felt someone approach him from behind. He turned and came face-to-face with Torres.

Torres had a broad smile on his face and said, "Dario, I'm Juan Torres."

Dario put his hand out to shake hands with Torres. Torres shook it. Dario said, "It's nice to meet you."

There were four men following Torres. "It's nice meeting you, too." In a whisper, Torres said, "These men will help me execute the kidnap."

Torres made the introductions and said, "Let's get going. We've got work to do."

"My SUV is in the parking lot. Once in the vehicle, we'll be able to talk privately," replied Dario.

"Let's go, then, amigo." They all piled into the SUV.

On the way to Dario's place, Dario said, "If you'd like, I can drive you by the place I think we'd have the best chance to grab the kid."

"That's why I'm here. I want to see this place," replied Torres.

Dario drove to the ice cream shop and parked. He

and Torres went in. The others stayed with the SUV.

Torres asked, "What flavor would you like?"

Dario was taken aback. It showed on his face. "What? You like ice cream?"

"Sure, I like ice cream. Who doesn't?"

"I'll have a double scoop of cookie dough," replied Dario. Dario continued in a whisper, "I thought we were here for you to see the place."

Torres said in a whisper, "I want to see how the layout works." Then in his regular tone he said, "I like rocky road." Torres went to the counter and gave the counter girl his order. "I want one cookie dough, two scoops. And two scoops of rocky road, please."

The server asked, "How do you want them...in a cup or a cone?"

Torres looked at Dario for an indication of his preference. "Cone," was Dario's response. Torres said to the waiting counter girl, "Both on waffle cones. Please." Torres paid and left a 20 percent tip.

"Thank you, sir," responded the counter girl.

"You're welcome," replied Torres.

Once they got their ice cream cones, Torres said, "Let's sit for a while and eat our ice cream." They sat down and slurped their ice cream. Torres said, "There's nothing like two scoops of rocky road after a long flight." Torres paid attention to where the restrooms were and the traffic to and from them. He made note of the traffic in and out of the shop. He saw people going down a hall and never returning. He made a trip to the men's room. He looked for and found the rear entrance. Once he was satisfied with what he saw, he said, "Okay, we can go. I've seen enough."

On the way to Dario's place, Torres said to Dario, "It'll be tricky, but doable."

"You really think this place is good to grab the kid?

We don't want a gunfight here. I'm sure you know the kid can't get hurt."

"Don't worry. No one is going to get hurt badly... especially Flores's son. I was told you had some men who're going to help," replied Torres.

"Yes. They're waiting to meet you. They'll be part of the kidnap team. They're waiting at my place."

When Dario and Torres got to Dario's, Fabio Iglesias, Chaco Lugo, Elio Cabrera, and Edwardo Vicario were waiting. Dario said, "I want you to meet Juan Torres." They all shook hands.

Once the formalities were complete, Torres brought in his team. "These are my men. They will help plan and execute the kidnapping. I will use you sparingly...if at all," said Torres.

Iglesias, Cabrera, Lugo, and Vicario let out a sigh of relief. They'd all made it known to Dario they didn't like being involved with kidnapping or using a gun. They told Dario before they met Torres, "We're college educated. We're aren't trained for this kind of operation. We're political scientists. That's what Mr. Flores wants from us."

After getting Torres and his men into a hotel, Dario brought his men back to his place and said, "It looks like you guys are off the hook. Torres may use you as drivers. You won't be in on the actual kidnap."

Cabrera said, "We can drive. We can surveil. But we don't want to use or carry a gun. Thank you."

"We know Hernández is not at her place. We are still watching it. She may show up unexpectedly. We want that information. I think all of you are due to relieve people at the Alvarez and Hernández place, aren't you?" asked Dario.

"We're on our way," answered Iglesias.

Chapter 51

Yanelli called Biscotti. Biscotti answered, "This is Biscotti, Director Yanelli. What can I do for you?"

"I've talked with the president. We've decided that you should start picking up all suspects regarding Secretary Alvarez, Miss Hernández and her son, and those surveilling Governor Martinez and her family, too. By the way, Gonzales and Chavez are in on this operation. Gonzales will go with Dick Henderson. Consuela is going back to her place. Chavez will go with Dave Osborne. He will take Chavez to Consuela's. He'll stay with her until further notice," answered Yanelli.

"I'm not sure about letting those guys in on this operation, sir. I know what they did to rescue the secretary and governor. Are they trained for this?" asked Biscotti.

"I had the same reservations. After giving it some thought, I figured these men are experienced combat vets. Considering what they did to rescue the secretary and governor, I think they can handle anything. Besides, the president ordered this," replied Yanelli.

"When do you want us to start?" asked Biscotti.

"Gonzales and Chavez are on the way to their respective teams. Once they're briefed and in place, you can start immediately. Once you've picked up those guys, I'll send two teams one to pick up Ortega and the other for Dario. I'll send two teams to New York to look for Remus Escobedo," answered Yanelli.

"I'll tell my people to do that. We've been ready to act on this for the last day or so, Director. I think you're right about sending two other teams to pick up Dario and

Ortega and two to look for Escobedo," replied Biscotti.

Biscotti called his team together and related the conversation he had with Yanelli. "Gonzales and Chavez are part of the operation. We've got to wait for them to join the teams they've been assigned to. Gonzales will join Henderson. Chavez will join Osborne. You know what they're supposed to do and where they'll go during the operation. You got that, Henderson and Osborne?"

Henderson and Osborne answered in unison, "Yes, sir," indicating they wouldn't move until Gonzales and Chavez were briefed and were in place.

* * *

"Where does the Alvarez woman live?" Torres asked Dario. "I want to see it for myself. I'll bring one of my men with me."

Dario answered, "I can have Cabrera show you. He's spent many nights there."

That night Cabrera took Torres to a place a few blocks behind Sydney's townhouse. He said, "We'll come from the back. I've checked this out myself. I want you to see the back of the house. The people who are trying to keep the Alvarez woman safe seldom come back here to check things out. They do come occasionally. It's random. There's no set pattern."

Torres asked, "Why don't they come back here?"

"I don't know for sure. As I said, they do come back here. It's random, though. Let me show you the door. It may be the reason. It's steel. The frame is steel. It looks like it's embedded in the brick and concrete wall. There's a window here. It's a little high. I thought I'd use the garbage cans to climb up and use a glass cutter to cut the windowpane, unlock the window and go in that way," answered Cabrera.

Once Torres saw the back door, he motioned for them to leave. He said, "Okay. Let's get out of here. I've seen enough."

The next night, he brought two of his men to see the back door and window. They approached the same way Cabrera had the night before. Torres was stunned with the lack of security for the back entrance.

* * *

Dick Henderson, Joe Bandy, Dave Osborne, and John Evans were the original detail assigned to protect Sydney and Consuela and her son, respectively.

After the meeting with the president was over, Gonzales drove himself and Sydney to meet Henderson. Henderson asked, "Are you good with this, Madam Secretary?"

"Yes, I am. Captain Gonzales is quite capable," answered Sydney.

"I know if you're up for this, Gonzales. We expect to make our move during the shift change. The people watching the secretary get relief at six in the morning. We intend to intercept both teams," noted Henderson. "Gonzales, I think you should go into the secretary's townhouse from the back. You do have a key with you, Madam Secretary?"

"Yes, I do. Why would he have to use the back door?"

"If they are watching and see Gonzales go in the front door, they may get in touch with Dario. Dario may call everything off. It's just a precaution," offered Henderson.

Gonzales and Sydney went to her place for the night. Gonzales got out behind Sydney's home. She gave him the key. He let himself in. Sydney drove to the designated parking place. She went over to CIA Agent Joe Bandy and said, "We'll be ready for anything. I know you and your folks will be, too."

"We don't expect anything to go down tonight. Maybe after midnight or early tomorrow morning. We'll be ready for anything that might occur," replied Bandy.

"See you in the morning."

Once Gonzales and Sydney were in her place, Gonzales said, "Syd, I think you should keep this with you tonight." He handed her a Glock. "You remember how to fire it, don't you? I took you to a range and taught you how to fire this weapon."

"Yes, of course I remember. I went to the range a few times when you were at the Mohawk Reservation. I practiced just like you taught me," answered Sydney. "If I may say so, I'm pretty good."

"Well, you weren't too bad when I took you. You were an easy teach," smiled Gonzales. "I hope you don't have to use it tonight—or anytime."

"Me too."

"Enough of this; we have to set ourselves up for tonight. I know we aren't expecting trouble until early tomorrow morning, but I like to get ready for any contingency. So, here's what we're going to do. I'm going to stay out here in the living room. You'll be in your bedroom. You keep that Glock ready, just in case," said Gonzales.

"Gonzales," said Sydney.

"Yes? I know the tone of your voice when you indicate something's on your mind, Syd."

Sydney walked over to Gonzales and put her arms around him and pulled him close. "Well, I can't tell you how happy I am when I'm with you. It was hard when you were gone. We were confident you'd get yourselves out of any trouble you found yourselves in. I've got to say, though, I was more than a little scared." She began to cry. "I can't bear it!"

"Can't bear what?" asked Gonzales.

"I can't bear it...if you go out again...I can't. I'm sorry, Gonzales. I don't want to see you in harm's way again."

"I don't think this is the time for this discussion, honey. We've got to be ready tonight. If it makes you feel better, I didn't like being away from you, either," replied Gonzales.

Sydney squeezed him more tightly and said, "Your feeling that way does make me feel better. And you're right, this isn't the time for this. I feel much safer now that you're here. I know the CIA is good, but you're much better."

Gonzales and Sydney settled in for the night. "I don't like sleeping alone," remarked Sydney.

"You think I like it?" asked Gonzales. "As soon as this is over, things will get back to normal."

"What do you consider normal, Gonzales?"

"Like it was before I left for the Mohawk Reservation. We'll be together again," answered Gonzales.

"You think that's what it means to be together?"

"I think that's part of it. What does it mean to you, Syd?"

"Well...I like the thought of being together, as you describe. I'm thinking of something more permanent—"

"Did you hear that?" whispered Gonzales.

"Hear what?"

"I heard a noise...there it is again," said Gonzales softly.

"Yes, I did. It came from the back of the house. I'm

sure the CIA checked it. I know the back door is locked. The door is steel, and it's been embedded in the stone wall," said Sydney.

"There it is again. I'm not taking any chances. I'll go check it out. You call Henderson...and be ready," said Gonzales.

As one of Torres's men crept into Sydney's kitchen, the leader said to his partner, "Try to be more careful. Keep your night vision goggles on."

Gonzales approached the back of the house. It was dark. He didn't have night vision goggles. He went through the kitchen toward the back entrance, an entrance that was seldom used. He heard movement to his left. He spun around to encounter the movement. Torres's man was standing right in front of him. Gonzales said, with his Glock pointed right at the man, "Stop right there."

The other Torres man said, "I don't think so." He had stealthily gotten behind Gonzales and put his handgun next to Gonzales's head. He said, "I think you'd better put your gun down."

"If I don't? If you shoot me, the CIA are right out front. There's no escape," responded Gonzales.

Torres's men were not ready for this response.

Sydney had covertly come into the room and saw that two men had engaged Gonzales. She saw the intruders were using night vision goggles. She had one hand filled with a Glock and the other on the light switch. She used the hand over the light switch. She flipped the light switch on and said, "Okay, you two, drop your weapons!"

When the lights came on, the two men immediately screamed in agony. They tried to tear off their night vision goggles.

By that time, Gonzales had moved into action. He threw himself at the men. They stumbled backwards and fell to the floor with Gonzales on top of them.

"Okay, you two. Stay down or you'll never get up again! I mean it!" shouted Sydney.

Torres's men didn't move.

"Gonzales, are you all right?" asked Sydney.

"Yeah, I'm good. Thanks for the help," answered Gonzales.

Sydney had called Henderson and reported someone was in the house. Henderson immediately responded to Sydney's call and was in the house as fast as he and his men could get there. "What do we have here?" asked Henderson.

"We found these two guys inside. They obviously were trying to kidnap the secretary," answered Gonzales.

"How'd they get in?" asked Henderson.

"Right now, I have no idea. Why don't we ask them?" replied Gonzales.

Before Henderson asked that question, he had one of his own. "Who are you? What are your names?"

The two men looked at each other. Neither man said a word.

Henderson asked, "How did you get in here?"

Garcia looked at Lopez and shook his head no.

Henderson said, "You won't show us? We'll find out ourselves. It can't be that tricky."

Sydney said, "There's a back door. It's steel and embedded in the brick framework." There was a glass cutter on the floor and a circle of glass with a suction cup attached to it.

Henderson picked up the glass cutter. "This what you used to cut the hole?"

"Si."

"When did you discover this back entrance?" asked Henderson.

The men said nothing. Henderson looked at both and said, "You can tell me now...or you can tell me later. Which is it going to be?"

Garcia and Lopez looked at each other again and said nothing. This time, Garcia broke the silence. "If we cooperate with you, will we get better treatment?"

"I can't promise you anything right now. What I can say is this; if you answer my questions now, I'll do everything I can to make things easier for the two of you. So, what's it going to be?"

Garcia and Lopez looked at each other. Lopez did not want to give Henderson any information. He feared Flores. Garcia was scared. He feared being locked up forever in the United States.

"Okay. I'll answer your question. You want to know who showed us this entrance? We came here last night with our boss. He showed us the window. He said the door was too secure. We should use the window," volunteered Garcia. Lopez had a stoic look on his face. He offered nothing but was thinking to himself, *Why shouldn't I talk. No one will help me.*

Henderson interrupted and asked, "Who is your boss?"

"Carlito Dario had one of his men show us the back entrance. Juan Torres is our boss on this job. His boss is el Gato. You know who el Gato is, don't you?" this time it was Lopez who volunteered.

"Of course I know who el Gato is...Benito Flores," offered Henderson.

"Si," said Lopez.

* * *

Fabio Iglesias and Chaco Lugo had just pulled up behind

the back door of Sydney's townhouse. Their job was to wait for Garcia and Lopez to bring Sydney out and drive them out of there. They had no idea that Garcia and Lopez had been taken down. They waited.

Two of the CIA agents who had been working the front of the house moved to the back of the house during the hubbub that was taking place inside. They moved on foot to the back door from the sides of the townhouse. They were mic'd up with Henderson, and knew what just went down in the house. They pulled their Glocks and ran to the front and back of the SUV that was parked there. Iglesias and Vicario were waiting in it.

One of the CIA agents went to the passenger side, which was occupied by Iglesias; the other went to the driver's side. They both hollered, "Get out of the vehicle! Get out of the vehicle! Do it now! Keep your hands where I can see them!"

"Okay! Okay! We'll get out! Don't shoot!" exclaimed Iglesias. They had never experienced fear like this. They were educated people. They were political scientists.

Iglesias and Lugo got out of the SUV with their hands in the air. They were greeted by the CIA agent's Glocks. One of the agents shouted, "On your knees! On your knees!" Once Iglesias and Lugo were on their knees, the agent asked, "Is there anyone else?"

He got no response. He shouted again, "Is there anyone else? Is there anyone else?"

Iglesias finally got himself together enough to answer, "No. Not here."

The agent said with his Glock next to Iglesias's head, "What do you mean, not here?"

"There're other people at the Hernández woman's house," answered Iglesias in a weak voice.

"Okay. Let's get these guys out front," the CIA agent said to his partner.

The CIA agents got Iglesias and Lugo into handcuffs and to the front of the house. They met Henderson coming out of the house with Garcia and Lopez.

Henderson asked the agents, "What do we have here?"

"We found these guys at the back door sitting in a SUV. I think they were waiting for their friends to come out with Secretary Alvarez. They gave us information concerning Miss Hernández's house. I asked if there were any more men here. This guy"—he pointed to Iglesias—"said not here. He said there are more at Miss Hernández's house," answered the agent.

"Welcome to the party, you two. Okay, get these guys out of here. We've got two other men in custody. Take them all to Langley," said Henderson. "I'm calling Biscotti to tell him what we've got. He'll be thankful for the information we've recovered about Miss Hernández."

Henderson made the call to Biscotti and related what just transpired. Biscotti said, "Good work. I'll report this to Director Yanelli. He'll have someone meet you at Langley."

As soon as Yanelli got the call, he reported to President Rivera. When he filled the president in on what just took place, the president said, "That's great work, just great work. And no one was injured. The secretary is all right?"

"Sir, the secretary may have saved the day. I'll tell you later, when I make my full report. Right now, I'm calling Osborne and tell him to pick up the men who are in front of Miss Hernández's home," said Yanelli.

President Rivera responded, "You do that. I'm looking forward to hearing your full report."

* * *

"Are you good with this?" asked Osborne.

"Of course I am," answered Chavez.

"Good. We're glad to have you aboard. Thank you," replied Osborne.

"No thanks necessary. I'd be here one way or another. That's what I told the president."

"I know what you told the president. We're glad you're here...just to set things straight. If you know what I mean," said Osborne.

"Yeah. I know where you're coming from. I might feel the same way. I may not want you in my operation either. That's settled. Now, how do we handle things from here on?" responded Chavez.

"Okay. They know you're here. We're being watched as we speak," responded Osborne.

"Yeah, I saw them when I came in. They don't know they've been made, do they?" replied Chavez.

"No, they don't. I just got word from Biscotti. We're supposed to pick up these guys as soon as possible. I'd like you to go in and stay with Miss Hernández. We'll handle things out here," said Osborne.

"If that's the plan, I'm in. When this goes down, I think Consuela will feel better if I'm in there with her. I'll be available for anything you may have for me," replied Chavez.

"Once you're inside and have Miss Hernández secure, I'll be in contact with you through the radio. It's inside. The frequency is set, so just listen up," said Osborne.

"Roger," responded Chavez.

Chavez went into Consuela's townhouse. She was expecting him. After she let him in and closed the door, she jumped into his open arms. She began to quietly sob.

"Now, now, Connie." When she heard him call her Connie, she held him tighter. "Everything is going to be fine, Connie," reassured Chavez. "Where's Alejandro and Lucia?"

After Consuela heard Chavez's reassurance, she caught her breath and got a hold of herself. She answered, "They're in Alejandro's room."

"Okay. Let's get them out and let's all get into your room," ordered Chavez.

She immediately called Lucia and Alejandro out of his room. She said, "Let's go into my room. Bob is here. That's where he wants us."

Once in Consuela's room, Chavez asked, "Do you know where the radio is, Connie?"

"Yes. It's right here on my nightstand."

"Good. Give it to me," said Chavez. He took the radio and turned it on. It crackled into life. The frequency was set. He spoke into it, "I've got everyone secure in Miss Hernández's room."

"Roger that, Chavez. We're about to start the operation. Sit tight," responded Osborne.

Osborne told his men to start the operation. The plan was to box the men in who were watching Consuela's house.

Osborne gave the order. "Move. Now."

When the command was given, a car moved beside the parked car, blocking the car's escape. Two of Osborne's men came up on either side of the car, which was occupied by Cabrera and Vicario. They shouted, "Get out of the car! Get out! Get out! Keep your hands where we can see them...get out of the car now!" Cabrera and Vicario, not being the standard MS-13 thug, turned green with fear. They got out of the car with their hands up.

Osborne met his men, who had Cabrera and Vicario

in tow, in front of Consuela's house. He said, "All right, get these guys to Langley."

Chavez saw what took place and came out of Consuela's house. He said into the radio, "It looks like you've got things in hand, Osborne."

"I think we did pretty good, Chavez," replied Osborne. "I think you should stay with Miss Hernández for a while."

"That's exactly what I was thinking."

Chapter 52

El Din sat on a log he'd found and waited. What else could he do? The no name man said to wait and someone would come and get him.

After a while, he saw someone coming out of the rain forest. He wore a military uniform and was riding a horse and had another one in tow. As the rider got closer, el Din didn't recognize the uniform. The uniformed man rode up beside el Din and said, "Get on this horse. I'll take you to the people you're looking for."

"Where are you taking me?" responded el Din.

"You told someone you wanted to get away from el Gato," answered the uniformed man. "If you do, then get on this horse and follow me."

El Din shook his head in disbelief. What else could he do? He got on the horse. Once he was on the horse, the uniformed man began to walk his horse away. He looked back to see if el Din was following. He was.

After a while, el Din asked, "How much further?"

The uniformed man didn't answer. He kept riding, and el Din kept following.

The uniformed man stopped. El Din pulled alongside of him, but said nothing. El Din thought, if anyone should say something, it should be him.

Finally, the uniformed man said, "We wait here."

After about half an hour, a man came out of the rain forest. He asked, "Are you Baha el Din?"

"I am," answered el Din.

"Okay. Follow me."

El Din asked, "Where are you taking me?"

"Out of here. To see the people you want to see," answered the man.

They rode for about two hours. When they came to a clearing, the man said, "We wait here. They will come."

"How long do we wait?" asked el Din.

The man looked at him and said, "Not long. Maybe fifteen minutes."

About twenty-five minutes passed and another man in a Mexican Army uniform came into the clearing. El Din thought this man was an officer. The man came up and introduced himself. "I am Colonel Nicolas Jimenez. You have information for Mexican authorities?"

"I do have information. I don't know if I should give it to you. I have no way of knowing if you are who you say you are. I need to get out of the rain forest before I say anything. I need proof you're Colonel Nicolas Jimenez."

The colonel thought for a moment. He wanted the information el Din had. The colonel knew el Din knew where Benito el Gato Flores was. He knew el Din wanted out of Mexico and wanted transportation back to his country. "Well, if I must prove who I am, you'll have to come with me."

"Where are you taking me?"

"If you want proof, you'll have to come with me," repeated Colonel Jimenez.

"Will you tell me where you're taking me?" responded el Din.

"Sure, I'll tell you. I'm taking you to people who will verify what I told you."

Again, el Din had little choice, "Okay, let's get going. I want out of here. I want to go to my home in Afghanistan." El Din got on his horse and followed Colonel Jimenez. He thought as he rode out with Colonel Jimenez, *If I get out of here, I'll never volunteer for those bastards again...never, ever.*

It took the colonel an hour to get to the destination. They came to a little Lacandon village. The colonel was met by a general, who asked, "Colonel Jimenez, is this man Baha el Din?"

"Yes."

"Very good," responded the general. He turned to el Din and said, "Welcome to our village. I'm General Antonio Padilla. We've been expecting you. How was your journey? I hope your guides treated you well."

"The journey was fine and the guides, as you call them, got me here. Now, I want you to tell me when I can go back to my country."

"You have information I want," responded the general. "You have to give it to me before I can let you go home."

El Din replied, "If I give you the information, how can I be sure you'll let me go?"

"That does seem to be a problem, doesn't it? You have some time to think about it. You must tell me this evening or I'll leave you here," replied the general.

"You can't just leave me here. We have a deal!" replied el Din.

"Yes, we do have a deal. First, you must tell me exactly where Flores is. Once we establish the exact location of Flores, I'll get you back to your family," responded General Padilla.

El Din knew he had little choice. "Okay. Flores is at a Lacandon village. The village is on the Usumacinta River, which is, as you know, on the border of Mexico and Guatemala. He uses the river to build his semisubmersibles. He's going to use the semisubmersibles to transport the heroin he gets from Afghanistan to the United States."

"We know about the village, the river, and the

semisubmersibles. We didn't know Flores was hiding there," replied General Padilla.

"Now you know where Flores is. I want to go home."

"It isn't that simple, my friend," said General Padilla.

"What do you mean not that simple? The deal was I tell you where Flores is, and you let me go home. That's the deal," said el Din.

"Before I can let you go, I first have to verify Flores is where you say he is. Once we determine that, you can go. I'll personally escort you to transportation that'll take you to your home. Now, if you will excuse me, I must get things going. You'll stay here until I get back. You'll be safe here. These people will take good care of you," said General Padilla as he walked away, leaving el Din sputtering to himself.

* * *

Bob Reynolds's office phone rang. His personal secretary answered. "Director Reynolds's office, may I help you?"

"This is General Padilla calling. Is Director Reynolds in? I've got important information for him."

"Can you hold for a moment, please?" asked the secretary.

"Of course."

"Director Reynolds, you've got a call from a General Padilla. Do you want to take it?"

"Yes, I'll take it," answered Reynolds. The secretary made the necessary hookup.

"General, what can I do for you?"

"I've got information on el Din and Flores. You may be interested."

"Let me have it," responded Reynolds.

"I've got el Din in custody. He told me Flores is hiding out in a Lacandon village on the Usumacinta River at the border of Guatemala. We've known about the Lacandon village. It's where Flores builds his semisubmersibles. We didn't know Flores was hiding there. El Din said he doesn't know the men who brought him out of there. He does know the man who set up his escape. He won't tell me his name. I've got a good idea who it may be. My best guess is the man is Chan K'in Viejo. He's an elder in the Lacandon village. We've known for a long time Viejo is very unhappy with Flores's taking control of his village. El Din won't identify him because if Flores finds out it was Viejo; it will not be good for him. Viejo wants Flores out of his village. Of course, el Din thinks I should let him go... put him on some transportation that will get him back to his home," replied the general.

"Thank you for the call, General. We've been working closely with you on this. I think President Rivera would agree that we should keep el Din under arrest. He has a life sentence to serve here for his cooperation in the nuclear attack in Chicago. He should be sent back to the United States," said Reynolds. "I'll call President Rivera and advise him on the situation."

"I'll hold el Din as long as you say. I agree, he should go back to your country and serve his sentence. Now that we know where Flores is, we can send one of our Special Forces military units to capture him," said the general.

"Let me talk with President Rivera about this. After I've spoken with him, I'll get back to you. Probably within the hour," replied Reynolds.

"I'll be waiting for your call," responded General Padilla.

After disconnecting with General Padilla, Bob Reynolds immediately called President Rivera. He related what General Padilla had said. The president responded, "Tell General Padilla to hold el Din until further notice. Tell him I'll make the necessary arrangements for his transport back to the States. I'll have FBI Director Madden make those arrangements. Since Flores's attempts to kidnap the secretary and Consuela failed, they are safe now. We should let them live normal lives. By that I mean, without any undo safety measures like a heavy CIA presence. Flores will be in a rage for the failure. All his main men in DC have been picked up. The men surveilling the governor and her family have been picked up, too. His leaders are off the streets and will be off the streets for a long time. They are being questioned as we speak. Having said that, I think the general should use Mexican troops to get Flores. When they capture him, I want them to send him to us. As you know, I'm having Covert Bravo and our committee here tomorrow morning. We can discuss the issue with Gonzales then. In fact, I'll call him after our call is done. I'll alert them to what we'll be discussing in tomorrow morning's meeting. It will give them some time to mull it over amongst themselves. If Mexico can capture Flores, that would be perfect. I don't want to send Covert Bravo back to Mexico. You call General Padilla and tell him everything except what I said about Gonzales and our meeting tomorrow morning."

"Will do, sir," replied Reynolds.

Reynolds made the call. So did President Rivera.

Chapter 53

Gonzales and Chavez were back at the farm. Sanchez, Ramirez, and Gomez were there waiting for them to return. They were not part of the operation to take down Flores's people at Sidney's or Consuela's.

"How did it go?" asked Sanchez.

Gonzales answered, "Pretty much as expected."

"So, not exactly as expected," responded Sanchez.

"When does any operation go exactly as expected? Never," said Gonzales. He related the early morning operation.

"So, Secretary Alvarez saved your bacon, Gonzales," chuckled Sanchez.

"You could say that, Sanchez. When she threw the light switch, I was just getting ready to deliver my stuff," said Gonzales with a chuckle of his own. "Okay. She did have a lot to do with bringing those guys down. I admit it. Okay. Since that's settled, I've got some important information from the president. Listen up." Gonzales related his conversation with President Rivera.

"So, he thinks that the secretary and Consuela are out of danger for the time being?" clarified Chavez.

"Yes, that's what the president thinks, right now," replied Gonzales. "I'm inclined to agree with him, too. Chavez, you'll be with Consuela most of the time. When she goes to school, she'll have some security provided by the CIA or the FBI. The president wasn't clear about which agency would take on that responsibility. Now that they know where Flores is, what do you think about having the Mexican military take charge of capturing him?"

Sanchez spoke, "I think it's their country and their problem. Why should we get the job?"

Chavez said in reply, "I agree with the Mexican military taking charge of capturing Flores. They already have el Din. I'm not too sure about the safety of the secretary and Consuela. I agree with the president about their short-term safety. Long-term is a little iffy. It's only a matter of time before Flores gets more people to fill the leadership positions that have been vacated. I'll be with Consuela at night for sure. But I'm not so sure of the other times. The secretary always has a security detail with her. So, I think she's good for short-term and long-term. Of course, if Flores is captured, we won't have to worry about Syd or Consuela."

Chavez then dropped a bomb on Gonzales and Covert Bravo. "I'm going to retire from the army. I've got over twenty years in service—"

This caused Gonzales to interrupt Chavez. "Hold it right there, Chavez. Are you seriously considering retirement?"

"Yes. I am. Like I said, I've done over twenty years. I'm not as quick as I used to be. I'm not old, but I think I'm too old for the Army Rangers. I may be a detriment to any operation. I talked with Consuela about this. This is what we both want. We want to start a life together," said Chavez.

"Well, that makes a big difference," responded Gonzales. "Does anyone else have anything to say?"

Ramirez and Gomez put their hands up. "Okay, let's have it," said Gonzales.

Ramirez spoke. "We don't want to appear ungrateful. But Gomez and I've been talking, too. We would like to be sent back to a Ranger unit. We'd still be available for any Covert Bravo mission you might need us for. We just don't feel right in our present set of circumstances. We feel out of place. Although the farm facility is fantastic, we feel out of place outside of an army barracks."

"Sanchez, what are your plans?" asked Gonzales.

"I'm good here with you, Gonzales. I'll do whatever is asked of me." Sanchez's ears and face turned red after he said this, prompting Gonzales to say, "This doesn't have anything to do with Pattie Hayes, does it, Sanchez?"

"Well, actually, it does."

"Have you talked with her since we've been back?"

"Yeah, I have," said Sanchez with a big smile on his face.

"Okay. I didn't see any of this coming," remarked Gonzales. "We've got a meeting with the president tomorrow morning. He'll get an ear full."

Gonzales and Covert Bravo were at the White House at eight o'clock the next morning. As usual, they were met by Pattie Hayes. She escorted them to the Oval Office. She asked, "Would any of you like coffee, Danish, or fresh-cut fruit?"

Gonzales looked at them. Sanchez raised his hand, followed by the rest of Covert Bravo. "What'll it be?" she asked. Sanchez said, "Coffee and fresh-cut fruit would be great." The rest of Covert Bravo said that would be fine.

"Well, that's different. It's coming right up," responded Pattie. She left and came back with an orderly carrying a tray of coffee and fresh-cut fruit. As she left, she gave Sanchez the look, giving them all a little chuckle and a few eye rolls.

President Rivera came in with his committee: Sydney Alvarez, Reynolds, Yanelli, and Madden. When the president came into the Oval Office, Gonzales and Covert Bravo stood up.

"Please, take your seats and finish your coffee and

fruit," said the president. "We've got a few minutes this morning." When they finished, the president said, "Let's go to the Situation Room."

Once in the Situation Room, the president related to Gonzales and Covert Bravo what he knew. He asked them, "Gonzales, you and Covert Bravo have had a chance to discuss what I related to you yesterday. We'd like your thoughts."

"Mr. President, we've talked about this matter at great length. I've got some news for you," replied Gonzales.

When Gonzales said this, everyone on the committee sat a little straighter in their seats.

"We're listening," responded the president.

"Sir, I can't beat around the bush." Gonzales told the president and his committee the decisions Chavez, Ramirez, and Gomez had made.

Sydney had spoken to the president about Chavez and his wanting to retire from the army. She spoke on behalf of Consuela. Sydney told President Rivera Consuela and Chavez wanted to start a life together. While speaking to the president about Chavez's retirement, she asked the president to find a place for him in the Secret Service.

After Gonzales finished giving his news to the president, the president said, "I wasn't expecting this. So, are you telling me Covert Bravo is disbanding, Gonzales?"

Gonzales answered, "Not really, sir. As I said, Ramirez and Gomez want to go back to a Ranger unit, the Special Troops Battalion. They said if you had any special assignments for Covert Bravo, they'd be willing and ready to answer your call. Sanchez wants to remain here with me at the farm. We'll continue to train there. Chavez is out. I can't say that I blame him. He and Consuela want to start a life together." Gonzales looked at Sydney when he said this. She returned the look.

"If the need is there, we still have a Covert Bravo, minus Chavez. Gonzales, will you be able to move at a moment's notice?" asked the president.

"You can make that happen, sir. If you issue a standing order that Ramirez and Gomez can leave any duty station, no matter where they are, we can and will move that fast, sir," answered Gonzales.

"I see your point, Gonzales. I can do that. Let's get back to the reason for this meeting. Did you discuss anything concerning my feelings about the safety of the secretary and Consuela and the Mexican military going after Flores?" queried President Rivera.

"Yes, we did, sir. We feel pretty much the way you feel. We think Secretary Alvarez and Consuela are safe in the short-term. We agree they should try to get back to normal lives. We feel it's just a matter of time, though, before Flores gets his leaders up and running again. That's if he's not captured first."

"As far as the Mexican military going after Flores, we think he's their problem and they should shoulder that problem. When they catch him, we feel the Mexican government should send him back to us, along with el Din. Flores and el Din have been convicted by our courts and should spend the rest of their lives behind bars," answered Gonzales.

The president said, "Thank you, Gonzales and Covert Bravo, for your service."

President Rivera looked at his committee and asked, "Do any of you have anything to add?" No one said a thing. "All right, this meeting is adjourned. Gonzales, I'll keep in touch with you and Sanchez. I want to extend my best wishes to Chavez and Consuela. Ramirez and Gomez, I want to take this time to wish you men good luck. Gonzales, would you stay for a moment? Chavez, would you wait outside for a moment? When I'm finished talking with Gonzales, I'd like to see you, too."

When everyone was out of the Oval Office, President Rivera said, "How do you feel about Covert Bravo breaking up?"

"As I said, sir, I don't see it as a breakup, sir. Ramirez and Gomez are available at a moment's notice. Chavez will be a big loss. It will very hard to replace him. He doesn't feel like he can cut it anymore. I would disagree with him. He may have lost a step. He more than makes up for it with his experience. He's really good," answered Gonzales. "I think the real reason he's dropping out is Consuela. He's fallen in love with her. I could tell in Mexico he was. I think it's a good move on his part. I wish them nothing but the best. They both deserve it."

"I can see your point. I'm wondering about you," said the president.

"About me, sir! Why would you wonder about me?"

"How long have you been in the army?"

"Twenty years, sir. I enlisted when I was eighteen years old."

"You've been in the field for twenty years. Is that right? By the way, how long have you been a captain?"

"Yes, I've been in the field for twenty years. And a captain for four years. I started as an enlisted man. I remained an enlisted man until the army sent me to the University of Arizona. I completed my degree in Political Science in two and a half years. Then went to Officer Candidate School. I made 2nd Lieutenant. If you don't mind my asking, sir, just what are you getting at?"

"Well, I think you're overdue to make major. I think you should consider getting out of the field."

Gonzales felt like he got hit with a sledgehammer.

"Why would I consider getting out of the field, sir? I love being an Army Ranger. I don't understand. You called me to do special operations for you. You asked me to bring some men, men I trust. I did that and have been successful. Now, you're telling me I should walk away? I don't understand. If that's your position, sir, I will go back to a Ranger unit with Ramirez and Gomez," was Gonzales's response.

"I'm not telling you to do anything. I just thought you may be ready to slow down. I want you here to protect our country from any threat...external or internal. That's why I sent for you. You're right on that point. So, you're declining my offer of getting out of the field?"

"If you put it that way, yes, sir, I am. I still don't understand. But I will not leave the field...at least not right now. I'll know when I should leave field operations."

"Okay, Gonzales. You are still working for me. I thought you'd respond that way. Thank you. Now send in Chavez."

"Thank you, sir," said Gonzales as he left. Suddenly, a thought came to him...Sydney Alvarez. She must have gotten to the president. At first, he was a little upset about her getting involved in his military affairs. Then he began to chuckle to himself.

He saw Chavez and said, "You're next," and walked away.

Chavez knew Gonzales was upset. He walked back in to see the president.

"Sit down, Chavez, and relax."

After Chavez was seated, the president said, "I just had a thought during our meeting. Would you consider going into the Secret Service and being on my security detail? I'd keep you here in Washington permanently. You'd never have to travel with me."

Chavez answered, "Mr. President, I don't know

what to say. It would be my honor to serve you and the country in that way."

"So, your answer is yes?"

"Yes, sir. My answer is yes!" exclaimed Chavez.

Chapter 54

Benito Flores wanted to speak with Baha el Din. He went looking for him. He looked in the Lacandon village and went to el Din's hut. He was nowhere to be found. Flores went back to his house and saw Dize Cruz. He asked Cruz, "Dize, I'm looking for el Din. I can't find him. Have you seen him?"

"No, Benito. Did you look in the village or his hut?" responded Cruz.

"Yeah, I looked for him there. He's not in either place," replied Flores.

"That's strange. He should be around here somewhere," said Cruz. "I'll go ask some of the people in the village. If anyone knows, it should be Viejo."

"You do that. Let me know," replied Flores.

Cruz saw Viejo and walked up to him and asked, "Have you seen el Din?"

Viejo knew this was coming. He had practiced his lie. When he told Cruz the lie, he looked him right in the eye. "The last time I saw him was the other day...or was it yesterday, when you saw us talking?" answered Viejo.

Cruz stared right back at Viejo. "If you see him, tell him Flores wants to talk to him. Okay?" Cruz bought Viejo's story.

"Sure, if I see him, I'll tell him."

Cruz went back and told Flores what he'd found out.

"He's got to be here somewhere, Dize. He'll turn up. Why don't you call Juan Torres? See if he's been able to hook up with Dario. He's been in DC for two days. Dario said he was going to show him the place. Torres should have had a chance to look it over by now."

Cruz punched in Torres's phone number and waited for him to answer. He answered as though he was in a frenzy. "Hello, Dize."

Cruz caught the strain in Torres's voice right away. "Okay. Slow down, slow down, Juan. Tell me what's wrong."

Torres related how the attempts to kidnap the secretary and Consuela had failed. He was still in DC and hiding out in a hotel.

"Hold tight, Juan. I'm going to tell Flores. Don't worry," responded Cruz.

Cruz related what Torres had told him to Flores. Flores sat for a few moments before he said, "You tell Torres not to worry. You tell him to come back to Mexico. Tell him I'm not angry. Tell him I've got another idea."

* * *

Torres was on a flight to Mexico. His flight landed at Mexico City International Airport. He was met by one of Flores's men, who drove him to a place as close as he could to the Lacandon village. From there, he and the man used an ATV the rest of the way.

Upon their arrival to the village, Cruz was waiting for him. He asked, "How was your flight and trip down to the village?"

"Uneventful, but good. The first-class section is really nice," answered Torres.

"Good. Flores wants to see you right away. He's waiting. I'll take you to see him."

"Okay," said Torres.

Flores didn't waste any time. "Tell me exactly what

happened."

Torres told Flores the whole story. "I'm sorry, Mr. Flores. The CIA—or whoever they were—made a move on my men before mine could make theirs. It was like they had inside information."

Flores said, "Don't worry. This is what I want you to do. Okay?" He put his arm around Torres's shoulder. "Don't worry about what happened. I'll have you make another attempt."

"Sure, Mr. Flores."

"You may go."

* * *

The next day, Flores asked Cruz, "Has el Din showed up?"

"No. I've been keeping my eye out for him. He's not around. No one has seen him. I hate to say this, but I think he may have made his escape."

Chapter 55

When Chavez got out of the meeting, Gonzales was waiting. They went back to the farm. On the way, they discussed what the president said to them.

"Are you kidding me?" said Gonzales.

"Yeah, he said he'd get me a job with the Secret Service. I'd be on his detail all the time and never have to go out of town. When I tell Consuela, she'll be so happy," responded Chavez.

"That's great, Chavez, just great." He told Chavez the conversation he'd had with the president.

"You turned down the president on his offer? It doesn't surprise me, Gonzales," said Chavez.

"Yeah, I told him I'd know when it was time for me to get out. Just like you."

When Gonzales and Chavez got back to the farm, they had to say goodbye to Ramirez and Gomez. "We've been through so much stuff. I almost can't believe we're parting and going our separate ways," was all Chavez could think of to say to Ramirez and Gomez.

"This isn't goodbye, Chavez. We'll be in touch," said Ramirez.

"You're a very lucky guy. You're about to start a new life with a very wonderful woman. Go for it. You deserve all the happiness this world has to offer. We hope all of your dreams come true," offered Gomez.

"When are you and Consuela going to get married?" asked Ramirez.

"We've never talked about marriage. But now that you mention it...it sounds pretty good to me," answered

Chavez.

"I'm sure you two will figure it out. We've got to catch a transport and get to our new duty station," replied Gomez.

After saying their so longs and goodbyes, Ramirez and Gomez were gone, leaving Gonzales, Sanchez, and Chavez looking at each other.

Gonzales thought about what President Rivera said to him and Sydney's possible involvement in it.

Gonzales said, "Well, I'm sure we'll see those guys sooner or later. I hope it won't be on a deployment from the president. Chavez, you'd better get over to Consuela's and tell her the news."

"Thanks, Gonzales. I was just about to get going over to her place. I feel like a little kid...almost giddy. I can't believe I just said that...giddy. I don't think I've ever felt giddy in my life! Especially after twenty-plus years in the Army Rangers. I can't wait to tell Consuela the news," said Chavez.

Chavez rushed to Consuela's. He noticed there wasn't any security detail on duty. She greeted him as he came up the steps. "Oh, Bob, I'm so happy to see you! I didn't expect to see you until tonight."

"Let's go in. I've got something to tell you," replied Chavez.

Consuela immediately said, "Are you going away again? That's what you want to tell me...isn't it. You're going someplace...aren't you? Okay. Let's go in and you can tell me," responded Consuela.

Chavez couldn't believe what he was hearing. He kept his cool and went in. Once in Consuela's townhouse, he said, "Consuela, please sit down."

Consuela gave him a very hurt and angry look. She did sit down and said, "You want me sitting so you can tell me you're going someplace dangerous. Aren't you?"

Chavez thought he'd get right to the heart of it. He said, "I just left a meeting with the president. Gonzales and the rest of us were there."

"So, I'm right. You're going away," responded Consuela.

"I'm not going anywhere, Connie. I'm staying right here...in DC. I told Gonzales and the rest of the guys I was going to apply for my retirement as soon as possible. This morning at our meeting in the White House, Gonzales told the president my decision to leave the army—"

As Chavez spoke, Consuela's eyes filled with tears. She interrupted and asked, "What did they say?"

"If you give me a chance, I'll tell you, Connie. After the meeting was adjourned, the president asked me and Gonzales to stay for a minute. I couldn't imagine what he wanted from me. He asked me if I'd be interested in joining the Secret Service. He said he'd keep me here in DC permanently."

Consuela couldn't contain herself. She asked, "What did you say?"

"At first, I was overwhelmed. But I said something like, yes, I'd like that very much."

Consuela suddenly remembered the talk she'd had with Sydney Alvarez the other night. She smiled as she replied, "That's wonderful, Bob, just wonderful! That means you'll be with me all the time."

"If you'll have me, I'll be here all the time," responded Chavez.

"You know I want you here. How could you think anything else?"

Chavez got down on one knee. "Consuela, will you marry me?"

When Consuela heard Chavez's proposal of

marriage, she was overwhelmed with emotion. She burst into tears of joy. "Yes, yes, I will marry you, Roberto. Yes. I can't believe it! I'm so excited."

"That's what I wanted to hear from you. Now, we can start our life together," responded Chavez.

Consuela came out of her seat and jumped into Chavez's arms. "That's what I want, Bob, to live my life with you," replied Consuela with tears in her eyes. Tears of joy.

* * *

After Chavez left to tell Consuela the news, Gonzales called Sydney. "Hey, Syd, how are you?"

"I'm well, Gonzales. How're you?"

"I guess you could say I'm fine," answered Gonzales.

"What's with you could *say* I'm fine? You either are fine or not fine."

"I should say better than fine. I know you had a busy day today. I thought, if it suits you, we'd go out to dinner tonight. What do you say?"

"I can't think of anything better. How about swinging by about five thirty. We can have a glass of wine before we go out for dinner," answered Sydney.

"Five thirty it is. I won't be late," responded Gonzales.

"You'd better not be late, Gonzales. I don't like being kept waiting," replied Sydney as coyly as she could. She heard Gonzales try to drown out a chuckle.

* * *

Sydney was waiting for Gonzales at the door. She jumped into his arms as soon as he closed the door behind him.

They kissed tenderly. She clung to him desperately. He did the same. A few moments passed before they came apart ever so slightly but still held each other lightly, neither one wanting to give up the feeling they each had for the other.

Sydney had a nice bottle of Merlot chilling at sixty degrees. As she opened the bottle of Duckhorn Vineyards Merlot she said, "This Merlot is from Napa Valley. There's a lot of special complexity to it."

"What gives it its special complexity?" asked Gonzales.

"It has fleshy and juicy layers of Bing cherries, raspberries, and plum. It hints of blueberry, cedar, vanilla, and clove highlighted by an elegant tannin—"

Before Sydney could finish her description of the Merlot, Gonzales interrupted, "Hold it, honey. I wasn't looking for a google explanation. Let me try it."

"Sure thing." Sydney had just finished opening the bottle and poured two wine glasses appropriately full.

Gonzales first sniffed the wine. Then he took a sip and swished it around in his mouth. Then swallowed it. "This is a very fine wine. It's the best you've offered me by far. You've been holding out on me...haven't you? What else have you been holding back?"

"Well, I can't reveal everything I know, can I? I've got to save something," said Sydney.

"I can't believe you're so good to me. How lucky could I be? This lucky...I guess," responded Gonzales.

They sat and drank the wonderful Merlot in quiet.

Sydney broke the ice. "Where do you want to go for dinner?"

"How about our favorite spaghetti and pizza shop? We haven't been there for a while. It isn't fancy, like some of the places you've taken me...but the food is really good," answered Gonzales, noting, "I see you have security outside."

"They're my regular security...nothing extraordinary. They'll follow us and either stay outside or come inside and have dinner away from our table," responded Sydney.

* * *

The seating hostess greeted them cordially and said, "It's very nice to see you, Madam Secretary. I've got a table in the back. You'll have more privacy there."

"Well, that would be very nice. And very thoughtful of you. Thank you," said Sydney.

"It's my pleasure. Follow me."

They ordered a nice Chianti before dinner. Sydney said to the waiter, "Would you please give us some time before we place our order?"

"Yes, of course. Take all the time you need, Madam Secretary."

Sydney and Gonzales sat there staring at each other for a few minutes. This time, Gonzales broke the ice. "I wonder what the staff in the restaurants we go to think and say about the Latino guy you bring with you, Syd?"

"I think they say, I wonder where she got that good-looking Army Ranger." Gonzales always dressed in his dress uniform when he accompanied Sydney anywhere.

"That's what you think they say about me? I think they say, how could a Latino army grunt get close to the secretary of the Department of Homeland Security? The most generous, caring, and beautiful woman in the world."

When Gonzales said that, Sydney blushed.

"Gonzales, stop being foolish...but I love what you just said." Sydney changed the subject. "How did the after-meeting go with the president this morning?"

"I'm not being foolish, Sydney Alvarez...not in the least. As far as the meeting with the president went, you know, it went okay," answered Gonzales.

"What was said?"

Gonzales was starting to get a kick out of this. He knew now Sydney had put the president up to what he had said. "Oh, the usual stuff. Why do you ask?"

"I was just curious...I guess."

"Since you're just curious, I'll tell you. He asked me if I'd consider leaving the field. He didn't say what I'd be doing if I did. I've been in the army for twenty years. This year marks the twentieth. He asked how long I've been captain. I told him four years. He said I was due for a bump in grade. That would make me a major. A field grade rank...as opposed to a company grade, which is what I am now...just in case you didn't know that."

"Well, what did you say?" asked Sydney with a hint of anxiousness in her voice. It didn't go undetected by Gonzales.

"I told him I wasn't interested in leaving the field. The reason I am here is because he requested me. He asked me to recommend a few other Rangers to join me. I did that. We have proved to be very effective. This came out of the blue. You wouldn't know anything about it...would you, Madam Secretary?"

Sydney turned away from Gonzales and looked down. Gonzales knew then that she had interceded for him.

"It's okay, honey. It's okay...really. I know we've talked about this...at least a little," said Gonzales.

Sydney looked up with tears in her eyes and said, "Yes. Of course, I spoke to the president. I did talk with the president about you getting out of the field. You deserve to make major. You've served your country a thousand times more than anyone I know. You deserve a break, Gonzales...

and so do I. I don't want you to be deployed to a dangerous place. I've told you that."

"Yes, you have. We talked about this very thing. I understand your concern."

When Gonzales said this, Sydney let out an *oomph*. "Do you! Do you? The Mohawk Indian Reservation was supposed to be a few days, with no danger. Look what happened. A few days turned into a few weeks. And you had to fight for your life to get out of there!" exclaimed Sydney.

"Hold up a minute, Syd. Hold up. You're right about the Mohawk Reservation operation. That's why I've been giving some thought to this. Even though I told the president I wasn't ready to leave the field, I've been thinking about our conversations. How I felt being away from you. If I decided to leave the army and take retirement, I'd like to know what I'd be doing. I don't think I could stand being cooped up in an office for eight hours a day...or even working nine to five. That's what bothers me...even scares me more than a little," admitted Gonzales.

Sydney was taken by surprise with this. She hadn't thought Gonzales would consider taking retirement. "Are you really thinking about taking retirement?"

"Yes, I am. Like I said, I've given some thought about what we've discussed. I just don't know what I'd do with myself, if you know what I mean. I don't have much money saved. My retirement will be fifty percent of my current pay, which is approximately six thousand seven hundred dollars a month. I'd get fifty percent of that. So, I'm looking at about thirty-five hundred dollars a month. That's not enough for one person to live on...at least in DC."

"Do you know anything about the defense industry? You might be able to get a job with one of those companies," suggested Sydney.

"I don't know anything about that. I don't know what I could do for a company like that anyway," replied Gonzales.

"Let me do some investigating, okay?"

"Okay. But I don't like depending on anyone for help. I've lived my whole life that way. All I know is the army. It's been my life. Then I met you..."

"I know exactly what kind of man you are, Gonzales...exactly. Your self-reliance is one of your best attributes. When I'm with you—and I know I've said this in the past—I never feel more secure. Let me see what company may need someone with your skills. We'll figure it out, okay?"

"Of course, we'll figure it out," said Gonzales. "Here comes our server. What are you thinking about ordering?"

"Last time we were here, I had pizza. I think this time, I'll try the eggplant parmesan with a side of linguine in a marinara sauce. I'd like the wedding soup, too."

The waiter came for their order. Sydney gave the server the order. The server asked, "And what can we bring for you, Captain?"

"I'll have the same, thank you. And by the way, we hope you make a lot of money tonight and that all of your dreams come true."

When the waiter heard this from Gonzales, he was a little taken aback. He managed to say with a beaming smile on his face, "Thank you, I hope so, too...on both counts. I hope your dreams come true, too, Captain. Thank you again."

Gonzales always looked for the name of the server. As he walked away, Gonzales said, "Thank you, Emile. I think my dreams are about to come true."

"That was very thoughtful of you, Gonzales...very thoughtful. What dreams are you talking about?" asked Sydney.

"The dreams we've just been discussing," answered Gonzales.

"You never cease to amaze me, Gonzales," remarked Sydney. Her face was radiant.

Emile brought their dinners. They ate and made small talk. After dinner, Gonzales said, "That was really good eggplant parm. But I can't wait to get back to your place."

"What can't you wait for?" asked Sydney coyly and with the same glow on her face.

"I guess you'll have to wait and see, won't you," replied Gonzales.

* * *

Sanchez was still shy about calling Pattie Hayes. He screwed up his courage and made the call.

When he heard Pattie answer and say hello, Sanchez's knees buckled.

"Hello, Pattie. This is Sanchez."

"I know who's calling me, Sanchez. I do have caller ID. What can I do for you?"

"Well, to start with, you can say yes to my buying you dinner tonight," answered Sanchez with a certain sound of authority.

"Of course, you can buy me dinner."

"I'll be by at five thirty. Be ready," said Sanchez with more authority.

"I'll be ready."

Pattie's doorbell rang at exactly five thirty. When she opened the door, Sanchez was standing there with a bouquet. He stretched his arm out and said, "These are for you."

Pattie was not easily caught off guard, but she was thoroughly surprised at the man she had privately nicknamed Shy Sanchez. She managed to regain some semblance of composure. "Sanchez, thank you. They're lovely."

"You're very welcome. Let's go back to the Mexican place. You know, the mom-and-pop place where we went the first time. Do you remember?" said Sanchez confidently.

"Sure. Let's get going."

Sanchez followed Pattie's directions to the restaurant. The daughter of the owner was the seating hostess. "If it's not a problem and one is available, we'd like a quiet table, or better yet, a booth," said Sanchez.

Maria said, "Yes, of course; I've got just the booth." She directed them to a private booth. It was just off the main dining area.

"Thank you," said Sanchez in a very confident but pleasant tone of voice.

"My, you've acquired some bravado, Sanchez," remarked Pattie.

"I've always had bravado, Pattie. I just never showed you any. I've been in some hard places in my life. Sometimes, I was scared out of my skin. My bravado always showed up at those times. I think my bravado has shown up tonight. You know, I was intimidated by you— or a lady like you—but no more. My bravado, as you say, is here...just in time."

Pattie listened intently as Sanchez spoke. "I always knew you had it...always knew it. I knew it would show up. I was just waiting for it. Let's order dinner."

They looked over the menus. Pattie said, "I liked

the Enfrijoladas the last time we were here. I'm going to order them again."

"I like them, too. They were almost as good as my mother's. Let's go for it," said Sanchez.

"Okay."

The server took their order. They sat together and made small talk. Sanchez asked, "Have you heard about Covert Bravo?"

"Not really. Why don't you tell me?"

"Ramirez and Gomez are going to an Army Ranger unit, and Chavez is applying for retirement...leaving me and Gonzales.

"Why are you staying?"

"I thought that was self-evident, Pattie," said Sanchez with a broad smile on his face.

Pattie Hayes was not one to blush. However, she turned beet red. She was smiling, too. She said, "I wasn't so sure...until now, Sanchez. But I'm very happy about you staying. Maybe you can work on going to college. You said you thought about that, didn't you?"

"That's exactly what I was thinking," answered Sanchez.

Dinner came. They made more small talk as they enjoyed the Enfrijoladas.

After dinner, Sanchez was able to get back to Pattie's place without help. He remarked, "How's that?" as he drove up to Pattie's door.

"Thanks for a wonderful dinner. Would you like to come in for a cup of coffee?"

"I thought you'd never ask."

"Sanchez, you're something else."

With that said, Pattie took Sanchez's hand and led him into her home.

Chapter 56

Benito Flores and Dize Cruz were sitting in Flores's house in the Lacandon village the evening el Din turned up missing. "You think el Din made a break for it, Dize?" asked Flores.

"We've looked everywhere. He isn't here, Benito... he just isn't here. I don't know what else to think. What do you think happened to him?"

"I don't know. If his countrymen find out he's no longer here, I do know the shipments of heroin will stop. My plan will be worthless."

"Come on, Benito. You are one of the biggest drug lords in the world. You've got more money than some countries. You've never let a little setback get in your way...at least, not as long as I've known you. He may turn up, too. We don't know exactly where he is."

"You may be right, Dize. No one in the village is talking. If anyone knows anything, it's Viejo. He says he doesn't know anything. If I lean on him, most of the people here will back him up. Most of them are very loyal to the elders of the village...like Viejo. They'll stop working for me. But I think he's gone. Unless he has help, he won't get out of the rain forest. He'd never leave without help. Someone in the village helped him. Viejo denied helping el Din. He's the only logical choice. He knows something. But if we get tough with him, the other elders will turn the village against me. So, I'm what people say, between a rock and a hard place," replied Flores.

"Where would he go? Even if he gets out of the rain forest, who'll help him? He can't go to the Mexican government...can he? If he goes to one of your politicians, he won't get far. You'll know about it. I don't see him going anywhere," said Cruz.

"If he did get help and does manage to get out of the rain forest and gets to a government official, he may try to make a deal with that official...even one I own. They're all for sale. He has wealth behind him in Afghanistan. If he contacts someone who wants him back and has access to large sums of money, he may be able to make a deal. The people in Afghanistan don't want him to give up what he knows about ISIS. It's possible. That's all I'm saying."

"You know, Benito, I never thought of that. He'd have to find someone who could get him in touch with a powerful person in the Mexican government...someone with connections. Someone who can set up communications for him...maybe someone in the military, or a governor of one of the states. You own most of the military officers and governors already. One of them may try to make a little fortune...on the side," responded Cruz.

"Dize, anything is possible. We should get ready to get out of here. We should be prepared to cross the Usumacinta River and get into Guatemala on a moment's notice," said Flores.

"Why do you think that?" asked Cruz.

"I don't know. I just have a gut feeling."

* * *

"So, you're going to send me back to the Americans, General? What if I told you I could make you a very rich man," said el Din.

"I'm already a very rich man...but I'm listening," answered General Padilla.

"If you can get me a way to communicate with my

people in Afghanistan, you'll be rewarded handsomely... my guess is, it'll be in the millions," replied el Din.

"There's not enough money in the world that would make me a traitor to my country. You come to my country with nuclear bombs and you send them to the United States. Then one of your people detonates one of the bombs in Chicago. Do you think I'm a fool? You must have thought it. Otherwise, you would not make this proposal. You, my friend, are going back to the Americans."

Having heard what General Padilla said, el Din lowered his head in defeat.

Colonel Nicolas Jimenez had brought el Din out of the rain forest to General Padilla. He was standing outside the door when el Din made his proposal to Padilla. He heard every word. Padilla called for him, "Colonel Jimenez, come and take the prisoner back to the village. He's scared to death of the rain forest. He won't try to escape."

"Yes, sir. He won't try anything. He doesn't even know where we are."

On the way back to the village, Colonel Jimenez said, "El Din, I heard what you said to General Padilla... and his response to you. What if someone else set you up to communicate with your friends in Afghanistan? What would you do for them?"

El Din was surprised by what Jimenez just said. "I tell you this. Anyone who can get me back to my family in Afghanistan will be paid very, very well. I guarantee it," answered el Din.

"What do you mean paid very, very well? How much money is involved?"

El Din started to think he may have a chance of escaping. "How much would such a person need to do this for me?"

Jimenez had been thinking about how much money

he'd want to do this for el Din. "How does fifty million dollars sound?"

El Din didn't say anything for a few moments. He mulled it over in his head. He knew the money would not be a problem. Finally, he said, "That's doable...not a problem. Who would take a chance like that? You know... it wouldn't go so good for that person if he got caught."

It was Jimenez's turn to be thoughtful. He thought it over for a few minutes. "What if it was me?"

"You would take a chance like that for me?"

"Not for you...for me. I'll have a cell phone ready after dark tomorrow night. Be ready, el Din."

"I'll be ready, don't worry about that. I want out of here...as soon as possible. I've got a few questions, Colonel."

Jimenez said, "Let's hear it."

"How are you going to get me out of here? How do you want to handle the money exchange? What means of transportation will I have to get back to Afghanistan? How do I know you'll keep your side of the bargain? If you get the money, how do I know you have me set up to go? Please tell me."

"Well, these are very good questions. I think we take it one step at a time. Let me bring the cell phone and you make the call. I understand your misgivings. I'll handle everything. It may take a week or so. The cell phone will be here tomorrow. I've got to go into the city on army business. I'll bring it back with me."

"If you can set up the communication, we've got a deal. I think that's what the Americans say."

El Din thought about this overnight and the rest of the next day. He thought his chances of pulling it off were 50 percent. It was better than 100 percent going back to the Americans, and jail. He knew the money was not a problem.

* * *

That night, Colonel Jimenez went looking for el Din. He found him sleeping in the quarters. "El Din, wake up, wake up. Let's go, man."

"What is it? Oh, it's you, Colonel. I've been waiting for you. I must have fallen asleep. I'm sorry. Do you have the phone?"

"Yes, I do...here it is. You make your call. I'm staying right here. I'll listen to every word. If you say anything that isn't about your getting back to Afghanistan and the money, I'll shoot you here on the spot. You got that?"

El Din was shaken by what Jimenez said. "Are you threatening me? Or are you protecting yourself? Why would I jeopardize my chance to get out of here?"

"I'm just saying. You get the money...that's all. Okay?" answered Jimenez.

"I'm about to make you a very rich man. Now give me the phone...give it to me. I hope it's fully charged. I'll put the phone on speaker. You can hear every word."

Jimenez handed the phone to el Din. "It's fully charged. You can call anywhere in the world with this phone. Now make your call."

"I have not called this phone for a long time. I hope it's still in service," said el Din.

El Din punched the number into the phone and held his breath. "It's ringing, it's ringing...Allah be praised."

The phone rang and rang. Finally, el Din disconnected the call. His heart sank. He looked at Jimenez with a dejected look and said, "It seems the number is no longer working. I didn't think they'd change this number."

El Din and Jimenez waited a few moments. "I'll try again. Maybe no one was around to take the call. It happens sometimes." He punched in the phone number again. He waited for the call to go through. It rang. It continued to ring. No one answered. El Din disconnected the call. "They must have changed the number," said el Din.

"Is there another number to call? There must be," responded Jimenez.

"This is the only number I have."

Jimenez took the phone and started to go out the door. The phone began to ring. Jimenez handed it to el Din. "Answer it."

"Hello," said el Din.

The party making the call replied, "Hello, who is this?"

El Din immediately recognized the caller's voice... Aafiya Abad. Abad was the bomb maker who'd taught the young terrorists how to make bombs. El Din said, "Aafiya, Aafiya, it is me, Baha el Din! I just called."

"Baha, where are you? We've been trying to locate you. We thought you were with Flores. We were trying to figure a way of getting you out of Mexico. Flores won't let you leave...will he. He said to us that he'd turn you over to the Americans if we tried to get to you. Now, you are calling me. How can you call me if Flores still has you? Don't tell me you escaped," said the bomb maker.

"I'm still in Mexico. I've escaped from Flores. I have a chance to escape from Mexico...with some help. That's why I'm calling."

"What can I do to help?"

When El Din heard this, he took a deep breath. "I've got a friend with me. I can't say his name." El Din looked at Jimenez. "He says if I pay him fifty million dollars, he can get me back to you."

"Do you believe him?"

Again, el Din looked up at Jimenez. "Yes, I do. I'm still a captive. I've been able to escape from Flores. I'm with Mexican officials who want to send me back to the Americans. That's all I can say. Will you help?"

There was a pause. Then the phone crackled to life. Abad said, "That's a lot of money, Baha."

When el Din heard that, his heart sank again. He looked at Jimenez. Jimenez just shook his head in disgust.

"But not to worry. We'll have it for you."

"Good; that's what I wanted to hear. We have to set up a way to transfer the money at the same time I get on the transportation to get me back."

"We can do that. What'll be your transportation?"

El Din looked up at Jimenez, who mouthed *boat*. "The man said it'll be by boat."

"Okay, Baha, I'll get the money together. It may take a few days...but I'll get it. Can I call you on this number?"

El Din looked at Jimenez for an answer. Jimenez nodded his head yes.

"Yes, you can."

Chapter 57

General Padilla called Bob Reynolds. "Director Reynolds, we are getting a Special Operations force together right now. It'll be ready in a few days. The men are Mexico's best. They'll go get Flores."

"I hope you're successful, General."

"We will be. Don't worry, Director. Like I said, we've got our best soldiers on this operation. We want Flores just as badly as President Rivera and you do."

"I don't doubt you will make your best effort. Flores has as much influence in your country as anyone. He is capable of anything...including slipping away from you. He escaped from us on the way to prison and took el Din with him," replied Reynolds.

"I know the history...I know it. He won't know we're coming. He'll be totally surprised."

"Again, I hope you'll be successful. Keep me informed, General. Good luck, and good hunting."

"I will, Director. Thank you. Goodbye."

* * *

A Mexican Special Forces unit led by Captain Izan Noguera, an outstanding Mexican Special Forces officer, crept in the still of the night into the Lacandon village. They were directed by the village elder Viejo. He directed Captain Noguera to Flores's house.

Captain Noguera whispered into his mic, "Sergeant Aamot, take two squads and go to the house. Have one squad enter the back and the other the front. Have two more squads surround the house. Watch every window."

"Roger that, sir," replied Sergeant Aamot.

Sergeant Aamot's team did as they were told. The squad leader who led his squad through the front door whispered into his mic. "We're in."

The same thing came from the squad who entered from the back.

Captain Noguera whispered into his mic, "Good. Now proceed to Flores's and Cruz's bedrooms. Quietly go in and be careful not to accidentally wake either of them before you take them. I'm sure each one sleeps with a weapon."

Each squad entered the bedrooms and moved quietly to each bed and found no one. Each squad leader was perplexed and whispered into their mics, "There's no one here...there's no one here."

"What do you mean there's no one there? They've got to be somewhere in that house. Search the building," responded Captain Noguera.

The squad leaders did as they were ordered. They cleared each room. They found no one. Each reported, "The building is secure. There's no one here."

"I can't believe it," said Captain Noguera. "Are you sure you cleared the entire house?"

"Yes, sir. We did. There's no one here."

"How could he have known...how could he? No one knew...not one single person knew we were coming. But someone had to know and warned Flores. Flores and Cruz escaped. Bring your men to the rallying point."

* * *

It was the middle of the night when Flores got word the Mexican Special Forces were on their way. Flores thanked his man for the heads-up. Flores ran to Cruz's room. "Dize, let's go!" shouted Flores. "Let's go! We can't stay here any longer. I just got word. The Special Forces are coming for us...we've got to go, pronto, pronto...let's move! I've got a boat ready to cross the river into Guatemala."

Cruz was groggy from a deep sleep. "What're you talking about, Benito? We've got to move right now?"

"Do as I say or I'll leave you here, by yourself."

Once Cruz heard that, he jumped from his bed and into his clothes as fast as he could. "Let's go, Benito, I'm ready. Who told you they were coming?"

Flores said, "I'll explain later. For now, we've got to get to the boat."

The Usumacinta River was not far from the village. Flores and Cruz made their way to the river and the waiting boat. They got in and Flores started the engine. It roared to life. Flores pulled away from the dock and headed to Guatemala.

"I beat them again, Dize. I escaped again! That's why they call me el Gato. Hey, what do you think?"

"I'll tell you this, Benito; I think I work for one smart man. Where do we go from here?" asked Cruz.

* * *

General Padilla got the news from Captain Noguera and was infuriated. "How is this possible?" asked the general.

"Someone had to know. That someone alerted Flores. He must have slipped out just before we got there. Just as we were approaching Flores's house, I heard the roar of an engine. It must have been a boat down by the river. It was just a few minutes after we arrived. I've questioned all the people who live there. None of them know anything. Someone in that village tipped Flores off. That's the only way it could have happened, General," responded Captain Noguera.

"Stay there till morning. You may be able to talk with someone who may know something. We know Flores is building semisubmersibles in that village. Find that place and find all the drugs he's got there," replied the general.

"Yes, sir. No one knew we were coming. How did they find out?" responded Captain Noguera.

"Thank you for the effort, Captain. Let's hope we find someone willing to cooperate with us. Someone knows."

General Padilla hated what he had to do next. He had to call Bob Reynolds.

"It doesn't surprise me, General. I know your men did their very best. Flores has a network working for him all the time...a very strong network. He is el Gato. We'll catch him eventually. His luck will run out sometime, somewhere."

"We'll destroy his boat-building operation and confiscate all the drugs we find there."

"That would be great, General. As soon as you find anything, let me know," said Reynolds.

Reynolds called President Rivera and told him the news. The president's only response was an exasperated, "He escaped again."

Chapter 58

Six months later

Consuela and Chavez made plans with Gonzales and Sydney to have dinner with them that evening. Gonzales drove his company Buick SUV to the front of Consuela's Georgetown townhouse. He and Sydney got out of the SUV and rang the doorbell. Chavez came to the door. "Hey, guys, how are you doing? It's good to see both of you. Come in, please, come in. I've got a bottle of Syd's favorite Chianti ready to open. Sit down. Connie'll be out in a second."

"Don't mind if we do," said Gonzales.

Consuela came out looking beautiful. Sydney said, "Consuela, you look terrific...I mean terrific."

Consuela was a little embarrassed by the compliment. "Oh, thank you, Syd, thank you so much."

They sat down and drank the bottle of Chianti and made small talk. Gonzales said, "Let's get going. Syd made reservations at our favorite pasta and pizza place."

When Sydney made the reservations, she asked for a cozy table. The seating hostess greeted Sydney's party. "Welcome back, Madam Secretary. I've got your table and server ready to take care of you."

"Thank you, Helen, that's very kind of you."

Helen seated them at a cozy table. A server came up with water glasses full of ice and water. "May I get anything else for you?"

Sydney said, "Not right now. We want to chat for a while. You could bring us your best Chianti."

"Very well, Madam Secretary. I know just the one."

The server returned with the Chianti and said, "When you're ready to order, all you have to do is ring the buzzer on the wall behind the Captain."

"That'll be just fine," said Sydney.

When the server left, Gonzales asked, "Chavez, how's the new job working out?"

"We haven't talked for a while, have we? The job is going much like I expected. I like working security for the president. The Secret Service is a great organization of dedicated men and women. Any one of them would give their life for the president. But enough of that. Connie and I have got some news to share with you and Syd."

"What is it?" blurted Sydney.

"Connie and I are getting married."

"How about that! That's great news. Congratulations to both of you. You two deserve nothing but the best this world has to offer," said Gonzales.

Sydney jumped out of her chair at the same time Consuela did. They hugged each other tightly. "I'm so happy for you, Connie! Words can't say how happy I am for both of you."

Sydney and Consuela were both in tears. Gonzales had jumped from his seat and grabbed Chavez and hugged him. "Congrats, my friend, congrats. When did you decide to get married? It must have just happened."

"We decide a while ago. We wanted to tell. But we decided to wait until I settled into my new job. Connie is close to finishing her degree at American University. We thought we'd break the news tonight. I've got something to ask each of you—both of you."

"Shoot," said Gonzales.

"Well, I'll let Connie ask," said Chavez.

All eyes fell on Consuela. "I'd like to ask Syd to be

my maid of honor."

After asking Sydney, Consuela looked at Chavez, who nodded his head yes.

"And Bob would like Gonzales to be his best man."

Gonzales looked at Sydney and she looked back. This time, Gonzales nodded his head yes.

"We'd love standing up for you two—if you agree to stand up for us," replied Sydney.

Chavez met Consuela's eyes. They suddenly understood what Sydney was saying. Consuela couldn't contain herself. "You're getting married?"

"Yes, we are," answered Sydney. "He asked me a few nights ago. I wanted to wait to tell you until we were all together. Hey, I just had a thought. How would you feel about a double wedding?"

"I never thought this would happen," remarked Gonzales.

Chavez said, "Me neither. I like the idea of a double wedding, though."

"Me, too," said Consuela.

"Well, that settles it," said Sydney. "Connie and I will make the arrangements. You guys sit back and relax. What do you think, Connie?"

"I like it very much. I was going to ask you for help."

"Chavez, why don't you ring the buzzer. I'm getting hungry," said Sydney.

The server came and took their orders and brought their food. Consuela and Sydney were giddy with excitement. Gonzales and Chavez were content to watch their women be so excited. They looked at each other with satisfaction and happiness neither had experienced in their lives. They knew without saying that four people with a common heritage, but similar and at the same time very different backgrounds, had been brought together by very strange circumstances.

* * *

The next day was Saturday, the day Alejandro took his swimming lesson. Consuela said, "Alejandro, are you ready? We don't want to be late. Let's go."

"I'm coming, Mommy, I'm coming," responded Alejandro.

"Give Bob a kiss and a hug," said Consuela as she walked out the door with her son.

She drove Alejandro to swim class. Every time she did, she stopped at that doughnut shop. Alejandro loved to go in and buy himself two jelly doughnuts. Consuela parked in front of the shop. Every time she parked directly in front of the shop, she let her son go in by himself and buy his doughnuts.

"I can go by myself," said Alejandro. "You parked in front this time."

"Yes, you may go in by yourself. But stay in front of the window so I can see you. Okay?"

"Okay, Mommy."

Alejandro went into the doughnut shop thinking, *I'm a big boy now.* He was recognized by the counter girl. She had seen him with his mother many times. She greeted him, "Hi, young man! How're you today?"

"I'm fine."

"What would you like today?"

"I want two jelly doughnuts, please."

Consuela could see Alejandro from the car. She checked her phone for messages; there were none. She looked up into the shop for Alejandro. He was gone and the counter girl was screaming.

Consuela went into the shop as fast as she could.

"They took him...they took him! He screamed, I want my mommy...I want my mommy! Some men came in and took him!" cried the counter girl.

Consuela knew they didn't come out of the front door. She ran to the back door and out into the alley. They were gone, and so was her son. She collapsed there in the alley.

* * *

When Consuela came to her senses, she was on the pavement. She knew she had to call someone. She couldn't think straight. *Bob.* She pulled her phone from her pocket. "Bob, they took Alejandro. They took him. He's gone... he's gone!" said Consuela, sobbing uncontrollably.

Chavez tried to make sense of what he'd heard. "Who took Alejandro?"

"I think one of Benito's men. It has to be him!" Consuela managed to say between sobs.

"Where are you?"

"I'm sitting on the pavement behind the doughnut shop. You know the one."

"Did you call 9-1-1?"

"No."

"Call it now," ordered Chavez. "I'm on my way."

When Chavez got there, the DC police were questioning Consuela.

Chavez jumped out of his car and ran to Consuela. "I'm here, Connie."

When Consuela saw Chavez, she broke down completely.

One of the officers said, "We've called it in. The counter girl gave us a description of the man, but not his vehicle. The description of the man is vague. He is Latino, with a medium build."

"Do you know who this woman is or who I am?"

"No, sir."

"I'm Roberto Chavez and this woman is Consuela Hernández, my fiancée. I'm calling Vincente Gonzales and Sydney Alvarez, the secretary of the Department of Homeland Security."

The officer thought a moment and the proverbial light came on in his head, "Yeah. Yeah. I remember. I'll call this in to my supervisor now. I'm sorry."

"No problem. Just get the information out to the right people. This is not an ordinary kidnapping."

"Yes, sir. I'll do that."

Chavez picked Consuela up from the pavement. "We should go home. Let the police do their job. I'll call Gonzales. I'll tell him to call Syd."

Gonzales was in front of Consuela's townhouse, waiting. "I got here as soon as I could. Syd's on her way."

* * *

Alejandro was screaming, "I want my mommy! I want my mommy!"

Juan Torres had made the grab. "Shut up, kid. I'm going to take you to see your daddy," said Torres as he put Alejandro in a waiting SUV. "Alejandro, if you don't stop screaming for your mommy, I'm going to go back there and hurt her," said Torres. "I mean it. You believe me, don't you?"

Alejandro knew that Torres meant what he said, because he knew his father and what he was capable of, although his mother had tried to shield him from it. This man worked for his father. "Okay, I won't scream anymore.

Don't hurt my mommy; please, don't hurt my mommy," said Alejandro through his tears.

"That's better. I'm going to take you to see your daddy. He wants to see you very much. Okay?"

Torres was headed to Reagan airport. He had two first-class tickets to Mexico City in his possession. He parked the car and left the keys in the glove box.

"Okay, Alejandro, we're going to get on a big airplane. We'll see your daddy soon."

"Okay. You promised me you wouldn't hurt my mommy...you remember?"

"Yes, I remember. I didn't go back, and no one else will. We are going to see your daddy...just like I said. Are you hungry?"

"Yes, I'm a little hungry. I want my jelly doughnuts."

Torres thought about that. He spotted a Sticky Bun vendor and said, "I don't think they have jelly doughnuts in the airport. How about a sticky bun?"

"I don't think I've ever had one. I'll try one."

Torres bought one and gave it to the boy. "Here you go. How's that?"

Alejandro took the sticky bun and took a big bite. His eyes lit up. "This is very good. Remember, you said you wouldn't hurt my mommy."

Alejandro was seven years old. He knew what Vincente Gonzales and Roberto Chavez did for his mother, him, and Lucia. He knew what the uniform Chavez used to wear meant. While he was with Torres, he saw a man wearing a uniform just like Chavez's. Torres looked away for just a second. Alejandro saw an opportunity. He ran to the man in uniform and said, "That man took me from my mommy. You're an Army Ranger. Help me."

When Torres looked for Alejandro, he saw him talking to the Army Ranger. He and the Ranger locked eyes. The Ranger knew the boy was telling the truth. Torres knew he'd lost and looked for a place to run. The Ranger saw Torres make a break for it.

The Ranger saw man who witnessed the whole thing. "Wait here with this man. I'll be right back."

The Ranger saw Torres run toward the main terminal. Torres was no match for the Army Ranger. The Ranger caught Torres from behind and brought him down. It was a matter of minutes before airport security was on the scene.

"What's going on here?" asked a security guard.

The Ranger looked for Alejandro. An older man who was next to the Ranger and heard what Alejandro said took charge of the young boy. He brought Alejandro to the security guard.

The Army Ranger answered the security guard's question. "This boy came up to me and told me this man took him from his mother. When I looked at the man, he made a break for it. I ran him down."

The security guard looked at Alejandro and asked, "Is that what happened?"

"Yes. That man told me he'd hurt my mommy if I kept calling for her. I saw the Army Ranger and ran to him. I knew he'd help me," answered Alejandro.

"What's your name, son?" asked the security guard.

"My name is Alejandro. I want to stay with the Army Ranger. I know he'll keep me safe."

When the Ranger heard this, he was dumbfounded. He asked, "How do you know I'm an Army Ranger, Alejandro?"

"Your uniform is just like the one Roberto Chavez and Vincente Gonzales wear. It's just like theirs," answered Alejandro.

The Army Rangers are a small group of men. The

Ranger immediately recognized the names Alejandro mentioned. "You know Chavez and Gonzales?"

"Sure, I do."

"How do know these men?"

"My mommy is going to marry Bob Chavez."

By that time, the DC police were on the scene. Once things were straight, the DC police placed Torres in custody and took him away.

One of the officers asked the Ranger, "Can you take the boy to his mother? He's comfortable with you. We'll call her. When she hears the news, I'm sure she'll be ecstatic."

The Ranger had missed his flight. "Sure. I'd be more than happy to take Alejandro to his mother. Do you know your address, young man?"

"Sure, I do. My mommy made me learn it."

"Okay. I'll get a cab."

Milton Jackson was an African-American Army Ranger who was into a second enlistment in the army. He'd been in the army for seven years. When the cab pulled up to Consuela's townhouse, Consuela, Chavez, Sydney, Gonzales, and Lucia were outside waiting for Alejandro. As soon as Alejandro was out of the car, he went running to his mother.

As soon as Consuela saw Alejandro, she burst into tears of joy. She squeezed him close to her. "Alejandro, Alejandro!" was all she could say.

Alejandro exclaimed, "Mommy, Mommy, I escaped! This Army Ranger helped me."

Consuela looked at her son with pride and joy. "Yes. You escaped, Alejandro. We were so worried. We thought we'd lost you!" said Consuela tearfully. "I can't believe it. You escaped from a very bad man."

"I know. He was a bad man. He told me he would

hurt you if I didn't stop calling for you. He was going to take me on a big airplane. I saw this Army Ranger and ran to him. I told him that the man took me from my mommy. I knew he'd help me. I knew it. His uniform is just like Bob's and Gonzales's."

Consuela looked at Milton Jackson. She let Alejandro go and walked over to Milton. She put her arms around him, looked him in the eyes and said, "Thank you seems so inadequate. I don't know what else to say."

"Thank your son. He did a very courageous thing. He's the one you should be thanking."

Chavez and Gonzales took it all in. Chavez said, "You ran that guy down. You had no idea if he was armed or not. Yet, you stuck out your neck for a little boy you didn't even know. I'm retired Army Ranger Chavez. This guy next to me is Vincente Gonzales, Army Ranger."

Jackson said, "When Alejandro mentioned Bob Chavez and Vincente Gonzales, I knew exactly who he meant. I put two and two together on the way over here. I know about your rescue of the secretary of the Department of Homeland Security and Consuela Hernández. And of course, Alejandro. The lady over there must be Lucia. You rescued her, too. At the same time, you captured Benito Flores and, if I remember right, ISIS terrorist Baha el Din."

"You've got a great memory, Jackson," remarked Gonzales. "Where were you headed when you were interrupted?"

"I was returning to 3rd Battalion 75th Ranger Regiment, Fort Benning, Georgia, sir. I'm probably AWOL; I missed my flight. I was home on leave to visit my mother. I don't want to be in trouble, sir."

"Not to worry, Sergeant. I think we can handle that—and then some. You now have friends in high places," responded Gonzales with a smile.

Gonzales looked at Sydney. She said, "I'll call the president. Like Gonzales said, not to worry. You have friends in high places."

Alejandro ran to his mother and exclaimed, "I escaped! I escaped! I escaped!"

- THE END -

Made in the USA
Monee, IL
20 September 2020